Dear Lorraine, Jason, Mia & Daisy

Greer

First Edit

ISBN 978-1-

Oct 2021

The Story continues

trust you'll enjoy it –

it may be on TV soon!

Best wishes + Love

Tracy.

For Rodney Love

‘The body is the mere visibility of the soul and the soul, the psychological experience of the body.’ – Carl Gustav Jung

‘I do not know what I may appear in the world but to myself, I appear only to have been a boy playing by the seashore diverting myself playing in now and then, finding a smoother pebble or a prettier shell than ordinary, all the while the great ocean of truth lay all undiscovered before me.’ – Isaac Newton

A Worldshift Genre

Prologue

Spring 1957 – Buryatia Autonomous Republic, Siberia

The young girl shielded herself against the harsh wind whistling in across the flat, snow-dusted landscape. Wrapped in the folds of her father's robes, she peered from his hip, an interloper, intrigued at the odd sight.

Monks were hacking at the frozen ground with their pickaxes, struggling about the task, their eyes fearful but focused on the present. Their practice of worship had been all but eradicated by the regime with just a few elders remaining to keep the flame alight. Now in the few years since Stalin's death, a tangible hope existed that Tibetan Buddhism would flourish unfettered again in Buryatia, as it had done before, for centuries.

Soon, they stopped and looked up at the man's muted saffron layers outlined starkly against the white flanked mountains. Frantic gazes were exchanged.

'Papa?' she uttered, gazing up at him, her pomegranate cheeks shining. He nodded to his peers, reassuringly stroking her hair, but his powerful hands were trembling and unusually cold. In the pit lay a wooden coffin the hewn larch lid of which was now being prized open by one of the brethren as the rest fell back. The youngster lent forward peering down into the hole, her nose pricked by the pungency of thawed earth and the sharp lingering sweetness of incense before turning her head away, to hide from the imminent sight of the carcass.

Death was not something to be feared in their culture but the reasons for exhuming a saint, supposedly dead for more than thirty years, whose acts had only strengthened their beliefs and given fortitude in the long dark days of Soviet repression, were something her young mind could not process. She shuddered, and her father hugged her tiny frame to buffer her fear as the ringing of tiny bells pulled her focus back to the monks now pawing away the rock salt from the large box.

They stopped, momentarily suspended in silent reverence at the sight, before falling to their knees and chanting. The chorus reverberated through her body causing her breathing to resonate with it and even in her young innocence, she knew she was gazing upon a mystery.

There, in cross-legged repose before them, a shrunken figure seemed to hover against the brown salt, its darkened leathery skin was still draped in the same spice-coloured fabric it had been buried in. Had the salt preserved this body from decay or was this figure somehow still alive? The doubt burned in each of the small gathering as they huddled, melodically reciting their sacred sutras in hushed tones against the chiming of metal bowls.

One of the older monks, in his middle years, then stepped up and held a small mirror close to the saint's docile face. The chanting faded and then ceased. The mood filled instead with a restless pregnant anticipation for some minutes as the monk periodically turned the silvered glass, his eyes darkening with expectation as he squinted hard at it.

Then his frozen expression broke in gratitude. A small cloud of condensation had formed on its surface.

'Papa!' The young girl tugged at her father's robes again, begging his attention. 'Is he alive?' His gentle eyes answered silently within a puckered smile that creased his hairless, berry face.

The exhumed holy man was in tudkam – a meditative and supernatural state revered by the monks as the pinnacle of their worship and the vehicle which would ultimately allow them an enlightened death. The Lama had foretold this day and better times but for the present, they were committing an act punishable by death or at least a life sentence in a gulag, tolerance of their beliefs being purged for good.

A growing fear now loomed, dampening their elation. With a signal from their leader, they began to pack the salt back into box to cover the holy figure once more, aiming to rebury him as quickly as possible. Snow would soon come again before the end of Spring, covering their actions and ultimately entombing this enigma until a braver world was ready to accept it.

One

May 2008 – Heathrow Airport, London

'Are you sure you don't want me to come in with you?'

'Yes, I'll be fine and anyway, you're in a hurry.'

'Gordon can wait,' Carty uttered.

'That's not very fair.'

He smiled and then cradled Lena's soft cheeks in his palms, kissing her passionately. She dug her nails into his shoulders and held on to him for too long.

'Lena...,' he called after her minutes later from the car's lowered window as she wheeled her small bag into the terminal's entrance. She turned and cocked her head, much like she had done the very first time they met. It never failed to charm his heart but a strained expression betrayed her soft smile and the shimmer of a smudged tear stirred his fears.

She held out a palm, blew across it and then turned away.

****

'How's Lena?' Gordon Green enquired as they sat in his study.

'Fine, thanks. I dropped her at the airport this morning. She's spending a long weekend in Dubai with her Russian girlfriends.'

'Ah, yes, I remember you mentioning it. It's a long way to go for such a short break. Was Jack happy about the risk of her travelling there?'

'He seemed to be. It's been two years since the madness and she needs a break, although she only dropped the news of it last week.'

'I'm sure she'll be safe.'

'I dare say the security services are still watching us.'

'You're probably right, but Jack will never admit to that.' Green shot an avuncular grin. 'Anyway, how's business?'

'So-so. I have some concerns about the price of carbon credits being overvalued'

Scott Carty's infamy in having been absolved of one of the City's largest frauds had brought a plethora of investors flocking to his recently formed environmental fund, *Sole Carbon.* Like the media, they too couldn't quite believe his recent history, nor ignore the huge publicity it caused which de facto, made him *the* man to go to for carbon reduction projects. The multinationals were already teed up with grandiose schemes to cut the five main industrial greenhouse gases, not due to ethics but because it was financially lucrative to do so. Now the rest of the market was racing to catch up, throwing caution and funds to the wind, eager to include this new class of asset to their portfolios.

'What's the worry?'

'My investors are getting twitchy. I can't put my finger on it but I feel there's going to be a price correction..., downwards.'

'But didn't that already happen?'

'Yes, a couple of years ago,' Carty fired back, 'but they've recovered since then and anyway, my projects in China and India produce a different type of credits called CERs.'

'I don't really understand. Are you saying that these CERs are valued differently?'

'Correct that's why they are in such demand from the big industries which are capped on the amount of CO_2 they can vent,' he said, gesticulating with his hands like some Mid-West evangelists, trying to convince Green of how brilliantly simple the scheme was. 'It's cheaper for them to buy my CERs than to refurbish their aging facilities and the funds flow to lucrative projects in developing countries. It's a win-win for everyone.'

'Hmmm, you know what I think of that whole process, Scott.'

'I know. And it could all come crashing down again, soon. The sentiment is that prices have already peaked.'

'And that's why your investors are nervous?'

'Possibly. They particularly like my landfill waste projects which capture and burn methane to produce electricity. The yields are very healthy, an expected 25% return on investment in the first year.'

'That's not to be sniffed at but it does seem too good to be true. Why is there such a high return in so short a period?'

'Because methane is about 30 times more dangerous as a greenhouse gas than carbon dioxide and so any projects curbing it earn this relative increase in credits. But the real cream comes from the sales of the electricity generated.'

'Well, if that's the case why are you even concerned with a drop in the price of the credits?'

'It's human nature. All investors get worried about rumours and any other bad news.'

'There's bad news?'

Carty's face flushed. 'Two of the Chinese projects have gone cold and the operator is bypassing us. We know it is selling electricity to the local municipality, but we're not seeing the revenues from those sales.'

'I see.' Green's frown was unnerving. 'That constitutes a major default in anyone's books. Have you visited to question the operator?'

'No,' Carty replied, crows-feet creasing his temples as he sheepishly attempted to grin away the reply. 'There wasn't time for me to travel, what with all the registration bureaucracy, let alone the IT systems we've been building to report to investors. I thought it would be easier to use a small industrial consultancy here in London. They're the experts and we trusted them to deliver a number of our projects on schedule, which they did.'

'How much is outstanding?'

'About two million dollars.'

The older man was already shaking his head, his expression semi-contorted as if he had swallowed something bitter. 'And how are you aiming to resolve it?'

'I'm threatening a visit but Nick suggested I talk first with an acquaintance of his. She's the niece of a Chinese industrialist who owns a number of manufacturing facilities in the Xinjiang region, where these projects are located. Nick has the impression she can help.'

'Well, whatever the outcome, you need to be on a plane pronto.'

'I know. Do you think Jack could help out with the local politics if I needed it?'

'You'll need to ask him yourself. Where exactly in China is Xinjiang?'

'North West. It's a huge province bordering Central Asia.'

'Near Kazakhstan?'

'Yes.'

'Be careful. We don't want to lose you there again.'

'Lena said the very same thing.' His postured straightened, remembering the sound of her sweetly accented voice.

'Do you mind if I smoke?' Green muttered through a half-formed grin, momentarily waving a cedar box at Carty.

He shook his head wistfully reaching for his coffee instead and staring into space, recollecting the harrowing experiences of his recent past. He still struggled with sleepless nights, reliving the several attempts on his life and the complete dereliction of his trust by his former boss, Arthur D'albo. It almost cost Carty his health and left him desperately fighting rear–guard, against a contrived fraud and smear campaign, in order to save his reputation.

'I am having a few problems of my own,' Green confessed, now already on his feet and flicking a match into life as he paced past the book-lined walls to open the French windows.

'Our Olympic Village proposal has been turned down,' he remarked, puffing repeatedly until the end of a cigar glowed into life. It was late afternoon and its pleasant odour was carried on the spring air now pouring into the room.

'Really? Why?'

'I'm not entirely sure. It seems that some subcommittee doesn't believe that zero-energy social housing is worth the investment.'

Carty's eyes widened. 'That's ridiculous!'

'But that's the madness we're facing. It seems everything must have an overriding value-for-money raison d'etre otherwise it's not deemed feasible. When are these people going to wake up and realise that the earth doesn't charge for its services.'

'I guess that also puts paid to your plans for the hydrogen economy happening anytime soon.' Carty said, recalling Green's impassioned environmental conversations during their first meeting in this very same room.

'Probably, although I'm hearing noises that with the North Sea's declining gas supply there's talk of producing hydrogen from sea-water and pumping it into the existing pipe infrastructure to keep the system operating.'

'Hah! The thin edge of the wedge?'

'It will be if bureaucrats don't hamstring it first. Anyway, Nick has been tinkering about with another method of producing hydrogen called Brown's Gas. It sounds too exotic to be true, a little bit like that vortex machine of yours,' he said, crouching down on his haunches to examine the spines of the books crammed into the lower shelves. 'Ah, there it is' He pulled out a tattered paperback held together with masking tape along its ridge. 'This is something I've been meaning to show you this for some time.' he blurted, tossing it to his friend.

Carty caught it and scanned the cover's title. '*The Secret of the Golden Flower?*' He uttered.

'It's an 8th century cannon of meditation and is what actually caused Jung to abandon his famous *Red Book*.'

Carl Gustav Jung, the pioneering Swiss psychoanalyst and his work on dreams and alchemy had fascinated Green for most of his life. And dreams had been the main reason Carty had sought Green out, just a few short years before, struggling with a series of lucid visions that in hindsight were warning him of the dangerous events about to unfold in Siberia.

'Sorry, now you're losing me.'

Green fanned smoke away from his face. 'Jung spent much of the First World War, deep in a practice of inward contemplation, entering into a drama with the figures that emerged from his unconscious. He recorded these experiences in journals but they proved so intense that it caused him a minor breakdown, forcing him to retreat from his other studies.

He later transcribed them pictorially into a specially prepared leather tome, the *Liber Novus* or, as it's more popularly known, the *Red Book.*' Green took another drag, catching Carty's eye. 'Those who have seen the original, and few have, marvel at its content and Jung's artistic prowess in producing the illuminated calligraphy.'

'So why did he stop working on it?'

'Up until then he had been researching early Gnostic Christianity with its philosophical problems of a dark and light God as well as the link with alchemy's union of opposites and the salvation of the feminine principle. When he received the text of *The Secret of the Golden Flower* from the German missionary Richard Wilhelm, he immediately recognised a direct source of information, more than a thousand years old, which was unfettered by the indecipherable symbols and language of medieval western alchemy. It gave Jung a window on to the Eastern spiritual mind, a parallel with which to confirm his own inner experiences as well as those of his patients' countless dreams. I suppose he had found what he was looking for and didn't need to continue with the Red Book.'

Carty was now thumbing through the pages, noticing the outline pictures of a seated figure in full lotus repose. 'These look like meditation postures,' he resounded.

'That's why I thought it would interest you. The practitioner is circulating his inner light...his *Qi.*'

Carty's face lit up. He had been taught something similar to help aid his recovery after the brutal attack in the Siberian forest. It had since become a daily practice.

'Yes, and while *Qi* seems to be a natural phenomenon, flowing through life, it's only when there's inward focus of the mind and the breath that it can be harnessed to sustain health.

'I see. Do you meditate, Gordon,' Carty probed, hazily recalling his friend sitting in lotus at the Iron Monger Row steam rooms some years back.

'Yes, mainly a Tibetan system. Have done so for many years.'

'And do you practice circulating your *Qi?*

'No, I silently let all my thoughts go, inviting the inner world to surface.'

Carty smiled as he rested the paperback on his thighs. 'So how does Jung's practice of engaging an internal drama come into all this? It seems the very opposite of silently letting go.'

Green raised his large palms as if offering a sacrament, spilling ash on the rug.

'On the face of it, yes, it does. However, he made the critical distinction in understanding that we Westerners are in general, extraverted by nature. By that, he meant that we need to *know* and cannot simply take the introverted path of acceptance as was commonly the case in Oriental practices. In fact, Jung believed that by blindly adopting an Eastern spiritual way of life in denial of one's own heritage with all its cultural implications, could trigger neuroses and ultimately, physical illness. *The body is the mere visibility of the soul and the soul the psychological experience of the body* was one of his most insightful observations.'

The comment had Carty yawning but then embarrassed, he quickly caught himself and grinned. Green ignored it.

'I feel that his concerns, although probably reasonable for the times in the 1920s, are outdated nowadays in our culturally globalised world. But coming back to your question, Jung developed a powerful technique not unlike meditation, to engage with his unconscious, which he called active imagination. The process of letting go, and allowing the unconscious in, is helpful, if not essential, to dialogue with and balance the warring opposites within ourselves. As you know, I believe that if humanity neglects these to pursue the monopolisation of nature for greed, then we will see more and more turmoil materialising in the world around us.'

Carty slumped back at the statement causing the book to slip from his lap to the floor with a sharp clap, startling him. Apologetically, he quickly bent to scoop it up, noticing a faded edge of paper protruding from inside the back cover which he innocuously pulled out. It contained an old print of a human outline, seated against a patterned background and with 10 circles positioned geometrically over its body.

'Take the book with you, if it's only to read Jung's brilliant introduction,' Green said, moving closer to sit at the other end of the Chesterton, curious about the page now in his friend's hands.

'I will,' Carty replied, tucking the paper back where he found it.

They locked gazes for some seconds and Green sensed his friend was troubled by something other than just the odd situation with his projects.

'Have you had any dreams recently, Scott?'

'Occasionally but they're a bit scant and I struggle to remember them, unlike those shocking ones I had just before I met Lena and the troubles in Russia.'

'I see. So nothing that might give an insight into this dilemma with your business?'

'Nothing, but maybe I'll have one tonight.'

Green casually flicked the cigar end as he attempted a smile. 'Just be careful for what you wish for.'

Two

Nick Hall's house – the next day

'Lisa should be here in the next 15 or so minutes,' Nick Hall announced, as he plumped up the worn cushions in an attempt to make his tired lounge more presentable. He hardly used the room now that there wasn't a woman in his life.

'Why did Lisa agree to come all the way out here?' Nick lived just north of London. 'From what you've told me she seems the type who would prefer to be wined and dined in Chelsea or Mayfair and I would be happy to pay. I'm the one asking for the favour.'

'She insisted on it. Perhaps she's bored with the glitz and wants to rough it with real engineers.'

'Careful, Nick I'm a physicist.'

'And you won't ever let me forget it.' Hall grinned as he touched Carty's forearm. 'A physicist who has a huge secret worth hiding!' he joked. His eyes shone in the afternoon light but his face was carrying a grey hue, possibly from sitting in the stolid atmosphere of his makeshift workshop for too long, neglecting his health. Carty swerved the comment as he looked around for a place to sit.

'Gordon told me that you're dabbling with hydrogen – Brown's Gas? I haven't had a chance to look it up yet.'

'You should. It has a connection with that transmutation technology you uncovered in Siberia.'

Carty placed a finger against his lips as if unconsciously signalling for Hall to desist. Ever since he had shared the secret of the machine with his friend, Hall seemed determined to raise it at any possible opportunity, as if it should have been him who Fate had chosen to receive such a poisoned chalice. Carty had chosen not to tell him the full truth about the technology's uncanny energy source which seemed to defy any rational explanation but it had been impossible to keep that from Lena.

Her grandfather, Ivan Yegorovich - the machine's inventor, had secreted its designs within the pages of some luxuriously bounds tomes sent to her in London, years before. The sudden thought of her shining face reminded Carty that she was more than three thousand miles away and still hadn't replied to his texts.

'So, what exactly, is Brown's Gas, Nick?'

'It's a specific mixture of hydrogen and oxygen.'

'Really. I've never heard of it!'

'That's because it's been suppressed. Corporate sponsorship has never got behind it although the military probably has.'

'Tell me more.'

'Yul Brown, a Bulgarian engineer who escaped a Siberian *gulag* during WW2, stumbled upon the gas by accident after winding up in Australia where he perfected its production. Experimenting with pulsed electrical vibrations during the electrolysis of water, he noted that the gases produced, when burnt, imploded rather than exploded and the energy generated was far greater than from burning hydrogen alone.'

Vibrations! Carty pondered, the word prompting memories of the technology he was hiding. *All matter is vibrating, so why shouldn't water ignite if its constituents are in an excited, unstable state?*

'And that's the reason why it's being suppressed?'

'Most likely. It's a game changer particularly if the electricity required for electrolysis comes from renewables.'

'If that's the case then, it warrants a Government R & D grant.'

'We're beyond that Scott.'

'We?'

'Yes, the industries owned by Lisa's family have already produced a working prototype and the science is now well understood. You and I see China as a burgeoning economy, fuelled by cheap labour and limitless State funding when probably the country is held to ransom by controlled crude oil supplies and debt. It would appear that while its politicians are playing along to the tune of the international financial system, there's a drive to be independent of both.'

'You're suggesting that China might switch to Brown's Gas for power?'

'In part, it's a possibility. In the USA and elsewhere it's already being trialed in auto engines, to improve performance.'

'And less emissions, no doubt?'

'The international shipping industry is the big play. It produces four percent of global carbon emissions, twice as much as aircraft traffic with much of the dirty fuel oil it uses being dumped at sea, devastating delicate marine ecosystems.'

Carty was nodding. 'I can see that you've done your homework.'

'Lisa's plan is to introduce modified marine engines into the market which can use a majority mix of Brown's Gas in the fuel oil.'

'Hmm...,and I suppose diesel engines will be next on her agenda. Every step in the transportation system depends on them in one way or another. Does this now mean that you've given up on your hybrid car and its magnetic motors?' Carty probed.

'For the while. Brown's Gas is so versatile. It can even be produced from waste water and it appears Jules Verne foresaw its coming in his novel, *The Mysterious Island*.'

'Utopia,' Carty blurted out, 'but why do you believe it has a connection with the transmutation technology that I discovered?'

'Well, it appears that in the early 1990s, a Chinese nuclear power station in Inner Mongolia transmuted some of its radioactive waste by incinerating it using Brown's Gas.

'And was it transmuted into safer, non-radioactive elements?'

'Yes, almost completely.'

Carty's face hung with a look of astonishment.

So, you see, I'm keen to compare all this with the Russian technology you're keeping so secret.' Hall's cheeks flushed with the chanced comment.

'I doubt if there's any likelihood of that,' Carty said. 'Any information I had is now with Government scientists with official clearance.' He was bluffing but as he eyed his friend a concern stirred. 'You haven't told Lisa about it, have you?'

'Absolutely not! You've sworn me to secrecy.'

'Good,' he uttered, attempting a smile but stopping short. He sensed his friendship with this man and the camaraderie they had once enjoyed was now being tested.

'Anyway, her family has invested heavily in renewables so you'll get a chance to chat about those with her.'

'What about my carbon projects, Nick? I thought you said Lisa can help me with the problems I'm facing in Xinjiang.'

'No doubt she will.'

'But does she really have high level connections?'

'Well, as far as I can ascertain, she does. Her father, a senior Chinese diplomat died when she was young and her mother is English, so she came back here to go to school. Now she's handling the international negotiations of her uncle's manufacturing empire, as one of the new entrepreneurs driving the changes instigated by the government.'

'And is that her?' Carty nodded, his wide-eyed expression focused somewhere over his friend's shoulder, prompting Hall to swing around to catch the women's legs gloriously unfold from the open door of a Mercedes convertible.

'Yes, that's her!'

Petite and athletically slim with jet black hair scrunched into a bun and held in place by a chopstick hair-pick, she hesitated along the old path to avoid ruining her three-inch peach stilettos.

Nick hurried out to the door leaving Carty hanging on to the vision.

'Hi, Lisa, come in and meet my friend, Scott Carty.'

'Hello Scott, I've heard a lot about you,' she announced in a lazy impeccable tone while breaking into a relaxed toothy grin.

'It's a pleasure, Lisa, and thanks for agreeing to see me.' Carty held her small hand for a moment, scanning the expensive but fashionably dated ensemble of Zaffre blue silk blouse and tight full length skirt, slit tauntingly up one thigh. Her open neckline was garlanded with South Sea pearls and her clear complexion exhibited all the finest aspects of an ethnically mixed DNA which, if not for the sculptured high cheek bones and slight narrowness to her eyelids, might have had him questioning her Chinese ancestry altogether.

'Shall we sit?' Nick invited.

She tilted her head in agreement and weaved her narrow hips over to the sofa. Carty followed in the wake of the overwhelming Chypre fragrance, to sit down facing her.

'So how can I help?' she announced after tea and several minutes of platitudes, in which she let slip her attendance at a top English boarding school and an MBA from a leading business school.

'I not sure how much Nick has told you already?'

'Why don't you just share everything from the beginning, Scott?'

He found himself briefly ensnared by her deep emerald eyes as he began to explain the projects' loss of revenues and the ineptitude of his agent to provide any assistance at all in recovering them.

'My investors are demanding that my fund takes legal action against the local municipality.'

'Legal action would be a waste of time and money,' she bluntly pointed out, wrapping one toned calf around the other. 'Enforcing any court's decision in that region is almost impossible and quite unnecessary, if you know the right people.'

Carty shifted in his seat. Her words stirred uncomfortable memories of Arthur D'albo and the brutal nature of doing business in the more remote areas of the world.

'You mentioned that your family's contacts could assist Scott in reaching a solution,' Nick waded in, shooting looks between them.

He's keen! Carty noticed.

'Your carbon projects are located near to Urumqi, understand,' she remarked.

'That's correct.'

'And have you visited them recently?'

'I was hoping not to but I guess that can't be avoided now.'

'Well, unless you do, your problems will only get worse...far worse. Our facilities are situated nearby and of course, we do know the right people there.' She masked a smile. 'Scott, are you prepared to come to Hong Kong first, to discuss solutions with my uncle before flying out to Urumqi?'

His breath stalled momentarily. 'Will you be there too?'

'I intend to be,' she retorted, running a hand up the nape of her neck to play with her suspended hair.

'Well, I need to wrap up some things in the next few days but...'

'I'm leaving on Monday,' she interjected.

'Which airline are you flying with?'

She glanced askance at Nick and then back to him. 'My family's private jet. You're welcome to join me.'

'I would be happy to,' he reciprocated, smiling.

'Good, here's my card. Call over the weekend and my secretary will arrange the details.'

Nick Hall nodded at her, almost bewitched by her nonchalant charm which seemed to belie a calculating persona, used to giving instructions and having them obeyed.

What's going on between these two? Carty questioned as they both stood up with her. In her heels she was almost as tall as him and stared back unflinchingly, offering her hand again.

Why has she come out here to meet me? He took it. *She can't just be doing Nick a favour. Perhaps they're having an affair.* Lisa was definitely a catch if, as the ring-less wedding finger suggested, she was unattached but whatever her motives were, the offer of help was the only tangible one on the table and Carty needed it badly.

Three

Situated several streets back from the public beach, nearer to the Creek and the malls, the four star hotel was a basic affair with dated fittings and ubiquitous dark carpets running throughout. Lena hadn't chosen it for its cheap tariff nor for the shopping but because it was a more discreet location used by those international travellers seeking love without any attachment.

Is this a mistake? she questioned, agonising over her guilt as the Gulf's intense sun dappled through the net drapes, suffusing the cramped place with a subtle light that inveigled her to wander out into this new Babylon. The ageing air-conditioning system left the stale whiff of nicotine hanging all around, tempting her. She hadn't taken a drag for years and the strain was palpable as she cast the thought aside and pulled at her tight blonde ponytail while staring hard into the mirror. She let the wet towel's knot slip from above her breast and fall to the floor in a heap so that she could wander her warm hands over her Junoesque contours. Massaging the expensively scented cream into her goose-bumped skin was an attempt to calm her nerves and second thoughts. Why had she agreed to come here without confessing to Carty about the handwritten letter received just a week before and the need to see a man she had once loved? A tear sprang and ran down her cheek. What was she thinking and how Carty must be suffering with her enforced silence, ignoring his texts each a little more desperate than the last? All she wanted was to be held in his arms and to be forgiven, but that gave little solace. Even calling to hear his voice or simply texting to put him out of his agony might endanger everything. The note's instructions were simple and clear: no one could know why she was here.

Soon a musical beep set her stomach clenching and she grabbed at her phone to read the incoming text. But this time it wasn't from Scott Carty.

'Yelena Yakovlevna?' A seated man called out in Russian as she stepped out of the lift. Halted by the polite use of her patronymic middle name she turned to scope the lobby in a practised way, noting the man's Persian blue suit and designer stubble before nodding silently. He pulled forward and stood, offering his open palm.

'I'm Rustigiyev,' he announced coolly through a vulpine smile, his eyes wandering causally over her white halter neck blouse and satin black pants tied off at the ankle.

'Where is Vladislav?' she asked.

'He sends his utmost apologies for being delayed but hopes that you will understand once you allow me to explain everything.' The Russian indicated for her to sit on the sofa opposite him.

'When you said he's delayed, do you mean he will actually be arriving in Dubai shortly, today or tomorrow, perhaps?'

He fingered his spectacles conscious of her scrutiny. 'I believe that he means that he will see you in Irkutsk.'

Lena's countenance froze. 'But I'm not planning to go to Irkutsk. The plan was to meet him here.'

'Tea?' Rustigiyev enquired, flashing the large sovereign ring on his pinky as he waved to the waiter. 'Believe me, Vladislav wanted very much to meet you here, but matters of State prevented him from doing so. He apologises for the secrecy, but you must understand why it was needed.'

'Not really,' she countered, bluntly, 'is my grandfather in danger?'

'Given his background we felt it would be best to be discreet.' The stranger stared back at her over the rims of his glasses and pushed back in his chair, triggering a wave of forgotten anxiety to tense her shoulders.

'His background?' she frowned.

‘Yes, surely you know about the commotion his research caused in the scientific world, some years ago.’ He paused allowing the comment to stew as he turned and ordered from the waiter, now hovering patiently nearby.

‘No. I haven’t seen him for many years and never knew what his work actually entailed. Can you explain to me what’s happened?’ she pursued, cocking her head and brushing the fine blonde strands back over an ear in an accomplished manner, disguising her concern.

‘I don’t know much at all. I’m simply a messenger.’ He leant forward, holding her stare to convey the legitimacy of the meeting. ‘I don’t wish to alarm you, but your grandfather is not well and has asked for you.’

Her eyes dropped and she bit her lip while stifling any visible emotion. She didn’t know this man and wasn’t sure she could trust him with her tears. But he was already drawing an envelope from his jacket.

‘This should explain everything.’

The handwriting on its face was in a casual Cyrillic and soon its contents revealed a short written message signed by Lubimov explaining that his friend, Ivan Yegorovich, her grandfather, had suffered a mild stroke but was recuperating and that he wanted her to visit as soon as she could.

‘Is this genuine?’ she uttered, fingering tears from her smudged lids. Rustigiyev glared back through the lenses and raised his palms as if to imply disbelief at her doubt.

‘Why would you think that it wasn’t?’

‘It’s just that I have never seen Lubimov’s handwriting or signature before. Tell me, what is your relationship with him and why did Vladislav send you?’

‘Well, I've known Lubimov – Oleg Matissevich that is, for many years. He employed my uncle within the medical research team at *Sphinx*, in its early days. I know that you used to visit when you were a young girl and also that you were recuperating there from an *accident*, just a few years back.’

Lena’s chin lifted in acknowledgement. Both Carty and she had indeed been saved by Lubimov’s genius after the near-fatal attack in the taiga. This stranger couldn't possibly have known that information unless Lubimov had told him.

'Because I'm an international businessman, Vladislav trusted me to deliver the note to you in England.'

'But how did you find my address and mobile number? Neither Vladislav nor Lubimov know them.'

'He asked me to be very discreet, and of course it did take my contacts a while to find you.'

'And why was Vladislav so sure I would have believed the contents of his note.'

'Only he can tell you that but evidently, in my opinion, he still loves you and just hoped that you would take it seriously. Clearly, if you hadn't, then he would have found another way to contact you directly.'

Lena squinted into her cup, swayed by a surge of forgotten emotions. She was desperate to believe Lubimov's letter and see her grandfather, but a doubt had her churning the man's story for a flaw.

'I just can't see why Vladislav couldn't call me once you had my contact details?'

'I think you do know why, Lena. He's still part of the system and cannot expose himself or you. The Russian agencies believe that you died at Baikal.'

'I should be dead. Lubimov's skills saved me.'

'Vladislav understands that you cannot travel into Russia via the usual routes so he asked me to escort you to Irkutsk on my company's corporate jet.'

The bleep of an incoming text drew her attention to the phone's screen. It was from Scott Carty and regardless of the pangs of guilt washing over her she felt the timing of the text was coincidental. Sucking in her cheeks she raised her eyes and searched the stranger's for any telltale sign that he might be lying. *Do I trust this man?* She wondered. *Is he playing a game to find out about the machine?* She decided her fears were moot and at the very least, Rustigiyev was aware that her grandfather had fled during the fall of the Soviet State, when his work was being stolen by so-called *biznesmen,* and that more recently, she had been working as an asset of the Russian State along with her former lover, Vladislav.

'So, run it by me again. How do you know Vladislav?'

A grin slipped the corners of his mouth. 'I didn't tell you that.' He reached for the teapot and poured the steaming brew over the slices of lemon sitting in their respective cups, then gently nudged one across the glass surface towards her. The diversion was annoying, but she played along.

'Vlad and I were friends at the academy doing our military service. We were both trainee officers.'

'Whereabouts?'

'Novosibirsk. At the end of our term, I went into my father's business.'

She slowly dipped her head at the euphemism. 'What line of business is that? It must be pretty lucrative if you have a corporate jet.'

'Trading commodities, but that's not relevant. Vlad instead joined the agency and we saw each other infrequently but when we did, he was not shy in expressing his love for you.'

'Did Vlad tell you how he met my grandfather?'

'All he said was that during your first summer together, you took him to stay with your grandparents at their dacha at *Sphinx* and that you were both smitten with each other.'

Lena flushed with the rush of unresolved feelings that were possibly in danger of undermining her new life. She bit her lip.

He continued, 'A year or so ago we realised that we both mutually knew Lubimov and decided to take a short fishing trip to Baikal to meet him.'

'And that's when you learnt about Ivan Yegorovich's health?'

'No. It was only recently that Vlad explained the situation and gave me the note and then Lubimov's letter, here.' He shuffled in his seat, his demeanour somewhat wooden as he puffed out his cheeks in an attempt to convey his honesty. She read him and concluded that his relationship to Vladislav and Lubimov was genuine, but that didn't mean he wasn't play-acting for other reasons. But then she understood the seriousness of the facts. Her grandfather may not have long to live and she had a choice to make: give him his last wish, despite the risk of incarceration by the Russian State for defecting, or return to London. Scott Carty could never have known that he had been her asset during their visit to Baikal and that she had subsequently given up vital information to Whitehall Jack in order to remain in the UK. For that betrayal, she could serve a lifetime in a Russian prison. But there was also another burning reason for leaving with Rustigayev, the possibility of being with Vladislav one more time, to see his smiling face, and to know if he had found love with someone else.

'I don't have my Russian passport with me.'

The stranger straightened, his practised nonchalance uncharacteristically surprised by her sudden statement, which seemed to convey her acceptance of his offer.

'It would cause you more problems if you did. We'll obtain a Russian tourist visa instead. It can be arranged here, in a day or two. Would you prefer to stay in a better hotel in the meantime? I can organise it.'

'No, I'm just fine here.'

'Harosho [okay], I will meet you here in the lobby after breakfast, to collect your passport and I'm sure that Oleg Matissevich will be pleased to hear that you have decided to return.'

'Could I speak with him?' she blurted.

The question drew his blank expression and for some seconds his silence, before he collected himself. 'Yes, shall we do that now?' he suggested, fingering the digital buttons on his phone and then passing it to Lena as the number rang. She took it and placed it to her ear expectantly.

'No answer,' she muttered a minute later.

'We can try again, before we leave. But please could I ask that you do not contact anyone regarding all these arrangements?' he murmured, straining a smile, but she was already standing.

Stepping into the lift Lena caught the reflection of his departure in the mirrored walls across the lobby. She shuddered. Perhaps it was his slick persona - not her desired taste in men - or more likely, the sudden impact of his news and the painful but inexorable choice she had made to dutifully travel home to Russia, to see the grandfather she loved for the last time. The phone vibrated in her hand causing her heart to jump as she pressed the button for her floor. It was a text from a girlfriend in London not from Carty, and her chest sank allowing her to settle her breath. Should she text him? All her instincts told her to do so, but a fear that it would cause him to respond, spotlighting her location and the loss of any secrecy, held her back. No, he would have to trust in their relationship and in her, and that the silence, however agonizing, only meant she was doing the right thing for them both.

* * * *

Lake Baikal, Siberia

Heavy clouds banking along the Eastern Sayan range muted the dawn light, and cast a sombre hue across the vast lake. The Buryat understood that a storm would soon be upon him as he tramped on over wet shingle, each step sucked into the unstable mass leaving a small pool in its wake. Next to his own foot fall he could clearly discern the outline of Ivan Yegorovich's having passed this way in the last day or so and he grinned at the thought that the octogenarian still ventured out so far. Boris had advised him to wait until Spring had well and truly arrived before straying down to the lake, but the old man would have none of it, preferring to escape as soon as possible from the claustrophobic hangover from the raw Siberian winter spent cooped up in his cabin.

A sudden sheet of hail caught the local man, stinging his high cheekbones and forcing him to pull his hood low over his bowed head and pick up his pace, but as he did, his breath faltered and he froze for some seconds, noticing something very odd. Then he rapidly dropped to his knees. Straining against the dimmed light, and oblivious to the icy gale whipping over the pebbled flats, he could now just make out that each print of Ivan Yegorovich's had been over-stepped. *The old man had been followed.*

No one has passed this remote beach without being known to the locals, but someone had done so and had attempted to disguise the fact. A cold fear wrenched at the pit of his stomach as he traced the outline of the much larger footprints and instantly, he leapt up, racing over the collapsing surface, startling gulls into shrill alarm as they flocked to the sky. Shortly, the ash-tinted frame of the cabin, one of the few testaments to man's presence on this stretch of Baikal was caught in a shaft of sunlight, bursting through the bleak squall. Tunnel vision gripped the Buryat to push hard against the chilled air rasping at his throat and exhausted, he flattened his drenched body against shack's outside wall struggling to listen for signs of life inside above the pounding in his ears and the makeshift door banging wildly against its jamb. Moments slowly passed allowing his panting to calm before he decided to act, slipping through the door, crouching low with a small knife in hand. But the place was deserted. A quick scout of the bed told him it had been slept in but was now cold to the touch as was the furnace oven causing him to scour the floor for evidence of a struggle. There was none. Confused, he closed his eyes and allowed a transcendent state to loosen his weathered features as his senses heightened to detect the energetic imprint of recent events in the room – the presence of two other men and the emotions of anger and fear. His eyes shot open and he paced outside, examining the ground to confirm his intuitions. There, behind the building and picked out against the shining wet stones, he spotted several dragged footprints leading to the forest, fifty feet away. His shock now turned into a quaking fear as he found himself struggling to accept the only explanation that held water: Ivan Yegorovich had been abducted during the night.

Four

Carty pulled at the oversized fluorescent zip tabs to his suitcase, thinking of Lena. It had been one of her Christmas presents to him. *Where is she?* He rummaged in his pocket for the phone to check the messages again, the fourth time in the last hour. It too, was a present that she insisted they both had so that they could surf the internet as well as call and text. He understood that a Russian woman shouldn't be seen with anything less and instinctively knew that the world of the smart-phone was about to explode.

Nothing! He threw it back down on the bed, frustrated. Almost two days had passed without a word and he cursed himself for only having the scantiest information about her stay in Dubai. *Perhaps she's lost her phone,* he mused but it didn't add up, she would have found a way to reach him. The stress of leaving for Hong Kong and possibly China, for several days, was playing on his loyalties. Should he cancel Lisa and travel to Dubai to find her? Lena might not be too enamoured with his sudden appearance when she was simply having fun, away with girlfriends whom she hadn't seen since her teenage years. He began typing a text telling that he respected her need for silence and still loved her madly, though the news that he had an urgent trip to Hong Kong could wait.

His attention then turned to the bag again and he began to fill it with various summer shirts and light trousers for the warmer climate in Xinjiang having gleaned from Google that it was mostly desert and mountains with some oases towns, staging posts on the route the Silk Road had once taken out of China. His carbon projects were sited outside its capital, Urumqi, now a burgeoning metropolis, part of China's economic boom from which Lisa's uncle had made billions. Her sudden appearance and offers of help presented a timely solution to Scott's problems yet, despite her assurances to look after him there, an anxiety simmered.

What if they can't help me?

Wiping away the moist patina from his brow, he caught his tense expression glaring back from the long dress mirror. He perched on the edge of the bed, pondering the possible outcomes and then trying to lift his spirits by summoning the same, all-pervasive joy that had consumed him the moment he was reunited with Lena and knew that he was free from the pernicious grip of Arthur D'albo and his Russian masters.

A rapping on the patio windows drew his attention but he couldn't see anyone outside and as he wandered over to investigate, a shadow moved in his peripheral vision. He yanked at the sliding doors and stepped out into the garden. The fragrance of roses stole his senses as it dawned on him that it wasn't the season for them to be in bloom nor was this his garden. Collecting himself, he focused to its far end, catching sight of a hooded figure moving behind the wild, tangled bushes.

'Basilides?' he called out, fighting a rush of blood to his head, excited yet fearful at meeting the revenant once more. He hadn't waited for a response and was already across the lawn, crouching low to push his way under the thorny mess and squeeze himself clear to lean against a wooden door. It immediately collapsed under his momentum and he fell through onto his knees, cursing, as he scrabbled up into a squat among the shards of rotten splinters. He was in ancient walled garden, its weathered red bricks barely held together with crumbling lime mortar, supported a mass of overgrown jasmine with its seductive fragrance momentarily overpowering his thoughts, distracting him from the reason he had been led here. Puzzled that he had lost sight of the figure, he pushed himself up and began to make his way through beds of towering Buddleia, towards a faint noise that he could hear just above the rampant birdsong. Soon the tumbling chatter of a fountain enticed him into a clearing overlooking an ornate pool, once

the feature of the garden with its raised, carved stone walls hung in ivy and split with weeds. A young woman was sitting on its far end, her feet dangling over its edge and her face partially hidden beneath dark tangled locks. The image confused him and then he drew nearer to find that she was transfixed at a point within the pool's churning waters. Following her gaze, down into the slimy water, drew his sharp breath. There, in the building agitation, a serpentine mass of writhing coils and dark scales seemed to consume the sunlight so that details of a huge creature's form were obscured. Fearful for both the woman's safety and his own, he looked back up at her.

'What are you doing here?' he gently called out, trying not to shock her out of the trance-like state she was in. But she remained motionless.

'She can't hear you,' came a strong male voice from somewhere in the background.

'Why not?' he pressed, guessing it was Basilides.

'Because she is under a spell.'

Muddled, he swung his gaze back down into the waters and then a terror gripped his whole being with the sight of the beast's demonic head just breaking the surface, its dark slit eyes boring into his.

'Aahhh!' he yelled out, jerking himself awake and sitting up, the petrifying image still etched into his mind.

What the fuck was that all about?

He slowly lumped downstairs spotting a folded note that had been half-stuffed through the letterbox and he pulled at it, tossing it onto the kitchen table not wanting to be distracted by his driven need to find something. Searching through his old possessions stored in the drawers of his office, which he rarely looked through nowadays, he soon found the leather-bound notebook in which he had recorded all of those seminal earlier dreams, and felt comforted. Then, he perched down, silently took a breath and steeled himself before closing his eyes to re-live the images that had risen with the dream so that he could record them.

After fifteen minutes of struggling with the few associations that came to mind, his mood had dropped. It seemed that a part of his being was still walled-off and secret, a wild once manicured place of natural beauty, now unkempt and forgotten. What gnawed at him, though, was that the imagery suggested that part of his feminine was still immature, uncommunicative and somehow linked to the lurking beast. Unable to do anymore and with a need for coffee, he filled the kettle and picked up the note which he unravelled.

MEET AT THE IRON MONGER ROW BATHS TOMORROW – ELEVEN AM?

He grinned. It could only have been left by one person.

* * * *

The next day: Iron Monger Row Baths

'Hi, Gordon,' Carty's voice echoed along the tiled walls of the changing rooms. 'Thanks for that cryptic letter stuffed through my door, yesterday.'

Green waved back in confirmation.

'What makes you so sure that I would have seen it and met you here?'

'I wasn't sure but I'm glad you did.'

'So am I.'

'You seem slightly flustered, Scott. Is everything alright?'

'Had a huge dream yesterday,' Carty replied, pulling at a plastic curtain and beckoning with a sideways nod for the older man to join him in the hot room. 'Anyway, what's so important that you wanted to meet me here?' he added.

Green shrugged, avoiding eye contact. 'It seems like it's a useful coincidence. Tell me about your dream.'

A knowing smile cracked Carty's demeanour and in the sweltering heat he began to recount it.

'Hmm, I feel that you're missing something, Scott,' Green uttered after some minutes.

'You do?'

'What was the young woman doing?'

'Looking down and attempting to dangle her legs in the water.'

'Yes, but did you see her face?'

'Not exactly.'

'Do you mean *exactly* that you didn't?'

'Yes. I do mean that.'

'Then say so! It's extremely important. Does she remind you of anyone?'

'No one I can think of...,' he frowned, 'except that something about her was reminiscent of a woman Nick recently introduced me to.'

'The Chinese woman? He mentioned her to me'

'Yes, Lisa Taylor? She's Anglo-Chinese.'

'Hmm.'

'I was petrified at what was in the dark waters..., an enormous coiled beast.'

'Can you describe it?'

'It looked like it had the head of dragon.'

The older man stretched an expression of surprise. 'Ah ha, and dragons are usually associated with which country?'

Carty rubbed away the beads of sweaty brine now freely running down his brow and stinging his eyes. 'Wales?'

'Any others?'

'Oh, I see what you're driving at. You mean China?'

Green simpered. 'And usually, in Chinese mythology, dragons roam freely across the sky, embodying the aspect of the spirit but in your dream, the creature is more like a demonic serpent, emerging from the unconscious.' His hazel eyes blinked back. 'I think we should take this into the steam room, don't you?'

It amused Scott Carty that Green found the muffled ambience of the small room an aid to accessing his deeper self and thus giving advice to others.

'What was the thrust of your conversations with Lisa, if you don't mind me asking?' the older man asked as he pulled up his ankles and wrapped them into a full lotus posture.

'As I told you the other day, she has family connections to big industry in Xinjiang and has suggested that I travel there with her, after first meeting her uncle in Hong Kong.'

'To retrieve the funds stolen from your projects?'

'Well, at least try. I don't have a better option at the moment.'

'She hasn't asked you for anything in return?'

'No, but I am guessing she'll push for a success fee.'

'And nothing else, I wonder?' Green quipped as his head began wilting towards his chest.

'Well, she's really not my type, if that's what you're suggesting.' A tell-tale hiss of steam interrupted. 'I'm still totally smitten with Lena.'

'Good, and it's curious that Basilides showed up again in your dream, don't you think?'

'I'm not sure. Last time he warned me of the potential danger with D'albo and the Russians. I suppose I now need to be careful in my dealings in China.'

'Doubly cautious. Remember who Basilides represents – the Self, the deepest aspect of your psyche.'

'That did occur to me.' Carty's head had also begun to droop.

'And you didn't go through that deeply difficult process without learning a hell of lot about yourself and the dark side of human nature.'

'So you think by his reappearance, there's more to learn.'

'Hah!' Green guffawed. 'There's always much more to learn and it seems that this time, you've encountered another aspect of your feminine.'

'Not another one. I thought that I met her –the maiden of my previous dreams.'

'You did, but when the symbolic feminine is split, as it appears that this dream is alluding to, then the dark aspect requires attention to bring it into greater consciousness.'

'How can it be split?' Carty asked, rolling his brows down frowning a little.

'Possibly a family complex passed down from one generation to the next or, more likely, a direct traumatic experience encountered during childhood, which has remained buried and unhealed in the psyche.'

Carty physically shuddered in the stifling airlessness. Green, true to his uncanny form, had struck a raw nerve, his words causing memories to flood back of the utter despair the young Carty had experienced with his mother's worsening alcoholism. They had been smothered by his grandmother's well-meaning love of the church, forcing him to forget his hurt and forge a future life of success.

'Is there anything I can do to avoid all this?'

Green placed a reassuring hand on his friend's shoulder, his eyes giving him away. A wounded healer, he had felt similar pain. 'Don't worry, Scott, you're not being given anything more than you can handle. Tell me are you still practising those esoteric martial arts that you learned in Siberia?'

'Yes, why?'

'As I hinted the other day, perhaps you're using these, unconsciously, in an attempt to make sense of your life, which is probably a mistake.'

'But...,' Carty balked.

'And before you try to defend yourself look at the symbols in that nightmare you've just had. The young woman is toying with a beast by dangling her legs above the water. You can't see her face but she's young, callow and supposedly spellbound, unaware of the danger or perhaps waiting to be consumed. Do these conjure up any other important associations?' His eyes seemed to powerfully bore through the hot haze. 'No? Then let's have a dip in the plunge pool. I'm cooked.'

The water was, as usual, freezing but the initial shock and forced gasped breaths were rewarded immeasurably by the slow ebbing of heat from their skin. Soon they were standing comfortably below the running water of the pool's oversized faucet.

'So, any thoughts, Scott?'

'Well, you believe the images are alluding to my practice of those arts but I can't see the connection.'

'Okay, ever heard of *Kundalini*?'

He shrugged, turning down his lips.

'It's the mystical coiled serpent energy of Hindu yogic practices. The ultimate goal is for the initiate to release its power up the spine to the head thereby becoming enlightened. The problem with this is that it requires careful instruction from an adept and there's no guarantee it might ever happen. Any type of focused energy work, like the *Qi gong*, will lead to an accumulation which at some stage must be released. The energy we're talking about here is of a watery nature and by that I mean it is tied up with the sexual function of the body, the potential to procreate in millions. It's a raw power, Scott, and clearly, to my mind you do not have the maturity or tools to handle it, as hinted at by the image of young woman who is hypnotised and in its grasp.'

'And the dragon is significant of this *Kundalini*, but from a Chinese perspective?'

'I believe so.'

'And nothing to do with Lisa being part Chinese, then?'

'Who knows? When it comes to the unconscious, synchronicity is often at play. I do think that you need to take heed of both your inner and outer worlds. As the alchemists taught, use the higher aspects of your mind to transmute those emotions that are slaves to this existence...,' he beamed, 'and enjoy the process.'

'Are you implying that the mind is everything?'

'Not the rational thinking of the brain but the complex heart-mind or *Xin* of Taoism. It's something that the ancients understood very well and encompassed within their teachings.'

'But lost today?'

'I wouldn't say lost but just not valued. In these arts the body is perceived to have three centres of consciousness, one of which is the heart. Recent research has demonstrated that the heart can react to physical events seconds before they occur, as if it had an uncanny precognition of them. This, quite incredibly, seems to have been known thousands of years ago and that a relaxed prepared body can instinctively react to a situation better that an anxious stressed one, hence the concept of *internal* boxing which is the epitome of all martial arts.'

I wonder from where he referenced that? Carty mused, looking down into the water, secretly fearful that the beast was lurking there.

'I also mentioned the practice of active imagination recently,' Green uttered.

'You did.'

'And so I suggest that you quietly sit and actively go back into that dream to ask the young lady a question.'

'What question is that?'

'I'm afraid I can't advise you. It needs to instinctively come from your heart-mind, at that moment.'

They both dragged themselves up the ladder and, wrapped in towels, Carty noted that surprisingly, over the last few years, his friend's face had become noticeably more youthful.

Back in the steam room the air was thick and heavy but the small place was still empty, although, Green knew it would soon fill.

'How are James and Diane?' Green asked, knowing that Carty still cared for his ex-wife and missed his son terribly.

'James is really very happy at school and I get to see him as often as he wants. Diane seems fine.'

'I knew that her liaison with Nick would be a disaster.'

'She never talks about it and really, we don't have much to discuss unless it involves James.'

'Well, at least you're on good talking terms.'

Carty shrugged and opened his arms out wide. 'Naturally, she saved my life!'

They endured a silence for some minutes, observing the boundaries of their bodies blur within the atmosphere before Green pulled his legs up again into the contorted lotus posture which prompted Carty's recollection.

'Gordon, can I ask you about the image on that piece of paper.'

'Which image was that?'

'It was just inside the cover of the book, The Secret of the Golden Flower that you lent to me - an odd hand-drawn outline of a human body superimposed with a lattice of intersecting of circles.'

'Ah, that must have been the *Qabala*.'

Carty retained his stare. 'So you didn't draw it?'

'No. It was in the book when I bought it second-hand, years ago. I had completely forgotten about it.'

He nodded. 'And what's the *Qabala*?'

'It's the Tree of Life, the main tradition in the practice of the Western esoteric tradition. Allegedly, it stems from the ancient Egyptian mystery schools although it was preserved and handed down within the inner doctrine of the Jewish faith during the middle ages.'

'Don't you think it's a bit odd that it was sitting in a book on Taoist meditation?'

'Perhaps, but it has everything to do with our conversations. The *Qabala's* ten sacred spheres, or *Sephiroth*, are linked together by 22 pathways, which interestingly all pass through the heart centre. Each is, in essence, a *temenos*, a sacred space used in active imagination to safely navigate the powerful archetypal energies expressed through our bodies, our psyches. What the adepts of old knew was, that to attempt to work with these energies without a formalised structure would leave us open to the possibility of our hidden dragons overwhelming our consciousness,' he uttered, puckering up a deep-creased smile. 'The *Qabala* is a powerful tool to be used alongside dreams in providing the individual the ability to communicate with the wider personality and absorb the projections of our darker natures. Why don't you bring the picture when we next meet and we can discuss its various aspects,' he added as the door jerked open on them, sucking the heaviness of his words out with the steam.

'Ah, Gordon?' a familiar voice chimed through the mist. 'Tom said you would be in here. Hello, Scott.'

Carty raised a palm, but his face carried confusion at the sight of Whitehall Jack standing there, stripped bare, with only a towel covering his waist, his slicked hair reflecting the muffled light of the place's one solitary lamp.

'Hi, Jack, it's a surprise to see you,' Carty replied, shooting a frown at Green. Clearly the man had arranged this and had kept it from him.

'A nice one, I hope?'

'Jack suggested meeting us here, if he had some news,' Green interjected.

'News?'

'Yes, Scott, and I wish it wasn't so vague.' The Whitehall man shook his hand and then sat, fixing him with his characteristic dispassionate glare. 'We believe Lena was tailed – followed at Heathrow.'

'What!' Carty barked.

Green gripped his friend's shoulder, reassuringly. 'Jack, you just said *believe...*, so how sure are you of your sources?'

'Pretty sure. The asset boarded another plane later on, bound for Dubai, travelling under a pseudonym. We're guessing that he's an agent from one of the CIS countries and we're having him followed.'

Carty was silent, his skin crawling, oblivious to the temperature and numbed, as if he was just a spectator to a cruel hoax, waiting for its punchline to come. He exchanged frantic glances with the older men, for seconds that felt like minutes and then the shock wave hit him.

'Jack, I can't simply stay here, I must go to Dubai to find Lena.'

'That would be a mistake.' The mandarin's voice was gravel.

'But why?'

'Because it would blow the cover and put her at risk. Anyway, we know where she's staying.'

'So you're using her as a decoy?'

'I suppose that is a crude description of the plan but don't worry she'll be safe. Tell me, when did you last speak with her?'

'When I dropped her at the airport. She's not been answering any of my texts since.'

'Did she give any indication of why she was going to Dubai or acted strangely in any way, before?' Jack probed.

'She really told me very little. Just that it was a reunion with some old college friends. I didn't want to pry.'

'Well she's gone there for a reason and not telling you about it, is troubling me. My hunch is that it's something to do with the transmutation technology. She knew about it but just how much, we were uncertain. Only you can shed more light on that, Scott.'

'I didn't discuss it in any detail with her.'

'Perhaps you didn't but this smells of a trap.'

'But why would anyone want to follow her?' Green interjected.

'To possibly detain her and then lure Scott in. He's the one who discovered this technology.'

'But like Lena, I simply learnt that it was operating in Russia and that D'albo was involved in organising shipments of nuclear waste to feed it. We know nothing about its actual functioning or where it's situated, so why would they need her or me?'

Jack rasped an in-breath and rubbed the beads of sweat from his shoulders. 'I don't yet have an answer but all my senses tell me that it's the reason why Lena has gone off radar.'

The door swung open again and two young city brutes barged in, loudly sharing their day's business. Green rolled his eyes and unfolded his legs to shuffle from his seated position, beckoning for Carty to follow him. Jack remained behind.

Once outside Green squared up, gripping his friend by the triceps and forcing eye contact, but Carty had silently shut his eyes to focus, churning over the news and trying to seek answers as all the while, an image loomed.

He was in the taiga again, lumbering over fallen boughs, the raw concoction of rotten wood and wet ferns pricking his nose and triggering memories of his fight for survival, just a couple of years before. A quickening of his heart heightened his senses as he moved into an opening and caught sight of Boris, standing motionless next to the cabin. Slowly, the Buryat turned at the sound of his approach, beaming a tranquil smile which instantly settled him. Then, he heard the man's voice, speaking as if telepathically, repeating one phrase, over and over: "Silence is the key to action."

'Scott, are you feeling well?' Gordon Green recognised the younger man's shocked state. 'Do you want to get out of here?'

'I'm good,' he whispered looking about to see who was within ear shot. 'Gordon, for God's sakes don't tell Jack about the books. This story with Lena could be just a ploy to get information out of me and you.'

'Don't worry they're safely hidden and Jack's people will take care of Lena. I'm sure she'll contact you soon.'

'What if she doesn't? What if others know about the machine's real function and she's being held against her will in order to give that up?'

Green tightened his grip. 'Scott, think for a minute. Jack said that she's safe in Dubai and she may have gone there for the very reasons she told you.'

The logic of Green's reasoning lingered as they moved on into the dry rooms.

'Given the situation, Scott, do you still need to make that trip to Hong Kong?'

'I don't think I have much choice. If I don't go the investors will be calling for redemptions, which we will not be able to meet, and then the fund will collapse.'

'But the projects will still carry on reducing greenhouse gases?'

‘Sorry, I can’t think about any of that now.’

Jack then appeared, surreptitiously scoping the few other men present, all supine on separate plinths at one end of the room, before sitting to face Carty.

‘Scott, is there anything that you’re not telling me?’ he asked.

Carty felt the tickling of perspiration slipping down his spine. ‘What do you mean, Jack?’

‘It’s clear from my question, isn’t it?’ he followed testily.

‘Not really!’ Carty muttered, numbed by the man’s statement as his mind revisited the dank cave at Baikal, succumbing to the ethereal image of the machine’s levitation within its blue nauseating aura. He choked and then coughed violently.

‘Are you feeling okay, Scott?’

‘Just a little light-headed.’ Feigning a gasp he slipped off the slatted plinth. ‘This heat is getting to me,’ he added, looking askance at Jack as a notion crept into his head.

He knows about the machine’s ultimate secret and soon, others will, too.

* * * *

Blue tits flitted in and out the hydrangea beds as Scott Carty stood motionless under a mature cherry tree, the major feature of his London garden. The hushed wind of their hovering wings and a cheery *tsu-tsu-hu-hu* call gave him some comfort against Whitehall Jack’s inquisition than the two cans of lager he had hastily drunk on his return. Boris had warned him of the dangers of practising the internal arts under the influence of alcohol but now, a temporarily inebriated mind helped him switch states in order to quell the nagging fretfulness caused by Lena’s predicament.

The spring evenings were lengthening and with them the ambient temperature, allowing him to relax into his being. Soon he felt that familiar welling-up of heat from the pit of his stomach, pulsating out through his limbs and digits, bathing him in an envelope of unruffled calm. The urge to move or to think was slowly dulled and he felt detached in a cocoon as if he might be observing himself from afar.

'Go back into that dream and ask the young woman a question.' Green's instruction of earlier that day resounded again in his head. Taking a breath, he galvanised himself as he closed his eyes.

In an instant, he felt he was falling, as if the earth had disappeared from under his feet, plunging him deep into the depths of that pool to face the beast once more. His lungs burnt as coils of leathery flesh writhed around his torso squeezing the breath out of him, while somewhere above the surface his desperate stare could just make out the young woman transfixed and powerless as the beast's head reared up to consume her. Frantically, with his last ounce of strength, Carty wrestled against the supernatural power imprisoning him, digging his nails under the creature's scales, but then, abruptly, the beast's body writhed and slammed him backwards, its mass smothering and dragging him, now spent, down in the inky waters.

'No!' he screamed, shuddering so violently that his legs gave way, collapsing him onto his back as he gasped at his breath. A chilly breeze, whipping across his sweat-drenched T-shirt pulled him from the hallucination, allowing the reassuring smell of the earth and birdsong to gently confirm that he was safe. Green had cautioned him of the dangers of dabbling with unconscious forces and instinctively, he now understood that he was facing a new trial, one which he might not have the character and strength of will to overcome.

Five

Turpan: Xinjiang Province, North West China

An arid wind whipped up dust devils along the path in the old woman's ramshackle garden. Even before the peak of the fast-approaching Central Asian summer, grapes were hanging in abundance from a rustic pergola that also acted as a porch to shade the house. Apricots and walnuts were also appearing to flourish a little earlier than usual and the reason, Ludmilla Anatolivna had persuaded her family and friends, was the special mineral-rich water she hauled up from an ancient Karez well that accessed underground streams from the nearby Flaming Mountains. Hafeza Bazareva gazed out on to the garden smiling inwardly in the knowledge that her ageing aunt's neighbours used the same water source without achieving similar results. Whatever Ludmilla Anatolivna's secret, Hafeza understood that the woman possessed unusual powers.

'Chai?' the old woman asked, scarved in floral linen as she waved the tarnished silver Ottoman pot at her niece, one of the few heirlooms from her former Soviet life in neighbouring Tajikistan. Drinking tea was a ceremony that could not be overlooked, and the young woman took great joy in pouring for her senior relative and then listening to her stories as the afternoon heat subsided and the fragrances of jasmine and roses filtered into the small house.

After some minutes of sipping in silence, Ludmilla Anatolivna stopped to examine her niece's smooth features and green eyes, recalling her handsome father and how his family had claimed, ridiculously, that his origins were Roman - his village rumoured to have been settled by a lost legion long before the Silk Road had forged a path through this desolate terrain. The vast region had in fact been settled by many different Indo-European peoples since ancient times. Even the Uyghur, a Turkic race that now claimed Xinjiang as its state, were latecomers. In truth, it had been much like Europe, once a gaggle of separate tribes overrunning each other or by outsiders, until critical mass was reached and nation states finally took hold with the Chinese Ming Empire, only partially annexing the region from the late 1750s. Stalin had even been tempted to invade its Eastern border in the mid-1930s, to merge it into a greater Turkestan with the other Soviet Central Asian States.

Hafeza Bazareva caught her aunt's unfocused stare and simpered.

'Is there an issue you wish to discuss?' the old woman asked.

'Yes...,' she responded, understanding that the mage saw beyond the veil of the ordinary. 'I've been having a recurring dream that troubles me.'

'I see. Then we must consult the pieces,' she answered dryly, her creased features hardly moving as she pointed to a hardwood box sitting on the crazed windowsill. Hafeza knew it well and collected it, drawn as ever to the lacquered chequered inlay that ran like a ribbon around its lid's edge.

'So, you know what to do. Take some pieces out and hold them while you ask for guidance.'

Hafeza nodded and picked four worn chess figures at random, caressing them between her palms as she closed her eyes while Ludmilla Anatolivna muttered a prayer in a foreign tongue, one that the younger woman did not understand. She had observed this same practice on many occasions as a young girl, when strangers struggling with life had sought wisdom and answers from her aunt.

'Now place them here on the table, in any order you choose.'

Again, she followed, setting them carefully down on their bases, quietly grinning as the fading light tipped the ambience into expectation and lent an almost mystical quality to her aunt's countenance. Then, the mage closed her eyes and began to move her arthritic hands, awkwardly grasping the pieces, and sliding them about, hovering their relative positions to each other a number of times in order to sense their energies. Short expletives were grunted here and there, in different tones, giving clues to her intuitions.

Within a few minutes she stalled, her face pained as if she doubted herself.

'What is it, Ludmilla Anatolivna?'

'Much more than you can ever understand is at stake. I see a conflict with two people – a man and a woman,' she uttered, taking her niece's hand. 'You must act from your heart when you are with them. Trust it and don't be fooled.'

The old woman's straggled cat rubbed up against Hafeza's leg as she listened. The reading was severe and unlike any other her aunt had given her in the past.

'Who are these people?'

'One is known to you and the other is a stranger, but I cannot see which is which, the man or the woman.'

'When will I meet them?'

'Soon.' The answer was sharp and she realised that her aunt was tiring.

'Thank you, Ludmilla Anatolivna,' she said, leaning over to kiss her cheeks. The older woman held her hands and smiled strangely, exchanging a look that beckoned questioning.

'You didn't ask me about the fourth piece,' she whispered.

'No, I didn't realise...'

'The dark always hides itself.'

Hafeza tilted her head. 'I don't understand.' The usual warm feeling of joy in being with her close relative was now overpowered by the same sense of fear that had stirred following the recent dream. In it, a stranger, a man, had appeared at her door with a book and frantically, had begged her to hide it, but she denied him.

'Interesting, isn't it. You chose the pieces but unconsciously ignored the fourth and its meaning. In Chinese culture, not ours, four is an unlucky number perhaps because when it is pronounced, it sounds similar to the word that means *death,*' she said, in her Farzi dialect that had prevailed in parts of Central Asia since before Alexander the Great's annexation, almost two millennia before.

'In all cultures there is an unconscious aversion to the fourth function since it brings all cycles to completion, forcing that which is hidden to be brought into consciousness. This is why the great mandalas of the Hindus and Tibetan Buddhism display patterns of circles within squares. They are even intricately sewn into our Turkish rugs!' she added, nodding. 'In the West, where much of its arcane mystery school imagery owes its heritage to the cultures from the centre of the world, they are fearful of the number 13: 1 plus 3, equals 4. The Thirteenth card in the tarot deck is the Hanging Man who, suspended upside down with one leg crossed over the other to form the number 4, patiently waits to be released by forces beyond his control.

Hafeza had listened patiently. 'Is this fourth figure interacting with these other two and myself?'

Ludmilla Anatolivna looked grave. 'The fourth piece is not a person. It is energy and it's outside of the others' control but feeds off their fears and emotions. That is why you must act from your heart and not be swayed.'

'It sounds as if this is very negative?'

'Energy is neither good nor bad but is shaped by the unconscious mind of humanity where the unexpressed dark shadows collectively engage with and consume life like a wild beast that has been trapped without food. Finally, as it breaks free, it has no understanding of the delicate nature of this existence and so tramples everything indiscriminately, underfoot.'

'So, I must focus to master my emotions as you have shown me?'

'Yes, silence, stillness and patience will also allow you to master your fears and see into others. But make no mistake, you will need to take great care because one of these people will be aware of your ability to see their darkness.'

'How will I know who they are?'

'The one with the pure heart will become obvious to you.'

Stars were now hanging in the unpolluted inky skies as Hafeza Bazareva closed the wooden gate and began to stroll the few hundred metres back to her apartment. In the warm breeze she could hear the roosting collared doves and sparrows calling among the jujube and ash, but she was still uncomfortably absorbed with her aunt's extraordinary warning. From the porch, Ludmilla Anatolivna watched her disappear into the night, conscious of the information she had held back, fearful that it might weaken the young woman's resolve or sway the clarity of her decision-making. But she was now deeply troubled at the events about to unfold, causing her to reflect on her own long life. Leaving Siberia at a much younger age than her niece, for a warmer existence in Tajikistan, she began working in a cotton facility, which gave her more freedom to develop her skills in provision for the times that were coming. Now she understood that they were close by and that her life's devotion, the deep meditation techniques taught to her by her father - a legacy of an undead monk in Buryatia - were to be put to the ultimate test.

Six

A private airfield, just outside London

The interior of the executive jet was smaller than the Tupelov 86 in which Carty had flown to Baikal with Lena, but while less decadent in its décor it made up for it in its modernity, especially the new flat plasma screens. Lisa's entourage, though, were less colourful – two heavies who looked like Mongolian wrestlers mocked up in undersized Buster Keaton suits with fat spilling over strained shirt collars. It was clear what their role was: to protect this Anglo-Chinese beauty at any costs, and despite Carty's slight frame and genial smile, his reputation as the man who took on the Russians evidently worried them as they eyed him suspiciously while patting him down.

'Sorry, Scott, my uncle never allows any breach of protocol, which I must admit is a little boring,' Lisa said in her laboured way, winking as she sat down in her skin-tight Gucci jeans and a T-shirt of a matching shade carrying the name of some fictitious baseball team. 'I'm rather pleased we have this chance to be alone.'

'Thank you,' Carty replied automatically, feeling somewhat awkward. It was already dark outside and he had buckled himself into a reclining tan leather chair opposite her, not knowing quite what to expect from the long journey ahead.

'Yes, there really is a lot to discuss. I admire how you came through that awful fraud case. Nick told me all the details that the media didn't report, and that's when I realised we probably have a common future in business together.'

Carty attempted a grin, recalling Nick's remarks about her aspirations.

'That sounds very intriguing, and I would be happy to talk through your plans, just as soon as I can sort out the projects and their stolen revenues.'

'Well, you can be sure that situation will be resolved.'

'I can?' His dissonant tone barely disguised surprise.

'Oh yes.' She wound one leg around the other's knee, tucking a foot behind her calf and then pulled out her hair grip, casually holding it in her teeth as she arched her crown forward to let her locks cascade down before tossing them back up, the strands narrowly missing his face. Then she began to twirl them, resetting the grip and poking in a pen, to hold it all in place. Carty froze at the sight, momentarily reminded of the stark expression of the young woman in his terrifying dream. She tilted her chin to look out of the window and then askance at him. 'But surely you must want to know more about my family's ventures and why your environmental expertise will be a perfect fit for us?'

A slight Asian woman with softer features than Lisa, appeared, placing a teapot and two, ornate handle-less cups on the mahogany table.

'Nick mentioned that you're involved in manufacturing.'

'Yes, we have been for over 30 years,' she said, pouring for him. 'My uncle and father set up an engineering facility in Xinjiang..., such a godforsaken place. Then, slowly with the economic changes, one thing led to another and now, we are one of China's main industrial groups but we need to expand, to move into hi-tech manufacturing and R&D.'

'Do you mean silicon chips and IT?'

'No, that's already a market saturated with so many producers in China. We're aiming to leapfrog it and embrace more advanced technology.'

'Not armaments?'

'Uh uh,' she shook her head, 'too risky and anyway that's controlled. No, we're looking to the future, to renewables.'

'That ties up with what Nick said..., something about Brown's Gas and your company's marine engines.'

'He did? So you're already familiar with that?'

'Not really. He's always on the periphery of new developments, and it's hard to keep up with him sometimes.'

'He said the same thing about you. I was thrilled when he told me about your solar heat-pumps and how efficient they are compared to existing technologies.'

Nick told me he hadn't said much to her. I just pray that he didn't mention anything else.

'Well, that's because they employ a patented new alloy and the reworking of an engineering concept.'

'I know. We've had our people look through the patent and suggest some modifications. I noted that you had applied for the patent after you returned from Russia.'

Carty flushed. 'What modifications have they come up with, exactly?'

'I'm not technical at all so can only tell you that apparently, the alloy is already obsolete.'

'Obsolete...really?' he stammered,

'Yes, apparently, and the engineering is not as sophisticated as one might think either, so the whole thing can be replicated quite cheaply and easily.'

Is she implying that the patent is worthless? Is this the price I have to pay for her help? Carty thought, attempting a feigned interest and trying to stifle his growing annoyance with her blithe manner.

'Although,' she continued, 'your technology could be a huge success in China in reducing pollution and the growing energy crisis.'

'But Nick implied that you're more focused on Brown's Gas to solve that issue.'

'He's right and we are, first in adapting it for use in our marine engines and then scaling up to build a small power station. The problem is that it's shrouded in controversy and opposition. I'm sure that Nick elucidated on that?'

Carty shook his head, unconvincingly.

'No? The claims made for transmutation of nuclear waste?'

'I really wouldn't know. I hadn't heard of Brown's Gas until Nick mentioned it, the same day I met you at his house. He led me to believe that it's just an unusual mixture of hydrogen and oxygen that burns more efficiently than hydrogen alone,' he responded, feeling that he was forced to verbally fence with her. 'Anyway, how did you first meet Nick?' he lunged back.

'Why do you ask?'

'I'm just curious. He seems to be really taken with you.'

'I see.' Her emerald eyes remained fixed on his, unimpressed as she was with the innuendo. 'We were introduced at a conference a week or so ago.'

That's odd. Nick implied that they had already been working together for some time.

Lisa read the confusion on his face. 'But our senior engineers have been in contact with him for some time.'

I suppose that's plausible.

'I notice that your patent is held jointly with a Lena Isotova.'

'Yes, she's my partner.' His eyes narrowed. Hearing Lena's name being mentioned threw up the painful frustration of still not knowing what had happened to her. Lisa read him again.

'Please forgive me. I didn't mean to pry.'

'You didn't.' He remembered his manners and why he had taken up Lisa's offer of help when no one else had or could. 'If you don't mind me asking, Lisa, just how do you intend to persuade my local partners to pay the missing electricity revenues and then ensure that they continue to do so?'

She grinned. 'Your emissions projects are extremely important to the local government in Xinjiang, and my uncle wants to support this. He will suggest to your local partners that our manufacturing group takes the electricity and pays what's owed, directly to your investment fund.'

'And why do you think they will co-operate? They haven't done so far.'

Her brows arched with a dismissive look that silenced his doubts. 'They will be given a short period of time to repay everything that is overdue as well as any interest owed.'

'It sounds like this has already been decided.'

'They don't really have a choice,' she uttered, her well-formed lips slowly rucking in to a wide grin that made him nervous. The solution seemed all too neat and echoed Green's remarks of a *quid pro quo* – what she might want in return.

'I am very grateful for your family's help and my partners will, I'm sure, agree to pay a success fee to you or your uncle's companies for resolving the problems. That's standard practice in my industry.'

His words were lost as one of the bodyguards lumped up, drawing her attention before bending to whisper behind a hand, into her ear. She unravelled her legs raising an index finger to excuse herself to Carty as she replied in an odd dialect, shaking her head and mentioning a familiar word that unnerved the Englishman. The minder bowed his head and then returned back along the aisle.

'Did I hear you say Dubai just then?' Carty queried.

'Yes, the plan was to land there to pick up a contact but things have changed. We don't need to now. We're flying straight to Xinjiang.'

'Not Hong Kong?' he asked, his expression hung in mild confusion.

'No, my uncle is already waiting for us in Urumqi.. Now, where were we?'

'Discussing a success fee.'

'That's a little premature. We should wait until the matter is resolved. I'm sure that our two groups can work together in future, to offset any fees.'

Carty balked and then bluffed. 'It is a very reasonable suggestion, and I trust you don't think I am being churlish but I would need to run it by my board to get an in-principle agreement before we could discuss any cooperation.'

'Naturally, Scott, but what you have to understand is that my uncle makes business decisions on the spot without the need for consensus. It's the way things are done in the East. We tend to act fast when our hearts tell us to and we also get upset if someone reneges on an agreement.'

The words seemed to slow down as they left her mouth, echoing their intent inside his head. Despite her unperturbed disposition and the disarming smile, he sensed her whole body was electrically charged and totally focused on any response he made to what seemed like her veiled threat. Her painted eyelids lingered closed for a fraction longer than they should over her piercing irises while her indulgent perfume wafted around him. Carty puckered his lips to the raised fingers of both hands, held in prayer in front of his face as if unconsciously warding off a spell as memories filtered back of his first encounter with Lena. She was so diametrically unlike the glamour puss sitting before him. There was something sullied about Lisa, a sophisticated persona seemed to shroud her, not quite allowing the freedom to be her true self. At that instant she blinked again but more rapidly and then pulled back, habitually running a hand up her slender neck to entwine the few locks that had escaped the hairgrip. Her lightly freckled skin was flushed as she gazed down at the gold filigree and sapphire rings on her delicate fingers. Then, chameleon-like, she was back in her comfort zone again, eyeing Carty for a reaction to her statement for some seconds until the slow constant buzz of a mobile phone forced her to sit up and answer in Chinese. It was an opportunity for him to quietly survey the woman's body language once more. Her frame was somewhere between petite and average and he understood that it was this divinely proportioned projection of elegance that was so pleasing to the male eye.

What is this charade all about? he wondered as she kept her gaze locked onto his. *If she's after the patents, then that can't be agreed without Lena's consent.* But that notion didn't ring true to his keen mind. Lisa had implied that her industries could manufacture his solar heat pumps regardless and that any legal penalties for doing so were not enforceable in China, not unless one had power. *So, what does she want?* The Brown's Gas technology, as Nick had advised, was already researched and would soon be functioning, and she was well informed about its possibilities. Carty doubted, though, if she knew anything about the potential of the machine he had uncovered in Siberia. *Nick swore he hadn't said anything to her.*

Her modus operandi still didn't appear clear and he felt on edge as his thoughts stirred for the other reason why, his heart told him, he was on this flight. It didn't come and for the moment, though, he had to accept the premise that her uncle wanted to step into the renewables sector in a big way, and by helping Carty, his group could spin out similar emission reduction projects all across China, probably pulling in huge government subsidies to do so. He was under no illusion, though, that for any deal, only the crumbs would be left for *Sole Carbon.*

His ruminations stalled with the reappearance of the maid, carrying a tray to collect the things.

'I'm going up to speak to the pilot and then catch some sleep in the forward cabins. You're welcome to do the same,' Lisa said, winding up her call.

'Thanks but I think I will stay here.'

'Very well. Simone will serve you a meal and I look forward to telling you about my environmental plan for Xinjiang, later. It's one, I believe, you're going to love.'

Plan? Perhaps she is genuinely interested in the environment, he concluded, *and that will be a good thing for whole world.* China was already flexing its economic muscle to rapidly increase production of its domestic renewables sector, reducing manufacturing costs and thereby global prices – all this triggered by fear of the huge environmental issues it was beginning to face as areas within its borders suffered the impact of climate change and desertification, the slow inundation of windswept sand swamping fertile land.

As Lisa stood, the two minders, seated nearby instantly rose. They had kept a close eye on Carty during the conversation, and now he felt an unsettling mood of helplessness descend.

Who had she been talking with on the phone and why had they cancelled the plan to land in Dubai? he pondered, watching her glide silently up the narrow fuselage. While the somewhat contrived conversations had provided a distraction of sorts, an anxiety had crystallised with mention of Dubai again, so soon after Jack's information that Lena had been tailed at Heathrow on her way there. *Is Lena being silent because she's trying to protect me...by selling out?*

Jack had implied as much but the notion was too much for him to process and he found his gaze once again drawn to the cockpit door where Lisa was stopped, her lips parted provocatively as she pulled out the clasp to let her hair cascade down to her waist. The offer to join her in the front cabin was there, if he wanted it. He closed his eyes to the woman and remembered his vision of Boris, seeking sanctuary in silence as he prayed that Lena was simply visiting friends and would be in contact when she could.

Seven

The taiga, Siberia

The path to the shack was rarely walked and had become overgrown with a tangle of meshed fern, rhododendron and brambles, forcing the Buryat's decision to climb up and over a huge granite sarsen and then scramble down on to its wooden roof. His motive was clear: not to leave any obvious evidence of his approach to the secluded place. Despite the dense pine foliage he easily scaled the rocks, but in pushing through its branches, was now smothered in the sticky resin from their cones. It mattered little to the native man, who had spent the night watching the location for signs of strangers under similar trees and within spitting distance. The plan with Lubimov was to leave dead boughs in a pre-agreed pattern, just off the main path, some 50 metres away, so that either of them would know to abort their meeting if danger threatened. But that hadn't been necessary.

Rusting padlocks were still holding the door tight and he squatted, calmly chewing a ball of *sera,* pine sap, his ears attuned to the forest's sounds. Soon the odd chattering of a jay called out and a knowing grin broke his heavy Eurasian features. Lubimov's signal was covert as he made his approach, stepping on fallen saplings as much as possible to make his way through the undergrowth. The men's mutual smiles told of an extended absence and as soon as they were within range, they grabbed each other in a bear hug.

'I thought you would have found a way inside already,' Lubimov joked, pulling at a set of keys from a chain on his belt loop.

'No reason to.'

The place's stolid musty ambience came to life, rushing at them as he pushed the door open and waved Boris inside. The Buryat coughed and blinked, adjusting his eyes to the dimness.

'How long has this place been closed up for?' he probed, clocking the background whir of electrical meters.

'A while. I've only visited a few times since Scott left.' His ageing features displayed nervousness. 'So, what's news, Boris?' The Buryat only ever contacted him with their pre-agreed code word, if something of importance needed to be discussed.

'Ivan Yegorovich has gone missing,' he responded, calmly.

'What! When?' The older man's ire rose with his heightened tone, disbelief shining back from his eyes in the low light.

'Yesterday, I believe, at the beach lodge. I took him there just days before.'

'But how has this happened? No one knows his movements, except you.'

'I'm certain we were not followed and from the few clues remaining, it wasn't a random incident.'

'You're implying it was planned. That someone has exposed him, possibly someone we know.'

'It's very likely. A party who knows that he spends the summer by Baikal but who also knows my movements.'

'*So what* do we do now?'

'I've already instructed my network to scout the trail left behind by the kidnappers, but there's not much to go on. Whoever took him did a professional job.'

'The trail dies out?'

'Not completely. We know that a helicopter picked him up about 250 metres along the beach. They couldn't disguise the landing marks and I don't think they cared too much about doing so, either.'

'They're after the technology.' Agitated, the scientist paced over the rug and its hidden trap door, trying to come to terms with the information. 'But who could have found out about it..., unless the Englishman has sold us out?'

'That's plausible. He might have been offered a price he couldn't refuse or was blackmailed into revealing it, possibly under pressure from CentralniySib's people.'

'Why do you suspect CentralniySib is behind this?'

'Because Lena was working for them when she discovered that her director, Kosechenko was behind the smuggling of nuclear waste into Russia. It's also likely that Scott subsequently told her that he had seen Ivan Yegorovich alive.'

'So, she too may have been compromised into giving up this information. I had my doubts about revealing the machine to Scott but all the signs told me he was the one.'

Boris smiled. 'And you're intuition wasn't wrong, I'm sure.'

Lubimov paused and parked himself against the bench. Boris' announcement had unceremoniously wrenched open a door he believed had been firmly closed. Scratching at the few grey strands on his weathered scalp he observed the monotonous flicker of one of the gauge's full scale deflection – still measuring an almost limitless amount of energy being produced in the cavern beneath their feet. Since Scott Carty's departure, he had tried to put the image of the enigma out of his mind and forget it existed at all. After all, he had no way of exposing it to an unprepared world and even if he had tried to, he and anyone linked to it, however remotely, would be found dead, as had his father and the rest of Ivan Yegorovich's team.

'This abduction fits with the information I received some time ago,' he remarked, suddenly.

'What information was that?' Boris quizzed.

'Ivan Yegorovich's original prototype has begun to rapidly slow down and will, in all likelihood, stop if it hasn't done so already.'

'So my hunch was probably right?'

'Yes, and it's all starting to add up. Kosechenko will never give up control of a highly lucrative yet very dark business transmuting nuclear waste. They must have got wind that Ivan Yegovorich faked his death and has been hidden all these years in the taiga. He's the only person who can solve their problem. We have to find him before they extract everything he knows, including knowledge of the second machine, here, below our feet.'

'Even, if we could find him there's a good chance he's already been forced to talk.'

'If that's the case, they will kill him and then hunt us down, and then its real secret - *overunity* - will be left in the hands of monsters.'

'I won't let that happen.' The Buryat said frowning as he eyed Lubimov with an uncharacteristic look of fear. While not a scientist, he instinctively understood that specific energy points existed on the Earth's surface which channel and enhance enormous forces. But he was ignorant of the recent advances in quantum biophysics that had begun to access this mysterious arena and accept that the energetic spark of life functions in a manner not measureable in research laboratories. Locating and accessing these energetic sites had been an inborn reflex of ancient man but as civilisation began to organise and take control of daily life, it became a hidden art nurtured and passed on only from shaman to shaman. Later, natural philosophers revered this esoteric skill in siting the holiest places of worship but with the march of mechanistic science and industrialised times, it had been almost lost. Here, though, at Baikal almost 30 years earlier, Ivan Yegorovich, a maverick scientist had located by chance one of these rare points of resonance and had developed a water vortex technology, harnessing limitless free power. Boris had no idea where the man's research papers were now, if they existed at all.

'But even if they do learn of your machine's existence they're only interested in its ability to transmute spent nuclear waste so that they can continue their business.'

Lubimov shook his head slowly. 'It won't take their scientific team too long to realise that something far more esoteric is being accessed at this particular place.'

* * * *

The cyclical drone of the twin jet engines had coaxed Scott Carty into a deep sleep for some hours but then the aircraft's steady banked decline caused his ears to depressurise and his eyes to flicker open for milliseconds.

In that brief moment he saw the shocked face of Lena Isotova, hovering in front of him and he lunged out to hold her but she remained a desperate phantom inches from his fingertips, her fearful eyes staring down at her feet. Something that took the form of a pool of tar was oozing across the aisle of the cabin and massing around their legs. A terrified urge rose from the pit of his stomach as he wrestled against drowsiness to wake up but he couldn't leave Lena and soon the black substance was up to their knees. He turned and span in the seat, struggling to release himself but the entity had begun sucking her into its shapelessness, strands of the stuff now entwining her body and looming over her, forming the loose form of the serpent's head.

His eyes shot open, horrified to find his hands gripping Lisa's slender throat.

'Scott!' she croaked, stunned by his paroxysm, and in that split-second, her minder was on him, landing a crashing blow across his temple and then folding his huge biceps around the Englishman's neck into a strangle-hold. Carty desperately banged on the thug's arm, for air as Lisa watched for some seconds, her countenance betraying a merciless glare, seeming to revel in the power she held over his life. Then, as he began to black out, his struggling stopped and he vaguely heard her bark instructions. Instantly he was released and unceremoniously dumped to the floor, face down. Choking, he slowly rolled over, his hand nursing his Adam's apple.

'What the hell just happened, Scott?'

Ignominiously, his eyes met hers. 'Lisa, I'm sorry. I had a terrible dream..., I don't know what got into me.'

'What kind of a dream would cause you to strangle me?' She fired back. 'Perhaps you need to find professional help?'

'I don't understand? What are you implying?'

'In behaving like that. There must be something serious that you're hiding.'

Carty slowly shook his head and pulled himself up to sit, protectively wrapping his arms around his shins and pulling his knees up into his chest as the minder loomed nearby. Lisa appeared puzzled at his apparent lack of concern.

Who is she, really? He wondered, cognisant of her slip in mien, reveling in wielding her authority like a hidden knife. How different she was to his Lena who oozed femininity and love from the core of her being, conscious of her effect, yet true to herself, unlike this woman's narcissistic shallowness.

'Well?' Lisa asked, nervously containing a reluctant smoker's cough, conscious that he was weighing her up. Carty sensed that her secretive nature did not suffer being exposed.

'I'm truly sorry, Lisa,' he responded with a half-hearted shrug. 'I've been under a lot of strain lately and I'm being haunted by a recurring nightmare.'

'Alright, I accept your apology.' She stood, and immediately switching her charm back on again she turned to the maid and insisted on tea before urging the Mongolian to help Carty back up into the seat.

As they mutely sipped from the cups, Carty tried to make sense of the vision's irruption. In his dream a day or so ago, the beast had been writhing in the pool, in the overgrown garden and had seemingly bewitched a young woman, the face of whom was hidden from him by her flowing hair. But in this vision, the serpent was emerging from a shapeless ooze about to smother Lena and himself. Green had alluded to the creature being linked with Carty's deeper feminine and that he wasn't yet able to handle the implications of stirring it up. Now, despite his fogged mind he sensed that whatever this beast's image represented and why it was making itself so violently present was somehow linked with the emergence of Lisa and that, as Green had implied, signalled something dangerous and dark.

The notion agitated Carty as he felt Lisa's crystal green gaze still surveying him as she casually fondled the rim of the porcelain cup.

'So, now perhaps you would like hear about my audacious scheme to *green* the Taklamakan?' she purred, blithely ignoring what had just happened. He nodded, recollecting the name of the desert from his brief scout of the internet, a day or so before. His fund's projects were just to its North East, in the Turpan Depression, one of the lowerest and hottest places on the planet. Quite why the fund had chosen to invest there, he had often questioned, but the quants' analysis had demonstrated very strong returns. What they had overlooked however, clouded by all their academic brilliance, was the human element of corruption.

'Why not,' he muttered, his temple still throbbing from the brute's strike.

'Good.' She pulled up the corners of her lips to form a well-practised show smile. 'Well then, the desert is a vast basin only slightly smaller in area than Germany and fabled for its huge shifting sand dunes, which cause rivers and lakes to disappear and then reappear in other places.'

'I read that it is locally known as the *Sea of Death,* a huge natural obstacle which confounded caravans navigating the Silk Road and forcing them to travel around, along its northern or southern borderlands.'

'Many people die there even today, wandering into it by accident.'

'But not from the radioactive fall-out then?' He uttered with a snort It was met with a stony glare. 'I meant because of the nuclear weapons testing in the region,' he added, attempting to correct himself.

She gently shook her head. 'That's at a place called Lop Nor, a dried up salt lake, but I don't believe there has been any testing for many years. Anyway, the area is sealed off under army control and has nothing to do with my project.'

'Which is to *green* the desert?'

‘Precisely. There are huge underground aquifers fed by the glacial run-off from the Kun Lun mountains along the edge of the Tibetan Plateau, to the south, and the Tien Shan mountains to the north.

The volume of water these aquifers contain is more than ten times that of the five Great Lakes of the USA.’

He arched his brows in mock surprise, hearing Oleg Lubimov’s voice in his head stating similar stupefying statistics about Lake Baikal. But Lisa was claiming that a body of water, ten times the volume of the world’s oldest and vastest lake lay beneath the Taklamakan. If it was true it was a numbing fact.

‘The only problem is that it’s brackish water, slightly salty.’

‘Yes, that would be a problem if you’re planning to irrigate the desert.’

‘Beijing has other ideas to develop the Tarim Basin’s many natural gas and oil deposits and plan for it to become the Houston of China, using these new water reserves.’

‘And you’re not happy with that?’

‘Not at all, but if through my family we can persuade government that this water can also be used to fertilise the desert, allowing lakes, grasslands and trees to be nurtured, then the climate in the region will change. That will then surely impact positively on the global climate and influence other arid regions around the world to follow suit. Just think about it, a vast desert at the heart of the world being transformed into a huge green eye.’

Carty pushed back into his seat, taken by the comment and Lisa’s exuberance. Gone was her corporate persona, dissolved it appeared by an almost juvenile rapture and wish fulfilment.

‘I understand why it’s *green* but why an *eye*?’

‘Because that’s that shape of the Tarim Basin when viewed from space. Our scientists believe that these underground reservoirs are responsible for the inexplicable systematic disappearance of carbon dioxide in the area.’

‘You mean that they are vast natural carbon sinks and that the Chinese government would need to ensure that they are not disturbed.’

'Or if they are, then they are replaced with another method for fixing carbon..., by growing hemp grass, shrubs and ultimately, trees.'

He grinned. It sounded perfect but, like so many other brilliantly simple suggestions, human nature and greed always found ways to leave them floundering.

I wonder how much of the natural environment needs to plundered before the corporate world gets the message. And then, will it be too late?

'Tell me, Lisa, how are you planning to pump up this water?'

'By using renewable energy, of course. The local area around Urumqi, is known as the wind tunnel of Xinjiang because quite often trains are blown off rails, and traffic has to stop until the winds calm. The government has sensibly sited one of the world's largest turbine farms there and is planning to increase its size, in time.'

'That's very encouraging to hear but what about desalination of the water. It's very costly.'

'We're proposing to build huge lagoons that are covered with transparent material like a greenhouse to collect pure water by evaporation and then use it in subsurface drip irrigation technology as has been used so successfully in Israel.'

'It's a massive vision.'

'It will take a generation to complete but it's my life's purpose.'

'And a very noble one too.'

'You'll see the turbines just before we land. The project has been coined the *three gorges of the sky* to emphasise the huge wind resource and the energy it produces.'

Carty forced a nod, aware of the Three Gorges Dam project on the mighty Yangtze River in Hubei province, one of the world's largest but blighted with environmental and social issues in its construction. The thought, though, was rudely shunted away as another one suddenly crashed his mind and he snatched a breath, incredulous at how fate was repeating itself.

'Lisa, do I need an entry visa for China?'

'Yes, if you are a British passport holder.'

Her response elicited a knotted sensation in his gut, leaving him feeling sick. Believing he had been on the way to Hong Kong, he had no need for a visa, but the sudden change of plans, mid-flight, meant that this was now in disarray. China was a completely different ball game.

'Well, I am and I don't have one.'

'Really?' She bit into her bottom lip.

Surely, she must have known this. He felt his heart start to pump in frustration, vexed by her quixotic reply.

'So how do you propose that I enter the country? It's impossible without a visa.' Anxious, he pressed her. 'There's no other option than to resume our original plan to go to Hong Kong first..,or possibly land in Dubai and apply for the Chinese visa there?'

'We're already well past Dubai, but there's no need to panic, Scott.'

'And why's that?'

'Because my family owns a private air strip outside Urumqi and no one will ever know you've landed or left.'

'But I'm not at all comfortable with that Lisa,' Carty balked. He had been here, in this same predicament before, in Russia. 'I cannot risk being deported. My position as the senior executive of my fund will be undermined, not to mention my credibility with investors.'

'Scott,' she replied concentrating her gaze out of the window, 'just trust me. Everything will be fine, and we'll have you safely back in London in a matter of days.'

'Huh!' he uttered in an attempt to quell his annoyance from boiling over, understanding that she wasn't going to be coerced into altering her plans. He toyed with calling Gordon Green secretly, from his mobile, to ask for Jack's help, but what would that achieve? An international scandal in which a UK national, formerly in the news for the Albion fraud, had boarded a private plane not knowing where it was bound and without a relevant visa, then accusing his hosts of deceiving him by any other name. That would impact badly on his reputation and his business, returning empty-handed, having lost Lisa's support in retrieving the missing revenues. He pulled his hands back through his hair, silently sighing and avoiding her gaze. Whether this situation was by design or just a coincidence, for the moment he would have go with it and trust that his instincts would guide him.

Eight

Urumqi – Xinjiang Province, China

The slight jolt of the landing gear meeting the desert runway sent up plumes of yellowish brown dust which obscured his view, and as the jet rapidly slowed, Lisa casually, unbuckled herself to stretch her arms high with an audible sigh. It did nothing to allay Carty's unease nor had her suddenly taking a call; speaking again in a tongue that was wholly alien to anything he'd heard before. Her two oversized colleagues were gabbling quietly between themselves, bending low to peer out of the small cabin windows, checking for signs of the marshalling crew and the portable steps.

Shortly, they had the fuselage door open and were standing to attention waiting to escort her off. She finished the conversation and unfolded her legs. 'Shall we go?' she asked.

What else can we do? Her question seemed absurd, but he simpered back and pulled himself out of the deep chair, catching the blank stares of the men surveying him for the slightest move. He was surprised at Lisa's largesse after just having had his hands around her throat and wondered if it was perhaps because of her now being back within her familial power base.

She hovered at the door, wrapping a sheer silk pashmina around her head and clasping it close to her mouth to block the dust-laden wind before theatrically flicking open the arms of her sunglasses. Carty watched, observing her manner in greeting a local man who, hung in an oversized shabby jacket, had just trotted up the steps offering her his hand. She refused, turning back to bark instructions at her entourage and fleetingly hold Carty's stare. Then, putting on the shades she stepped out, away from his view onto the mobile staircase.

His chest tightened and sweaty patches were now uncomfortably obvious on his tailored shirt as he rushed forward in case he was left alone on the plane without her protection. A perverse comfort greeted him, though, as he squinted into the bright sunlight of the Xinjiang afternoon. Two SUV jeeps with darkened windows had timed their arrival perfectly to meet them and Lisa, already being shown into one, had stopped to look back up at the Englishman.

Shortly after, as he climbed into the vehicle to sit beside her, he met the image of his strained jawline thrown back at him in her mirrored lenses.

'You see, no customs formalities here,' she uttered, cocking her head sideways.

He glanced back over a shoulder to check if they were being followed and naturally threw his arm behind her head rest in the process.

'You don't believe me?' She moved closer, softly squeezing his thigh.

'Of course. I'm just a little cautious.' His expression read alarm and she gently patted his leg.

'As you can see there's nothing but desert and this one road, for some miles. The journey always terrifies me.'

'It does?'

'Yes, imagine getting stranded in this place.' She pulled her glasses off and began arranging her hair again into a Japanese style top-knot.

'How often do you visit here?'

'Every month or so.'

He settled back into the dark leather seat, thankful that the authorities had not been alerted to his arrival.

It was a further 10 minutes, before he could make out the myriad box-shaped buildings forming the skyline of Urumqi, the provincial capital, blurred in the haze of the afternoon's heat. Fields of green vegetables and vines had suddenly replaced the ubiquitous dull earth and young families of farmers were attending their fine wool and fat-rumped sheep herds alongside cotton bushes sprouting their unmistakable white bolls. Huge electricity pylons with splayed arms resembling giant mantises stood along the roadside, stretching far off into the distance, like an image between two mirrors receding away into infinity. The wind was notoriously gently wailing, driving the vast sea of turbines erected either side of them, throughout the flat hardened dessert, the syncopated movement of their blades creating a mirage of technological wonder that impressed Carty. He had always felt that wind, as a renewable energy source, had unfairly benefitted in subsidies over solar and that the horizontal axis turbines were inefficient as a opposed to vertical axis, which took up less space and killed less birds. Now, though, he stared in marvel, recalling statistics he had read, that wind power in China would soon be competing with coal-fired generation. That would be a stunning achievement, if not a paradigm shift, for the country. Beyond these and the approaching urbanisation, the horizon was filled with low uplands and just visible, the snowbound peaks of the 'celestial' Tien Shan, the furthest inland range in the world, forming the border with Kazakhstan. As disquiet rumbled inside him, he silently prayed that this journey would be much quicker and far less troublesome than the last time he was in such close proximity to them.

Lisa had remained silent after replacing her shades, and he guessed she may have been napping, which was not surprising as he was himself fading. A quick glance at his Komandirski told him that in London it was 7:11 am and puzzled, he searched for the sun's position in the sky, through the dimmed glass windows.

'It's just gone two o'clock in the afternoon,' she murmured, one of her plucked brows lifting, 'although that's not the real time.'

'The real time?'

'China has the same official time zone all across the country. So when its 1:00 pm in Beijing it's officially 1:00 pm here, too, more than two and half thousand miles to the west.'

'Isn't that a bit difficult for the locals?'

'Yes, it is. Imagine trying to run regional train and bus timetables here or having to contend with a setting sun at midnight. It doesn't work so most locals pay lip service to officialdom and use a system that is two hours behind Beijing.'

Carty sensed from her off-hand tone that she had little time for the imposition of the One Party State. This was wild-west China, remote from the capital and still untamed, although, the relentless pace of modernisation and an influx of Easterners on a promise of a better life, was challenging the indigenous ways that had hardly changed since the Silk Road's heydays.

With the discovery of those vast underground aquifers, this place is going to be transformed very quickly, he mentally noted.

The increasing clusters of small buildings marked the beginnings of Urumqi's suburbs, linked by a myriad of tangled telephone cables, streaming in every direction from baked wooden posts that seemed as old as the culture. Most of the dwellings were not recent, judging by the faded painted exteriors and dated architecture with ubiquitous air-conditioning units precariously slung to their exteriors as an afterthought.

The vehicles slowed and then swung off the road in a wide measured arc and up an earth ramp to reach the rust-proofed gates to a compound. The perimeter walls were several metres in height and constructed of hollow concrete blocks roughly thrown together and un-rendered, exposing solid mortar bulging like lava from their joins. The driver revved his engine, sounding a horn in successive pips and suddenly a motor kicked into life, unhurriedly winding one of the gates sideways, along a fixed rail. Carty glanced over at his host, but she remained phlegmatic as the SUV pulled forward into the confined shaded courtyard.

At its far end a steel staircase led up to a platform that extended along the wall, above which sat a bank of modern doubled-glazed offices. A triangulated frame of welded steel struts stood proudly on the roof's edge, overlooking the place and to which a number of Chinese glyphs had been erected.

As they were led from the vehicle towards the stairs, something caught his peripheral vision forcing him to take a second look up, squinting and placing an open palm to his brow to shade out the sun. Above the glyphs and in English, were the words:

DRAGON PEARL COLLECTIVE

The sight captivated for some moments.

'Aren't you coming up?' Lisa uttered, prompting him to follow her.

'What does that name signify?' He pointed, as they reached the platform. The temperature was in the high 20s forcing him to pull off his suit jacket and sling it over his shoulder, suspending it by its hanging loop from his finger.

'The dragon is a mythical beast in China, symbolic of the breath of heaven and capable of everything and anything. Legend tells that each one of them carries a pearl under its chin, a secret prize for the most worthy.'

Carty grinned as the image of her necklace of South Sea pearls floated into memory again, giving him reason to wonder if she was worthy of wearing them. 'And can dragons live in water?'

She frowned intensely. 'Why do you ask that?'

'No reason,' he uttered, understanding that it was better not to pursue the question. 'But what's the significance of the word *Collective*.'

'It's a hangover from the communist days. My uncle ran the local party office here, during the Cultural Revolution when citizens all over China were sent back to the land to grow crops for the population. In some areas it was food, but here he mainly oversaw the management of cotton, hemp and livestock.'

'And he's turned it into a business in recent times?'

She stifled a laugh and turned to walk as she continued. 'Not exactly, but the trade in these products with the Soviet Union gave him a base to begin a substantial enterprise when the time was right.' Her manner and carefully chosen words were clearly subterfuge, but the Englishman thought better of prying further. He was after all, her guest and an illegal alien.

'Why hemp? Is it an important crop here?'

'Only for the last 6,000 years, in making ropes, paper and medicines. China is the world's biggest producer.'

The half-glazed door ahead of them opened abruptly, and a small, darkish man stood in its frame, garbed in slacks and a brilliantly white short-sleeved shirt, its creases starched pressed. Lisa surged forward to embrace the man's meagre frame leaving Carty in no doubt that this emotionless, slight man was family.

'This is my uncle, Mr Ong,' she said, noticeably shy in his presence. For that moment, the Englishman didn't appear to exist but within seconds he was on the end of the man's reluctant smile and clammy handshake.

'Welcome, Mr Carty,' Ong pronounced in a practised English.

'Thank you, Mr Ong, for inviting me here.' Carty was visibly impressed but while towering over his host, he detected an inscrutable searching in the man's beady gaze, feeling as if the local had looked straight through him. Carty turned to Lisa but she was acting the subservient niece and for some seconds, there was a prickly silence before Ong, inexpressively ushered them both inside. His facial features were more akin to Caucasian than Chinese with the exception of his eyes, and his skin colour, a mustardy hue. What seemed odd to Carty, though, was the very humble nature of the surroundings and the man's attire compared to the extravagance of his niece's lifestyle and the private jet they had just arrived in. The place was filled with a small army of mixed staff sat at formica-veneered desks with chromed cylindrical legs beneath strip-lighting, silently poring over piles of stamped documents and periodically glancing at the screens of their box computer terminals. Whirring fans supplemented the droning air-conditioning as he was led through the middle of all this without catching anyone's eye. Ong's unimpressive glazed office was situated in the corner, built it appeared, as an afterthought with is stud walls and hollow sounding door which shut behind them.

Tea was already waiting in a decorative blue pot sat in the middle of a round table laid out with a linen cloth, which was ruffled as if lunch had been recently eaten there. Lisa immediately placed out three small cups and poured for them.

'The weather is very pleasant here.' Carty attempted small talk.

'It's been a warm spring and we expect the usual hot Central Asian summer,' Ong retorted, signalling for Carty to sit. 'Has Lisa taken good care of you?' The question seemed veiled.

'Yes, she has, and it was most gracious of you to provide your company's jet,' Carty added, accepting a cup from Lisa. 'I hear that you have a very successful manufacturing base in this region.'

Ong waved his small hands with a modest indifference that suggested a skill at handling high-powered politicians. 'We do produce a variety of goods for export and Xinjiang's economic strength is growing rapidly,' he responded, then making a guttural snort and pulling on a tissue to cover his mouth in order to spit out the contents of his nose. Lisa had turned away apparently nonplussed, to stare at her phone. 'After lunch, Lisa will arrange for you to visit our research centre at Turpan,' he continued lobbing the balled tissue into a small bin by the closed door.

'Ah, and I'm sure she has already told you about my carbon projects nearby?'

'Yes, I have, Scott, and we can discuss all that in due course,' she interjected, 'but first we should eat.'

'Of course.' He was still confused by jet lag but was hungry, having hardly eaten on the journey. She punched a number on Ong's desk phone and a voice immediately replied over the speaker prompting Lisa to bark out something. Carty took the moment to survey Ong while the man was nodding at his niece's instructions. Tar-stained teeth indicated that he was or had been, a heavy smoker and the inside of his forearms carried small faded tattoos suggesting that he had been a worker, not part of the ruling elite and must have risen to accumulate great wealth through grit and fortitude as well as being in the right place at the right time. Lisa seemed a subservient pussy cat in his presence and although nothing about his persona projected his power, his eyes bore a cold ruthlessness. This and his lack of conversation left the Englishman muddled, not sure if the man was hiding his true character or just culturally shy, unusual for someone who had such a good command of the English language.

The office door sprang open without a knock and two scarfed, middle-aged women routinely wheeled in a trolley, the kind Carty recognised from the restaurants in London's China Town, laden with bowls of soups, noodles and dim sum baskets. Lisa began serving, her uncle first and then Carty.

Any further communication dried up as they ate, and he wondered if it was taboo to even attempt to make pleasantries. The food, though, was delicious and, well fed, a quarter of an hour later, they moved back down to the car. Ong had stepped out on the platform above them, the Pearl Dragon signage hovering above his head as he blew cigarette smoke into the air, ignoring Carty's wave.

One of the Mongolians, suited and glazed, was waiting for them, standing in the full force of the sun. Lisa's importance to the organisation was clear and now her body language had reverted to the confident woman that he had almost forgotten existed. Clearly she was a chameleon, but being so far away from England, in this barren, ancient place and now shattered, he was having trouble focusing on the reason why he had come here.

'Your uncle is a quiet man.' He broke conversation as the car filtered out of the compound and back onto the dust-strewn highway.

'He is with strangers but changes once he gets to know a person.'

'I do hope that will happen while I am here. I must say, though, his English is very good. Is he from Xinjiang?'

She let out a light laugh. 'No, in fact he was born in Hong Kong, but his ancestral roots are in Central Asia. You know the indigenous peoples here are more closely related to an Indo-European gene pool rather than to the Han Chinese. There have been discoveries of ancient mummies buried all along the

Tarim Basin, some in tartan clothes, resembling a Celtic tradition.'

Carty shook his head, his eyes wide in disbelief. He hadn't got that far in his background reading.

'Over the millennia many tribes and cultures from Russia and Asia settled the region, first living alongside earlier peoples and ultimately warring with them in an attempt to colonise an expanse that even successive empires of Persians, Greeks, Romans and ultimately Chinese, struggled to rule. Xinjiang has, over its history, become the melting pot of Eurasia.'

'But I understood that it's always been part of China?'

'It is now but for the last two thousand years, China's dynasties maintained just a presence here with small forts at the end of the Great Wall, as it was impossible to control what is essentially a dessert landscape. Successive dynasties succumbed to bribing the various tribes, allowing China's merchants free passage to the lucrative Silk Road.'

Staring out into the vast dryness, the Englishman could clearly see how that would have been the case. 'So, are you saying that Mr Ong is not wholly Chinese?' he quizzed, intrigued by her story and own genealogy.

'Not Han, which has been the dominant tribe in China. No, he is a mix of Hakka and Uyghur. The Hakka are an ancient nomadic people that lived throughout the empire but were eventually marginalised to the South East and Hong Kong and largely make up the majority of the Chinese communities overseas today.'

'And what about the Uyghur? Are they a different tribe altogether?'

Her hidden eyes seemed to be staring through him as she paused to choose her words, recognising that she had slipped into her own secret fascination for Carty and for a moment, lost her well-honed edge.

'Yes, they are.'

'But you, yourself obviously have Chinese roots.' he added.

She sighed in an arrogant, almost throwaway manner that could only have been perfected during an English boarding school education. 'As you probably know, my father was a senior Chinese diplomat and my mother is English. Now why don't you tell me your potted history?' she spat, dismissively putting him on the back foot. He shrugged and threw in a wry smile.

'You already know about my recent history, but I must confess, my genealogy is almost wholly English, with a smattering of Irish, Scottish and Norman thrown in. My father was an investment banker and came from Cambridge while my mother is a Londoner.'

'You said you father *was* a banker – is he retired?'

His sandy brows lowered as he glanced away through the window. He felt that he had dealt with his father's early passing but now found himself wincing emotionally, in contemplation of the unequivocal response. 'No, sadly he died some years ago.'

'Oh, I am sorry to hear that.' She turned her head, casually pulling her glasses up to show an expression of solidarity. 'And are you married...to Lena?'

'Not yet. I've been divorced and we're in no rush to tie the knot.'

'I see,' she uttered with a curt smile.

He didn't quite understand the timing or relevance of the question but sensed insecurity camouflaged by her crafted manners and practised rhetoric. The conversation, though, left him aching to call Lena, but he would have to wait until he was alone.

The relatively vibrant greenery of Urumqi was almost a memory as the road lead out through a wide, shallow gorge in the foothills of the Tien Shan. Windswept sand moved in shifting ridges across the sweltering tarmac as it began to descend onto an extensive plain where the Gobi and Taklamakan deserts converged. The vehicle's on-board gauge was now registering a dramatic increase in the outside temperature causing him to put a palm to the window pane, consciously swallowing hard against the intensity of the heat and the image of the harsh, arid landscape. *And she wants to green this place!* He sighed inwardly and sucked on one of the bottles of water provided in the armrest.

'Lisa, when do you envisage starting your scheme to make this place fertile?'

'In the coming months and it will be executed in manageable stages.'

'I see. You've really thought it through.'

'I may be a woman, Scott, but my background and my uncle's resources provide all the tools I need to oversee the project's requirements. Added to that, the federal government's bureaucrats have tested the models and approved our plan to be eventually, self-financing, albeit not in the same time periods or to the same high returns, as your local carbon projects.'

'I am impressed and please forgive me, I didn't even ask about your profession but I am interested to learn what it is.'

'I'm a bio-physicist from Kings.'

Carty was stunned. 'That's outstanding!'

'It's of no consequence. I'm mainly involved in business nowadays, but did do some initial DNA research with Chinese conglomerates.'

'Can I ask what kind?'

'If you must. There's some concern about the uncontrolled spread of genetically modified crops contaminating the natural ecosystem. Why any scientist would want to support or allow that to happen purely for financial gain, is madness.'

'But I understood there is a lot of value in creating these GMOs to prevent disease in grains and improving harvest yields.'

'That's the marketing hype, but what we're hearing is that some of the crops might produce seeds that are impotent.., they terminate themselves.'

'What's the point of doing that?'

'Exactly, unless of course, you want to hold farmers in the developing world to ransom.'

He caught her hardened gaze. 'Are you saying that's what's going on?

'On the Indian subcontinent and in various other places, we believe subsistence farmers are given loans to buy these seeds along with weed-killers that eradicate all of the vegetation around. After the produce is sold, the farmers must pay back the loan and then buy further seeds to plant the next crop. All it takes is a drought or crop failure and then they and their families are destitute. Many end up taking their own lives.'

'I never knew any of this.'

'Of course, because most of us are caught up in our tiny worlds, worrying about the next TV series, car purchase or fighting over which school to put the kids into. You and I have a responsibility from our privileged position to hold ground, to protect and preserve the earth's natural processes, for generations to come.'

Now Nick's collaboration with her on Brown's Gas makes sense, he reasoned, appreciating the scale of the task she was up against.

'But I doubt if anyone can avert the corruption that is endemic, particularly in the developing nations.'

She had now turned to face him fully, her legs entwined in the cramped space. 'You're right, we can't, but I am damned if it's going to happen here. That's why the first stage of my greening campaign will start with hemp.'

The Englishman raised his palms, shrugging in ignorance.

'It's extremely versatile and easy to grow under the right conditions.'

'Wait a minute.' A light bulb had gone on in his head. 'Isn't hemp part of the cannabis family?'

'It is of the same genus as cannabis, but no, it does not contain the same psychotropic chemicals although, various governments would like to perpetuate that myth.'

'They would?' He screwed up his cheeks guessing that like Nick, she tinkered with conspiracy theories.

'Obviously you don't know its history so let me bring you up to speed. Hemp has probably been humanity's most useful and versatile of crops. The entire civilised world had relied on this one plant mainly for clothing, food and medicine and later, fuel, rope-making and paper production But that all changed dramatically with the advent of the petroleum age.'

Carty bristled almost guessing what she was next about to tell him.

'In 1900, at the World's Fair, when Rudolf Diesel ran his newly developed car engine on peanut oil and later demonstrated hemp oil as a practical alternative, the world listened. Then, in 1917, George Schlichten filed a US patent for his decorticator, a machine which could not only process the tough fibres of the hemp plant without damaging them but dramatically reduced the intensive labour costs for doing the same job by hand. It also provided a stalk waste which stood poised to revolutionise the paper making industry.'

'But let me guess. Some vested interests stopped the decorticator from being commercialised?' He sighed, recalling the conversation with Nick regarding Diesel and Tesla and their inventions being stonewalled by powerful industrialists at a similar moment in the early 20th century.

'You could say that! Schlichten spent more than 15 years and a small fortune on the invention, driven by his desire to prevent the felling of virgin forests for paper production. He failed to find the investment needed to bring it into production and died a broken man in 1923. The conspiracy theorists claim that allegedly, powerful interests supporting the DuPont Chemical company along newspaper magnet William Randolph Hearst, mounted a campaign to discredit hemp by creating confusion about it being an addictive drug, cannabis. Hearst was heavily invested in timber and paper while Du Pont had recently invented its new synthetic fibre, nylon. They, along with other oil industry players saw that hemp and Schlichten's machine posed a threat. Finally, in 1937, the Marijuana Prohibition Bill was pushed through Congress and within three months the outcome ruled in favour, devastating the domestic US hemp industry by banning its growth.' Lisa was slightly out of breath. It struck the Englishman how spirited she was and that perhaps he had misjudged her.

'Just think about it,' she continued, 'we are now experimenting at our research centre with raw hemp waste in the manufacture of a super-capacitor and in a new generation of cheap fast-charging batteries. Henry Ford is rumoured to have manufactured a type of plastic from hemp and we have recreated that here. In fact we could produce a whole car, both from it and powered by it. Now can you see why greening the desert is so important for the future?'

'Yes, I can. It will be a remarkable feat if you can pull all this off.'

'I will, and perhaps you will join me in replicating this model around the world.'

The offer caught him off guard and he felt hemmed in, having to remind himself again of why he was there. 'That's very exciting, Lisa, but one thing at a time.'

There was a short silence as she sucked at her cheeks. 'Is that a no?'

'I came here, to resolve the issue with my projects.'

'And I told you that there was no need to concern yourself. The problem has been dealt with already.'

'It has?'

'Of course, shortly after we met.'

'Then why did you invite me here?'

'To show you, first hand, in the hope of persuading you that it's worth pursuing this with us..., my family.'

'I'm flattered.'

'Don't be. There are others we're considering.'

Her veiled malice irked, forcing him to question why she traded in power games in stark contrast to her obvious passion for the environment.

'Well, as I'm here, I should meet with the local operating partners as a matter of routine, just to satisfy my board that I've ticked all the boxes.'

'Everything in your project's contracts will remain unchanged, my uncle insisted on it, but of course, if you want to meet with them we can organise it. They're going to be surprised to find out you're here.'

He feigned a grin, ignoring the frisson that goose-bumped the skin of his forearms. The whiff of mafia machinations didn't sit with him well, even though he had to accept that while he didn't do business in that way, that was the way it was done here. If he was honest with himself, he was actually relieved that the headache had been dealt with so easily, but still couldn't shrug off the nagging doubt that a price would be extracted from him, in some way.

Perhaps I can offer some consultancy to her group, calculating the long term carbon reductions from her hemp fields, he ruminated, believing it might be wise to make this proposal in advance, as a show of thanks and to mitigate any plans she or her uncle might suggest as payment. *I'll raise it when I thank Ong for his help.*

His Komandirski was now showing 8:54 am, prompting him to pull at the black rubber clasp, unfastening it so that he could hold it in both hands to unwind its crown. As he did, he caught her peering askance from beneath the rims of her shades, causing him to toy with the bezel and rub away some imaginary smears on its glass face before tilting it away from her. Then, he adjusted the hands forward seven hours to Beijing time, ignoring her proud statement about Xinjiang's unorthodoxy. As soon as he did, he began to feel the drowsy effects of jet lag surreptitiously relinquishing the hold on his eyelids.

The SUV's smooth passage suddenly began to stop-start, jolting him from a brief nap. They reached Turpan's hinterland and became stuck in a ragged queue of local traffic with its cacophony of blasting horns. He surveyed the scene, bemused by the haphazard parking of tractors and trucks along the pavement-less road, where the dirt desert met meagre tarmac. Around them dodged and weaved a multitude on bicycles and mopeds, most of which were precariously overladen with food and goods or with one too many children as passengers. The explosion of gaudy colours in their unmatched garments seemed to express unworried cares for their jumbled existence. A teenager, riding pillion, stopped alongside and momentarily pressed his nose against the mirrored pane, unaware that only few millimetres of glass separated his from Carty's. A small dark felt cap hung onto his crown, its edges decorated with light floral embroidery and beneath it, his weathered amber face held a timeless expression, both curious and yet blasé. Then he was gone, his teamster shooting the moped down the wrong side of the road. Lisa's chauffeur, impatient with the hold-up and knowing that few would argue, decided to follow suit and pulled out abruptly into the oncoming traffic, ganging the vehicle down a chevroned central reservation. Eighty yards on, he swung it abruptly in between two trucks and then paused, snatching glances on either side before slipping up a side street, wide enough only for one vehicle. The man at the wheel was obviously a local and slowing the SUV to a crawl, took them further into the maze of narrow alleys populated with the joyful laughter of children playing with stray cats and the odd donkey. Carty turned to glimpse back over his head rest at the rapidly disappearing concourse and felt a lump gather in his throat. Sunlight had been dampened in the shade of the rough plastered buildings, their timeworn contours hugging a thick mask of dust and soot while overhead, looped between each block, black telephone cables hung in tousled catenaries that further obscured the sky's blue brilliance. He glanced uncomfortably at Lisa, but she was silently maintaining her boarding school composure leaving him to assume that she had seen this all before and was oblivious to its stark reality.

Some minutes later they pulled out on to another thoroughfare, less busy with traffic but instead thronged with people, carts and livestock.

'They're going to the market,' Lisa muttered. He drank in the scene as they nudged forward through the massing crowd and then pulled into the tree-lined carpark of a very recently constructed glazed building.

As the gates closed behind their vehicle she turned to him and raised her shades pulling a tired smile.

'Now we can relax.'

'Where are we?'

'The research centre and also our guest house. We have all the modern facilities you can think of here.'

She personally showed Carty around the apartment's exquisite decor, snatching a coy smile at him before quietly pulling the door closed behind her. He dismissed it and slung himself on the bed, content to leave unpacking and showering for later while letting his slowing mind pore back over her conversations. It seemed that Ong had solved the difficulties with the local partners, but something about his story of how it had been done, still left him asking questions He couldn't risk leaving without having met them and visited the projects to satisfy his hunches. Then he would push Lisa to be on a plane and out of this dust bowl within a couple of days.

A picture of Lena's beaming face stirred again and he took up the phone, already knowing that there would be no text from her. He was correct. *Where the hell is she?* Frustration prompted him to text Green.

There's been a change of plan. I'm now in Turpan, not Hong Kong

Then he sprawled out in an attempt at slumber but Boris' urgent expression appeared through the curtain of his eyelids, triggering the vision he had had of his friend while at the Baths. '*Silence is the key to action.'* The recollections of the man's words gave him comfort as his left brain tried to argue with them. But once again, it dawned on him that he had no power to control the outcome of anything and must instead quietly place his trust in his own intuition, allowing events to unfold. Doing so still felt foreign and illogical but it was all he had at this moment and succumbing to it gave him some temporary peace.

Nine

The Irkutsk Oblast, Siberia

The old man was sat on the metal framed bunk, back propped against a rough stone wall, his unkempt snowy hair hung from a slumped head as a continuous strand of saliva streamed down onto the lapel of his crumpled jacket. He hadn't slept in days, just snatching moments of unconsciousness before being routinely woken with a violent slam of a door. There were no windows to the rough rendered room and the constant catatonic flicker of strip-lighting had stripped away any sense of the passage of day and night. He understood the form, why he was here and what they were seeking. Worryingly, he also knew that it was only a matter of time before they would use other methods, ones he could not even contemplate, to glean his secrets.

'Ivan Yegorovich, wake up!' The voice was harsh and the request, an order. 'You will shortly have a visitor.'

Who could they mean..., Boris? Lubimov? He struggled with the thought, his bleary eyes trying to focus on the face of the bulky man filling the door. 'Who...,who's coming?' he slurred

'You will soon find out but for now, why don't you answer our questions, and then we can all leave this place and get on with our lives.'

Isotov now caught the man's glinting stare and recognised that beneath the paper-thin politeness lurked a nature not at all shy in using absolute violence to achieve its ends. A cold distress gripped his whole being, his mind aching with exhaustion as he tussled with his captor's intimated threats. Had his old friends been incarcerated too, slowly being tortured with sleep deprivation and lack of water and food to pry out information that could be played against him?

Boris would never break...but Lubimov is another matter. He scrunched his eyes closed against the shocking notion of his friend being brutalised into giving up the location of the machine. But then he reminded himself that this was purely supposition on his part and that he couldn't be sure of anything the brute was feeding him with.

'So, Ivan Yegorovich, are you ready to tell us everything about your invention.'

'I've already told you everything. The technology was decommissioned many years ago and my research programme discontinued.'

'After you refused to decommission it yourself and then fled.'

'Anyone passionate about their life's work and watching it being destroyed would have done the same.'

'Spare me the emotion,' the Russian barked, 'and tell me about this.' He dropped a dog-eared manila file onto the small table and then flipped it open, scrutinising the old man's reaction as he sat down to face him. 'Do you recognise these reports? You should, your signature is all over them.'

Ivan Yegorovich blinked profusely, his cheeks flushed. It was palpable that he did. 'Those are classified,' he murmured defiantly.

'They *were* classified but as the Soviet Union is now defunct, they have been made available to the highest bidder.'

The old man shook his lowered head.

'And can you remember what you reported in these pages?'

'That was more than 20 years ago. I reported many things.'

The interrogator's hands slowly clenched into fists as they rested on the table's surface, his patience testy. 'Well, let me guide you, shall I? You stated that your research evidenced a critical phenomenon, did it not?'

'Do you mean the transmutation effect?'

'Yes, as well as the claim for free energy production.'

'That was spurious at best as we could never prove it.'

'Then why did you report it as being a critical factor that required military backing for its further research at the expense of any of your other work?'

'Because that's what my controllers within the Kremlin ordered me to report. They were worried that the existing funding would be dropped. It didn't help, though, as it was shut down and decommissioned anyway. Some years later, I heard a rumour that it had been reassembled in another part of the region solely for the transmutation of nuclear waste.'

'It was and it's now starting to critically fail.'

'That was one of the problems I foresaw.'

'And so now we need your help to design and build a number of new machines.'

'But I'm not able to without any of the original blueprints and help from my team members. My memory is too poor nowadays.'

'Don't worry, Ivan Yegorovich,' he glared almost manically at his captive, 'we have the very best people and your project will be handled with the highest level of funding. You will become famous for your pioneering work.'

The comment played to the ageing academic's ego. He had been slighted before, his life ruined by the emergence of *new* Russians, craving wealth from the wholesale theft of the State's military-related industries.

'If that's what you wanted, then why did you kidnap me?'

The question threw the interrogator and he pulled back, his eyes widening just enough to show his frustration. 'Because there are foreign forces looking for you.'

'Really, but you're treating me as if I am a convict.'

'We haven't even begun to treat you badly.'

The cutting remark sent a shiver through the old man, his resolve now on a low ebb and sensing an agenda that hadn't yet been raised. He looked straight at his adversary, seeking the motive behind his expression. It lasted for some seconds before the interrogator faked a grin and pointed at him.

'Of course, the reason we need the machines is not just for the transmutation but for the free energy they will generate.'

'But I just told you that it wasn't researched. I was simply the team leader and didn't fully understand how it had occurred, if it ever had.'

The man wagged his finger. 'Come, Ivan Yegorovich, both you and I know that isn't true.'

'Whatever do you mean?' Fear had now become a terror that was clearly etched in the aged man's craggy face.

The finger stopped. 'We have evidence here to show that you pioneered *overunity* and demonstrated it at *Sphinx*. At the time, it was considered a military secret and for that reason had to be removed from your team and investigated elsewhere. However your decommissioned machine never did exhibit the phenomenon again and so we want to know why.'

'As I said, it was simply a story to secure our funding. I admit that it was wrong but I was under orders.'

'That doesn't tally with the statements of the other members of your team who were coerced into telling everything before they died in that fishing accident.'

The poor souls! He thought, realising that thankfully they hadn't been aware of a key secret – that the machine had to be situated exactly on a specific coordinate, a node point, before it would run by itself and generate almost limitless amounts of energy.

'They might have admitted things under torture that were never proven. The phenomenon was not even tested.'

'That may be your story now, Ivan Yegorovich, but you will tell us what we need to know sooner or later. I'm sure your visitor will want you to.'

Ten

Turpan – Xinjiang Province, China

'Scott, please meet Hafeza Bazareva our head of R&D,' Lisa announced standing close to a slight, younger woman gowned in a lab coat that appeared to be slightly tighter than it should, hugging her curved figured.

'I'm very pleased to meet you, Hafeza.' Carty offered his hand in a sweeping gesture, recognising the awkward body language between the two women. She nodded and placed her right hand over her heart momentarily before bringing it back to shake his.

'Welcome, Mr Carty,' she responded, smiling economically. 'Madame Taylor has told me a lot about your work with the environment.'

'Ah, really?' He grinned, somehow humbled by the refreshing quality of this bright woman's persona and her command of his language. 'Ms Taylor has also told me a little about the activities here, which sound very exciting and I hope to learn more about them,' he added, still gently grasping her hand as he stole a sideways look at his host.

'Hafeza will show you around,' Lisa interjected, coolly, in a practised manner before breaking off into dialect with her. The Englishman looked on silently, uncomfortable at Hafeza's overly deferent respect for her boss. She was younger than Lisa, probably by just a few years and much smaller in height with a shining face that was different in shape and tint to those he had seen on the streets outside, but which hinted at a strongly spirited demeanour.

'Right, Scott, I have some urgent matters I must attend to so I will see you a little later.'

She turned and swanned out of the lobby leaving behind her tell-tale hint of Chypre.

'If you would take this protective coat and these safety glasses, I can show you into our research laboratories.'

He dipped his head courteously obeying Hafeza's request as he reached for the garment.

They passed through several glazed security checks where he was requested to empty all his pockets and leave them in a security tray to which he begrudgingly obliged. As he placed down his phone, his thoughts turned to Lena again and no matter how hard he tried to qualm it, an apprehension stirred in his gut that all was not well with her. He removed his shoes, replacing them with spotless galoshes and then followed Hafeza in covering his hair with a plastic cap liner.

The first room they entered consisted of a several induction furnaces where a similarly attired team were busy.

'This is the beginning stage in developing our new material,' she announced.

'Hmmm, can I ask what it is?'

'Yes, it's a form of carbon, similar to graphite. We're producing strands here that will go into the *clean* laboratory for vapour deposition. I'm afraid I cannot take you in there.' Her disappointment was obvious.

'That's OK, but what is the name of the end material? Is it called *graphene*?'

She blushed, her eyes avoiding his as she tried to give the company's verse. 'I believe that is what the inventors have called it, but we have also been researching this material for many years.'

His nostrils flared. 'It was discovered in England some years ago, and I believe it is protected by an international patent.'

'That doesn't stop our work. Our patrons have invested a lot in its development.'

He tried to hold his incredulity at the blatant abuse of a patented discovery.

Is this Mr Ong's doing or his masters in Beijing, I wonder?

'Well, I suggest you don't publish your findings in any international journals, if you want to avoid a lawsuit.'

'Oh no, we never do that. These operations are completely secret.'

'So, you're suggesting that you discovered this material long before anyone else did?'

'I understand that much of the theoretical work was done in Russia, and with the backing of the local government in Xinjiang, we were able to establish this facility and make rapid progress in its actual production.'

He sighed, visibly concerned at the blithe practices that Lisa was obviously aware of but had been turning a blind eye to. He had vaguely followed the rise of graphene, since its discovery at the University of Manchester in 2002, by two Russian physicists, and learnt that it was the almost perfect two-dimensional material, a single layer of carbon atoms forming sheets with amazing properties: electrical conductivity 100 times better than copper, 100 times stronger, pound for pound than steel, ultra-light and more flexible than rubber. It had been predicted to completely revolutionise the modern world but neither Carty nor his former scientific colleagues, had seen real evidence of that happening anytime soon.

'We originally used the waste material from processing hemp to create a cheap graphene-type material from which we've produced a prototype supercapacitor. I can show you that in one of the other development labs here,' she added proudly, her large almond eyes holding his for a fraction. He warmed to them as if she too understood the pressures of holding back information that could change the world, powerless to divulge it without her or her family livelihoods being forfeit.

'Lisa..., Miss Taylor did mention that to me on the way here. So, does that mean it's not really graphene?' he probed further.

'Well, we have refined the process and I believe that it is one and the same material.'

'Incredible!'

'And it is much cheaper to produce. The lack of a low-priced and efficient supercapacitor has been the main hurdle to the mass electric car market.'

She's obviously not aware of the fossil fuel lobby.

'It will also transform many other industries particularly in the storage of electricity produced from renewables like your hybrid solar heat pumps.'

'You know about them?'

'Yes, our team looked at the patents you had filed. If the alloy can be replaced with our hemp graphene, then you'll not only see a huge increase in efficiencies, but they will cost a fraction less to produce and will be so flexible that they can be incorporated into any building surface to harvest sunlight.'

'And is that what you're planning to do here, to use my patented design?'

'We would very much like to work with you on modifying your technology as I have explained, and then rolling it out throughout China,' she said, smiling.

Has Lisa instructed her to tell me this? he pondered, meeting her gaze, taken by the clear opalescent whites of her eyes and understanding that she was wholly dedicated to her projects. Just then Hafeza's mustard cheeks seem to flush slightly and his thoughts returned to the business opportunity she had implied existed. It was tempting indeed. China's enormous domestic renewables sector and political will to maximise their deployment, meant that if a new start-up company produced a step-change technology cheaper and more efficient than anything current, it would have immediate listing status on the world stock markets. Financially, he would be made for life, but the climate and humanity would be the main winners. Then a reality kicked in.

Why do they need to share these enormous profits with me? Lubimov's alloy is redundant compared to their graphene. They could simply ignore the patent and copy his heat pump technology, incorporating it within their collectors.

The thought was sobering and had him questioning again why Lisa and her uncle were helping him at all, let alone offering him the chance to make a small fortune.

'The Chinese government has a different research facility experimenting with other, two-dimensional materials that in combination with our graphene, should demonstrate superconductivity at ambient temperatures.'

'Really!' he visibly balked at the comment. 'And if that's demonstrated, then the global energy paradigm will change for ever.'

'It's the vision that Miss Taylor has for this region and we're fully behind it.'

He felt vindicated. Green's comments those few years before had persuaded him to keep a lid on *overunity* and not to reveal it to a humanity that was not yet conscious enough to honour the lofty philosophy of free energy for all. Indeed, Green had intuitively felt that breakthroughs in renewables, like the new super-materials Hafeza had mentioned, could not be held back for much longer. It would be these that would crack the nut of a cheap and sustainable energy supply, not the sledgehammer of free energy.

'You said for this region, not for the whole of China?'

'Mr Ong's business base is here, in Xinjiang and so naturally, this is where they wish to start. Shall we move on?' she added, glancing at her watch and then towards the double-partitioned exit. The small team had their heads down, busying themselves, hardly acknowledging their presence as she pressed the door release button.

She led the way, moving elegantly in her slacks and low heels down a long, airless corridor barely a few feet taller than Carty and which also lacked any windows. At its far end, a huge lever served to secure an unpainted galvanised steel door, and as she cranked it open, a sudden rush of warmer, dirtier air hit his senses. The place beyond was a large workshop with concrete brick walls, roughly painted in an odd shade of lime green and onto which were fixed plywood shelves and hooks suspending all kinds of mechanical components, up to the high ceiling's steel struts among the air-conditioning ducting. At the centre of the shop, some 150 feet away, he saw a team of men clad in crisp boiler suits, working on an oversized industrial engine secured to the solid floor by huge bolts, which were clearly visible from where he was standing. Hafeza had already waved to a supervisor who in turn signalled to the band of workers to down tools. They did so, pulling up visors and smearing the oily sweat from their brows onto their forearms as they gawked emptily at the foreigner striding towards them.

'This is our test rig for the marine engines.'

'Modified to run on Brown's Gas?' he blurted, surveying both the machinery and the motley group. He had never seen such an engine up close and was taken by its complexity.

She nodded.

'And is there any noticeable increase in performance?'

'There is, and it's far more efficient than using diesel alone.'

'Fascinating, how long has this one been tested for?'

'A number of months so that we could fine tune the mixture to achieve maximum output. It's so impressive that we've recently gone into full scale production, retrofitting a number of the engines in the Dragon Pearl's shipping fleet.'

'The company owns a shipping fleet?'

She frowned, confused that he didn't appear to know this fact. 'Yes. Madame Taylor's aim is to completely replace the dirty bunker oil they use, which also contains all manner of toxic contaminants.'

'With a mixture of hemp oil with Brown's Gas injected into it?'

'Of course, and this combination will massively reduce the carbon dioxide and other poisonous gases emitted.'

Carty had heard it all from Lisa on the way here but was now captivated by this woman's verve. She had it in her heart, more obviously so than her boss, to make any change she could to help preserve the natural balance of the planet.

'I understand that Brown's Gas can be produced from the electrolysis of water,' he enquired as they began to stroll back out.

'That's correct, in the next laboratory, but it's not any ordinary process.'

Her comment left an unfamiliar clenching in his stomach as she opened the sealed door and invited him into another corridor, one much shorter than the last but glazed so that he could see out onto a dirt compound. He remained silent, pondering her comments as he followed his host. Another set of sealed doors opened with a hiss and they stepped into a vast laboratory to be met by rows of stainless steel containers, each the size of a small car, rigged with sheathed power cabling and rubber tubes fitted to their sealed lids. A muffled tone hummed though the chilled air and partitioned away in a box-like office, a lone lab assistant sat immobile, staring at a screen. Hafeza gently knocked on the glazing and was instantly greeted by a smile, the young man springing up, grateful to have human company. Carty had recognised the industrial sized electrolysis chambers and realising Lisa's research team were intently serious, was now intrigued by the claims for Brown's Gas and whether it wasn't all simply a hoax. There had been many in his time but the one that stuck in his head was that of *Cold Fusion*, reported by two scientists, Pons and Fleischman, in 1989, when they observed that super amounts of excess heat was being produced in their electrolysis experiments without any viable explanation. They put this down to the water's hydrogen atoms fusing together in a low energy nuclear reaction, but this was deemed unthinkable by the scientific community of the day and when the results could not be replicated by other leading institutes, the revelations were thrown out, and the investigation pronounced dead. He recognised that here he was again, staring down the barrel of scientific heresy, a position few scientists would ever contemplate facing. Yet, he had seen with his own eyes only a few years before, a similar phenomenon and his mind was now open to any possibility. But that wasn't going to stop him quizzing her for hard evidence to support the claims for Brown's Gas.

The assistant shyly shook Carty's hand and indicated that he would guide them around.

'Can he show me the input and output data on his computer?'

She broke off into a foreign tongue with the man, the question causing him to glance nervously back at the Englishman.

'We can later, but let me show you the apparatus first,' she followed as he she peeled away to follow the man down one of the aisles between the buzzing contraptions, beckoning to the Englishman to stay close.

'All these electrolysis cells are fed with electricity from the grid and as you may know, much of that comes from local wind power.'

'I saw the turbines on the way here. Vast arrays of them, very impressive!'

'Now that we've perfected the technique, we're aiming to produce the gas using solar electricity alone.'

'Really? Solar can provide enough power?'

'We believe so. The main principle behind this process is the exact vibrational frequency that's introduced, which generates an odd chemical combination of hydrogen and oxygen,' she said straightening. 'But the confounding anomaly, for which we don't yet have any explanation, is the vast amounts of these gases generated – much more than with the ordinary electrolysis of water. That's what makes it commercially viable and a replacement for fossil fuels.'

He grinned. 'But you don't have any conclusive research data to explain why this anomaly occurs?'

'Not conclusively!' she said, hesitantly, pausing to collect herself.

She's not telling me something.

'Do you have any more questions?' she probed.

She's avoiding showing me the data, he thought, but didn't want to press her, sensing that she couldn't. 'No. That's fine, thanks.'

'So, would you now like to see the Sea Water Farm model?'

'Should I?'

'I believe that you would find it interesting.'

'Lead the way.'

They strolled through a sequence of passageways, all pneumatically sealed from each other by the same large steel doors, as she explained more about the research facility and her time there.

He listened, but all the while his mind was busy playing over the images of what he had been shown here and why?

Eventually they were led out into a small annexe room to de-robe and remove the plastic covers from their shoes and heads before entering an open plan lobby.

The place seemed to serve as a visitors' reception area and was modern, decorated to a high quality with mirror-polished dark marble flooring, teak furniture and fittings, and plush leather upholstered Barcelona chairs sitting alongside glass coffee tables. On the walls hung framed photographs of central government members and local politicians surrounded by paintings depicting scenes from Venice, London and Vienna. Positioned at its epicentre and lit by an atrium was a large raised pedestal platform, a metre in height, finished with a huge glazed box sitting atop it. Inside, clearly was the model she had been referring to.

'Here we have a scale mock-up of the *Green Eye* project.'

'Impressive,' he muttered, glancing down at the incredible attention to detail: mountains, small oasis towns, including Turpan, and the two cities of Urumqi in the East and Kashgar to the West. 'Just how big is the area of land the project will cover?'

'There will be an initial pilot scheme of 5,000 square kilometres, planted with hemp and drip irrigated using water from the underground aquifers. It will take two years to complete and when successful, another sector will start, aiming to complete 20,000 square kilometres within another five years. The plan is to cover approximately 100,000 square kilometres of the Tarim Basin within 15 years. To put that into perspective, it's about half the desert's size.'

'That's a very ambitious plan. Tell me is Turpan included in this?' He was concerned for his own projects' longevity and if they may be stymied by Lisa's altruist goals.

'No, it's over here,' she pointed, 'lying in a depression beyond the Tien Shan Mountains, which border the desert.'

He winked, lowering his voice to ask a burning question. 'And do you believe this project is actually achievable?'

She faltered, affected perhaps by his gentlemanly charm, which caught her off guard and lit a florid sheen across her cheeks. It seemed her library of practised dialogue and answers had no space for personal opinions.

'There's no reason why it shouldn't be,' she remarked, her eyes holding his.

'That's good to hear,' he replied, noticing her vulnerability and kicking himself for forcing her to challenge her loyalties. Even so, he sensed that she wasn't fully convinced with the plan she had outlined.

'What's that over there?' He indicated to the other side of the five-metre square layout. 'It looks like a large lake.'

'It's the sea water farm I talked about earlier, situated in the desert landscape. What we're showing is that with the expertise our company will develop here, in the Tarim Basin, we can export it to any desert region around the world. These sea water farms were first developed by indigenous cultures along the pacific coastlines of New Mexico by letting the tides flood the flat desert plains and inlets, then damming them to form a series of lagoons. This allowed the harvesting of shellfish, seaweed and salt production onshore, completely changing the local habitat and microclimate.'

'How so?'

'The brackish water encouraged plants and mangroves to remerge, followed by settling birds and mammals. Shellfish excrement is an excellent fertiliser and so in the few places where sea water farms have been established, both the environment and employment have benefitted enormously.'

'They sound like excellent sinks for fixing carbon emissions too.'

'Yes, just like our hemp fields. We plan to grow salicornia, a salt-tolerant plant like samphire in some of the lagoons. It contains the only vegetable oil that in tests, withstands the freezing temperatures of the high atmosphere. This means it can be introduced into jet fuel to impact the net carbon emissions from global flights, which as you may know, along with shipping, are a major source of CO_2 in the atmosphere. I believe that is why Madame Taylor would like you to work with us.'

Carty's expression went blank in now understanding what Lisa's group were aiming to achieve; not only a commercial revolution in the way energy is produced and used, but the whole-scale approach of letting nature show humanity what the real solutions were, by assisting it in partnership, rather than just raping it for short term profit. He wanted to ask more but was feeling sluggish with the change of hour. It was now late evening in Xinjiang.

'Ah, Scott, there you are!' Lisa's familiar tones rang across the empty marble behind him. Immediately, Hafeza's warm expression shifted to a stony seriousness and Carty spun around to find the vision of his host draped in a hugging beige trouser suit which left little to his imagination and with the length of her toned legs amplified by six inch suede stilettos of a matching shade. 'I've had my assistant looking for you and hadn't realised Hafeza had taken you around the complex so quickly.'

'I'm pleased she did. This model really does provide a good idea of your vision.'

Her countenance softened with the honest flattery and she stepped closer, parading herself as if on a catwalk. 'That's very encouraging to hear, coming from you. I hope what you see changes your mind,' she purred, now in his space, and momentarily confusing him before he understood that it was the offer to work with her and her family, that she had meant.

'It would justify my reviewing the vast carbon emissions saved by the seawater farms and the fields of hemp. These alone could provide some of the advanced funding for the projects.'

'Hmmm, the funding is already in place, but we never say no to more.'

'Well, it's the least I can do, Lisa. After all, without your help, my fund's investments here would be in jeopardy.' As he finished the sentence he detected a strange feeling as if a cold wind had blown in and he glanced over his shoulder to find the local woman bristling next to him. Lisa caught their exchange and muttered casually to her for a few seconds.

'I must leave you now, Mr Carty, but I hope you've enjoyed your tour of our centre.'

'Thank you, Hafeza. It was very inspiring indeed. I trust we'll see each other again before I leave.'

'Yes, you will, Scott. I've asked her to show you around the market in Turpan tomorrow morning, and my uncle has arranged for your local partners to meet you here after lunch.'

'And when are we scheduled to return to London?'

'In the evening, so it will be a busy day, and I suggest that we have supper now and then get a good night's rest.'

He was too tired to attempt to suggest that Hafeza join them and succumbed to collecting his valuables and the notion of then taking a shower.

Switching his phone back on, the thrill of seeing a text message, received while he was on the tour, set his heart racing. But it had been from Gordon Green.

Nothing to worry about but need to talk on a secure line when you're able to – Gordon

Quickly texting back, he advised that he was well before stopping to quiz himself what a secure line was and where exactly he could find one in this place? He simply typed that he would try tomorrow. *If it's not urgent it can probably wait. I'll be back in London, in a day or so.*

As he entered the apartment again, the fine hairs on his neck prickled, forcing him to shake off the tiredness and look in his case. His passport was still there along with his cash and travellers cheques, but someone had carefully rummaged through it.

I guess that's common practice here.

He had after all, experienced the same shenanigans in Kazakhstan and Siberia but the audacity of it irked him as he lay back on the bed and threw his feet up, wondering if Lisa was aware of it. His thoughts, though, soon filtered back over the odd events of the trip, which kept prodding at him. The manner in which Lisa had suddenly changed the flight plan and the fact that he lacked a Chinese visa and was in effect an illegal alien, now diluted any sense of satisfaction at the resolution of the projects' missing revenues. Exhausted and faltering, he slid into the hinterland of sleep and a swirling kaleidoscope of myriad pictures crossed his inner screen. Then suddenly, one of them crystallised - the sign above the office: *Dragon Pearl Collective.* The synchronicity of the beast appearing in his dreams and now in words, in such a short space of time, unnerved him.

Eleven

Dubai

Lena Isotova had spent those two days a prisoner of her own making, watching endless drudgery on cable TV and only leaving the hotel room once in the morning and once in the afternoon, for the roof pool to fast swim a kilometre each time. It was there, while drying off, that Rustigiyev showed up, hovering by the wall under the frayed linen canopies that spanned the unpainted pergolas, clearly temporary constructions that had been left to weather the climate and the second-class clientele.

Towelling down her white-blonde hair she felt self-conscious among the other young woman, lounging out in bikinis, waiting for local men in *dishdasha* to leave small but expensive presents and an invitation for dinner. She then caught sight of the Russian's blue suit and momentarily froze before attempting to casually scoop up her locks with a head band and then collect together her phone and toilet bag. Wrapping the sarong around her shoulders and toeing herself into her flip-flops drew the unwanted attention of the poolside guests, wondering who this mysterious woman was who swam like an Olympian yet disappeared before she could be approached.

'You now have a visa' the Russian said quietly as he handed back her UK passport.

'Thank you,' she replied, securing the latch to her room's door and turning, stone-faced, invited him to sit. 'When do we leave?'

'Today, just as soon as you can be ready.'

She nodded. 'The cash for the room is in there,' she uttered, pointing to the safe within the wardrobe.

'I will organise it. There's no need for you to pay,' he responded.

She picked up on his copious expensive cologne and caught him eyeing her figure still masked by the sarong. His calm manner was well-practised but betrayed edginess.

'Is everything alright?'

'Yes. I'm just thinking how to get you out of here without anyone noticing. The easiest way is to take the elevator to the basement and into the carpark. How long do you need?'

'30 minutes.'

'Good. I will be back then.'

As he left, she turned and leaned back against the closed door gazing at the few items of clothing folded on the bed while quickly formulating a plan. She would leave the phone in the room hidden in a drawer, with the SIM removed and destroyed so that anyone tracking her would have lost her physical trail, believing she was still in Dubai, days after slipping out of the country.

Twelve

Turpan

A frantic knocking woke Scott Carty and he pushed a hand out to the side dresser to find his watch or his phone or anything that could tell him what time it was. His eyes were still bleary with a veil of moisture from his puffy lids and he rubbed at them with the heels of his palms while his fingers scratched at his forehead. It was 10:04 as the sound came again, more violently this time and prompting the sudden memory of where he was.

'Okay, okay, I'm coming,' he mutely answered, pulling himself up and then swinging his legs off the bed. In opening the door, the minder's expression told him that he had overslept.

'I'll be 15 mins,' he stated in a deliberate syllabic manner to the man who just frowned back, clearly frustrated, forcing Carty to think on his feet, holding up an outstretched fingers and thumb and alternately contracting them into a fist and back out again three times. A grunt and gruff nod confirmed an understanding and he pushed the door back closed, trying to recall what had happened the previous night against the throbbing of his temples. Clearly there was drinking involved, despite his promise to Lena that he had kicked his habit with the exception of the odd glass or two at celebrations. How much he had imbibed, though, was a mystery, but it appeared enough to have completely dulled his memory to most of the evening with Lisa.

Towelling off after the briefest of showers, his phone rang, and an unrestricted excitement had him diving to answer it, hoping it was Lena.

'Good Morning, Scott.' It was Lisa. Downcast, he put her on loudspeaker while flipping into his messages.

'Morning, Lisa. Sorry, has my tardiness caused a problem with the schedule?'

She muffled a sigh. 'A little, and it means skipping breakfast if we are to get you to the market this morning. Anyway, you'll find plenty of food stalls there and will be spoilt for choice. You need to eat to keep your strength up.' She giggled in a perverse way. 'I'm waiting in the car at the compound main entrance, don't be long.'

There was still nothing from Lena and his focus had slipped.

'Er, okay. I will be out in ten minutes, maybe less.'

He skipped into the black Mercedes jeep and shut the door with a reassuring clunk, to find Lisa positioned facing him on the wide leather seat, her jewel eyes sparkling within a reserved grin.

'He..llo, Mr Car..ty,' she uttered in stressed syllables, cocking her head. She was somehow different.

'Hello, Lisa. I'm so sorry about the mess up with times. Is everything well with you this morning?'

'It is now.' Her upper lip pouted, the tip of her tongue seductively touching the edge of her prominent incisors as she pulled back on her mane and tousled its ends against her high cheek. He smiled, confused and yet slightly turned on by her manner before recollections of her haughty and sometimes capriciously manipulative character dowsed the chemistry. He glanced out onto the network of backstreets that they had negotiated the day before wondering why Lena had been silent and what Green might want to speak to him about. Just then he felt Lisa's warmth and startled, shot his head around to feel her fingers raking the back of his head, her hypnotic eyes captivating his. He tried to pull back but her slight body was already pressed up against him and her wide mouth closing in on his. He allowed her tongue to gentle embrace his lips as she writhed and ran a palm over his chest and down to his groin.

'Whoa!' he cried, grabbing at her hand and it pulling back to his thigh.

'You didn't act this way last night, Scott?' she blurted, her hot close breath into his face.

'What do you mean?' He gasped at his own words.

'You can't pretend that you don't remember.'

'But I don't.'

She shrank back shaking her head and simpering disdainfully at him. 'I thought you were different, but you're typical, just like all men.'

'I'm sorry, Lisa, but I really don't understand. I don't recall anything about...,'

Her small palm now blankes his retort and her manner couldn't have been any diametrically different to that of just seconds before, leaving Carty muddled and somewhat vulnerable. He hadn't encountered such volatile capriciousness in a woman before.

She remained silent for the rest of the journey behind her large shades, and he was left gazing onto the streets outside. Shortly she barked a command to the driver and the car swerved into a stream of mopeds to pull up between a group of small trucks and three-wheeler vans, all parked haphazardly and piled high with farm produce to sell.

'Hafeza will meet you here within five minutes,' she announced as she slipped her sunglasses down from her forehead, avoiding eye contact. 'We will collect you from this point in a few hours. Make sure you're here.'

The instruction was curt and cold and the vehicle roared off as soon as he had slammed its door. He dipped his stubbled chin and sighed into his chest in disbelief of his host's bizarre behaviour, clearly worried that she was playing a game, the rules of which he had to discover. The notion, though, was jostled away by busying locals swamping him. It appeared as if the majority of town's citizens had come out on to the streets, some cycling and others with small handcarts, weaving precariously between the flocking pedestrians.

'Mr Carty!' Hafeza called out to him. He spun around and waved, relieved to see her smiling countenance. She gesticulated for him to stay put as she trotted across the road dodging vehicles.

'Madame Taylor just called to tell me that you would be waiting here.'

'Yes, she had a last-minute change of mind, which appears all too common for her,' he responded with a grin.

'Shall we go to the market?' she pressed, the veiled joke lost on her.

They filtered into the buzzing milieu, partially shaded by the ash and poplar in full leaf, their trunks marked with a dirty whitewashed band from the ground up to waist height. He was taken again by the wealth of so many different faces, a few definitely being Han Chinese but the majority, a fusion of Asian and European physiognomies: berry toned with softer contours and rounder oval shaped eyes. They resembled those he had encountered in Kazakhstan which bordered this region some 400 miles to the north. With his slightly higher stature, what stood out most, though, was the plethora of caps that presented the image of a swarm of square shaped locusts bobbing across the heads of the men around him, their varied and intricately patterned weaves denoting both ethnicity and Muslim faith. The women too, mainly wore silk scarves of delicate turquoises, buttercup yellows and crimsons to adorn their simple cotton robing and trousers.

'Lisa...,Madame Taylor mentioned that she is partly Uyghur,' he spluttered, momentarily choked by the air now thick with fumes from revving mopeds - all cheap Chinese brands - that had slowed to navigate the throng of the market proper. 'She didn't have time to tell me much, but I understand that this is the main culture here.'

'The Uyghur claim this region as their motherland, but in fact their roots are based in Southern Siberia, around Lake Baikal and the Yenisey River.'

'Baikal?' Carty's eyes widened.

'They were a nomadic tribe, which due to famine and conflict, were forced to move away and ended up in the Tarim Basin, in the 9th century during China's golden period - the

Tang dynasty and while they are the majority ethnic race, there are officially 54 others including mine.'

'Which is?'

'I'm mixed – Russian, Tajik and Uzbek.'

'So how come you're now living in China?'

'What you may not know is that this area only fully came under the control of Beijing following the communist liberation in the late 1940s. For millennia before that, many cultures occupied Xinjiang especially as it was a major artery of the Silk Road.'

'Ah yes, Lisa did comment on that.'

'My grandparents were brought here to escape the Soviet expansion into Central Asia in the 1930s.' Her words rang with a pleasing soft accent which seemed to vibrate from her whole person.

'There's been quite a lot of tension after 9/11, with the locals who believe that Beijing is socially engineering the region by moving young Chinese families into the area, giving them jobs, housing and other benefits while the indigenous peoples, the majority of whom are *Hui* or Muslims, seem to be treated as second class citizens.'

'Are you *Hui*?'

'By birth, I am an Ismaili Shi'a but I don't practice. Generally, Muslims here are peace loving and follow Sufism, a different, less strict form of Islam, unlike the extreme Wahhabism that was imported into Afghanistan in order to fight the Soviet influence in the 1970s and '80s.'

The Englishman attentively listened while he snatched stares of elderly men sat on upturned fruit crates, smoking while their fingers energetically played with Mah Jong and chess pieces between piles of rank Yuan notes, wagers held down with stones. Just beyond them several young Han couples were lazily practising their ballroom dancing steps, dressed in western suits and skirts, absorbed and oblivious to the little attention paid.

'I don't claim to understand the local politics but what I can see here are many cultures enjoying the ancient tradition of visiting the market.' He coughed again as the smoke of the locally grown tobacco caught the back of his throat. She nodded and pointed at the stalls of spices on which hundreds of small jute and cotton bags were laid out in a vast jumbled array, displaying fabulously coloured seeds and powders. Traders beckoned to him, dropping small samples into his palms to try. The fragrances were pungent and almost overwhelmed the ubiquitous sweet waft of pomegranates and tomatoes but were also fascinating and entirely new to him, clearing his head from the excesses of the night before. True to Lisa's words, though, he was now craving other smells nearby and the breakfast he had missed.

'Can we eat something?' he asked, pushing his six-foot frame sideways through the crowd to a stall across the way. Hafeza followed in his wake and translated to the owner who instantly carved meat from a skewered roasting lamb into a flatbread and loaded it with salad.

'Aren't you having one?' he shouted above the noise.

'Thank you, but I've already had breakfast.'

'Mmmm!' He chomped on the greasy mix, catching its contents from spilling out with a napkin.

'I'm glad you like it,' she said, laughing earthily like a woman much older than her years, letting her guard down for the first time. 'Why don't you try some *Musailaisi* to wash it down?'

He shrugged, noticing a group of men all staring at the taller foreigner, grinning and swigging back the vine-coloured liquid. 'Is it alcoholic? I need to be careful. I drank too much last night.'

'No. It's a grape juice that's concocted with many things to give a lift to life.'

'And just what are these things?'

'Berries, rose petals, saffron and cloves are just a few. Try it. There's a legend that Alexander the Great originally brought grapes to this region.'

The locals waited patiently; eyeing him, she swigged it down and then beamed.

'Hmmm, it's similar to mulled wine. We drink it warmed, around Christmas time.'

'We do the same in the colder months.'

'Does it get cold here? I thought it was one of the driest and hottest places on earth.'

'The Turpan Depression is the second lowest place on the planet and so in June and July the temperatures are unbearably hot but during our winter, cold winds blow down from three mountain ranges and its freezing.' Her words were drowned out by the wailing piped from the huge minaret announcing *Dhuhr*, one of the five sacred prayer times, its sound filling the space and bringing a sense of commune to all, regardless of faith. Carty searched his pockets and flushed, grasping that he had no money at all, not even sterling, to pay for the food but, before he could speak, Hafeza had pulled out a grubby note and handed it to the stall trader.

'Thank you. Please let me pay you later when I collect my things.'

She shook a finger, mischievously. 'Don't even think about it. You're a guest of Madame Taylor, and it's my pleasure.'

He knew there was little point in arguing as they ambled on. Young children joyfully shrieked and giggled, running between them and attempting to hide behind his legs as Hafeza ran her hands over their rich brown locks with love. These moments at the market, sharing in the energy and life of this place, calmed his anxious mind, reminding him that no matter how pressing his world was, it was illusory and required balance with his inner world. He wiped his mouth and caught Hafeza's gaze, discerning how her eyes shone with the deep harmony that she seemed to carry within her.

'I would like you to meet someone. Is that acceptable?'

He attempted a smile but clocked that seriousness had crept across her countenance. 'Yes, of course. Is it to do with business?'

She ignored his comment and casually turned her head to look behind them for some moments before grabbing his forearm and forcefully leading him into a side alley. He was shocked that for her size, she was deceptively powerful.

'It's not far,' she uttered, picking up the pace and momentarily glancing back again behind him.

'Is someone following us?'

'I'm not sure yet. In China, most foreigners are followed or have a *guide* to manage their trip.'

'But why would they want to follow me.'

'Many reasons.' Her voice had hushed, 'you're all over the internet.'

'Because of the Albion fraud?'

'Yes, but there are also other reasons.' Her word echoed in the passageway as she stopped and turned to face him.

Who is she? A tingling shot up his spine as he visibly shrugged in feigned denial of her statement. Her outstretched palm touched his chest as if to pin him to the wall, although, he immediately noticed there was nothing behind him except an open doorway.

'Hafeza, what's going on? Where are you taking me?'

'Please trust me. I want you to meet someone who can help you with the truth.'

'What truth?' The words were lost in the ether as she pressed him into the cool darkness of the small building and then swung around to clock if they had been trailed. Her body language was electric and agile like a cat's and not that of the calm academic researcher, prompting him to wonder if like him, she too, had a secret.

Thirteen

They stood, their breathing hushed as she watched from the window, half hidden behind a wooden dresser, the only piece of furniture in the room, save for a chair that Carty decided he was going to sit on.

'Don't!' she ordered. 'Are you carrying a mobile phone?'

'No, I left it in the apartment with my things.'

Whitehall Jack had advised him some years earlier, that a mobile phone could easily be triangulated, giving away its location and that of its owner. But why would he need to worry about that here? The last thing he wanted was to get lost in this country without a passport and sucked into a local's political and cultural issues.

'Hafeza, why are we hiding? I really must insist that we return to the market.'

'Scott,' she sighed and frowned. 'You came here for a reason, and it wasn't just to recover the revenues stolen from your projects.'

'Now you're talking nonsense.'

'Am I, or do you think the dragon is just a nightmare?'

He froze with the same feeling of dread that had gripped him in the dream.

'Who are you?' he slowly mouthed.

'I can explain that another time. Now we need to leave, we've only an hour or so before Lisa returns to pick you up.'

What the hell! It was the first time he had heard her mention her boss by name informally, and somehow he found himself nodding his consent.

Within seconds they had slipped into a tight hallway and then down some rough timber steps to a basement. She flicked a switch and a string of filament bulbs, suspended on a bare cable fixed to the rough brick stanchions, lit a subterranean passageway stretching out under the building for some 200 feet or more. The air was cool and fetid, forcing him to breathe hard and then cover his mouth against retching as he crouched low, fighting his pained knees in the struggle to follow her smooth movements under the low concrete ceiling. She was way ahead of him when she stopped to place an ear up against the wooden timbers before banging loudly on them. Almost instantly a hatchway opened, and she was lit in a shaft of light as two hands appeared to pull her up and out of sight. Carty stumbled along on all fours, his palms sinking into the sandy detritus of the earthen floor while openly sucking in the stench of rodent droppings and leaking sewage. Hafeza's face lowered, upside down, and she offered her palm to him, encouraging him to hurry. Soon, he was being crudely hauled up and finally stood to brush himself down in front of seven or eight locals who had been dining around a table but were now embracing and kissing her as they made exchanges.

'These are my extended family,' she affirmed as the sun-worn faces now ogled him with friendly curiosity.

'Wash your hands and then put these on,' she ordered. 'You won't look so conspicuous.' She passed him a long, traditional velveteen coat, woven from cotton and of a luxuriant dark green, along with a small fez-type cap similar to those sported by the local men. He smiled, eyeing her in an attempt to seek answers, but she wasn't about to indulge him.

Shortly, they were moving outside again, hanging close to doorways for some minutes shading from the sun and scrutinising the inhabitants of the small backstreet. The air was still and sweltering, stretching his patience in the agitated silence until she took his hand and stepped out, hurriedly crossing over and into a gated garden shaded by a pergola's canopy of vines. Once inside its space, things appeared to settle, and he felt calm despite a raised heartbeat. Her gentle rap on the glazed door was an excuse to enter without waiting. In the small hallway, bent and propping herself with one hand against the peeling wall, stood an aged woman, her countenance furrowed and shining in the muted light.

'This is Ludmilla Anatolivna, my aunt.' She prompted Carty to walk forward. He was nervous, scared that his handshake might break this fragile person but all the same he put out a hand while removing the cap with the other. She said nothing, just held his fingers with her gnarled, swollen knuckles as she examined him, glancing up and down at his appearance, his chinos dirtied at the knees, his shirt patchy with sweat and shrouded in the local garment. He flinched as an odd prickling sensation ran up his arm, something like a low electric current felt as if it was emanating from her grip, which was not soft or firm but felt inexplicably weird, almost magnetic, preventing him from letting go. He immediately thought of Boris' uncanny abilities and she cracked her mouth open in a smile that showed the majority of her yellow mottled teeth still intact. He feigned a smile still bemused as to why he had been brought here to meet her, but then she spoke quietly and intermittently to allow the younger woman's translation as the Englishman nervously shifted from foot to foot.

'My aunt welcomes you and invites you to have tea with bread. We should sit for a quarter of an hour or so with her,' Hafeza rejoined, pointing to the salon, which looked out on to the garden.

They sat, and she poured black tea, placing a dollop of jam in the semi-filled cup before passing it to him. He grinned: Lubimov, the Russian, had done the very same thing as they desperately discussed Carty's escape plan from Siberia, back to the UK.

Ludmilla Anatolivna proudly pointed at a round of salted flatbreads, stacked in layers like pancakes, dominating the tiny lacquered coffee table and all obviously her own handiwork.

'It's more of a Russian custom,' Hafeza piped in, aware of his growing bemusement as he gently broke off a piece.

'I don't understand..., is your aunt Russian?' he asked, observing the mage's pearl grey eyes peering from within a face that was clearly different to the locals.

'She was born there but moved to Tajikistan with her family when a young girl during the Soviet collectivisation. She is mixed race: Russian and Buryat.'

'I know about the Buryats,' he interrupted. 'One of them saved my life,' he said, stunned as the words left his mouth with the synchronicity that, in the space of an hour he had heard mention of Baikal and Boris' indigenous clan that lived around it. The coincidence was not something he was able to easily dismiss as he dunked the bread in the tea with the old woman nodding, her eyes transfixed on him.

'Your intuition is keen,' she murmured to her niece in old Fazi. 'This man carries a special responsibility.'

'I saw the dragon around him.'

'Then you need to take heed of what I told you recently. He has great potential and I believe that his ancestors and mine are somehow protecting him, but this alone is not enough to keep him safe in the task he has set for this life. His heart does not yet fully believe in his own abilities.'

'Hafeza, just how did you know about my dreams?' Carty blurted, interrupting them.

'I sometimes see things that other cannot ordinarily perceive,' she rejoined. 'My aunt is a master of these things too.'

'So it runs in the family?' he quizzed as he swigged the tea to wash away the salty remnants of bread, but the jam had made it overly sweet and sickening and he yearned for a glass of Burgundy.

'She comes from a long line of adepts who have pledged to help humanity.'

'How?' He frowned, snatching a glance at his watch.

'By suspending themselves in deep meditation, in a place between life and death.'

'Really! For how long?'

'For as long as it takes to achieve balance in the world.'

The mage quietly sat, the cup grasped tenderly in both palms, her contemplative look leaving a doubt in him as to whether she really did understand all that was being said in English.

'And do you practise this as well?' he asked.

Hafeza's gaze altered. 'Ludmilla Anatolivna's father was a Buddhist monk, taught from a young age by a master who, as we speak, sits in near-death state – *tukdam* – in Siberia.'

'I'm not sure that I understand the relevance of that.'

'The master was buried in 1927, well into his 70s, in a state of deep meditation. He was exhumed, just after Stalin's death in the 1950s but quickly reburied for fear of retribution. Then at the turn of this century a scientific party was organised to exhume him properly..., still alive.'

The corners of Carty's mouth dropped as he walked his eyes to the ceiling, mentally churning the maths. 'That would make him more than 150 and still alive. It's impossible!'

'Only in your world but I sense that you believe there is another.'

He shrugged. 'I have seen and experienced a number of unusual things.'

'Such as?'

'The Buryat, I mentioned could perform mental and physical feats that I still find unfathomable.'

'There are many phenomena that we humans can only perceive and utilise through heightened states of awareness. The energy arts that you have learnt have prepared your mind and body for deeper insights – those of manifestation that can only be fully experienced through the practice of silence.'

'Manifestation?' He felt the gaze of both women as the words tripped from his tongue. Hafeza's open smile showed a keenness to share with him. 'Yes, all matter, all life is vibration and can be materialised, changed and dematerialised through the manipulation of the thought-forms that bring it into being.'

'What you're saying is nothing new.' He grinned, recalling the dialogue with Lubimov on the very same subject. 'Quantum physicists have been stating this much for more than a century, but I'm not convinced that thought alone can bring things into being.'

'Ah, then that is something that you need to experience.'

The old woman coughed, and then turned to face her niece as she quietly placed down her cup upon its saucer. Carty watched having no idea how old she was but clearly understood her mind was sharp from her unwavering stare, which carried deep warmth. Then she began to speak in melodic tones, intriguing the Englishman to ask what was being said but he knew to remain silent until she was finished. It took many minutes.

'My aunt wants you to understand that human existence is under threat from unconscious outmoded patterns being repeated and preserved, due to fear of change. Paradoxically, these patterns are being perpetuated by those intent on their own short-term gain, little realising that they too will be consumed by the same fate. There is a rebirth coming that will honour nature and its quiet forces but this will require a huge change for humanity and its behaviour. Many will not be able to stand the transition.'

Carty sat stock-still in awe. Lubimov and Boris had conveyed the same message as had his friend, Gordon Green, and now he was hearing it again, almost verbatim.

'I am aware of these changes, but what can any of us do?'

'It seems that you have forgotten the recent lessons that you learnt so harshly.'

'I don't think that's true. You know that I've originated a number of projects around the world as well as here, in Xinjiang, that reduce huge amounts of carbon dioxide entering the atmosphere. I can't do much more than that.'

She shook her head slowly. 'Ludmilla Anatolivna believes that you have a special responsibility..., a hidden truth that you carry, and that at some stage you will have no choice but to reveal it.'

'Is that so?' He nonchalantly rubbed at his reddish stubble. He hadn't shaved in his rush to leave that morning and now the growth had become obvious.

'You know it is.' Her expression gave no quarter for doubt. 'If you trust in yourself and the timing of your actions, the forces for balance will support you, but your journey will not be straightforward and will contain many deceptions, making you doubt who you are and who you can trust. Your dream of the dragon is warning you of this.'

'But I really don't understand how you can know anything about my dream. It was a personal one, warning me I believe, about the dangers of the psyche.'

Hafeza dropped her eyes, her head swaying from side to side for some moments as if seeking the exact translation she needed. Carty meanwhile vaguely smiled at Ludmilla Anatolivna in a vain attempt to convey his gratitude for her words.

'Wasn't it Jung who stated that the psyche of mankind was the all-coming great danger and that if it was not contained and made conscious by each individual, threatened to wreak havoc?'

'You've read Jung?' He was surprised by the unexpected mention of the famous Swiss analytical psychologist, here, in such far-flung reaches.

'Of course, Scott. He also thought that anyone of us could be the makeweight that tips the scales and shifts the planet into a whole new reality, and you do have knowledge that can make that shift.' She paused again her cheeks now florid with the mental exertion.

The clock quietly ticked in the void left by her rhetorical statement, shooting his thoughts back to Green's analysis, shortly after the harrowing escape from death, in Russia. They had agreed then, that the *overunity* machine should be left to the long distant future when hopefully, a more balanced consciousness had emerged, or failing that, in the event of a worldwide catastrophe, such as another Carrington Event. But Whitehall Jack was now chipping away at the edges of that secret truth, his intuition keen that Carty had not given up everything during his debrief after his return. It seemed uncanny too, that Hafeza was now alluding to know more than she possibly could, forcing his rational mind to doubt her intentions. *Is she spinning a ruse, trying to trick me into revealing what I know? It would explain her bizarre secrecy in bringing me here.*

Just then the mage leant forward and indicated for him to do the same, so that she could place her withered hands around his temples.

He flinched from her touch again. 'I don't wish to be rude, Hafeza, but shouldn't we start moving back soon.'

'There's no hurry. Lisa will not be on time. She wants to teach you a lesson by making you wait.'

Carty blushed, unsure that if this woman knew the reasons why.

'Ludmilla Anatolivna wants you to close your eyes and relax.'

He tried to follow her instructions but was still anxious that Lisa would be close to arriving at the market to collect him. Suddenly, all that was immediately lost to the same prickling impression he felt earlier, as it swarmed over his crown, dimming his eyes and giving him the sensation of floating.

He was back in the taiga once again, standing with Boris and testing the man's standing stance, forcefully pushing at him, only to be effortlessly shot away as if he was a flimsy nothing. Pulling himself up off the grass, the distinctive fresh fragrance of wet flora filled his nose and the pleasant recollection of how it revived his energy seemed all too real. Oleg Lubimov then stepped out of the bushes, pointing in the directions of the ramshackle cabin and magically, they were transported back into the cavern that only they knew lay below it. He stepped those same steps again, along the dripping granite path, towards the azure brilliance lighting up the grotto ahead as his chest cavity pulsated with the ultra-low resonance generated from the machine. He shuddered but then felt his hand being taken by a feminine presence that he could not resist, as if to reassure him that he must trust that he was being guided.

His eyes shot open, his countenance momentarily frozen as they met Ludmilla Anatolivna's expressionless glare.

'How did she do that?' he stuttered, obviously stunned.

'She simply allowed you to remind yourself of the experiences you've had and the path your spirit has chosen in this life.'

'But how...?'

'Nothing we do, think or say is ever lost but simply remains within our psyche as lessons for another time. This has been known to all cultures for as long as mankind has existed, but in modern times has only been kept alive within traditions that wish to preserve truth.'

'What traditions are those?' the Englishman piped up, cocking his head, unsure of what had just happened and her remarks.

'History..., mainly western history, labels these traditions as *Gnostic*.'

His face seemed to register the word as she continued.

'Gnosis is the Greek word for knowledge of truth but on a deeper level, not the rational or even a philosophical knowledge of truth, but the mystical insight that arises from the heart and is revealed through meditation and focused reflection.'

Carty mulled her words swallowing a sip of tea and picking again at the flat loaf, still shaken by the experience the old woman had engendered.

'This region we're in was a crossroads, a meeting place where the ancient religions and cultures fertilised each other. Several hundred manuscripts written in Syriac, an ancient tongue, were unearthed at a monastery site not far from here dating from the early medieval period. They provided unadulterated evidence of a proto-Christian gnostic doctrine and were considered heretical; they were altered to fall into line by the orthodox dogma of the Western Christianity, which was essentially laid down in AD 325 at the Council of Nicaea.'

His eyebrows arched at the comment.

'Besides the Nestorian Christian sect which flourished on the fringes of the Eastern Roman Empire, Persia and here in China, the main contender to early Christianity was from Gnostic Manicaeism - followers of Mani, a Persian prophet who, more than a hundred years before the Council of Nicaea, had several revelations that the teachings of early Jewish Christianity, Buddhism and the much older Zoroasterism, were incomplete. He taught that these religions had lost or purposely removed the gnostic truth of the equanimity of man and woman and their eternal struggle to redeem the spiritual light trapped by the forces of darkness in the world of matter. He believed that it was humanity's path to understand these opposites – effectively an allegory, teaching that the divine was within reach of all, through the spiritual practise of realising one's own true nature, not from the following of blind faith.'

Carty nodded. *Sounds very much what Jung had gleaned through his studies of alchemy and the analysis of his patients' many dreams.*

'Manicaeism spread all the way into Northern Europe, Egypt and Africa with its teachings of the dualism of man and woman and a God who embraced both good and evil. It was outlawed in the fourth century by the Christian Emperor Theodosius I, and its practice made punishable by death. It did however continue to survive in the East for a thousand years, flourishing in Babylon, Tibet and northern India until being marginalised as a forbidden faith when it became the source for uprisings. The Uyghurs were among the many followers of Mani, until being converted to Buddhism and finally Islam centuries later. Eventually, it died out but not before leaving its mark as a heresy practised by the Bogamils in Bulgaria and then later, the Cathars in southern France.'

'Weren't the Cathars wiped out by Simon de Montfort in the 13th century?' He remembered this gruesome date from his school history classes.

'I believe so.'

'So, are you a follower of Mani?'

'No, but we do practise many of the ancient ways that were forbidden or lost as the great religions fought for hegemony and control of the masses' minds. The heart of gnostic practice is the involvement of the body: physical rituals and exercises that open up its chakras to greater consciousness and the ability to hold the inner aspects of the personality together rather than their being projected unconsciously onto the world.'

The words sent a shudder through him. *Too many coincidences.* It was confirmation again of Boris' philosophy. In his heart he knew that these local women possessed skills and insights that could only reflect truth.

'That resonates very much with Jung's work. He rediscovered this same silent and self-reflective technique from the alchemists, which he called *active imagination.* I now see why many people called him a gnostic and...'

The old woman warbled a few words, interrupting his flow. Hafeza turned to listen, respectfully deferent in her soft features.

'Ludmilla Anatolivna has asked me to show you one of the techniques she has taught me in order that you can reach your full potential.'

The quixotic suggestion drew his shrug. 'I would love to, but we don't have the time, do we?'

She grinned. 'Time is relative when we explore its opposite pole, the nature of space.'

Carty remained wide-eyed, his facial expression stuck awkwardly in a weak smile, endeavouring not to let his doubtful thoughts leak through. But he knew it was useless, as the older woman peered at him muttering something inaudibly, which prompted him to turn to Hafeza for an explanation.

'She's asking you to sit comfortably and then put your hands in hers.'

Timorous, he tilted his face to Ludmilla Anatolivna, the memory of the startling vision of just a few minutes earlier while under her influence were still too fresh. The mage's smile, though, inveigled him to hold his palms out.

'Close your eyes and let any thoughts and images you have pass by like clouds, without a care..., and then invite silence,' Hafeza advised.

What does that mean? His mind wrestled for some seconds as he felt the sensitive touch of the older woman's fingers on his. It seemed as if the ticking mechanism of the wall clock's antique pendulum became amplified, drowning out any stray thoughts, forcing him to focus through his closing lids.

The light became sublime, penetrating all the room's corners and shadows, casting a billion microscopic dust particles into an eternal side-show, wafting with the eddies of unseen forces. Odours of the baked bread, tea and the flowering bushes at the window were mixed together yet each distinct, all making perfect sense as if he knew that these were underlying truths obfuscated by his rational mind. Then with that realisation, they fell away, and his focus was on a single miniscule point of light to which he was traveling at an impossible speed. Suddenly, everything slowed, and he found himself hovering in blackness, suspended in a vacuum as the silence surreptitiously consumed him, stripping any meaning to his existence as if time itself had stopped.

Before him, the shining point continued to grow infinitesimally slowly and while he knew he was still in that room holding the mage's hands, he had no conflict with the notion that his consciousness could also exist in another place, a timelessness that transcended the materiality of his world. Days or months might have passed until the source had grown into the unmistakable image of the earth, its tilted shaded surface spinning deliberately into daylight. He was now hovering serenely way above continental outlines, witnessing Lake Baikal glistening like a holographic thin blue eye at the centre of the lurid red and purples of the dramatic weather patterns ravaging the planet. They appeared to be pulsating with an increasing rhythm, faster and faster, taking on a familiar and terrifying shape – the body of a dragon squeezing the life from the world. Yet he suffered emptiness, a lack of compulsion to act knowing that he could exist here forever. But within the seething mass of tightly woven eddies and swirls, a tiny homunculus reached out to him, growing rapidly in size, wrapped in woven silk robes and stirring his heart with her loving face. He could see clearly that she had emerged a goddess, fighting to prevent the beast's head rearing to engulf all in its mouth.

Abruptly, a huge cataclysm sent him shooting across space, the earth becoming a familiar pinprick of light in the vastness of the cold void, its rare warmth and life threatened by the possibility of annihilation. Soon he heard words spoken in another tongue that needed no interpretation. 'I de suda' ['Come here!']. The old mage was calling out to him in Russian, to step across the veil and back into his world.

His lids flickered and then slowly opened. Ludmilla Anatolivna had loosened her grasp, smiling with a loose-toothed lilt. He felt strangely calm and unchallenged by the experience, which he couldn't seem to quantify in a timescale that he understood – it had felt like many lifetimes – yet in turning his wrist to note the face of his Komandirski, less than a minute or more had passed in this world.

'And now we must leave. Lisa will be arriving soon,' Hafeza uttered.

He stood and turned to the door, viewing the rustic room's collection of Sino-communist memorabilia and the jaded interior decoration. Above the entrance's split wooden lintel sat a medium sized picture, framed with its glazing blurred by the years of dust and heat. Despite this he could still make out the beautifully curved geometric lines painted in ochre against the scant gold leaf background and he unconsciously halted his breath for some seconds in awe at the synchronicity again. There, in plain sight, was a similar image to that drawn on the paper wedged in Green's copy of *The Secret of the Golden Flower.*

Hafeza drew inquisitively to his side.

'That picture..., it's bizarre, but I saw it just a few days ago,' he stated.

'The Flower of Life?'

'Is that what it's called? The one I saw contained the outline of a human body at its centre with the Qabala superimposed upon it.'

'The Qabala's Tree of Life gives birth to the Flower of Life.'

'You seem to know a lot about it.'

'It's an archetypal pattern contained within the esoteric practices of Judaism and Christianity and comes from a very old spiritual tradition that places the human body as a fractal reflection of the cosmos. Some researchers claim that the earth's *dragon lines,* those that energise it, are ordered in a Flower of Life pattern across its surface.'

'And what about the node points?' A curious sensation gripped him recalling Lubimov's claim that his machine only exhibited *overunity* because it was positioned on such a point, at Baikal.

She lowered her eyes fractionally, before grinning.

'Those are where the great meditators sit in *tudkum* and listen to the cries of the world. While the mystery schools demonstrated that the underlying nature of reality is ordered by mathematics unfolding within its own beauty, the human soul is undefinable and not bound by the same laws. It's like a ghost in the creator's machine and can only be truly known through individual inner experience.'

'And that's why they sit in silence?'

'Yes. The gnostic traditions, taught that the common person is stuck in life like being in a valley in the fog, blind to their fate, while the person who has attained enlightenment, is up on the mountain summit in sunshine. The paradoxical nature of reality, though, suggests that both states are true, and that The Flower of Life demonstrates in a pictorial manner, the mysterious link between all life and all souls.'

'That's sounds like quantum entanglement - two states existing at the same time but in different places.'

'The issue now facing us, as a race, is that will be soon meeting the singularity point for humanity's collective unconscious.'

'I don't understand. When is that?'

'We have an opportunity to reverse the effects of our actions by 2012, but after that there is no going back. We must do what we can to bring awareness that our collective fate is the fabric of this reality. Materialism is no longer the saviour and the sooner this is understood, the more rapidly changes can be implemented to protect the earth and mitigate the threat to our civilisation.'

Carty was stunned. Here was that same eschatological warning being promulgated once again, echoing the wisdom shared with him in the deep Russian forest. It had only been a few years since, but he had let its import slip away with the distraction of modern living.

'Well, the coincidence of seeing the Flower of Life again is incredible.'

'Perhaps its appearance is to show you proof of your thought forms being manifested.'

'But I wasn't even thinking about it.'

'You will see,' she added, winking cheekily at him.

He shrugged as he pulled on the cloak and then the cap. 'Do we have to go through the same underground passageway, again?' His expression was strained.

'No, we can walk back to the market via the side streets.'

He instantly looked relieved. 'So why did we have to go through it in the first place.'

'Because we were being followed, and I didn't want anyone to know that I had taken you to see my aunt to spare her a visit from the authorities. She's an old woman and an ethnic here.'

'And you?'

'I'm not worried about them but just to be sure, wait here.' She grinned, leaving him in the doorway to stroll casually down to the gate, remaining just out of view behind one of the pergola's timber stanchions. Carty was not fully back in his world yet, his mind poring over the extraordinary visions experienced in the presence of the old mage, uncertain as to what they signified but rocked by their graphic detail and possible implications. The brief meeting revealed that these women were holding ground in a battle beyond the usual.

She caught his gaze and beckoned him forward.

Within seconds they were across the road and walking back into the melee of side streets.

'Can I ask you some questions?' He craned his neck. Despite her diminutive frame her energy gave her the appearance of being taller and more powerful than she actually was.

'Of course, but I can't guarantee that I can answer them.'

'You and your aunt claim to know my dreams and that I have a special responsibility, but what are you doing here? You're not just a technologist working for The Dragon Pearl Collective, are you?'

'My job isn't necessarily my life, Scott. My family line has been burdened with nothing less than the guardianship of consciousness. Soon Ludmilla Anatolivna will go into *tudkam*, she wanted to some years back but has been inexplicably waiting for something.'

'Something?'

'Yes, possibly your arrival.'

His eyes glared like two full moons. 'What have I got to do with anything?'

'I don't fully understand it myself but hopefully the silent experiences you had with her, will give you some guidance.'

'Do you mind if I share them with you?'

She shook her head in accord.

'The second time I took her hands, the dragon appeared again after a long sojourn in space. It was wrapping itself many times around the earth, squeezing its life away in an attempt to swallow it.' As the words left his mouth he wondered how his friend Green, would analyse this vision and what questions he might ask.

'Is that the end of the vision?' she retorted.

Exactly what Green would have said!

'No. A being - a goddess of some kind, was standing her ground, growing in stature.'

'How did she appear?'

'I don't understand?'

'Her appearance, can you describe it.'

'She was robed in satin and silks and despite her dilemma, looked incredibly calm.'

'Oriental looking?'

'Yes, possibly.'

A smile peeled her lips apart into a beaming smile. 'Well, that is useful.'

Carty's brow furrowed, confused by the statement.

'You've invoked the Bodhisattva *Kuan Yin* - the one who observes the cries of the world,' she added. 'She's a deity worshipped across the East for her mercy, compassion and love, but I can see from your face that you've not familiar with her.'

'I'm not. So why would I unwillingly invoke a goddess I've never heard of?'

'Perhaps because you've tapped into the collective unconscious of this place. Buddhism entered Xinjiang in the 1st century, from India, and took hold for many centuries alongside Manichaeism. The 1,000 Buddha caves in the Flaming Mountains to the Northeast of the Taklamakan were a main centre for Buddhist worship, and it is in such places, and other mountain ranges at the centre of the world, that monks have sat and still sit, in *tudkam* - hearing the cries of humanity.'

'Do you actually believe that?'

'Do you believe that you have invoked a goddess you've never heard of? You had the vision, not me.'

He nodded in defeat. 'So, tell me more about *Kuan Yin.*'

'She is androgynous and synonymous with the Bodhisattva *Avalokitesvara*, the male Hindu deity of compassion and mercy. It is said that a Bodhisattva is one who has achieved Nirvana, defeating the wheel of karma and the need to reincarnate but then vows to stay among humanity until all beings are saved. They have the power to appear in any life form required to relieve suffering. *Kuan Yin* is revered much like the Virgin Mary of Christianity.'

'Well, she seemed to be holding back the all-consuming dragon.'

'And perhaps this dragon you speak of signifies the all-consuming and unsustainable passions of modern civilisation, which are undermining the fabric of nature and all life. Now can you see the reason why my aunt was waiting for you?'

'I'm sorry. I really can't.'

'Because she understands you will have a part to play in keeping the dragon under control and transforming the situation so that it instead, metaphorically holds the pearl delicately in its mouth.'

'I guess I'm doing my bit with the carbon projects, as I told you.'

'They're not enough and cannot possibly deal with the enormous issues resulting from the corporate world's unchecked plundering of the planet.'

'So, you're implying that I should join forces with Lisa to promote Brown's Gas, graphene, hemp and any other crazy technology that your research team comes up with, as if they can solve the issues?'

'No. I am not condoning that you do that. You just need to look into your heart and not ignore its message. I think it was Jung who also said words to the effect that if a person does not follow their own destiny, Fate drags them there by the hair, screaming.'

She seems to have read a lot of Jung, he ruminated, looking down at the road, mentally churning a recollection of the revenant Basilides, who, he had learnt from Green, was an early Christian gnostic, and who in his dream, had led him to the pool in which the serpent was lying in wait, to devour the young woman. The images stirred the same sense of helplessness that the nightmare had, but also awareness that, through the visions induced by the mage, he had moved beyond the arts he had learned in Siberia. And then it hit him. *'Silence is the key to action,'* – the words that had been telepathically imparted in the recent vision by his friend Boris. Gordon Green, too, had very clearly mentioned that the practice of silence and deep contemplation were the necessary tools to uncover his own inner personae; the shadow, anima and Self. He would need to contemplate his experiences and share them with Green on his return, but for the moment, the pressing urgency was to get back to Urumqi, meet with his local clients who Mr Ong had so kindly *persuaded* to return the missing revenues, and then, as planned, board Lisa's plane for home. And with that thought Lisa's lazy gapped-tooth smile slipped back onto the screen of his mind. It had only been a couple of hours or so since she dropped him there, but the uncanny experiences with Ludmilla Anatolivna had distorted his sense of time, leaving him both anxious and exposed as to how his host might now act, given her claims that they had been intimate the night before. It was a bizarre conundrum which grated against his logic whichever way he pondered it. Had he really been that drunk or had she dropped something in his wine to blur the events, allowing her to tell any story she wanted?

But what would her motive be for doing that? The confused thought brought an uncomfortable surge of emptiness and a longing to be with Lena.

Hafeza had been scrutinising his brief silence as they strolled, wondering exactly what it was that this man possessed, in order that her aunt would had waited to meet him.

'Ah, isn't that Lisa's jeep?' he blurted, pointing ahead to where the narrow street opened out onto the square he had been dropped off at earlier. The darkened vehicle looked familiar and he quickened his pace, stepping out of the shadows cast by the ancient buildings, to find Lisa hanging from the door in another change of outfit: tight blue denim jeans, a loose silk blouse and a bright yellow chiffon scarf tied under her chin, like a fifties actress might have done.

'There you are!' she announced, waving in a relaxed way as she slid back onto the vehicle's leather seats and the driver simultaneously stepped out in preparation to open a door for Carty who had already begun thanking Hafeza. But the

Englishman became confused by a sudden blurred movement rushing past his host and he instinctively leant to pull her out of the way, but she had already reacted, moving like lightning, stepping around him so swiftly that he had lost focus on her. Then a swish of air to the side of his head caused his panicked flinch, turning to catch two thugs bearing pickaxe handles down on him. Hafeza, though, had stepped inside their swings, kicking to the inside of one of the men's knees, causing him to crumple and domino against the other. Carty used that second to engage his spirit to fight. The loud crack of a pistol shot rang out nearby, forcing his frantic dive behind the men legs. Across the small arena people were wildly scrabbling for cover into doorways and behind upturned market carts, their produce scattered underfoot. In the middle of it all Lisa's driver sat floored against the Jeep's oversized wheel, clutching at the unmistakable bullet wound to his chest, his last gasps of life spent staring in shock at the claret oozing from his light shirt onto the dirt road. Carty desperately scanned the scene for Lisa who had vanished from sight, but then a short grunt behind him sharpened his senses, forcing him to spring up into a loose guard stance and instantly rotate on the spot to avoid a club's swing aimed at his torso. Using the empty space and momentum he instinctively stepped in, chopping the man's clavicle and feeling it splinter underhand. But in simultaneously dropping to the floor from the blow, the hardened assailant had wildly flipped the end of the wooden handle up, catching Carty smack in the groin and he crumpled, gasping at the excruciating pain. Drooling saliva and on all fours, he expected no mercy but quickly registered that the killer was now laid out on his back. The other assailant, though, was closing on him with his crude weapon, but then unexpectedly, froze in mid flow. Hafeza had punched into the man's kidneys, temporarily halting his momentum. Grimacing, he lurched around and towering over her, vented his fury with a wild assault. Surprisingly, she held her ground, skilfully dodging two of his lunges before returning a full heel-stamp to his sternum, stunning him. Then, in what appeared to be an act of sheer madness she suddenly stood stock still, her outstretched arms circling up over her head and back towards her centre, playing out like slow motion film frames. Slightly rocking herself forward, she exploded her arms out, her mouth wide open as if she was screaming. Carty's dazed mind couldn't quite comprehend what he was witnessing as her attacker was propelled back, six feet or more. It was if he had been hit by a silent hurricane, pinning him to the ground, his blood-soaked palms vainly shielding his shattered eardrums as his eyes rolled upwards in agony. The Englishman, still grounded, gasped violently as the unseen shockwave rapidly sucked his breath away and soon, he too slumped onto his pained face, unconscious.

Fourteen

Irkutsk Airport - Siberia

The passage through border control had been smooth for a provincial airport accepting international flights. In effect the only passengers had been her, Rustigayev and his two cohorts, but that hadn't lessened the churning stomach and anxious few moments in which Lena's documents were scrutinised by the ubiquitously sour-faced official, checking her details against a computer's entries. Clearly, she was a native Russian who had acquired a foreign passport. *How bizarre*, she ruminated, that here she was in the country of her birth, Mother Russia and yet she was now just an *inistranitz,* a tourist, to all intents and purposes. The surge of love she felt in being back had never been lost to her in these few years away, only left bubbling beneath a veneer of cultural respectability in a new country she called home. It and the comforting smells, distinctive faces and aura of authority in the arrivals hall gave her some respite against the fear of being found out and imprisoned. There were no second chances for turned spies.

Her steps were carefully traced by the stares of several of the armed guards as Rustigayev purposely paced alongside her in his expensive attire, speaking quietly about the weather. His bodyguards in tow, sent an unspoken message that they were not to be interfered with. One exuberant conscript did step forward at the exit and Lena froze for a fraction of second before understanding that he was opening the door for them. The gesture, forced her lips into a measured smile at the man, that her shapely form and classic blonde braids was fully appreciated, something that had slipped into insignificance for her during these last few days of anguish and unknowing.

Outside, the continental summer had arrived early, allowing her to bask in the balmy ambience, squinting into the sunlight across the broken tarmac as they waited for the transport.

'Can we call Vladislav now?' she asked her host.

He curtly shook his head once, his downturned mouth leaving her in no doubt. 'Nor Lubimov, not here, it's far too dangerous. We need to get out of the city before we can rendezvous with Vlad. But he already knows that we've arrived.'

'How long will that take?'

'An hour or so, depending.'

'On what?'

'If we have to make unplanned detours to shake off any trails.'

'Do you think we will be followed?' Her shoulders stiffened, and he read the fear that had resurfaced after being so masterly stifled.

'There's no need to worry. It's highly unlikely that anyone else knows of your arrival, but you do understand Russia, and that we may receive some unwanted attention by bored members of the security services, keen to know why a beautiful English woman is visiting Irkutsk of all places. We did arrive in a private jet after all!' he uttered, cocking his head and taking her arm to help her up into the people carrier. She returned a mute smile but found that despite his smoothness, she couldn't warm to him.

As they set off she panicked, rapidly patting at her pockets and then nervously searching in her bag. Rustigayev was about to ask her what she had lost, before she stopped him, nodding to herself as she resumed a calmer countenance.

'It's okay. I forgotten I had left my smart phone in Dubai.'

The Russian gazed back, understanding her unspoken reasons for doing so. But a leaden sadness had pulled at her heart as, through her own choice, her tie with Carty had now been severed along with the tentative joy of knowing he was there, even if she couldn't have answered his texts or calls.

I have to do this. She dipped her head, fearful that she may have risked losing the one man whom she truly loved and for what? *I shouldn't have kept the reasons for my coming here, from him.* She breathed deeply, trying to halt the welling-up of confused tears. But they came anyway, accompanied by a sobbing gasp, the frantic reflex of a palpitating diaphragm. Rustigayev, shuffled uncomfortably, attempting to calm her with a cold hand around her shoulder but she pulled away, turning her face into the leather upholstery.

The familiar sites, memories from her youthful holidays, arriving by train to be collected by Ivan Yegorich, shouted back at her from beyond the vehicle's rear window. The wide boulevards and their walkways were lined with a collage of ageing Soviet-era concrete frontages, interrupted every so often with older, brick-built building and the rustic architecture of traditional wooden houses painted in bright blues and yellows as if to ward against the bleak dark winters and sheer rawness of the huge wilderness, beyond the edge of the city. A golden onion-shaped orb, atop a wooden church spire, rose above the tangle, reminding her just how much she loved this place and its people. Their faces seemed to be carrying a muted collective excitement at the prospect of the longer summer days and she felt touched by a sense of belonging, momentarily soothing her inner turmoil. The orb gleamed in the morning sun for some time as they moved out to the harbour where they pulled up alongside a throng of moored vessels. Rustigayev pointed across to a tired looking power boat, its uncleaned hull streaked with remnants of diesel.

'That will take us up the river towards Baikal,' he confirmed. 'It's inconspicuous and shouldn't attract any attention.'

Her eyes rounded in slight shock at the statement. 'We weren't followed?'

'No.'

The Angara's waters unspoken depths brought serenity, allowing her to be more centred as thought streamed of that last trip from this very same harbour when, not yet in love with Scott Carty, she watched him travel on ahead, with the fated CentraliniySib business delegation, on board an *Ekranoplan.* She glanced around, seeking signs of that Cold War relic, a hulk that could not ordinarily be missed but it wasn't there, and she guessed that the gigantic technological platypus might be on another trip or more likely, had been sold for scrap.

The robust current soon found their small vessel struggling full kilter to make headway, and a trip of only a few miles took more than an hour. The master finally pointed over to their destination on the shingle coastline and changed course towards it. As they rounded a cliff bank and its overhanging birch copse, the flow became distinctly calmer and in the still air the acrid odour of wood-burning raised a sense of relief that they were nearing their journey's end. Dead ahead, spangled beams of sunlight streamed through the forest, exposing the lighter coloured timber of a few cabins nestling, some way back from a small bay into which a small brook gently spilled into the world's mightiest lake.

Within minutes they had banked and she was being helped off into the lapping shallows.

'Is Vladislav here? I can't see him around,' she fired, her anxiety now transformed into an almost perverse excitement at the expectation of seeing her former lover again.

'He should be. Follow me up to the cabins.'

'You seem to know this place. Have you been here before?' she asked.

'A few times, fishing.'

He marched on, pushing aside branches of larch and pine saplings allowing her to pick off small pieces of sap and moss and chew them together as she used to, following her grandmother's advice that they were health-giving. The billowing smoke from a chimney tumbled down the sides of a *dacha* and hovered in a torpid mist over the small meadow, signalling that a furnace oven was in full flame, in preparation for dinner. She toyed with what might be cooking; a *borscht* perhaps, or pork-filled *pilmeni* dumplings in a nettle broth finished with coffee and a dollop of the ubiquitous *gorshconia molako* – sweet condensed milk, settling thick at the bottom of the cup..., and then she saw him, tall and fuller than she remembered, with one arm wedged skyward resting against the door frame. Rustigayev moved ahead to his waiting friend whose unflinching eyes never wavered from hers triggering a wave of pent up emotions. She struggled to calm her heart and a small tree took the brunt of her lunging grasp as her legs began to crumple below her, but the man was already there pulling her up into his strong familiar embrace. Her fingers fondled his hair as he slowly kissed each soft cheek in turn and then he threw her up so that he could carry her inside, all the while staring into her eyes.

'Chai?' Rustigayev offered. Lena took the cup in both hands and sipped, allowing an unfettered grin as she sat on a bed with her back against the wall.

'How have you been?' she asked, examining Vladislav's hirsute toned chest beneath the unbuttoned lumberjack shirt.

'I'm fine and very pleased to see you.' He held out a palm to her temple and she wanted to allow its caress but stopped herself.

'Sorry for all the games in getting you here,' he added.

'It was only to be expected,' she shrugged as she spoke. 'Are you still with the agency?'

He cocked a brow and then grinned: the agency was where they had first met and fulfilled a number of tasks together as intelligence gathering operatives.

Rustigayev gulped down his tea. 'I'll need to leave shortly,' he announced, 'the captain needs to get his boat back, and I have some business to attend to.'

'Thank you, Maxim..., for everything.' Lena pulled herself forward and moved to grasp him, but he pulled back, his hand pushed out instead to shake hers.

'You have to eat before you go?' she announced, ruefully.

'I would love to but not today.'

Vladislav playfully grabbed at the man temples, fixing them between his large hands to gently tap foreheads together as he stared into his eye in a gesture of solidarity and appreciation. Rustigayev had risked a lot in bringing her home and de facto being complicit in harbouring an enemy of the State.

The roar of the launch's outboard motor had them waving to Maxim Rustigayev for many minutes until it rounded the bluff and they were alone again, together in the wild stillness.

'Now, can you tell me about Ivan Yegorovich. How is he and when can I see him?'

Vladislav held her gaze for some seconds and then indicated with a slight sideways nod that they sit on the rough chairs around the porch.

'I don't know how to tell you this...,'

'What?' her voice strained.

'Ivan Yegorovich has disappeared.'

Lena face read desperation as she tried to question him, but his palm stopped her. 'Listen, I mention that in the letter otherwise you might have panicked and done something stupid.'

She scowled at him. 'You lied to bring me here!'

'Believe me. I thought through every possible option to deliver the news to you.'

'So, where is he?'

'I've had all my contacts searching through their networks but he appears to have slipped off the face of the earth, for now anyway.'

'But he's a very old man and may be in serious danger,' she barked. 'We must find him quickly. Where's Lubimov?'

'At *Sphinx*, he's aware of the situation but doesn't know you're here. Nobody does.'

'Huh!' she expelled her frustration, jumping up. 'I need a rifle and some provisions.'

'You and I need to calmly discuss this, first,' he said restraining her arm. 'Is there anything you can think of that may have caused his abduction?'

'Abduction! Why do think that?'

'A man in his eighties just doesn't simply vanish without telling anyone. Lubimov also inferred that while Ivan Yegorovich's things were untouched in his cabin, there were signs of a struggle outside. For the last 25 years everyone, including me, thought he had died in the taiga but clearly, both Lubimov and you knew otherwise.'

Lena's felt the blood drain from her face. 'Lubimov admitted that to you?'

'He had to. He needed my help to search for him and given my background, knew that I could achieve that without the regular authorities being involved.'

Where's Boris? The unexpected thought had her wondering if the Buryat was aware of her grandfather's quandary. If anyone could find him he could, but she doubted that Vladislav knew of the local man and a niggling hunch stopped her from asking.

'Vladislav, even though we were in love, I couldn't tell you that he was alive, it was too risky.'

'And then your disappearance,' he probed, his countenance taking a more severe tone as if he had slipped back into his interrogation training. 'Thinking that, for these last few years, you had been killed when in actuality, you were in London with another man..., it hurt me, Lena, more than you'll ever know.'

'I'm truly sorry.' The words tumbled out as she tussled with the reasons why she couldn't have communicated with him while knowing that with his privileged position, he would have understood those anyway. 'But all this brooding on the past isn't going to help find Ivan Yegorovich. We need to come up with a plan to do so.'

'I've already called on a specially trained team to meet us here first thing in the morning and then we'll begin the search.'

'I'm coming along too.'

'That's your choice, but it will be hard-going in the taiga. You know, I'm confused as to why Ivan Yegorovich faked his own death all those years ago and why anyone, now, would want to kidnap him.' He uttered, searching her eyes. 'Do you have any idea why?' His expression betrayed a quiet confidence which seemed strangely untroubled by Lena's clear distress at the drastic circumstances her grandfather might be in.

'You forget that I was a teenager when all that happened.'

'Ah, yes.' He reached out a palm again to stroke her face and this time, nervously, she let him.

'And I had the odd impression that somehow, your sudden leaving was connected with him or his work.'

Her huffed exhalation sought to dismiss the statement as conjecture, but his stare wouldn't consent it.

'Did it?' he pressed.

'What are you driving at?' She pulled away, her breathing vexed as she unconsciously played with her braids, trying to sooth herself.

'Lena, you and I can never have secrets from each other..., you know that.'

She found herself nodding. 'And...?'

'What was Ivan Yegorovich hiding?'

She straightened, steeling herself, her breathing now regular as she had been trained to do. 'He didn't want to give up his research and the prestigious funding that went with it. When they forced him to resign and disband his team, he refused.'

Vladislav's dark eyes narrowed and he feigned a smile. 'But that doesn't explain why three of his team died mysteriously in a fishing accident before he fled, does it?'

'I don't think he murdered them, do you, Vladislav?'

'No I don't, but the facts, Lena, they don't stack up at all.'

'Is it really that important? Why don't we find him and then you can put all these questions to him directly?'

'Yes, I suppose that will be one solution.'

One solution! What does he mean?

Fifteen

Turpan

Light trickled through Scott Carty's lids as sluggishly, he began to come around and recognise the prominent features of a familiar face watching over him. Some seconds later he recognised it as Hafeza's.

'How are you feeling?' she whispered.

'Bad.' He raised his head slightly and then dropped it back onto the course pillow, nauseous with the throbbing that pulsed through his groin and down his legs.

'How long have I been out?'

Her silent, yet grim expression did little to answer him or hide her disquiet as she passed her hand under his head to support it while the other placed a cup to his lips. He resisted.

'You should drink this. It really will make you feel better.'

'What's in it?'

'A tea made with herbs and roots.'

The comment had him attempting a grin, but it faltered with the intense pain, which felt as if his skull was being squeezed in a vice. He took a large sip and then forced himself up onto a forearm, breathing deeply and rubbing his neck as he took in the surroundings. It was the same room that Hafeza had brought him to earlier that day, and her family members were buzzing around the place, seemingly oblivious to his presence.

'What happened in the square earlier?' Confused images of the shocking events had now begun to swirl back into his mind's focus and he tensed with the recollection of the brute's strikes. She reacted, stroking his arm, her sullen gaze meeting his.

'We were attacked, and Lisa was abducted.'

'What! Why?'

'Most possibly because her uncle is a billionaire and her kidnappers will very likely be seeking a ransom for her release.'

'Do you know if she was hurt?'

'In the panic I couldn't see what happened to her and wasn't sure if there were any other witnesses.'

'That's shocking. What do we do now?'

'We remain here for the rest of the day.' She glanced away towards the window. It was still light outside.

'How long have I been out and how did we get here...? I mean shouldn't we be reporting all this to the authorities?'

She swung back, her expression taut. 'Believe me, Scott, we don't want to be anywhere near the authorities. They cannot be trusted and as an ethnic minority, I would be under immediate suspicion. But to answer your question, you've been out cold for a few hours. Some friends carried you here in their car and they're now trying to find out who undertook this assault.'

The tea seemed to have already taken effect, somewhat alleviating the grogginess but as he struggled to bring his legs around to sit up, an excruciating pain shot through his inner thighs again. Wincing, he collapsed back on the bed.

'I will make a special preparation for your injury to alleviate the bruising.'

He wanted to smile but a grimace consumed it as he attempted to wriggle into a more comfortable position on his back, his head propped up on the folded pillow remembering the attack and how Boris' *neijia* training had probably saved his life, again. Then the details became hazy.

'Hafeza, just how did we escape? I can't seem to recall exactly what happened before I passed out.'

'You don't remember anything?'

Vague pictures surfaced, stalling his reply as their impact rendered him momentarily speechless. 'I can't quite believe what I saw and heard,' he eventually stammered.

'Try to explain it to me,' she said, her voice calm.

'You just stopped in the height of the melee and then appeared to scream but there was no sound, just a huge shockwave.'

'A *spirit shout,*' she uttered.

Carty's brows peaked, over his moon eyes. 'Is that what it was? It felt more like a nuclear bomb going off!'

'And that was the purpose. That thug was about to finish you.'

'I know, but what you did defies any explanation.' His words triggered a recollection that he had said pretty much the same thing to Boris after beholding the man's similarly incredible feats.

'Not really. It's an ancient technique – expressing the *Qi* as a resonant sound vibration. Ludmilla Anatolivna taught me.'

'But I didn't hear anything.'

'That's because its pitch was beyond your hearing range.'

'Can she do it too?'

'Naturally.'

'Ah.' He grinned. 'I thought there was something special about you when we first met and I can now see that you're also a martial artist, the way you evaded that guy and kicked him,' he said, pausing. 'But did that attacker survive your..., spirit shout?'

Her eyes lowered. 'Unlikely, and that's why we need to remain in hiding for a while.'

'How did you learn these arts?'

'I've been practising most of my life in the Tibetan White Ape monastic lineage, a form of energetic Kung Fu. In essence it's a means to train the mind and body to transcend the normal and tune into the higher vibrational frequencies so that an opponent's intent can be sensed. The spirit shout then occurs spontaneously without any effort and can be devastating, but as you'll probably understand, neither the shout nor the fighting are the art but are vehicles to more sublime states of consciousness.'

A delicious savoury odour had begun to fill the room and the family members were now milling around preparing for a meal.

'Are you hungry? You should eat something,' she uttered as strands of chestnut hair fell across her face, loosely shading her wholesome attractiveness.

'A little, perhaps.'

'Good.'

She stood and then called out to a young lad, who had been laying the table. He stopped and listened to her instructions respectfully before trotting out of the room. Carty studied the short woman's stature as she spoke, noticing that her whole being seemed to resonate in expressing her words and actions. It was the something that he hadn't been able to put his finger on up until now but understood that he was in the presence of a highly evolved person and it comforted him. Quite how she had floored that killer and left him unconscious or possibly dead was still beyond his left-brained thinking, but it had occurred, of that he was sure.

What of Lisa's fate, though? He was now shocked back into the reality of the moment. Without her he was stuck in this foreign country, visa-less and an accomplice to an unlawful death even if it was in self-defence. With the herbal tea now rapidly clearing his head, his intuition strained at the whole odd episode leading up to and during his stay in Xinjiang.

'What is going on here, Hafeza? I can't help but think that Lisa and her family have another agenda to the one she's been spouting.'

'Hmmm,' the local sounded forcefully through her pursed lips. 'It's interesting that you say that. I've had my own suspicions for a while.'

'What are they?'

'A few months ago, there was a lot of activity at the research centre. I and some of the team are involved to a limited extent in a Thorium nuclear pilot project situated just outside Urumqi, in the desert. I am forbidden from mentioning it to anyone who has not been cleared by the Government and so couldn't tell you before.'

'But you can now?'

'I've made an executive decision to do so.' She broke into a measured smile. 'Anyway, it appears that there was serious tension between Mr Ong and the local communist party leaders resulting in his exclusion from a very lucrative business deal.'

My God! A lightbulb had gone on in Carty's head. 'And let me guess; is it to do with nuclear reprocessing?'

'I can't be sure. The rumour was that small amounts of spent nuclear waste were being shipped from a repository, in the Southern part of the Taklamakan desert, possibly Lop Nor, across the border into Kazakhstan. Apparently, Mr Ong was handling this murky operation for many years and my hunch is that he's been ousted by jealous Party members.'

'Ha! That's very interesting. Lisa had also raised Lop Nor with me recently, saying that it was a dried up salt lake where nuclear weapons testing had been carried out underground and that the area was now sealed off, under the army's control.'

'Well, she must also know about the power clash, as federal funds for the Thorium pilot facility have stopped.'

'Does that make any sense? I can't see a connection.'

'It does if you know that Mr Ong has control over the supply of Thoria, a mineral sourced from local Xinjiang deposits, which is the feedstock for the test facility,' she continued, 'and once the process is demonstrated as feasible, he wants to have the same exclusivity to supply it to all the new Thorium nuclear plants built throughout China. This alone would make him one of the country's wealthiest businessmen.'

'I see, some in the Party want to prevent his control so that they can keep the huge revenues for themselves. Greed is a good enough reason to kidnap his niece as a bargaining chip, in order to change his mind.'

'That's a likely explanation. Lisa had persuaded Mr Ong to allow her to focus on environmental issues, and these new Thorium reactors seems to go half way in achieving that and solving China's emerging energy problems. Thorium is many factors less radioactive than Uranium and has very little waste material associated with it, unlike current reactors. More importantly, though, these new reactors can consume some of the spent waste from decommissioned reactors, and also from warheads.'

The teenager's cough pulled her attention. 'Ah, chicken broth and bread. Perfect!' She thanked her nephew as he placed it down on a side pedestal next to the Englishman. Carty nodded his gratitude. The concoction he had drunk earlier was working wonders and he now relished the thought of eating. He picked up the bowl and placed it on his lap.

'Then that would make for a perfect scenario, consuming China's many years of stored nuclear waste while replacing its huge number of dirty coal-fired power stations with cleaner electricity generation. I can't see why the UK is not doing the same thing,' he uttered, slurping on a spoonful of broth. 'But surely the Chinese state can go ahead without Ong's involvement?'

She silently noted his comments, staring into his eyes to catch a *tell,* that he may know something more than he was letting on. Satisfied, she continued. 'The powers that be are nervous of upsetting influential local businessmen who could ignite political unrest in this mainly Muslim region. Anyway, politics aside, there's still one thing that seems out of place,' she added.

'What's that?'

'The shipments of spent waste transiting the border into Kazakhstan.'

The spoon hung in his fingers. 'I don't follow.'

'I mean, why ship it there when it can be processed in the near future, in domestic Thorium reactors? There's no urgency or danger to anyone if its left where it is, stored in the middle of the remotest desert in China before these new plants are built.'

'I suppose it's because it must be more lucrative to sell it to Kazakhstan if it is also developing its own Thorium nuclear industry and wants the waste for that process.'

She mocked a frown. 'I haven't heard about any Thorium programmes in Kazakhstan and if there is one, it would be relatively recent; the shipments, however, have been going on for many years. No, there's another reason why it's being shipped there, I just can't put my finger on it.'

The spoon now dropped and from her demeanour he understood the implication.

'You think that I'm somehow linked to this business, don't you?'

Her expressive eyes grew. 'I overheard Lisa talking with Ong about bringing you here after she discovered that your fund had financed those methane capture projects outside Urumqi.'

'When was that?'

'About a month ago.'

'What!' The Englishman felt his cheeks flush. 'That doesn't stack up. I only just met her in the last few days.'

'Well, Ong now owns your projects having forced the local partners to sell their shares to him.'

'But that's impossible. My fund is the majority owner and the legal structure cannot change without the Board's say so.'

'Your rules and business etiquette stand for very little here.'

He rose up, ignoring the soup and the pain. 'So, the lost revenues from my projects weren't stolen at all, just held back on the instructions of Ong?'

Her face remained impassive.

'When did you find this out and why didn't you tell me?'

'I am not immune to their power, Scott. If I had let slip any of this, I would not be talking with you now and anyway, I was hoping that Lisa's desire for you to collaborate on greening the desert was the main reason she brought you here. It now appears that it wasn't.'

'Does it?' he uttered, flexing his lips and lowering his eyes to focus on the soup spilt on the bedsheet as he processed her comment. Lisa had played him, and that now explained her odd behaviour. *Bitch!* Clearly she had spun her manipulative charms to achieve her goals which also, peculiarly, included environmental projects. Somehow, though, extortion didn't really seem to suit her or explain Ong's pretext for the expropriating the local projects. *Surely he couldn't have found out about the technology?* The notion sprang into his head, but he dismissed it. Even if Ong was aware of where those spent waste shipments were going and why, he was now out of the loop having been usurped by Party members as Hafeza had surmised.

'She brought you here without a visa so that they would have you at their mercy.'

'You know that I don't have an entry visa?'

'Of course, and clearly, you know far more than you're saying about the shipments of the nuclear waste.'

Carty frowned in disbelief, but she continued.

'Some months back, I had a series of recurring dreams in which a foreigner appeared at my door with a book, frantically begging me to hide it.'

'And did you?'

'No, I refused to help him. Ludmilla Anatolivna foretold that the book symbolically represents knowledge of some kind, and that if that falls into the wrong hands it may threaten the balance of world power.'

'Well, I'm certainly grateful to you for saving my life earlier,' he declared, stunned at the synchronicity. His beautiful Lena had been given the books years ago by her grandfather without knowing what they contained until Carty discovered their unsettling contents: the blueprints for the construction of the machine. He sighed, wanting to open up to Hafeza with his secret, but hesitant for the reason that she had no real power to help him escape this mess and the country. *What would Lena do?* Instantly, he wondered how she was and how she would handle this situation. The earlier vision of the goddess *Kuan Yin* then floated onto his inner screen reminding him that Ludmilla Anatolivna and Hafeza had shared their arcane knowledge and neither had any reason to do so other than out of open-hearted love. He glanced up and caught the woman's simper, as if she had just read all his thoughts.

'Okay, Hafeza, you told me earlier today that you wanted me to meet someone who can help with the truth, didn't you?'

She cocked her small head, not entirely sure what he was implying.

'You have been very open with me so let me share what I think it is you need to know,' he followed. 'I'm seeing a picture in which Ong may have been a middle-man in the trading of spent waste through Kazakhstan, and on to the Russians.'

'Does that mean that Russia is also developing Thorium reactors?'

His eyes narrowed, accentuating his characteristic crow's feet. 'I'm not sure about that but what I do know is that there is a technology operating in central Siberia which transmutes nuclear waste into safer, non-radioactive elements.' He paused, registering the woman's transient confusion. Her muted oriental features then broke into an incredulous smile.

'Are you joking?'

'No, I'm deadly serious and just knowing that it exists has completely changed my life and how I view the world. As you may know, I was *lost* in Siberia for some weeks a few years ago after stumbling too close to this technology. There was an attempt to eliminate me and Lena, the woman I love.'

'But you both survived.'

'Yes, thanks to the help of some unusual men with unusual powers, not unlike yours and Ludmilla Antolivna's.'

'That is coincidental.' Her fingers rubbed her chin, supporting her logical machinations. 'I think your hypothesis also fits nicely with the other facts.'

'Which are?'

'Over the last few years we've had visitors to the research centre from Russia and the former Soviet countries.' She paused momentarily as if to access her thoughts. 'There was a business delegation possibly four or five weeks ago, and I remember that one of the guests grew quite agitated as he was leaving. I could see it in his body language but unfortunately, I was behind the glass wall in the research centre and couldn't hear what was being said. Mr Ong seemed distracted for days afterwards, and it was then that Lisa left for a few weeks.'

'Where did she go?'

'I've no idea but it was definitely out of the country.'

'Did she return here before arriving with me?'

'Actually, no, she didn't. The first time after that was yesterday, with you.'

'Then she could have gone elsewhere before visiting England, perhaps to Russia?' He was now fully engaged, the events of the day lost to the moment. 'Do you recall the visitors' faces and their appearances, perhaps?'

'There were four men. Three were fairly young but the main representative was probably in his 60s, short and fat with a bald head.'

Kosechenko! He felt his skin goose up. *But could it be him? That would be too much of a coincidence.*

'Was he the one who was stressed?'

'That's right.'

'I wonder if that was because Ong had lost the business?' he muttered, questioning himself out loud, 'because the corrupt Party members have moved the goal posts, stopping the shipments. They've probably circumvented Ong and now hold all the cards, and if the Thorium pilot plant is already operating here in Xinjiang, they will make their black money by overcharging the State twice: once for processing the waste and second, for supplying it as part of the raw material to the reactor: it's a win-win. There must be many tons of it and the fees lucrative, meaning that they don't need to export it to the Russians anymore.'

'You seem to know how this corrupt practice works, very well.'

'I've had first-hand experience of these shenanigans!'

The woman drew a blank at this comment and was instead now glancing trance-like, past his shoulder, into space. Carty turned to look at the wall behind him, resisting the temptation to openly question what was holding her attention, deciding instead to continue eating the remains of the soup, which while delicious, was now lukewarm. But as the spoon reached his mouth, he noticed that her unfocused stare had not changed, absorbed as it was with an inner world.

'They didn't want her,' she susurrated, her gaze still indistinct.

'Sorry, who are you referring to?'

'That attack today. They were coming for you, not Lisa,' she added, shaking her head. 'Yes, I can see it clearly,' she continued.

'Really!' Stunned at the comment, the Englishman's felt his breath fleetingly suspended. 'Why me? Was the attack something to do with the Russians?' he probed as the image of Kosechenko's ugly face filled his head again. The thug was doubtlessly, still carrying on with the transmutation business.

The local woman sucked at her cheeks, her opal eyes still vacant and unresponsive.

'They've probably convinced themselves that I'm here to sell know-how of the transmutation technology to Ong,' Carty ventured.

'Perhaps, but it feels that they want more than that..., as if this technology will be a game changer and yet, as I see it, in the wrong hands it will cause greed, war and desecration of the environment. It's what Ludmilla Anatolivna foretold – you're carrying a secret that could alter the future. Your vision of the *Kuan Yin* is prompting you to sacrifice your worldly ambitions and walk a path between your own concepts of good and evil, to manifest what is latent in the collective unconscious for the benefit of humanity. It's the next stage that the ancients spoke of, a new cultural tune that is emerging, possibly triggered by the recent increase in frequency of the Schumann Resonance – the planet's electrical heartbeat. Nature and the ancestors are supporting you, although the outcome will not be certain and even if the technology is embraced, it may not be used in the way you perceive it will be.'

Carty's jaw was now hanging in shock as he registered her words. They prompted yet again those moments in the remote Siberian forest around Baikal learning of Ivan Yegorovich's incredible machine and the possibility of *overunity*: limitless energy production. He had since shuttered the episode away in his psyche, hoping that instead, his environmental projects and emissions derivatives trading would kick-start a revolution in abating climate change, raising consciousness for a new generation. But it had been a pipe dream. The world had carried on. His young son, James, along with his peers, was already an internet consumer and it seemed that they were being slowly severed from the natural world, doomed to accept globalisation's anthems and the soundbite shibboleths of politicians with their mantras for progress. He shook his head and the images, away.

'I don't understand...,it will not be used in the way I perceive it will be?'

'I can't tell you anything more than to advise you that your dreams and visions are the means by which you will receive guidance.'

He pulled at a long breath, unclenching his fists. Her statement echoed those of Green's. Despite his temporary amnesia of the last few years, it appeared that the serpent dragon had reared its head, reminding him that there was no escaping his destiny.

'Hafeza, do you think can we make it back to Ong's compound?'

Her features had momentarily hardened in toying with the options. 'Not now. Are you sure that's the right plan anyway?'

'It's the only one. I can't officially leave the country without a visa, and he certainly has the wherewithal to obtain one for me or fly me out, the way I came in, on his private jet.'

She blinked in accord. 'I could organise a driver to take you there during the night, but I cannot come with you, it would be too risky. I'm now a wanted person.'

'And what will happen to you?'

'I'll lie low for a few weeks and then escape into the mountains. There are communities there who will hide me.'

'But you can't run forever and what about your important research?'

'It would be a shame for it to stop as my teams are on the verge of several breakthroughs. Perhaps if and when Lisa returns safely, Mr Ong will be able to resolve the issues with the authorities so that I can return to my work.'

Her words struck Carty hard, sympathising as he did, with her dread at mistakenly being branded a criminal on the run, and wondering how she would cope with the unimaginable stress caused by the interrogations of her family and friends. Her predicament seemed, on the face of it, to have been ultimately caused by Lisa's tainted motives in bringing him here.

As his strained mind pored over his enigmatic host's antics that last evening he was still perplexed at what, deep down, drove Lisa. Was she simply striving for fame and status with her ambitious environmental plans under the cloak of a femme fatale, or did she really have knowledge of Ong's furtive business activities? He had no clue, but any concern for her current predicament was soon submerged in a fretful angst, stirred by thoughts of Lena's whereabouts and how she was coping with their enforced mutual absence. An inner feminine voice, though, quietly soothed his fears, convincing him of her immutable love. Juggling the gnawing emotions with the pain of his injuries and the urgency of the situation had left him shattered.

'Vodka?' Hafeza offered. 'It will help you sleep for a few hours and then we will leave.'

He shrugged. 'Anything to help dull the pain.'

Sixteen

The City of London

The crazed varnished steps had Gordon Green firmly gripping a cast iron balustrade, as they spiralled down into the dim beer cellar. Not much had changed in the few years since his last visit, with its nicotine-stained floral wallpaper and grimy ambience. He loathed the place but understood that Jack's suggesting it meant one thing, secrecy above and beyond all else. His watch showed just after 11 am and as expected, the place hadn't yet filled, but he knew that within the hour it would be heaving with old-school city types, a rare breed nowadays, eager for their steak'n'kidney pies and a pint or two to wash them down.

Green spied his friend holed up in one of the alcove seating areas.

'Good to see you, Jack.' He flourished a wave.

The man remained seated. 'And you, Gordon. Family all well?'

'Fine thanks. Yours?'

'They're good.' Jack's beady eyes smiled over his thick-rimmed glasses as Green firmly shook the man's hand to reaffirm their bond and then parked himself unceremoniously on the leather bench seat.

'It's a bit early for lunch, isn't it?'

'They start taking orders in about 45 minutes, but we can have coffee in the meantime?' He leant forward to take a cautious glance around before flashing a hand at the waiter who was busying himself preparing tables nearby. A request for two cappuccinos was quietly announced.

'Right then, Gordon. There's a lot to share and as usual, it's sensitive,' he uttered, extending his index finger to slowly push the specs back up his aquiline nose. Green understood the formality but arched his brows anyway in ironic disregard.

'Have you heard from Scott recently?' the man asked.

'Only a text, a day or so ago. Why?'

'What did it say?'

'That he was well and that he would call on a secure line when he could.'

'And did he?'

'Not yet.'

'What if I told you that he was in Turpan, Northwest China?'

'I understood that Lisa Taylor was taking him there via Hong Kong.'

'Well, that didn't happen. She diverted the destination to mainland China, mid-flight. They landed in Urumqi, in Xinjiang'

Green's eyes widened. 'He did say there was a change of plans but I didn't grasp that they had changed destinations. Is that a problem?'

'It presents several problems not least that Carty doesn't have an entry visa for China. I'm guessing he was planning to organise that in Hong Kong.'

'The stupid idiot! Didn't he learn anything from his experience in Russia?' Green squeezed his eyes together, tightly.

'It may have been pre-planned, which smacks of trouble.'

'Why?'

'It seems that Scott's past is catching up with him.' Jack's sober utterance triggered a look of fear in his friend's countenance. 'Tell me, Gordon. Have you ever met Lisa Taylor?'

'No, I haven't. I know that Nick had introduced her to Scott on the proviso that her well- connected family could help him solve some issues with his projects.'

'What kind of issues?'

'Default on payments. The local partners failed to collect several months' electricity revenues, which for some reason suddenly stopped being paid into his fund's designated account.'

'And has Nick known her for some time?'

'Not long, I believe.'

'Do you have your phone with you?' the Whitehall mandarin asked, drily.

'Of course, why do you ask?'

Jack paused as the coffees were placed down between them and waited for the waiter to saunter away.

'Would you call Scott now, please?' he instructed removing his glasses and pointing with them.

Green squinted at the request but complied, punching at the Nokia's button and then pressing the slim wad of black plastic to his ear.

'No ringing tone,' he stated, after a few attempts. 'Either its battery is dead, or he's deliberately switched it off.'

'Yes, we came to the same conclusions.' Jack brows puckered. 'Through satellite triangulation it's been pinpointed to Xinjiang, so we reckon Scott must still be there.'

'Just what are you driving at, Jack?'

'Don't you think it's a little too coincidental that this woman, Lisa, suddenly turns up out of the blue in London and offers Carty help in a remote area of China where her uncle just happens to wield influence?'

'I suppose it could be construed as such.'

'And at the same time Lena goes missing in Dubai.'

'Missing? I thought she was at a reunion with some old college friends and that your guys were watching her.'

'Yes, but she's given us the slip. According to our sources she is no longer there.'

'Just how sure are your sources?'

'You know the answer to that!'

Green snorted. 'So, what's the plan to find her?'

'Our people are using all the diplomatic channels to obtain as much information as possible. Her new smart phone was recovered in the hotel bedroom after she had checked out. Make of that what you will. We think it was a deliberate action – that she didn't want to be contracted or traced.'

'Do you think Scott has done the same thing and that they may be secretly rendezvousing?'

‘That did cross my mind, but my gut tells me that it’s not the case. Carty looked too shocked when we met up at the Baths and I explained that she had been followed at Heathrow. By the way, we now know that it was a Chinese source, possibly their intelligence, trailing her.’

‘Has she been kidnapped?’

‘That’s likely and all my instincts are still telling me that it’s connected with the technology.’

‘But we still don’t know if Scott has gone missing.’

Jack pursed his lips, his laconic demeanour tensing slightly. Green clocked it.

‘What is it? What are you not telling me?’

‘Word came in earlier today that Lisa Taylor was abducted. Her driver was killed in the melee and Carty was seen nearby.’

‘And you waited to tell me this!’ Green was agitated. ‘Has Scott been injured too?’

‘All that we know is that he’s vanished.’ Jack blinked in succession. ‘Gordon, it’s probable that other forces believe that Scott and Lena know more about the technology than they actually do.’

‘Really, I find that hard to believe,’ Green muttered in an attempt to hide his knowledge of the truth.

‘But surely you remember how agitated Scott was when I asked him if he was holding something back? Our top research people now believe that the water machine he claims to have seen in Siberia, produces energy as well as transmuting radioactive nucleotides.’ He slipped his spectacles back on. ‘They’re talking about the implosion of water causing a form of low temperature nuclear reaction called *cold fusion,*’ he rejoined, ‘I don’t understand such things with my scant scientific knowledge but apparently, and I know this sounds incredible, the technology Scott described to us can tap into higher dimensional states – the quantum flux, liberating vast quantities of energy. It might be this that others believe he and Lena know something about.’ He picked up the cup then slowly sipped. Green followed suit, the words preying heavily as he shook his head.

‘Sounds implausible.’

‘You’re right, it does, but there’s no other viable hypothesis at this moment.’

‘And you believe that Lisa Taylor somehow knows about this technology?’

‘It’s likely, given the murky past of Lisa’s uncle, Ong. You’ll recall that Lena escaped from Russia, into China after the attack on her and Carty, at Baikal.’

‘Of course I do.’

‘The Chinese agencies bent over backwards then to help us find out more about the shipments of nuclear waste into Russia from Japan and where it was being dumped. They revealed that a trial shipment of their domestic nuclear waste had been shipped into Kazakhstan, bound for Russia. Since then they’ve clammed up..., radio silent.’

‘And Xinjiang province has a border with Kazakhstan, doesn’t it?’

‘Correct, it does, and so now it’s all starting to add up.’ Jack pulled a hand over his shiny greased hair. ‘Ong is effectively a Chinese oligarch with a vast business empire controlling much of Xinjiang’s mineral wealth and links to corrupt Party members.’

‘Sorry, I still don’t fully follow how Ong and Lisa are involved.’ Green frowned.

‘We now know that Ong had contact with Arthur D’albo, who acted as the go-between for that trial shipment bound for transmutation in Siberia.’

‘Ah, I see, and was Ong involved in D’albo’s death?’

‘No idea, but the connection to the technology is too coincidental.’

‘You can say that again and in putting this all together, you’re implying that both Carty and Lena have been coaxed into visiting these places because of what they might know.’

The Whitehall man’s eyes glared back, like a barn owl’s, through his lenses.

‘Gordon, did Scott ever mention anything to you about *overunity* or zero point energy?’

The question had him stumped and he realised that if he lied, Jack would see it in his eyes and then their long-term bond of friendship would be inexorably threatened.

'Yes, yes..., I think he did mention those terms,' he replied, reaching for the cup but suddenly remembering that it had been emptied a minute earlier. 'Scott suspected that the Russian water technology was able to produce it, but I completely dismissed this as nonsense and I believe he did too.' Green sighed silently to himself, choosing not to divulge that he was safekeeping the blueprints for the machine's construction within a set of leather bound books entrusted to Lena by her grandfather, some years back.

'So, I was wrong.' Jack huffed. 'He and possibly Lena do possess this knowledge. Why didn't you tell me about this before, in confidence? It would have allowed me to put a full security operation in place which, no doubt, would have saved them from this predicament, whatever it is that they have got themselves into.'

'Sorry, Jack, but I gave him my word. The important thing was that he did divulge to you what he had heard about the technology's ability to transmute nuclear waste. It was one of the underlying reasons why he was set up by D'albo and probably why the Chinese were interested. It wasn't until much later after the Albion's fraud case was resolved, that he told me about his suspicions of *overunity* and as I just said, it seemed a ridiculous assertion.'

'What if it wasn't? What if both the Russians and the Chinese want a limitless energy machine?'

'It would certainly stir things up, politically, on planet Earth!' Green simpered. Jack had no idea of the ideological conversations he had struck up with Carty on the very same subject. Deployment of such a machine would change everything and therefore could never be allowed to exist, not at least in the current economic paradigm.

'I can't believe a rational man like you, is even contemplating such a thing. It could never be held secret, not least by Scott Carty.'

'But I didn't say it was...,' Jack halted his words as two men walked past booming about the events of their morning. The place was beginning to fill up fast. 'Can I ask you to meet with Nick Hall and challenge him about what Carty may have told him?'

'Surely, Nick can't know anything about all this?'

'If he does it's unlikely he will yield anything to the agencies, but he may to you. It's vitally important that he tells you everything he may have said to Lisa Taylor. Both Carty's and Lena's lives may depend on it!'

Seventeen

Irkutsk Oblast, Siberia

A light mist lingered over the clumped bilberry shrubs, stirred by the faintest rays of the dawn sun, which had also prompted the Buryat to rise from his overnight lair. He hadn't remembered falling asleep in the early hours, having transcended, allowing the ancestors to guide him in his search for the old man. His gut sent queasy messages telling him that he was either close to finding him or he had eaten the wrong herbs and roots, but he had no choice but to continue as he had done, more than 15 years earlier, when searching for Lubimov's missing father. Then, he had discovered the place, of the man's murder but not his body - the physical remains were not important inasmuch as the energetic aftermath from the struggle and final blows, which told the Buryat everything. His quest now, though, had been made easier. Witnesses had indicated the landing site of a helicopter in a forest meadow a few kilometres away, and he had used it as his starting point, allowing his other *self* to take him on the spirit walk, surrendering any cogent sense of time to merge into a heightened state of consciousness and supernatural awareness. He had no idea of the date or how long he had been in the taiga but simply that it was now morning and that with the rising sun's heat, the rich odour of pine was pricking his nose bringing him into the present.

I know Ivan Yegorovich is close. The thought had him rolling up onto one knee, the mist now all but vapourish and transpiring through the foliage around him. Then the sound of branched snapping froze his action. Someone or something was pushing through the shrubbery nearby, behind him. The Buryat bristled and hunkered down behind the bushes, panther-like and steadying his breath as his eyelids hung almost closed. *These men have no reason to be here,* he reasoned, listening to their slurred voices and turning his head immeasurably slowly to scan their gnarled scarred visages, as they passed just yards away, oblivious to his blended presence. Only hunters or rangers were out this early, so far into the forest, and neither of these men fitted those roles. His suspicions were then confirmed, overhearing their conversation, twanged with regional accents. These were hired mercenaries from European Russia and the coincidence of their appearance with his sensing the old man's presence was all the evidence he needed that he was on the right track.

As soon as they had moved out of sight into the green, Boris moved, padding onto the trodden-down moss, silently stalking their footsteps, mentally noting every aspect of these strangers and the weapons they were carrying as they tramped on. At one point they stopped in a patch of recently cleared timber, perching down on hewn stumps to roll tobacco and smoke while continuing their brazen dialogue. Their purpose he now gleaned had been to clear any remaining traces from the landing site, a job that could take any number of days and being their own masters, they were taking as much time as possible to relax.

That's a mistake.

The Buryat waited for the moment to present itself before coolly pulling away the low branches and stepping out behind them, hovering. They turned, frantically scrabbling for their holstered pistols.

'Don't!' he barked, having simultaneously snatched up one of their rifles, aiming it at them. 'Drop your weapons.'

They gingerly complied, and he stepped forward to kick the guns away.

'What is your business here in the forest?'

'We're hunters,' one grunted the obvious answer, wiping his shorn head with a huge hand.

'Where are you heading?'

'Why do you need to know that?'

'Because I'm pointing this rifle at you.'

'We're moving to a camp an hour up this path and we don't want any trouble,' the other snarled, shooting a grisly glare. 'Who are you, anyway?

The Buryat nodded slyly, clocking the man's unusual neck tattoos, recognising their connections to prison and possibly mafia. These thugs knew about intimidation and death no doubt, but so did the Buryat. 'I'm a local ranger,' he bluffed, 'there's been some unlawful trapping of bears around here recently so that's the reason for the questions.'

His answer caused the slow shaking of their dipped heads. He now faced an impasse: should he lower the rifle and return it or simply keep it focused on them as he backed away? The strong waft of alcohol meant the decision was obvious: they would kill him without a second thought if he gave them the chance. He retraced his steps backwards, still facing their glares beneath lowered brows

'We need our rifle, now,' one threatened.

'I'll return it in a day or so, to the camp you mentioned..., if it exists.' He knew it didn't 'Make sure you're there if you want it back and, by the way, I will be with my comrades.' His utterance met with florid sneers and half-grins. They knew he was bluffing and began inching forward. He instantly fired two rounds at their feet, forcing their halt.

'Stay back!' he yelled. 'I'll maim you both and then leave you for the bears.'

They obeyed but glances were shot knowingly between them and then one defiantly chanced it, diving sideways towards the downed pistols, forcing Boris to let off a shot, wounding him in the thigh. He rolled about screaming, clutching at the pumping claret while in the diversion, the other had run at the Buryat but pulled up as the gun's barrels were swung rapidly back to aim at his face.

'You'll get the same if you take one more step. Now get on the ground and tell me exactly what you're doing here.'

The creased face remained sullen, its hooded lids shielded cold eyes and a lip had leered to reveal blackened teeth. The Buryat, unperturbed, waved the barrel to enforce his orders but then sensed a sharp presence at his rear. He spun to narrowly avoid a rifle-butt, aimed at his skull, but which rammed into his shoulder instead and momentarily, he was knocked off balance. Forced to drop onto his hands, he instantly shot out a kick into this third attacker's groin and then jumped up, his forehead smashing the thug full in the face and exploding his nose. The man fell but as he did, Boris was jumped from behind, an arm pinioning his neck while a blade was violently swiped sideways with intent to slit his throat. In the same instant the cold metal touched the Buryat's skin he had spun again, his speed matching its trajectory while his arm simultaneously spiralled up between their bodies to keep the weapon away and his other hand clamping the blade's edge between his palm and fingers. The killer's face registered an uncanny fear as he urgently attempted to pull it free, but Boris's drove his free elbow into the mercenary's sternum as his fingers simultaneously gripped and twisted the man's windpipe. The figure crumpled and then suddenly slumped as a round rang out. The first man, still floored, had aimed poorly. The Buryat's face screwed into a grimace for a millisecond as the bullet, passing through the assassin shielding him, grazed his tricep. He flipped the knife blade in his fingers to feel its centred weight and then launched it. It met its mark, squarely in the chest of the pistol-wielding gunman, just as he let off another shot. Instinctively, Boris was already diving low as his peripheral vision caught the other bloody mercenary's aimed weapon. Rolling across the short space into the man's legs, took him down and the rifle flying into the undergrowth. They tussled, the seasoned assassin righting himself on top of the winded Buryat, grinning and spitting blood from his shattered nose while pinning the local's arms down with his knees and leaning, full weight via his forearm across his windpipe and carotid artery. The Buryat struggled but couldn't break the hold and his wide eyes spoke of death for some seconds before his body slowly went limp and his breathing ceased. The assassin laughed arrogantly, released his pressure with a mock salute of victory. But then, in terror he realised his crucial mistake: his victim was no ordinary man. The Buryat had appeared to have come back to life, instantly arching his back up to shake the killer from his superior position. Panicked, the man lashed out with a fist but missed as Boris' palm delivered an electric shock causing the stranger to spasm violently, his demeanour registering hell. The Buryat quickly rolled sideways to crescent his leg up so that his thigh was now wrapped around the stunned assailant's neck. A quick jerking snap and it was over.

Boris breathed in sharply, his years *of neijia* training and acquired esoteric skills had given him an unrivalled edge, but the sense of victory was fleetingly. He couldn't relax knowing that the gunshots would have alerted others and he hurriedly raced over to the two men. Both had expired and with them a lost opportunity for interrogation to find out Ivan Yegorovich's possible location. All he could do now was search them for clues before arranging their bodies and weapons to suggest that they had argued in a drunken state and then lethally fought each other. It wouldn't fool those investigating for very long, before they called for a search of the area, but that would give him the time he needed to become invisible once again, within the taiga.

* * * *

London, later that evening

'Tea or perhaps something stronger?' Nick Hall enquired, grinning as the older man sat.

'Tea's fine thanks.' Green's polite acknowledgment seemed strained.

'Is everything okay, Gordon? It's quite rare nowadays that you visit me here at home.'

'Well, since you've raised the question, I must admit that I am concerned about Scott and this unscheduled trip he made into China.'

'I don't think you ought to worry, he's being chaperoned by an acquaintance of mine, Lisa Taylor, with the backing of her very wealthy and influential uncle in Hong Kong.'

'That's the problem, Nick. Scott never landed in Hong Kong. Her corporate jet took a detour mid-flight and landed in Xinjiang province where his projects are.'

'Really?' Hall caught his friend's stare as he slipped the cup onto the table and perched on one of the high wooden stools, facing the man. 'I guess she didn't want to waste any time in helping him. He's been facing some financial problems with those projects in the last few months.'

'I know. He explained everything to me before he left. Have you heard from him since?'

'Come to think of it, no, but then that's quite normal with Scott. Sometimes we don't speak for months.'

'Well, he's not responding to calls or texts, and my sources tell me that he didn't have an entry visa for China. He was probably planning to do that in Hong Kong.'

'What! He's in the country illegally?'

Green nodded calmly. 'Nick, tell me about this woman, Lisa Taylor.'

'I know that look of yours, Gordon, but I can tell you she's totally genuine if not a little showy.'

'Showy?'

'Stunning.'

'I see. She's captivated you with her charms, but what's her background?'

'As far as I know she's from a Chinese diplomatic family with an English mother, went to a boarding school here in the UK and then studied Biophysics at University in London. From what I understand, her uncle is a very successful businessman, and she's been drafted in to assist him with negotiations and to be the public face of his companies overseas. I mentioned Scott's difficulties to her and she offered to help. I believe that behind the scenes, her family has powerful influence and can reach Scott's Chinese partners.'

Green fingered his chin. 'You didn't quietly question yourself about the possibility that her uncle may be involved in criminal activities.'

'Come on, Gordon! You know better than most how the developing world functions. There's no way I could have raised that as an issue with Lisa. She would have never spoken to me again, if I had.'

'So tell me again, how did you meet her?'

Nick Hall fidgeted, crossing his legs. 'At a technology conference. Her family's facilities are pioneering research into a number of new promising areas one of which is Brown's Gas and, as you know, that's a subject close to my heart.' He smiled openly but Green was nonplussed.

'When was that?'

'About two months ago. Why?'

'I'm trying to understand when you raised Scott's issue with her.'

'Oh, that's easy, at the conference when she told me where her research facility was situated.'

'In Xinjiang?'

Hall bobbed his head in affirmation.

'I see. So she had approximately two months to investigate Scott's background and business activities in China.'

'Why would she have bothered to do that?'

'Because I believe that her chance meeting with you was too much of a coincidence,' he announced lowering his gaze. 'Nick, I know you're aware of the technology.' The words hung as Green eyed him for a while before smiling reservedly.

'Do you mean Brown's Gas?'

'You know what I'm talking about. Scott told me he had mentioned it to you in confidence.'

'Ah, that's interesting. He didn't tell me that you also knew.'

'How do you think he was released from D'albo's fraud so quickly? He had to advise the intelligence agencies of what he found in Siberia. Did you mention anything at all to Lisa about it?'

Hall's usually ruddy expression drained at the enormity of what was being implied.

'Not directly.'

'What kind of answer is that?'

'She raised the issue of the transmutation of nuclear waste hinting that Brown's Gas could initiate it. Thinking back, it was a rather random topic to bring up with someone she had only just met. Being me, though, I may have been over zealous in my response.'

'What did you say to her, exactly?'

'That I was interested to hear more about her company's research as I had heard rumours of similar technologies operating in Russia.'

'Did she offer you some involvement in her Brown's Gas business?

'Yes, she ventured to seed-fund a start-up business, based in London, which would pull in further capital to launch her company's technology worldwide. It was very tempting, and I accepted.'

'Damn!' Green thumped his fist edge down on the table causing the tea to spill. 'She's played you and Carty very smoothly!'

'I doubt that very much,' Hall said, mocking nonchalance.

'Don't be a fool, Nick. You don't have any special intellectual properties or patents concerning Brown's Gas. Why would she need to offer you funding when her family owns industries and trading businesses worth billions? They could do it themselves.' He rubbed his worn hands over his eyes. 'Sorry for my outburst but I think it's obvious she was after something else other than starting up a business with you. With all the international publicity surrounding Scott, Lisa and whoever she's involved with must have heard inklings of what he had learned during his time in Russia. All she had to do was ask you some roundabout questions concerning transmutation and see how you responded. Almost nobody would have reacted to her specific line of enquiry, but you evidently did. You were superbly taken in.'

‘I can’t quite believe it. Where is Scott now, and how do we alert him?’

‘He’s disappeared. No one knows where he is except that he was recently subject to a kidnapping incident. Lisa was taken but not him.’

Hall was shocked. ‘That’s crazy and just doesn’t make any sense, particularly as you’ve been implying that she was playing us both. What is being done to find them?’

‘Everything that can be done without being too overtly obvious,’ Green answered, quietly scanning his demeanour. A niggling hunch was eating away at him about his friend’s story.

‘Have you spoken to Lena? Perhaps Scott’s been in contact with her?’ Nick piped up.

He obviously doesn’t know that she’s missing too. Green mulled, thinking it unwise at this juncture to tell Nick Hall about her vanishing.

“Not yet. I don’t want to worry her and I suggest that you don't speak with her about this either.’

Eighteen

Turpan

A sharp nudge shook him from a fitful sleep and he blinked in the dull light, not sure where he was and why sharp pains were shooting up his torso from his thighs.

'How do you feel?' the local woman asked calmly.

'Better, I think.' Carty winced in trying to get comfortable. 'What time is it?'

'Just after 1:20. Do you think you can walk?'

Carty swallowed hard. 'I could try. Why?'

'The authorities are making house to house searches nearby and it's likely they'll come here soon so we need to move back underground as fast as possible. Here, let me help you stand.' She reached out a hand and he reciprocated, sensing the uncanny energy in the young woman's grip and reminded exactly of what she was capable of, if challenged.

The trauma from his injuries had lessened considerably, probably due to her earlier insistence on administering an unusual liniment infused with alcohol and having him drink the herbal teas and then the vodka, which had sent him to sleep. He took hold of her shoulder, though, as she led the way with a small hand torch down into the confined basement space below the buildings. The torch batteries were obviously failing, and the scant lighting had not been switched on in order to avoid detection, leaving him squinting in the darkened environment as the floor panel was closed up behind them. There had been no farewells, the family members behaving as if this was routine, carried out on a regular basis to defy the authorities' attention. Unease gnawed that he had inadvertently fallen in with a renegade group who might have been responsible for Lisa's abduction. The notion was lost quickly with the screaming pain in his lower back as he forced himself down onto all fours and crawled. Each movement of a limb left no respite, and the few hundred feet in the putrid ambience began to exhaust him, but he gritted his teeth and pushed on, in the certainty that what lay ahead was the better option than being hauled in by the police.

Soon they were close to the stairs leading up to the tenement house that he had ventured into earlier that day and she signalled for silence, poised on her haunches. With his breath hushed and heartbeat throbbing in his ears, he trusted that it would not be long before they could start up. It wasn't. Another of her close group had signalled by tapping, followed by a wall opening and then, again, they were upstairs in that now darkened, ground-floor room, looking out on to the scantily lit, deserted thoroughfare. Hafeza broke into conversation with an older scarfed woman whose placid eyes and beautifully rounded cheeks relayed a sense of peace to the Englishman, allowing him to accept that his host's help was genuine. He collapsed, sinews yelling, into a low chair, its vinyl cover cool in the sticky atmosphere.

'Good,' she said turning to him and simpering softly. 'The authorities were here earlier but are now up the street. They shouldn't bother us.'

'And what do we do now?' he asked, his worried expression lost in the long shadows cast across his face.

'Wait for the car that's coming to collect you. I don't know how long that will take but I suggest you try to rest in the meantime.'

He took her cue and rested his head back in an attempt to blank out the stabbing throbs of discomfort while focusing on the buildings beyond the window. Then the brutal attack began to replay itself as if it was on a continual film loop in his mind, compelling him to reflect on the shocking event. Just how Hafeza had disarmed and possibly killed one of the killers with a shout..., a spirit shout no less, left him bereft of any logical explanation. He was in no doubt it had happened, although how she had executed it was a mystery, as had Boris' unbelievable skills been.

The trundle of tyres over the broken road heightened in pitch and although he could not yet see the tell-tale beams from head lights, he knew the car was close by. Within seconds Hafeza was positioned askance, her face registering signs of relief as the vehicle emerged, its lamps extinguished, to pull up just across the street.

'Time to go?' he quizzed.

'Let me check the situation,' she murmured, cracking the door open onto the road and poking out her face to capture the driver's attention. Carty immediately pulled himself up, bringing his eyes to window level to observe the car's lights flashing once back at her.

'It's safe.' She peered over her shoulder at the Englishman, somewhat tense. 'I want you to casually walk over there, open the rear door and get in. Do not look back or act suspicious in any way, understand?'

'You're not coming..., for part of the way at least?'

Her gazed lowered fleetingly, trying to muster the words. 'I can't, Scott.' She placed her soft palm on his jaw, in a disguised gesture to sooth the effect of the attack, but their shared glances knew it was something else as his hands reached for her tiny waist. She flung her arms around his neck and slipped her cheek alongside his, her entire body trembling, and he then understood that in her culture she rarely had the chance to be this intimate with a man she was not destined to marry despite all the rhetoric and appearances of being a modern, professional young woman. He pulled back to face her.

'Will you be fine?' he asked.

She nodded, frantically rubbing her fingertips across the purple rings beneath her eyes, embarrassed that she had shed tears. 'Once you're in the car the driver will take you directly to the Pearl Dragon Collective..., and after that, I will not be able to help you. Mr Ong should be around as he rarely travels nowadays. You will need to explain to him that you and I escaped the attack and hid after which I arranged for the car.'

'But won't he ask why you didn't come with me?'

'No doubt he will, but let him know that I will be in contact shortly to explain the issues. He will understand my reluctance to get involved with the police, who may try to implicate me for whatever corrupt or connived reasons they have.'

'Does that mean that you'll continue working for Ong's research facility in the future?'

'Who knows? I would guess that he's desperate to find out what's happened to Lisa and to have her returned safely as fast as possible, rather than your or my predicament.'

'Well, I will feel a whole lot safer once I'm there. I can then contact the British Consulate if the circumstances require it.'

'I would advise against it, Scott. It will embarrass Mr Ong, if not compromise his position quite badly having allowed you to fly in on his corporate jet without a visa. He will be made to accept the full force of the authorities for doing so and then his enemies will begin to circle.'

'But I may have to contact the British authorities if he can't fly me out of the country by the same way that I came in.'

She shot him a wry look. 'This is all academic and it's not worth wasting time discussing. Now you better go. I wish you much luck, Scott Carty. Don't forget what you have seen and learnt here.'

'Will we meet again?' he blurted, searching her face for some recognition of the possibility.

'I hope so,' she whispered, her lips tremoring within her strained smile as she gently manoeuvred him towards the door.

He did as instructed, slipping rapidly over to the ancient Toyota and squeezed himself in onto its mottled fabric seating. Its atmosphere was heady with foreign, aromatic pungencies as a pair of dark eyes fixed firmly upon him from the driver's mirror, prompting Hafeza's instructions to say nothing. Instead he simply indicated with his index finger to move on, causing the shabby chauffeur to let the vehicle roll forward down the gentle incline for some 30 feet or so before flipping the ignition key and smoothly engaging first gear, all without headlights.

From the partially opened door Hafeza watched, her breath high as the car moved off slowly, praying that her insights about the kidnappers' target not being Lisa, but Scott Carty, had been misguided.

The vehicle weaved through back alleyways, inching along here and there, narrowly avoiding scraping its sides and scattering the plethora of wild cats that had made their homes there. The man's strategy was nerve-grindingly tedious but avoided road blocks or police cordons and ultimately brought them to a dirt track that crossed a thin strip of desert on the outskirts of the town. Shortly, they were joining the main road north to Urumqi and Carty sighed loudly, cracking open a window to relieve the stuffiness. The rush of cool air had him immediately hunkering back into the seat, bringing on the uncontrollable trembling of post-trauma shock. The faster speed, though, gradually settled his state and had him staring unfocused out onto a barren landscape of ubiquitous small hills now lit by a waxing moon – a backdrop to his mental churnings. Shattered and physically broken, the incessant lumber of the wheels over the highway's uneven surface was hypnotic, enticing his eyelids to hover barely open as Lena's charmed and loving countenance surfaced behind them. His last glimpse of her magical smile at the airport seemed to be calling to him and all he really wanted was to be with her, away from this place and the mad responsibilities thrust upon him. But in his heart he understood that he would never be free of them or his destiny as Hafeza's words seemed to echo again across the desolate plain. *Or Fate will drag you there by the hair, screaming.* They had remained a puzzle to him until now, but in the recesses of his mind he registered that he had been drawn once again, unconsciously it would appear, into similar circumstances to those that had led to his near assassination in Russia. Those had also brought him face to face to what could have only been described as the incredible: the supernatural skills of the odd characters arriving in his life to save him, and a technology so earth-shatteringly shocking to his sensibilities that it should have been experience enough for several lifetimes. Both Lisa and Hafeza, though, had revealed that other less exotic developments were threatening the hegemony of a fossil-fuelled future: Brown's Gas, graphene, supercapacitors, hemp plastic and even the potential to green a desert to replenish the planet's already dangerously diminishing oxygen levels. Had he, as Hafeza inferred, simply been a catalyst for manifesting all this in a cosmic quickening that would always be beyond his full understanding? The synchronicity of The Flower of Life appearing twice in such a bizarre manner and within the space of a few days seemed to signify that she was correct. Also, those few special souls that had come to his aid were on the face of it and despite their idiosyncrasies, driven by the love of humanity and life: their selfless actions had maintained a window of opportunity for civilisation to evolve and preserve those priceless gifts above all else. It meant huge change, not for those who had little but those who stood to lose their false gold. *Is that what was meant by the meek inheriting the earth?* his exhausted mind quizzed. *But what if the serpent Dragon doesn't want to relinquish its hold?*

He slumbered, sometimes jolted partly awake by the vehicle's sudden swerving to avoid pot holes or small animals that had strayed onto the tarmac. Saliva, dribbling in gooey strands from his half-cocked mouth, had left a soaked patch across the front of his crumpled shirt, and as they came to an abrupt stop, his head shot forward and then recoiled back into the chair, forcing him into a shocked wakefulness.

'Are we here, yet?'

The driver did not respond but simply turned his head, looking sternly at his passenger and pointed. Carty rubbed a palm across his eyes and peered out in the direction, noting that they were clearly back in the industrial hinterland of Urumqi, parked in the shadows at a deserted junction of two roads, away from the scant municipal street lighting. Confused, he glanced back at the man who was now waving the back of a hand dismissively and with some urgency, signalling for the Englishman to leave. Carty peered out again, recognising the ancient scaffold stanchions above a white-washed building a football field's length away, which supported the huge steel-sections spelling out: DRAGON PEARL COLLECTIVE. They reminded him of the makeshift advertising hoardings, leftover remnants of the Soviet Era, positioned on the roofs of offices and factories that he had briefly driven past in Almaty and Irkutsk. It prompted his questioning why, with all the wealth Ong possessed, more modern neon signage hadn't been erected in its place, but then he quickly concluded that he was measuring the man by his own Western standards. Ong had no need to promote anything and the apparent dilapidated state of the exterior walls and hoardings hid the real nature of his wealth and the very modern, research operations he was funding.

The chauffeur's expression was now agitated as he began to speak in raised monosyllabic tones, indicating that it was urgent that the Englishman left. Carty took the cue, rapidly grabbing the man's small hand to thank him before cranking the door open and stepping out onto the road. As soon as he had, the vehicle sped off door still ajar and then it dawned on Carty in his exhausted state, that the driver had taken a huge a risk in bringing him here given the possibility of the vehicle's licence number being captured, implicating both him and possibly Hafeza.

Pulling himself together against the unusually cold breeze now blowing in from the mountains, Carty limped slowly up to the corrugated iron entrance gate where he paused. Drawing a long breath he considered the consequences of his next action – there was no going back – so he pressed a button on the intercom panel.

'*Weihee*,' came the curt response seconds later.

'Hello. This is Scott Carty. Is Mr Ong there, please?'

There was a mute pause, but it was obvious someone was still on the line, listening to him.

'Mr Ong..., Ong!'

Again silence. Carty rested his forearm against the gate and then slumped his head squarely on to it, wondering if he had been understood and realising that Ong was probably in bed at this godforsaken hour. Then a shuffle of footsteps inside, across the yard, grew louder and came to an abrupt halt, leaving a pregnant anxiety with in the Englishman as the electronic buzzer again came to life. A small door opened within the gate and a shrunken uniformed man stuck a head out, sharply cocking it at the foreigner.

'Mr Ong..., I need to speak with Mr Ong,' he pressed.

The man rapidly nodded while raising a palm to desist Carty's begging as the other hand held a cell phone to his ear. He appeared to be listening to instructions and timidly replying with one word affirmations. Then, nodding and hanging up, he ushered the Englishman through into the familiar yard once again and escorted him through to the staff refectory.

An older woman wearing a brightly flowered scarf turned to give him a semi-toothless grin while she busied herself cutting vegetables over large industrial aluminium pans, all steaming away furiously. She pointed with her sharp knife at a teapot on one of a series of covered trestle tables along the far side of the room. He poured it gratefully, watching her repetitive formicidaen duties and how she both accepted and handled preparing food for the various shift workers with zen-like ease. As he sipped a sensation of relaxation allowed him to drop his guard and take in his dishevelled attire, desperately brushing at the dirt-stained chinos. He stunk of a grimy sweat and rubbed at his stubble and lank sandy hair as he moved to one of the other basins, sticking his head under the industrial-type faucet to refresh his tired state. The woman raised her knife to protest but was overshadowed as the compound's main lights suddenly came to life outside and the familiar rattling of its gate kicked in. Ong's Mongolian minder and a colleague had stormed into the refectory, neither acknowledging the Englishman's presence but focused instead on a Mercedes Jeep that had pulled in. Carty observed from the window, registering the familiar petite frame of Lisa's uncle emerging, sporting the simple white cotton shirt and trousers held up with a belt that seemed too long for his painfully thin girth. Clearly in command, the man strolled effortlessly into the building escorted by the huge men, and then the Englishman's feeling of ease evaporated. *Have I made a mistake in coming here?* He wondered, recalling Ong's laconic, cold behaviour towards him during their last meeting, and the fact that he was now aware that the oligarch had stolen ownership of his projects.

Ong's lack of urgency in calling Carty to his office only accentuated his nervousness, but after what seemed like an age, the Mongolian entered the hall and brusquely waved at him to follow. He did, gingerly climbing the metal staircase one step at a time wincing, as his lead leg bore his weight, all under the eyes of his minder, hovering unsympathetically from the top platform, his swollen biceps folded across his chest. Carty kept his nerve, refusing to be intimidated and telling himself that Ong could wait. The wait soon finished as he pulled himself into the office to find the boss finishing a call.

'Hello, Mr Carty,' he uttered through an inscrutable expressionless smile. 'Where have you been? The authorities have been searching for you. Are you okay?'

'Just about thanks. I'm sure you know that there was an attack at the market in Turpan, I was almost killed, and Lisa was taken. Have you heard any news about her..., is she safe?'

Ong's face didn't flinch. 'She's okay but a little shaken. She's resting now.'

What? Carty tried to mask his confusion. The comment flew contrary to the report Hafeza had given him and what his vague recollections knew to be the truth.

'I thought she had been abducted. I saw her bodyguard being shot.'

'Do you need a doctor?'

'I probably do but can I ask where Lisa is?'

'As I said, she is fine and resting in hospital. You will be able see her in the next day or so.'

Carty shook his head stunned by the man's blithe response. 'Then, she wasn't kidnapped?' he quietly pressed.

'We have dealt with those responsible.' Ong bared his nicotine stained teeth in a smile that bore little empathy. 'But what I would like to know is how you evaded the authorities to arrive here?'

Carty was on the back foot and decided to bluff, telling how, apparently, a group of local men pulled him and Hafeza from the fracas into a car and drove them out of Turpan.

'I was knocked unconscious during the attack and don't have any recollection other than what I just told you.' He pulled at his sodden hair and then rubbed the back of his neck in the sticky environment, emphasising his injuries.

'And where exactly, is Hafeza now?'

'I have no idea. Once I became conscious and could sit up, she decided that the best place for me would be here. She said that you would understand.'

'Did she believe you were in danger?'

'I don't believe she did, but she was scared thinking that Lisa had been kidnapped and that as a westerner, I might also be a target.'

'She was correct. The Uyghur rebels are causing us many problems in this region.' A phlegmy cough had him reaching for the box on his desk.

Interesting! He obviously doesn't realise that I know of his background.

'They feel that too many jobs and benefits are given to the Han Chinese and so organise disruptions to vent their frustration.' He spat into a tissue.

'But it wasn't just a protest or disruption; it was a well organised attack with...,' Carty paused. A sudden fear had swamped his being. *How can he not know what really happened?*

'With what?'

'Er..., with automatic weapons.'

'Well, we can report all this to the authorities in good time. For the moment I suggest that you get some rest. Your bag will be brought here from the research centre, and I will arrange for the company's doctor to give you a complete check over then.'

'Thank you, Mr Ong,' he replied, understanding that with the late hour fogging his logic, probing any further about Lisa and what really happened might irritate the oligarch and that might then jeopardise his exit from the county.

The penthouse of a local boutique hotel had all the mod-cons he could want but they were lost on him with the desperate need for a hot shower and sleep.

He woke with his throat and nose stuffed with mucus, a reaction to the extreme cold setting of the air-conditioning, which left him chilled, forcing him to limp to the shower once more in order to warm up. As the steaming water played across the tender and colourful bruises, he pored once again, over the conflicting stories of Ong and Hafeza. He instinctively knew who he trusted but that didn't shine much clarity on Ong's rational for lying to him. Lisa had definitely been abducted and her minder shot dead. The blood, gore and his injuries were all too real and he rubbed his face with handfuls of water, mulling Hafeza's claim that Ong had taken control of his projects. If it was true, it made little sense. With all his wealth the man didn't need their comparatively low income streams or the carbon credits, however profitable they might be. But then he recalled how they had chewed over a crazy hypothesis, one in which Ong, in his dealings with the Russians over shipments of nuclear waste, had learned of the machine's ability to transmute that same spent material. Somehow, he had also gleaned that Carty was privy to this knowledge and thus has to be coaxed into a trap. The presumption seemed far-fetched, yet his gut told him it wasn't, as the sharp ring of the doorbell sprang him from his thoughts. In a towelling robe, he cautiously padded over to answer it, to find that his case had been delivered. Immediately he opened it, emptying its contents across the carpet. Elation registered as the familiar burgundy UK passport came into view and then his phone. He fingered it in an attempt to fire it up, but it was dead and spreading out the few clothes, he was unable to see the charger or its lead. Frantically, he unzipped the inside pockets of the case – nothing. They were gone and now the hope of seeing a text from Lena or the opportunity to contact her or Green had been quashed.

All it needs is few minutes charge, he thought, resigning himself to asking one of Ong's staff to help but that would not be for some time, probably after he had seen Lisa. His thoughts gravitated back to the brutality of her kidnap, wondering exactly what state she must be in, regardless of Ong's dismissal that she was fine. *What is he covering up?* Even if she was, then it would make little sense to quiz her about it. Instead, Carty's focus had to be on persuading Ong of the urgency of his own return to England. Any conversation as to his knowledge of the projects, switching hands was moot and would only endanger Hafeza. That could be better handled later, through Sole Carbon's lawyers, once he was back in London.

The doorbell chimed again and buoyed he opened it to encounter an attractive and unusually tall Chinese woman in a black business suit dotted with bright-red pinstripe, visibly blushing at his exposed hairless chest.

'Mr Carty?'

'Yes..., what it is?'

'The doctor is here. May we come in?'

He stood to one side allowing a suited local man to enter. Avoiding eye contact with the Englishman, he set down a typical doctor's bag on the dressing cabinet.

'I can translate if it's required,' the woman added.

'Okay, just let me get dressed, first' he said, grabbing the spare trousers and a shirt from his bag.

He emerged from the bathroom a few minutes later, to find the doctor indicating for Carty to sit on the edge of the bed, facing him as the woman hovered nearby in her oversized heels.

'He will examine you now,' she instructed.

The various standard tests were all carried out: pulse count, blood pressure, iris inspection and when finished, the local man muttered something.

'The doctor says you have slight concussion, but you are generally in good health.'

'Would it be fine for me to travel today?' he countered.

She looked puzzled but relayed the question. The man immediately answered by shaking his head.

'When, then?'

She quizzed the man again and then answered Carty. 'He recommends in a few days or so.'

Fuck that! The Englishman grinned politely back. *I'm leaving much sooner than you think.*

'He is going to give you a Vitamin C shot to help you recover faster.'

Carty shrugged. 'Okay, why not. Perhaps you could also ask him if he has any painkillers too.'

She did so as the man reached to unfasten the blood pressure sleeve and then take a syringe from his case. He ignored the question but slowly filled the syringe at eye level, rapidly squirting any air out before dabbing a vein with a cotton wool bud soaked in surgical spirit. Carty hated injections but in his lowered state he would take anything to speed the recovery, especially if he was to fly.

After the slight pin-prick he felt relieved, standing to shake the doctor's hand and thank them both, but then he felt a sudden head rush and perched dramatically back down on the bed, his mind spinning. The woman seemed to be speaking in a distorted voice, as if a 45 rpm record was being played at 33 rpm and as her smile swayed in and out of focus, her eyes seemed to hold a hellish stare. Carty blinked and violently shook his head, trying to dispel the episode, but it was growing worse. Soon the experience of looking down a telescope from the wrong end found their faces incessantly contorting into a kaleidoscope of hideous caricatures while their voices continued to become ever more slurred. As his head began to give way to its own weight and his eyes rolled skywards, she picked up her stilettoed heel and forcefully placed it into Carty's shoulder, shoving him backwards onto the duvet.

Nineteen

Lake Baikal

It's all a lie, Lena mused, still brooding over Vlad's comments as their lunch settled and he had vanished inside the *dacha* to take a customary nap. She had expected their reunion to have been a joyful sharing of memories followed by time spent with her ailing grandfather whose health, she had been led to believe, was failing fast and that their moments together might be short.

For whatever excuses he had given, Vlad had lied to her about Ivan Yegorovich's circumstances and his lack of empathy in quizzing her on what she might know, left her both empty and scared. Why had she not seen through his invitation from the first or at least thought to tell Carty or Jack about her plans?

The view out through the trees onto Baikal mollified her immediate fears for her grandfather, but the sense of uneasiness being here in Russia again, still hung around her as recollections began to stir. In her young 20s and experiencing her first love, her judgement was blinded to Vladislav's passive abuse: tell-tale hints of calculating ruthlessness and possible psychopathic tendencies. Now, though, it was clear to her that a joyous euphoria along with an exposure to power in working at the agency, having access to privileged information were the attributes she was mistakenly in love with, not him.

Then it all changed with the appearance of Scott Carty. At that time, she couldn't have grasped the magnitude of what she would begin to feel for the Englishman or the sequence of events that were about to unfold in their lives, but her feminine nous had sensed that destiny was at play and that she had to save him.

Shaking out her braids, she attempted to re-plait them all the while engrossed by the thoughts of her Englishman and being enveloped in each other's auras with his soft lips on hers.

I hope he'll truly forgive me for running away, without a word. The emotion revisited her with frisson and she closed her eyes, hoping to reach him to say she was lost and needed his help.

As the light of the long summer's day started to fade into oranges and reds behind the mountains on the far coast, she was woken by stirrings in the room. Vlad was cooking a hearty broth, one that he knew she loved, and hunger enticed her into the small scullery to catch the charming smile of her host.

'Are you hungry?'

'I'm starving,' she retorted.

The Russian ladled the broth and a piece of pork into a bowl and lowering her head, she wafted her nose over the rising steam, sighing outwardly in appreciation of the rich aromas.

'Vladislav,' she asked, sweetly, 'when can we begin the search for Ivan Yegorovich?'

'As I said, we'll start tomorrow just as soon as the team arrive.'

'Anyone I know?' she persisted.

'I doubt it.' He dropped a spoon into the soup and handed it to her, avoiding eye contact as he turned back to fill his own.

'It's as good as it's always been,' she joked slurping loudly and for a brief moment she was lost in her native world, a weakness Vlad knew how to play only too well. After some minutes she was helping herself to seconds and joining him out on the veranda to take in the dusk and the stillness.

'What did you mean earlier when you said *one solution*?' she asked.

'Did I say that?'

'Yes, when I said that we should find him so that you can put all your questions to him directly.'

'Ah, it must have been a figure of speech.'

'But is there any other solution?'

'I can't think of one at this moment.' He smiled and stood, picking up his dish to venture back for more. She sensed that he wasn't being fully open with her, which reinforced her resolution that once they had begun looking for the old man, she would make her way to Lubimov to enlist Boris' help and to get word to Scott that she was well.

Vlad re-emerged shortly, carrying the filled bowl and a pot with two mugs on a battered aluminium tray, which he balanced on the veranda's thin wooden balustrade. He grinned wildly at her.

'What?' she pressed, unsure of his behaviour.

He suddenly produced a large bar of Kraznoyarsk 98% cocoa chocolate, waving it in her face.

'Thank you!' she beamed, leaning in to take it but he pulled it sharply away, clowning around and then dangled it again in front of her nose. This time she snatched it from his grasp and held it in a childlike grip close to her chest. It was a tease he had always played and while it reminded her of happier times, she refused to allow the associated emotions to let her guard slip.

The sky displayed the softened hues of indigoes and blues as they sipped and ate tabs of the confectionary, watching bats criss-cross over the open space in the waning continental heat. Vlad had been continually lacing his tea with *balsam*, a traditional concoction of herbs steeped in alcohol and aged for a number of years, and while he sipped, he nonchalantly placed an arm around her shoulder in his familiar way. For a brief moment she was comforted, wanting to snuggle into his shoulder but an inner voice reminded her of Carty, causing her to slide forward, excusing herself as she trod down the few steps to head off in the direction of the makeshift toilet hidden away in the trees.

'I'm going to bed,' he called after her.

She raised a hand in response but didn't look back.

The only light was from a small kerosene lamp that Vlad had hung from the porch as a beacon to guide her back along the small track past his jeep. As she approached, she slowed her steps to stand at the entrance to the *dacha*, pondering her position here alone with her former lover. *Surely he understands that we've both changed and things can never be as they were?*

Once inside she dismissed the notion and popped her head into one of the two bedrooms where he was lying asleep.

She showered and spent time examining her face and naked body in the mirror, un-braiding her long hair so it flowed down to mask her full breasts. Tensing her toned stomach, she turned to view herself from various angles wondering how her shape would change when she had her child. Scott didn't yet know she was pregnant, in fact she hadn't found out herself until arriving in Dubai, believing that her cycle was late due to the stress of the secrecy and the concern for her grandfather. Ironically, in the room next door was the man she always believed she would have children with. *Life is odd.* She mused at how wrong that would have been. The door had creaked open in the light breeze and in the shadows, she caught the vague outline of Vlad standing, observing her. Shocked, she spun around and grabbed for a towel to wrap around herself in weak defence as he moved towards her, his eyes boring deeply into hers with lust.

'Lena. You know you're mine. We're supposed to be together,' he slurred.

'No, Vlad,' she said calmly, fixing him to the spot, trusting that their connection would win through. 'That was the past. I love somebody else now.'

The words had hardly left her lips when the back of his hand sealed them with a stinging swipe knocking her head back against the shower glass. She held up one arm to keep him away while the other nursed her busted gums. He caught her wrist, twisting it so that she buckled in pain to her knees. Somehow in her submission she believed she could reach him to stop this violence. That was a vain hope. He took a handful of hair, yanking her up, forcing her scream.

'Stop, Vlad! You're hurting me.'

But he was deaf to her or her charms and blindly driven to take what was his. Pushing her out to the bedroom he slapped her face so viciously that a welt sprung from her cheek bone almost immediately. She squealed, and he forced her down on to her back, sobbing loudly and trying to scream. But her lungs had let go of hope and she found herself weak and helpless as he fell on her, pinning her arms and squeezing his legs inside her thighs as she fought to cross them, screaming more loudly for him to stop, her eyes recognising a possessed obsession, which terrified her. She momentarily broke one hand free and dug its manicured nails deep into his temples, gauging them down to his cheek. He winced and then laughed as he violently pistoned her, his blood now dripping onto her milky skin. She gave in and sent her mind to a place that was safe, in London and in the arms of Scott Carty knowing that she could not risk losing his baby.

Then, he grunted grotesquely and ceased to breathe for some seconds as he collapsed and lay on her, trying to stroke her splayed hair as the full impact of his crime stunned his tortured mind. He had taken what he thought was his but realised that he could never have what they had once meant to each other. She pushed at him, forcing him to roll away and then she pulled herself up in one quick motion and staggered to the shower, locking the door behind her.

The hot raining water gave her some respite, consoling herself that the act itself, between them, was not foreign, but his cruel brutality was and could never be forgiven. She shuddered, her eyes screwed up in sheer anger. If she had a revolver, she would despatch him and leave him for the bears she thought, and it took all of the agency's training to keep her measured calm, knowing that she had to buy time and escape at the appropriate moment.

Loud blubbing could be heard as she closed off the taps and wrapping herself with a towel tucked across her breasts, she ventured back into the bedroom. To her disbelief Vlad was curled up, crying into an arm. Still dazed, a frisson of loathing engulfed her as she watched the pathetic scene, realising that this was the moment to flee. She took it, stealthily retracing her steps, suffering the raw pain of his ruthlessness, to the shower room to grab her bloody clothes from where she had left them.

A light panned across the small room, freezing her to the spot, fleetingly believing that in her sullied state she had imagined it. Then she strained at a sound, the faint, yet distinct rumble of heavy tyres, possibly from a truck, up the stony track. Vlad had become silent once more as the vehicle's headlights panned over the varnished pine walls and shot shadows around the room. He gathered his knees into his chest to rest back against the wall, a cruel smile now visiting his face as she reappeared.

'I'm sorry Lena.'

'Don't!'

'For everything that is now about to happen.'

She shot him a cold stare. 'What is that supposed to mean?'

He dipped his head, clearly in a delusional state, and she understood that he had given up on the man he once was.

The thud of truck doors being slammed was then superseded by several pairs of heavy footsteps that paused at the closed entrance. 'Vladislav?' a Russian voice called out. 'Are you there?'

Lena's look searched his, in terror.

'I'm here.'

The rough door was flung open to reveal a large silhouetted individual, aiming a pistol.

'You can put that down,' Vlad barked.

'Is she armed?'

'No.'

Terror and confusion gripped Lena. *Who is this stranger and who is he referring to..., me? Why would Vlad let anyone know I was here?*

The answer came swiftly as the man's gnarled features grew nearer with each step, his untroubled stare keen.

'Ah, Lena Isotova. Your grandfather will be pleased to know you're back in Mother Russia as will many others.'

'What do you mean?' she stuttered, firing a glance at her former lover. Vlad shrugged feebly, resigned in his wickedness.

'I see. Vlad hasn't told you.'

Her heart was in her mouth, unable to catch her breath and trembling with the absolute betrayal.

‘What about the letter, Vlad?’ she blurted. ‘Is Ivan Yegorovich really ill or did you simply invent that hoax to bring me here to sell me to the highest bidder.’

The stranger roared, his booming laughter filling the small hut as his two-man team bore down on her. ‘I suppose he hasn’t told you what the price was, either?’

Head shaking, she turned to make a dash into the bathroom, but her hair was grabbed by the brute yanking her back. He then stepped closer to spin her around to face him, grabbing her powerfully by the neck. His forefinger and thumbs squeezed viciously into her carotids as he lowered his face to examine her bruised beauty.

‘I suppose you’ve had her one last time,’ he sneered, shifting his gaze towards Vlad.

She was now desperately struggling to pull away from the grip, panicking from the lack of oxygen and imminent fainting. *I must save my baby.* She formed a fist, supported by her thumb locked behind a folded index finger so that its knuckle protruded like a blunt knife, then violently, she jabbed it hard into the side of his throat as she had been taught, and then again. Stunned momentarily by her unusual power, he released his clasp, but his over-developed saurian muscles had easily absorbed her blows and he wildly swung his knuckles across her temple in retaliation. The room grew dim as the burning agony of impacted nerves shot across her face and knees buckling, she slid down in a heap. His cohorts stepped in quickly to each grab a shoulder pit and drag her out to the waiting truck. She was crudely humped up and laid across its floor on a rough blanket, only just conscious as the loud crack of an un-silenced pistol shot sent roosting birds scattering from darkened canopy of trees. In her wrangled state, her slowly fading mind understood that the visitor had put a bullet into Vlad.

Twenty

Urumqi

'Scott! Scott!'

The voice sounded familiar he thought as he came to, waves of pain now deluging his mind with sharp burning sensations running across his shoulders and arms. In trying to move, it slowly dawned on him that his wrists were brutally cuffed behind his back to a metal chair on which he had been seated for some time. His skin carried a patina of sweat and from the drooping corner of his mouth, saliva was streaming in a continuous thread onto his stripped chest.

'Scott, can you hear me?'

Slowly, he titled his head up in the direction of that voice, his bleary eyes squinting.

'Lisa?'

'Yes, it's me.'

Shocked, he struggled to sit up, fighting the agonising throbs that racked his legs and lower back. While his mind was a blur of odd memories and tormented by numbed pounding, he could clearly pick out the pungent stench of his urine-soaked trousers. *I was drugged.* He slowly closed his lids and took a slow breath, juggling with the predicament of the situation and the likelihood of escaping alive.

'Are you alright?'

'I'm not sure,' he murmured, rolling his shoulders. His eyes now began to focus and in the dimmed light he could barely make out the outline of the woman sat across the room. 'Where are we?'

'In some kind of warehouse.'

'And are you injured..., hurt?' he probed.

'No, just scared. I'm cuffed too.' Her usually haughty tones were broken and clearly hinted at distress.

'Who's holding us? Are they bandits?'

'I don't know.'

He bent his knees and pushed with his feet to rock the chair. It was not fixed down and with a huge effort he stepped the legs successively across the stone floor to within a few feet of her.

What the hell?! The sight froze him rigid: she was naked, with her arms like his cuffed behind her back and her ankles secured with chains to the chair legs. A cool fear bumped his wet skin as he scanned her features, trying to disguise his anguish. *That bastard Ong. Why did he lie to me about her being safe? What's his game?* Confusion reigned in his reasoning. *She obviously doesn't know and I mustn't tell her. She'll give up hope.* He threw her a weak smile.

'Don't be afraid, Lisa. Your uncle has his people searching for us. I was with him before they drugged me and brought me here.'

'But how did you escape the attack at the market?' she asked, reciprocating with a feeble simper.

'By pure chance. Hafeza helped me.'

'And where is she, now?'

'I don't know.' His focused had switched to scan her position again. 'How long have you been trussed up like that for and why?' he asked, trying to not stare at her modesty and wondering why her captors had done this.

'A few hours. You were here but out cold when they brought me into this room. They've been rough but they haven't raped me, if that's what you meant.'

'Do you know who they are? Locals, perhaps?'

'I think they belong to a Xinjiang separatist group wanting to break free from the yoke of China.'

'So why kidnap you..., us?'

'To obtain ransom funds for their cause, I suppose.' Her eyes glared back at him, glassy green, capturing the light from the one overhead lamp way across the room. He garnered from them a sense that she was a lot stronger than her position dictated and his mind nagged, still uncertain as to why Ong had spun that story about her being safe when clearly, he must have known she wasn't. Either Ong was too embarrassed to admit to the Englishman that she was in grave danger, or he was playing some strange game to kidnap his own niece and then pay out funds for her release.

She dropped her head in despondency, trying to move her legs.

'Are those chains painful?'

'Yes, they're cutting into my skin.'

'Then we need to get some attention.'

Carty arched his head back to the low hung ceiling. 'Help!' he shouted. 'Help us!'

He felt the lingering desperation of his cries echo down through his throat and sternum and then waited in hollow expectation for a response. Nothing, just silence.

She blinked and then shrugged, her black mane hung in a sweaty matted mess against her shoulders and bare breasts, humiliated that her petite and almost perfect curves had been so crudely exposed. He looked away. A day ago, she had outright accused him of taking her, something he could not remember at the time, and had felt insulted, thinking her a wanton man-eater but now she had been reduced to this.

His neck muscles softened allowing his chin to gradually relax and sink towards his clavicle. Mulling those arcane arts revealed to him in his short life, skills that defied the rational processes of the sciences he cherished. He found himself suddenly much calmer, transported back to the encounter in the old house with Ludmilla Anatolivna and sensing her uncanny silent presence as if she was now close by. A glowing scintilla registered in his peripheral gaze, its intensity growing rapidly from somewhere across the dark space of the room. He bristled with a heightened sense of awareness, lifting his eyes to watch the wisp of light swirl in extended tails, coalescing together into a formless shape behind Lisa.

'Scott, what is it?' she blurted, shaken by his vacant gape, but he was gone, drawn into his inner world to which she was not a party, and fixated as the intangible slowly became defined into the thing he already knew it was: the haunting serpent-dragon of his dream. It grew, gravitating around and then engulfing her form as if its goal was to possess and then control her words and actions.

Watch for the serpent. It is present everywhere. Ludmilla's voice sounded around him.

'Why does it keep appearing – what is it trying to tell me?' he uttered out loud.

Because you have manifested it. The elderly Russian's words echoed back at him.

'Now, I'm really frightened!' Lisa shouted to him in a tone that pierced through the veil of his vision. He returned her scared glare. *Why had the dragon settled around her?* He fathomed that he if had manifested the beast again, then he had to be mindful in everything that he was about to say in this situation.

The sudden jangled noise of bolts being forcefully thrust open, spiking his readiness. Three brutish figures pushed through the industrial sized doors and moved on Carty, one swiftly pulling the leg of his chair away while pushing his shoulder, upending and crashing him backwards to the ground. Still cuffed, his elbows took the brunt of the fall and he yelped on impact, noticing that his projected voice seem to freeze the men for seconds, their expression harbouring confusion. *What just happened?* He seemed have given an uncontrolled spirit shout, and angered, the same small muscly brute pulled at the Englishman's hair, jerking him up squarely in front of Lisa and then locking his jaw between small vice-like fingers to point his face straight at hers. Carty scanned the others' squat ochre faces and understood that these men belonged to an ethnic clan not wholly Chinese. Clearly the hatred in their black eyes was driven by reasons other than any ransom Ong could pay, and now the terrifying notion that this was not going to end well, registered in his countenance. They toyed with her, laughing callously as they unzipped their trousers in her face while forcing her head down to perform fake blow jobs in a warm up for the real thing. She tightly rolled up her eyelids and writhed, screaming out to Carty. But he was helpless; forced to watch as they pawed her delicate body and rubbed the barrels of their pistols along her inner thighs in a sick mock foreplay.

'What do you want?' he brazenly shouted to one of them and for that he felt a cuff from his captor's fist across the nape of his neck.

'Arrgh!' His slumping forward only caused his restrained arms to twist his screaming tendons further. The man wrenched at his hair once again, putting his face close to Carty's and shouting foreign, unintelligible commands in a stinking breath.

Lisa's cries were hysterical as they twisted her locked arms, just close to snapping the joints and letting them go before thrashing her face with the full force of back-handed swipes, flinging out a spurts of blood from her split lips.

Shit, they're going to kill us. His eyes gave away his desperation.

One of the assailants had now pushed his face into Lisa's, dragging the weapon against her cheek before pushing it into her mouth. Tears streamed down her cheeks and ran into the lines of claret blood as she sobbed unrestrainedly. She was a mess, and Carty was driven to act. All he could do was shout again and trust that it would have an effect but as he sucked air into his lungs, the thug stopped, turning his stubbly cheek close to hers and barking words in a strange tongue as he glared at The Englishman. She nodded.

'Scott,' she fumbled to find the translation through her trembling. 'They want the details for the construction of an energy machine. They're claiming you possess them.'

His stunned muteness met her terror as he shook his head.

'Please, Scott, I beg you. If you know anything about this, tell them,' she whimpered, her fear palpable yet Carty was now trying to calm his breathing, erratic from the intense battering his body had taken in such a short space of time. The local grinned evilly and harshly placed the gun's nozzle over one of her naked nipples, then shouted something again as his comrades let out raucous laughs.

'They're going to gang rape me in front of you and then kill us both.'

As he registered her total despair, he was playing out scenarios in his head. Even if he could somehow break free of his bonds, there was no way he could save her or himself in fighting these men. He was broken, and the choice was now obvious.

'Yes, I do know about the machine,' he quietly answered, his blue eyes holding her gaze to lessen the sheer terror of what these men intended to do. But in her translation the man seemed inexplicably stumped, as if Carty had given in too easily. He looked back at him and after some seconds fired out more questions.

'He wants documents, plans and all the information you have in order to build the machine.'

Carty locked gazes with the brute. 'Tell him, they're in London.'

She shook, agitated. 'Where?'

'With a friend.'

'Who? Nick Hall?'

'No, a member of the intelligence services.'

Her eyes bulged. 'Really, Scott?'

'Tell this arsehole that the agencies know that I'm here with you in Xinjiang and probably will be searching for us right now. This bunch doesn't stand a chance of living unless they let us go, now.'

All three thugs stood motionless listening blow by blow, as she translated his foreign words. Then the leader screwed up his face, shouting back his demands at Carty as the thug behind slammed a forearm into his neck to reinforce the message. He crumpled. She recoiled in her seat, wincing at the obscene viciousness.

'He doesn't care about your threats and if he doesn't get those documents he will carry out his own.' Her sobs punctuated the drowned reply. 'Our bodies will be dumped deep in the Taklamakan never to be found and these men will simply disappear into their daily lives.'

Carty nodded once, grudgingly. 'Okay. He can have what he wants as long as we are freed.'

Lisa hysterically fired off into a long trail of words following which the leader angrily waved a hand to one of his group. The instructed man moved behind Lisa unlocking her cuffs and then released Carty's.

Within seconds the mob had left slamming the doors shut, bolting them again.

Carty was left confused. 'What did you tell him?' he probed, rubbing his wrists as she moved to hug him.

'Scott, I'm so scared.'

He was distracted momentarily by her naked sweaty legs stepping astride his.

'We're not free yet Lisa..., what did you tell him?' he pressed, again.

'They will return soon. Then I will be allowed to contact my uncle to explain that, in exchange for our lives being spared, he will have to fly you back to London on his jet. I will be held as collateral until your return. Obviously, I cannot tell him about the documents you will bring back.'

Carty was stunned. 'I can't just leave you here, what guarantee is there that you won't be killed by these mad men?'

'There's no guarantee but this might buy us some time so that my uncle and the authorities here can locate me.'

'You realise that I will have to tell the authorities in the UK.'

'That would be a mistake. They can't help and will no doubt stop you from flying back here.'

He shrugged. Thinking on his feet wasn't a solution in this instance. 'But what if I can't produce these blueprints, Lisa?'

'Then they will rape me until they have exhausted their enjoyment and then cut of my digits one by one before brutally killing me. They will then post a video of all this on the web along with your name as the person who was responsible for my grisly death.'

Her answer sickened yet while Carty hadn't understood what had been said in her translation to the kidnapper, he was struggling as to how she could have received such a detailed plan of action in what had been so few words.

'So, you see, Scott, there isn't a choice,' she said, pulling her fingers through her unkempt hair, coyly touching his cheek and then moving them to stroke the back of his neck. 'You're the only person who can save me.' She steadily rubbed her bare breasts on his chest while her other palm caught his cheek and their lips met. The warmth of their intimacy after the trauma of their ordeal slipped his guard for a jot, but then the salty taste of her bloodied mouth shook his senses and he pulled away.

'Lisa, this really isn't a good time.'

'Of course, I'm sorry.' She straightened herself. 'I don't understand what they want with this machine they claim you have knowledge of.'

'Nor do I?'

'Have you seen it working?'

'No, and it may not exist, but some technical plans were sent to me after my ordeal in Russia,' he bluffed, aware that the dragon vision of earlier was reminding him to stay guarded.

'Why?'

'To keep them safe, I suppose.'

'But what makes the technology so unusual. Does it use Brown's Gas?'

'Apparently it uses spiralling water to transmute nuclear waste.'

She rolled her eyes. 'Ah, that story again!'

'You've heard about it before?' he asked playing dumb, aware of Hafeza's confirmation about Lisa's meeting with the Russians before her trip to London.

'A little, but I'm worried that this gang will not be satisfied. That bastard kept claiming that the machine is revolutionary, producing free energy.'

'That's impossible!' Carty uttered.

'Then, why was he insisting on it?' In her shattered state her eyes carefully scrutinised his for a *tell.*

Carty shook his head in disbelief. 'Lisa, is that what was really being asked by that thug?'

She shrugged. 'I don't understand what you're saying. He knew exactly what he wanted and somehow he knew that you have the instructions to build this machine,' her eyes widened and began to well up again. 'Please don't tell me you were bluffing..., you do have them don't you?'

Tired, he succumbed to the questioning. 'Yes, they're in London but not in my possession.'

'But you can get them Scott, can't you? These men are killers.'

'I will make sure I do.'

'Thank you.' Her smashed lips kinked into a cruel smile as her words left them and then she began to chuckle hysterically, placing a palm on his bare chest and tugging at his sparse hairs. Carty stared quizzically at her, locking onto her eyes and questioning if the attack and the vicious threats had instilled a delayed trauma. But her laughter grew more bizarre all the while grinning madly as she wriggled on his legs. Then, her mask changed into one of cool callousness as she called out in local dialect.

Instantly, in response, the bolts clanged again, and the corridor's light streamed into the room, silhouetting the leader's figure as he stood in the open doorway. She moved to him and wrapped her arms around his neck, plunging into a deep kiss with the man.

Carty looked on stunned to his sickened core, his flesh crawling with frustrated loathing. He wanted to shout at her, but words were lost to the fermenting disbelief of cold betrayal as it dawned on him that she was the serpent, and he was now at her mercy. It was as if she had read his thoughts and emotions and thrived on them, turning back to glare wildly before ordering them to bolt the Englishman firmly in.

Twenty One

Siberia

The shot resounded in Lena's head, playing over and over again on a never-ending loop as she faded in and out of consciousness. She had lost track of all time and could barely register being carried from the truck into a cave complex and flung down onto a decrepit sofa.

Soon, freezing water was thrown over her bringing her abruptly into the moment to face the same smooth-talking hulk,

'What did you do to Vlad?' she blurted.

'He's in a better place!'

'You killed him?'

'He had a choice to either give you up or we killed his family. What would you have done in his place?' he said grinning loosely and sitting opposite her.

'Bastard.' She spat at him.

'Not at all. Vlad broke too many rules and understood that he had to pay the ultimate price.'

Despondent, her head dropped. 'What do you want from me?'

'Ah, the correct question actually, is what do we want from your grandfather?'

She pulled back up, terror gripping her expression. 'What have you done to him?'

'Nothing yet.' His smarmy practised way was dark. He snapped his fingers and a cohort stepped forward, handing him a compact video camera. 'Would you like to see him?'

A chilling sense of terror gripped her breathing and she struggled to catch it as the man simply continued, pressing a button and turning it to show a previously recorded clip on its small side screen. The images justified her horror. Ivan Yegorvich was bound to a steel chair in a place not dissimilar to where she was now, sitting with two men standing over him, slapping his face so violently that he couldn't hold up his head and his scant white locks were caked with crimson splayed across his bald head.

'What are you doing to him?!' she screamed. 'He's an old man!'

'We know that, but he's very stubborn and won't speak. We thought that if he sees you being treated in the same way then he might loosen up his tongue.'

'But what do you want?'

'Lena...,surely you must know the answer to that.' He gripped her cheek bones, squeezing them between the fingers of one hand. She resisted the excruciating pain, wildly punching at his face but her fists bounced off his toughness as he slammed her backwards, onto the sofa.

'Now we have some questions for you.'

A brutish colleague took her arm, roughly pulling her on to an old chair, thrown into place by his mate, securing her limbs with oily rope to its legs. She threw her head back defiantly and spat at them again.

'Now, Lena, why don't you tell us about the machine your grandfather developed.'

She eyed him for a second. 'I don't know anything about his research. It was classified, you know that.'

'Yes, I do know that, but the problem is that he doesn't want to share it with us. We think that you and that English boyfriend of yours found about it and then ran away from your homeland to hide with him, believing that you were safe.'

'I ran away because there was an assassination attempt on both of us.'

'Because you found out about the technology and its workings when you shouldn't have.'

'I don't know what you're driving at, but you're completely mistaken if you think that.'

'It doesn't matter; we'll soon learn what we need to know once we've shown him a video of you being beaten.' His chilling tone caused her tired muscles to tense, expectant of the imminent blows that he had threatened.

Was Vlad quizzing me to find out if I knew about the machine and its workings in order to give this information instead of me? She wondered, thinking what might have been if she had shared her knowledge with him. But it was too late Vlad had been murdered. *I must protect this baby,* she reminded herself, ruminating on giving up what she knew to these men to ensure the sanction of hers and her grandfather's freedom. *What am I thinking?* Logic chided against her fogged mind. She had been away too long and forgotten the ruthless nature of these types; they would never allow that. Then another notion filled her head. *If they are holding Ivan Yegorovich then why did they need to show me this video clip? They could have easily put us together in the same room and beaten us until we spoke.* This brute's threats, while terrifying, were weaker than he purported them to be. *Perhaps he doesn't hold Ivan Yegorovich perhaps the old man has escaped or even been saved!* The wild idea was soberly quashed as the thug smiled cruelly again, readying his fist to harm her already damaged beauty as the filming rolled.

Twenty Two

Boris' search of the assassins' clothes proved his suspicions, their documents showing that they were both Ukrainian mercenaries hired in to do the dirty work. Now the tangled mess of their bodies flung deep into the bear pit had him reflecting on the outcome.

What if I had succumbed to their attack? It was a rare analysis, which caught him unawares as he hastily dragged back into place the thin stripped pine logs to make a loose framework over which to pile the brush he had removed earlier. *Would anyone else take up the search for Ivan Yegorovich?* He wondered, as the cadavers' vanished from view under the last armfuls of leaves and ferns. *Now's not the time for such thoughts.* He banished them, conscious that the foreigners' associates, having heard the few shots would already be making their way towards this place.

The darkening overcast cover meant heavy rain that morning, which would make tracking and lying low tricky. Rolling away into the bushes, he then began a short hike up a brook, shortly reaching a limestone outcrop, dirty yellow-grey and shrouded at its lower level, by ancient cedars. *Perfect!* With his boots slung around his neck, on their tied laces, his fingers slotted into the fine fractures that delineated the surface rocks and then attempted to defy gravity, pulling his torso up, knees tucked to his chest so that he could place his bare soles onto the sheer face. Then, arching his back, he allowed his legs and arms to fully extend and sucked in a deep breath, sensing he had little time to scale the thirty-foot section of the wall to reach a ledge where he could lay unseen, able to survey the scene of the attack. His forearm tendons stood out in iron bands as he wearied halfway up, noting the fluttering of birds in the distance caused by a disturbance among the foliage. The mercenaries' cohorts were closing in and he understood that if they glanced up he was a sitting duck. He drew on a mental strength that had carried him through other, if not tougher, ordeals and pushed on to the shelf now clearly above him.

A shout went out after a short duration, from one of the four-man team scanning the area, alerting them to the discovery of their fallen comrades and, from the remoteness of his vantage point, Boris observed with his pocket glasses, their angered body language. They were soon covering the faintest traces of his movements though the brook and wooded area to the bottom of the outcrop as the rain now came down in sheets. Staring up at its height, they knew someone had passed that way, but the slippery nature of the rock's surface meant that without ropes, it was unlikely they could scale it. The leader hung around talking loudly on a satellite phone for many minutes leaving Boris to surmise that they were calling in a helicopter and if they did he would have to act fast. He cast an eye over the narrow ridge for an escape route or at least a hiding den and then he spotted just above him the dead carcass of a young bear, which had recently fallen to its death. The rain had temporarily called off the carrion and he slid snake-like on his torso towards it, drenched through from the rivulets cascading down the tight ravines above him. Quickly reaching the rotting shell, he grasped at its intact fur skin, dragging it down so that it covered him as he lay in a small depression, the rank hum of the remains of the recently stripped flesh was almost too much for him to bear and he gasped at the wet air passing through a slit he made where the beast's belly once was. *It could be worse*, he kidded. The animal had been dead for a number of days and most of its internal organs and muscle had been scavenged, leaving the putrefying husk of its fur and skeleton as perfect cover for the Buryat. He needed it fast, as the clacking from a Mil Mi-8 helicopter sounded overhead making a reconnaissance sweep of the outcrop. It passed overhead again, twice, before landing in the clearing. The team had already retrieved the bodies and wasted no time in loading them on to the aircraft, which had kept its rotors spinning keen that they should leave the scene in haste. The Buryat watched on as it rose vertically and tilted in the squally winds, then with it heading rapidly away, he threw off his cover to survey it for some minutes with his binoculars, as it headed straight back towards the foot hills and then hovered just above the tree-line before it vanished from sight. He estimated that he could walk to the location before nightfall but was confused, having earlier sensed that Ivan Yegorovich was nearer than where the aircraft had just settled. *There's no other option,* he concluded as he sat and hung his legs over the precipice, turning to face the rock wall and lock his iron fingers' once more into its narrow fractures, to cantilever his way down its sheer face.

Twenty Three

Xinjang

The unforgiving steel chair soon became unbearable and he quickly discovered that it was more comfortable for his body, still racked with the pains from his injuries, to lie on the coarse concrete floor, cool in the intense summer heat. The impact of Lisa's duplicity had rocked him and in his sense of sheer revulsion, he couldn't quite believe what she had just done.

Was it just a ruse to trick these men into freeing her? That didn't make sense. What did, though, were Hafeza's concerns about the Russians visiting just before Lisa left for England and her hunch they had been discussing the transmutation business together. *Damn! Has Hafeza shopped me to Ong and Lisa?* Despite his scepticism at the grating thought, given how he had just been so ruthlessly played he couldn't rule out anything, however far-fetched. *No, this is to do with overunity,* he reassured himself after considering the conversations he had had with the local woman only the day before, and the odd questioning Lisa had spun while under apparent threat of being gang raped in front of him. It seemed the obvious explanation. Lisa had to verify that fact by suckering him into divulging that he had the blueprints in London. *But why would the Russians believe that I had them?* Desperation of his plight now filled him with the realisation that no one knew that he had been abducted and that Lisa understood this only too well.

A sweltering blanket of air now hovered above him and with the knowledge it wouldn't get any cooler for many hours, he scrabbled up on to his haunches, his bare torso drenched with sweat. In the scant light he could make out that the place was an old brick warehouse and 50 feet to each side of him was cloaked in darkness. He reasoned not to venture into those areas as he sought another door or some loose bricks in the wall through which he could attempt an escape. But it was becoming clear that the intense temperature was sapping his ability to make the simplest actions and soon his mind began wavering, forcing him back down to rest his lobe on the floor. The air was both dry and dusty causing his throat to swell in the absence of any water to drink. *How long can I stay alive in this place?* The terror of being left here to die now broached his still rational thoughts, but reassurance then came. *Lisa needs those plans and without me she'll never have them,* he surmised as he began to fade. Shortly, and true to his hunch, he could make out the sound of the bolts being released once again, and the light being tripped followed by Lisa's stiletto heels clacking closer to his head as she ordered her coterie of men to lift the Englishman.

Propped up on a chair, freezing water was thrown onto his dipped face and then she took the pleasure of taking an ice cube in her sharp nails and running it over his muscled chest before slipping it beneath the belt of his trousers and into his underpants. He shook his head upright, blinking as she mothered him, placing an open bottle of chilled water to his chapped lips.

'There you are, Scott. Drink slowly..., that's much better, isn't it?' Her tones were deliberate and now confused him into thinking that the whole previous episode was just simply a nightmare.

'You didn't think we were going to let you die in here, did you?'

He shook his head slowly, avoiding eye contact as the same loathing sensation for her came flooding back.

'We want you to see something, just so you understand how very serious we are, Scott.'

A snap of her fingers brought a laptop alongside her, its screen flipped out in readiness for her to press the play prompt on the emailed video clip. Another of her cronies took the back of his hair in order that he couldn't look away as it started with a woman's screams. He focused in on the image noting that she was gagged and bound in some dingy place as a man threatened her with a leather belt, whipping it across her shoulders, repeated as he walked behind her, forcing her frantic pained yelps. The camera had zoomed in at that moment to capture Lena's panicked eyes. Carty visibly flung his arms out at Lisa to grab her in anger, but the heavy forearm of her associate pinned around his neck, restraining him as he watched the belt whip Lena again and again. Then the video clip ended.

'You're a cruel bitch, if you don't already know that!'

'I've been called worse but what I'm doing is for the greater good.'

'What nonsense.'

'Really, Scott? Don't tell me that when you already believe in such nonsense as *overunity*.'

'Look, I've told you I will give you the blueprints. Please, don't let your men hurt Lena. She knows nothing about it.'

'Even though the machine was her grandfather's creation?'

'As I told you, the machine is supposed to exhibit the transmutation of nuclear waste. How it does it, I have no idea.'

'Oh yes, we know that, but the *overunity* is more interesting.'

'I can't help you with that.'

'Maybe you can't, but we will hold Lena captive as insurance until we have those instructions safely in our hands. Then we might consider releasing you and her.'

Carty exhaled loudly. 'Why are you even doing this, Lisa? You're an heiress to a business worth billions. You don't need *overunity*.'

'I have my reasons,' she quietly stated, capturing his stare, 'and I must have that technology.'

She snapped her fingers again and a chromed medical trolley rattled towards them.

'But what you're doing is criminal. There's nowhere for you to hide.'

She chuckled, picking up a syringe and holding it to the light to flick its translucent body with her nail. The action stirred the memory of the Chinese woman who had recently drugged him.

'And just what do you intend to do with that?'

'Find out the truth so that we avoid any more silly stories.'

‘Lisa!’ he shouted, his expression spiked with a dread that in her madness, she would stop at nothing. ‘Please, I give you my word that I will hand the plans to you without any complications. I don’t need them and frankly they’ve only ever been a curse to me.’

‘I’m sure that you’re telling the truth and very soon we’re going to find out.’ With her sharp sideways nod, the men moved in to pull his forearm out to one side despite his resisting.

‘Good,’ she chuckled insanely. ‘Here’s a vein that looks like it was recently lanced with a needle.’ Her nails flicked at his skin a few times and then, holding the syringe skyward, she squirted out a shot before laying the needle flat on to his skin.

He tensed, his eyes widening as she paused to enjoy the sense of panic the theatre invoked. ‘Don’t worry,’ she said, winking, ‘All the men I have fallen in love with have gone through this.’

Twenty Four

Siberia

The Buryat's assumption was correct in reaching the location where he had last seen the chopper drop from his sights and with a canopy of stars filling a moonless sky, he had enough light and equally enough cover to venture stealthily without fear of detection. The area appeared undisturbed, and an odd sensation ground at his being, urging him to rest and refill his small water flask before scouting out the possible location of this group of mercenaries.

He squatted down next to a rivulet, scavenging for berries and roots, silently chewing on what he found as he adjusted his energetic levels to this place and the challenges that lay ahead in finding the old man. *Ivan Yegorovich, where are you?* His silent, inner words were left to find their own way through the ether however long that might take, despite the Buryat's burning urgency to free his friend from these professional killers.

Heavy rustling just ahead, alerted his senses and he remained stock-still, knowing that it was a beast of the forest but all the same vigilant as a male musk deer eyed him and then passed on. He slowly removed his boots, clipped his flask back onto his belt and felt for his knife then effortlessly sprung onto his feet without a sound. The creature had halted some metres into the dense rhododendron, craning its head back to maintain a visual on the human, but the local understood it was a numinous message to follow, and with that unspoken accord, the animal continued its passage into the undergrowth, pausing from time to time to graze, highly attuned to any signal to flee. The Buryat mirrored its movements from a safe distance, barely able to see it in the shadows but aware of its aura and its path as he padded in bare feet. Shortly, a feeling of grief took hold of him and unable to sense the deer's presence, he decided that he must stop at that spot and tune into its meaning. As soon as he did a part of himself was violently catapulted into the unseen world surrounding him, in a way that had happened only once before. Luminescent swirls of energetic vibrations engaged and guided him deeper into the undergrowth and he sensed the worst, knowing what he was to be shown: the ethereal imprint of Ivan Yegorovich's dead body as it lay nearby. As he closed in he heard the man's voice in his head. *I died of a heart attack as they tortured me. It was a happy release.* The Buryat collapsed to his knees, a choked wail of grief remained lodged in his throat as he felt for the corpse of the man, one of the great pioneers of science, dumped like unwanted waste, his half-eaten remains hastily hidden under a covering of fern and branches. He sobbed hard. *I'm gone but will always be nearby.* The old man's words sounded again giving him solace and resolution. He would find the men who did this and dispatch them knowing that it would not be the end, just a small battle against the corrupt greed and power that was the other side of the machine's legacy to set humanity free.

The whole night he sat in meditation, calling on the ancestors and spirits to protect Ivan Yegorovich's passage to the other world and then guide him in his actions. *If I die, then it will have been worth it.* The thought tripped as the slightest glimmer of morning lessened the milky star-scape and the deer's head reappeared in the muted light, munching on new leaves. It raised a smile from the man in recognising the living metaphor of his friend's soul at peace and at home. *And if I live, then I will return to bury your body,* he mentally murmured to himself, in preparing to avenge his friend's honour.

He took advantage of the dawn's faint light to track up the stream and then onto the jagged granite protuberances, catching sight of broken fern stems and depressions in the moist sand.

They've been this way. His heart picked up a beat as he lay to the floor turning his ear to the earth. *Now very close,* he grinned stoically and crawled through the bilberry clumps until a sandy clearing was visible in the near distance and a lump of a mercenary, seated on a boulder, drinking from a half-sized bottle. The Buryat was forced to manoeuvre to his left in spite of the fear of being detected, to reconnoitre with his field glasses what it was the figure seemed to be guarding. Then it became clear: an oblong wooden door twice the size of the man and built into the rock wall was covering a cave entrance. A strategy was formulating in his mind but it was a risky one. He had to incapacitate the guard and then force him to divulge who killed the old man.

Twenty Five

Xinjiang

Soon, the pain of the injuries of the last days merged into a warm feeling of calm and intense pleasure, as if all of Carty's cares had dissolved in the space of a short moment, leaving him free to explore in extraordinary detail, the room and those standing in it. One of the men had excessive nose hair and Carty found himself, in his delirium, wanting to pick up the pair of medical scissors alongside him on the trolley, to trim it but as he reached out he was pushed back into the chair.

Lisa pulled at his lids, to shine a torch into his eyes, examining his pupils before breaking into a smile, like a grotesque clown, leaving Carty's impacted mind with the notion that the real Lisa was hiding insecurely behind that mask.

'Scott,' she warbled in a disturbed manner, forcing him to blink and stop his head from rolling about as he reached for the bottle of water. She helped him drink and placing it to one side, began to speak to him again. But he had problems in hearing her, her speech appeared overlaid by somebody else's, a female who was not in the room, and he strained to recall who's it was as its deep tone grew stronger. He could clearly see Lisa's mouth opening and closing, her features growing agitated with his apparent reluctance to respond. Just behind her, he noted a funnel of air had coalesced into a cloud that was growing extraordinarily fast. Then he heard the other woman's voice enter his head, and soon the image of Ludmilla Anatolivna materialised from the mass, telling him that she would answer the questions he was being asked. He broke into an infectious chuckle, infuriating Lena, before his mouth uncontrollably started to spurt out words.

'Yes, Lisa. I believe the machine can exhibit *overunity*, free energy but I have no experience or evidence to prove it.'

The woman was taken aback.

'But did you see the machine in operation?'

'Yes, it was apparently transmuting spent nuclear waste from Japan, Russia and China.'

'Where exactly was the machine when you saw it operating?'

He stalled for a second to slurp at the water bottle again most of which ran down his chin as his head swayed under its own weight. The drug had slurred his mechanical actions but not taken total control of his mind as it was supposed to. He had a spiritual ally helping him from somewhere as she sat silently in *tudkum*.

'I was blindfolded but I know that it was operating somewhere in the Irkutsk Oblast.'

'Who was operating it, Isotov, its inventor?'

The words came pouring out without his conscious control, managed by the angel who was Hafeza's grandmother. 'No, they had relocated the machine to a secret location.'

'Who are *they* operating the machine?'

'A man called Kosechenko.'

Lisa glared at him and then smiled. Her suspicions had been confirmed. Kosechenko had met with her and Mr Ong months before, in Urumqi.

'Does Lena Isotova know about this machine and what it's capable of?'

'She knows everything.'

Lisa's eyes widened with the comment. 'And do either of you know if Isotov is still alive.'

He chuckled wildly. 'I was told his dead body was found in the forest in the 1990s.'

The woman frowned. Carty's superficial rational process was heavily under the influence of the pharmaceuticals, but she sensed he was toying with her as if his greater mind was sitting somewhere in another dimension. Shrugging, she couldn't bring herself to accept that the Englishman could resist the drug's powers as she sought pieces of evidence to fill her jigsaw. Clearly the Russians had offered her and Ong part of their business in transmuting nuclear waste and had shared the video clip of Lena being brutally treated in exchange for Carty being handed over to them. But she wasn't about to trust the Russians or co-operate. She had spent months using her access to money and the Chinese security system to investigate the machine's myth further and could not have cared if Lena lived or died. But by some bizarre twist, she had just been told through Carty's own words, that Lena knew as much as he did and now understood that she had to ensure that Lena stayed alive in case anything happened to Carty before she had her hands on the blueprints.

The serene vision of Ludmilla Anatolivna's beaming face hanging in the ether just behind Lisa kept Carty anchored and safe in his uninhibited state.

'And there's something else you should know,' he blurted.

'Yes, yes!' she responded.

'You can't trust Koshechenko.'

She stared back blankly at him.

'He ordered mine and Lena's assassinations.'

Lisa tucked her billowing hair back over her ears, the bruises from the beating now accentuated in the light, along with the shock registered on her face as she flung glances around at her comrades. But they hadn't understood his English or why she now looked so uncomfortably nervous in entertaining the notion that Carty, under the effects of a highly potent truth drug, had unintentionally turned the tables and apparently read her thoughts. Astonished, she began to wonder who this man was, sitting in front of her. The stories she had heard before concerning his narrow escapes from death in the taiga were, she had decided, fiction but now having complete control over him, she detected a hidden strength as if somehow, he was protected. Nausea rose from the pit of her stomach. *It's all just trite mumbo jumbo*, she mused in an attempt to convince herself, but the Eastern side of her psyche refused to ignore the very raw feeling she was experiencing. Scott Carty seemed to be exhibiting strange abilities the nature of which perhaps *he* didn't even understand or recognise himself.

Twenty Six

Siberia

As the Buryat ruminated on the almost impossible task, a loud crack sounded across the forest, diametrically opposite to where he lay, causing him to swing the glasses around to view the threat in the same instance that the guard's attention had been pricked. At first, he couldn't spot anything unusual, but then a grin split his oval face. The deer had brought its family to the hinterland of the forest, out of sight yet audible, troubling the guard so that he had to down his splif and ready his pistol from its holster. This was the one chance Boris needed and he seized it, sorting through the ground for suitable-sized pebbles he grabbed at two and then stood up as the thug reached the edge of the trees. Swinging one of the stones around his head in a sling made from a neckerchief, the Buryat leapt over the stunted pine and berry bushes so that the man was in closer range, and then flung the stones, simultaneously diving for cover. *Shit!* The projectiles shot past the man's head, narrowly buzzing him and spooking the deer, which frantically shot away into the bushes. Thinking the animal was the source of the disturbance, the guard turned to make his way back but met with the end of log smashing into the side of his head and reacting, let off a random shot, the Buryat had instantly dropped the man's legs with a sweep and then fell on his windpipe with his elbow. For a worrying moment Boris believed his victim to be dead but checking his vital signs, understood he had little time to question him as the guard's Walkie Talkie crackled into life and an accented voice questioned the commotion. Boris picked it up, toying with it as he pressed the response button.

'*Da, Da, Vsur harasho*,' [All is okay.] he mumbled, coughing several times to mask his voice. It appeared to work but he was not hanging around as he yanked out the batteries, pocketed them, and threw its carcass way over into the undergrowth. Then he took the man's pistol and let out a sharp exhale, gripping the hulk's ankles to drag him away into the trees. The job was backbreaking, and it took several minutes to get to a place where he could momentarily take a breather, tie his quarry's hands with a piece of wire that he carried in his army issue sack and then stuff one of his socks in the man's mouth, in case he came to and gave away their location. Then he picked up the legs again, taking the body down an incline through tough shrubs until he met the river. He stopped to take stock and psych himself for the tough part–yanking the assailant up over one shoulder to wade across the current. The sharp cold, even in summer, drove him on and reaching the far bank he collapsed in its shallow waters, his captive groaning as his face hit the pool. With superhuman effort Boris hauled him over the fallen trunk of an ancient cedar and then he stripped off his shirt. The sound of the chopper loomed again and he sank onto his knees as it broke above the tree line further up the valley. Not sure if the alarm had already been raised, the Buryat scanned the arena with his binoculars, seeking a suitable place to hide. Then he caught sight of the deer feeding off the young shoots growing in the bank just a short distance away where a small cascade poured over a limestone ridge. It was an obvious place to hide but was it too obvious that he might be easily found? He had little time to decide as he forced the soaked shirt over the man's face, choking him so that he would become more conscious in his desperation for oxygen. His tight menacing eyes showed he was ready to kill as he yanked on the length of wire securing the guard's wrists before pushing the revolver's barrel into the victim's nose. The hulk jerked with the pain of the jagged barbs piercing his skin, and with the gun to the back of his head, was forced to walk the few hundred feet along the shallows.

The calls of his comrades sounded as the helicopter's rotors became louder again, and sensing that despite the odds the man would try to break free, the Buryat pistol-whipped his quarry's skull, instantly dropping him so that he lay in the water, face up.

'Did you torture the old man?' he uttered close in to his captive's face.

The eyes were empty and unremorseful as they stared back.

'You know, I don't need this gun.'

Still the eyes were unyielding so he waded them both out to waist depth, leaning all his weight sharply onto his hostage's throat so that his face submerged. Soon the eyes registered desperation and then urgent panic as he struggled with his bound wrists to break free, but it was useless. The Buryat held him down with supernatural strength until finally, letting him up, half dead, gasping in air through his gagged mouth.

The aircraft had already passed over the area and they had been missed, unnoticed, and the voices too, had become more distant, leading the Buryat to suspect that his associates had found the walkie-talkie and followed in the wrong direction. It had bought him some time but not much before he and his prisoner would be found.

'So, tell me,' he asked again, 'who killed the old man? Was it you?'

The man, a seasoned professional, attempted a muted laugh in defiance, understanding that the Buryat wanted information so wouldn't kill him. But Boris, scanning his prisoner's disfigured shaven head and tattooed neck decided that he had lived only for death or the destruction of other people's lives, as he cocked the gun and stuffed its barrel in the man's face again.

'You don't need to live. I will find out anyway and if it was you, then I will have already done the right thing.'

His utterance was met with a shudder, the captive understood the language. He garbled something, inaudibly, through his blocked mouth, but Boris simply pushed his head back under the surface and forced him down, waiting for the wriggling and writhing to end. It soon came. *They're all responsible regardless of who tortured the old man.* But the thought didn't console him. A primordial revenge had been let out of its deep lair and was driving him to kill each and every last one of these mercenaries for what they had done. For them it wasn't personal, just a job to collect a fee and that made it all the worse.

He held the cadaver under the water, leaning his body weight on it as he waded deeper into the main body of the river to let it be carried away by the current. It would be found but not for a day or more perhaps, that was of course, if the man's comrades survived.

The cooler current sharpened his senses bringing him back into the moment and he sank beneath the surface, slipping under a passing tree trunk, clutching on to it for camouflage as the water's powerful flow took him.

The mercenaries arrived at the bank just as the river's bend pulled him out of sight into a ravine. The churning waters sapped every bit of strength he had as he pushed at the log to bring it around so that its length was perpendicular to the flow. He only had seconds to act as it lodged itself between the blocky cairns strewn in its path and he pressed himself up onto its slippery rotating circumference. Then, reaching out, he leapt onto the smooth granite rocks, as his vehicle, battered by the churning waters, span up and broke free, hurtling towards the main rapids only seconds away. Boris was now on terra firma again, behind the stony outcrop where earlier, the mercenary had been guarding the cave.

Twenty Seven

Xinjiang

'Scott, how do you feel now?' Lisa asked, as she stepped back into the room, her luminous eyes carrying just the hint of an unspoken secret.

'Yeah.' Carty slurred a reply, his eyes still unfocused. It had been some hours since she had left him to shake off the effects of his ordeal.

'Here, you should drink this.'

'What, more drugs?'

'No, fruit juice with a high dosage of Vitamin C to help you recover.'

He shrugged, verbally expelling a breath. 'Did you find out everything you needed?'

'Yes, you were very helpful,' She laughed, flashing a maniacal grin at him. 'You know, I'm sure I can persuade you to stay here and bend you to my will.'

'How do you plan on doing that?'

'By holding Lena as a hostage indefinitely, until I'm satisfied.'

'Lisa, I will do whatever I can to satisfy you,' he responded, cocking an eyebrow, understanding that he was dealing with unpredictable psychopathic behaviour on a par with D'albo's. She thrived on power and control, getting what she wanted or destroying it if she could not. His only chance of Lena's safe return was to humour this woman and play along until a moment would present itself to turn the tables. That moment he sensed, would be in London.

'Really,' she purred. 'We could make such a good team, you and I. Think about it, Scott, with your background and my research facility we could change everything.'

'Everything?'

'Yes, everything.' Her aura fired up, possessed as if by a powerful daemon prompting the image of the dragon-serpent to soar again in his mind's eye. 'We could build the machine here in Xinjiang and create a utopia where the Taklamakan would bloom with hemp fields and then grain and small forests. We will show those other desert countries of the world how to bring food and prosperity back into their own hands.'

'But you could do that anyway with Brown's Gas and the other cutting-edge technologies being developed at the facility. All you need is continual funding from your uncle and the Chinese State.'

Her face turned stony. 'That was the plan but now I see something much bigger. Once I had heard the faintest rumour that the machine existed, I hatched a dream to develop it here and then share it with other friendly countries to shift global economics from the neoliberal bondage of debt killing this planet. Western capitalism is unsustainable and is coming to a natural end while the so-called communists of this country only ever played at socialism in some bizarre mind-game, blithely experimenting with economic plans that wreaked disaster on its people and turned them to capitalism by another name. Don't you see? Within less than a generation a perfect storm of climate change, ageing demographics and the burgeoning migration of young unemployed men from the developing world, will tip the balance of western civilisation into melt-down. Experts are already warning of the fragility in the bloated derivatives markets collapsing and triggering the beginning of these events in the near future.'

Carty's lips had parted to mouth words but remained speechless. She was displaying similar emotions much like he had done when he first learnt of the machine's true purpose and at the same time had been warned of its consequences. There would be no smooth transition to a post-capitalist economy, just a huge and sudden collapse led by those holding the hegemony over free energy, shaping a dystopian future of control. Even if Lisa did obtain the blueprints to build the machine, she had no idea of the pitfall: that *overunity* was only feasible at certain co-ordinates–energetic nodes–on the planet's surface, points which may not even exist in Xinjiang. He had no intention of telling her this information, not if he wanted Lena to remain alive.

'I don't disagree with you, Lisa. Believe me, I've played these scenarios through in my head time and time again, but it's only when enough individuals become conscious to want a change that the machine could ever be implemented.'

'We could make that change together, Scott.'

'It is feasible,' he added, still trying to mollify her, 'but wouldn't it be more practical to go step by step, developing the machine's transmutation potential first. Long term storage of spent waste is not an option for those countries with large dependency on nuclear power, and they will be willing to pay any price you ask.'

'Are you suggesting that we use the transmutation business as a smoke-screen to fund and test the free-energy?'

'I suppose I am,' he answered coolly, pausing to take a sip of the juice. Her gaze never left his, and it felt it was the moment to ask the burning question.

'But can I ask you how you came to know about the machine?'

'I met the Russian businessmen who handled the spent waste from this region. The Party has recently banned its export, and these Russians were panicking, offering to start a joint venture company with my uncle to share in the profits they were making. I simply probed them on the technology.'

A warped sense of satisfaction stirred. *Hafeza and I were spot on in our hypothesis.*

'And you didn't mention Brown's Gas to them?' he followed.

'It made no sense to reveal one of our most secret technologies.'

'I see, and did your uncle agree to form the company?'

'He couldn't, mainly because he doesn't have the power within the Party to reverse the ban but he didn't let on to them. However, in their desperation to work with us, we learnt that their technology not only exhibited transmutation but also *overunity.*'

'They told you that?'

'Money and alcohol both talk! It was also disclosed that you had been hunted down in Russia after discovering this other secret.'

'So, from day one, you planned to ensnare me.'

'It wasn't planned that way, exactly. I simply researched your business activities.'

'And you discovered Sole Carbon's projects here in Xinjiang...,' he whispered, catching her grin, 'and then stopped its revenue streams from being paid.'

'I couldn't resist the temptation but if it means anything to you, Scott, I really do respect your brilliant mind.' She placed her index-finger delicately on his cheek and ran it down to his chin. 'I hope you'll reconsider my offer to return here after London.'

Her comment enticed the same nauseous sensation that he had felt only hours earlier, with her betrayal. His dream had told him everything from the start. *Yet how could I have known that Lisa would be the serpent?* It truly did appear as if fate had dragged him here by the hair screaming.

'I know you see me as a pure materialist, enjoying the benefits of my family's wealth but I have no illusions about the decadence of the expensive brands I'm wearing,' she pushed out her grossly imbalanced stilettos. 'Or their true cost of production in some sweatshop in South East Asia, at a mere fraction of the retail price. This iniquitousness cannot continue.'

Despite her callous and ruthless manner, he felt an uncomfortable resonance with her stark philosophy. He too, understood that the current paradigm was creaking at the seams, its fragility camouflaged by media humdrum, but having considered the machine's dark side, its dystopian potential, he had instead strived to make small changes in cutting emissions through his fund's investments. He feared now, though, that with Lisa, there was no stopping the machine's release to the world and the opening of Pandora's Box.

She coughed lightly. 'And now, Scott, it's time to get down to business. You should take a shower and have a rest before we leave.'

'Really!' Carty placed the glass down. 'When?'

'This evening.'

Twenty Eight

Siberia

Squatting on the ledge to catch his breath alongside the cascading ravine, the Buryat was drawn to the beautiful chaos of the churning waters as the sobering realisation hit that he had narrowly escaped certain death. The space around was limited and narrow, quickly tapering to nothing after only a few feet which prevented his climbing around the granite sarsens that rose almost vertically through the atomised mist. It appeared that his only passage was up and over them, an almost impossible task, given that their sheer surfaces were rendered smeary. But as he glanced up through the spray to survey the challenge, he spotted a possible line of attack, a split in the huge rocks about a house's height diagonally above him, which caused them to splay out like petrified feathers. Bolstered, he felt around the slabs for fault lines, to seek a fixing grip so that he could use the cantilever approach again. There were many and pressing his soles flat against the rock's surface he hauled his mass up then treaded gingerly one foot ahead of the other, his hands simultaneously sliding and gripping along the ridged crack ahead. He reached the vantage point more easily than he had imagined, allowing him to slip into the giant fault's space to temporarily rest and plan. The climb ahead would now be almost vertical between rising slab walls and the strain on his system had been enormous, having not eaten properly for days. But his mind was now in flow, blanking out any doubts as he stretched out, using the counter pressure of his hands and feet pushing on the opposite parallel facing surfaces, to begin to slowly walk himself up. Then, ten or so paces in, he felt his limbs deaden and a burning sensation run over his scapula threatening the flow state that had carried him this far: he was close to his natural limit and terrifyingly, a cold sweat soaked his skin with the very real fear of dropping to his death.

Consciously, he sought a slow quiet breath to maintain the outstretched agonising position of his limbs and reset his mental state, allowing his inner being to take over again, reminding him that he had handled the challenges so far and not to lose sight of the objective–avenging Ivan Yegorovich's murder. He pressed hard into his three limbs and moved the fourth, alternating them one at a time to deliberately scale the eighty feet to the outcrop's summit. Then clamping the top of the ledge in his iron grip, he dramatically let his legs drop and swing down below him, bouncing with the balls of his feet as they met the sheer wall. He held on desperately for dear life, sucking air into his stinging lungs before steadily pulling himself up and over the ridge to collapse, face-down on a weathered plateau.

The exertion had pushed him to his physical limit, but then the threatening immediacy of discovery by the helicopter had him rolling weakly across the coarse terrain to partially hide under a clump of dwarfed pine trees. Sunshine had pieced the veil of clouds and poured through the branches as he lay there on his back for more minutes than he cared to think about, challenged to bring his breath back into a calm rhythm. Gradually, it slowed and with that, his stamina returned. He moved back on to his belly, reaching for the binoculars to take in the rough location of the mercenaries below, noting that there were three of them, searching for their comrade and whoever else, in the taiga.

Good, they have no idea I'm up here.

He then scoped out possible paths down through the split sharp cairns, which were tricky and would enlist his total energy again, a challenge he was nervous of taking if he was to face these men in combat later. He had a hunch that one or two of them had remained behind, inside that cave entrance and that Ivan Yegorovich had been held there. But he couldn't see how he would achieve that, especially with the chopper's sudden appearance again, hugging the forest's canopy in the near distance. What he needed was a distraction. Causing a landslide was not an option, as the debris of shattered rock might block the entrance, and the disturbance would draw the attention of those out searching.

He continued scoping with the glasses and then noticed that the backdrop of blue sky appeared strangely blurred in one particular location, a moss-laden bluff about 12 metres to his left, causing him to pan back and forth over that area. Then he spotted a pillar of hazed air that seemed to be emanating from between the boulders. Curious, he guessed that it was man-made and that he would need to take a closer look before the Mil Mi-8 passed over. Holding a palm over his brow to shield the sun, he sprang up, timing his crouching run towards the point, to dive for cover, between the scarps. Glancing down over their edges he discovered a precipice, a tangled natural chimney venting the distinctive fumes from a wood fire somewhere below him. The narrow passage twisted down sharply so that he couldn't see any light or fathom how deep it went but reasoned it was a safe place to hide temporarily and possibly an entrance to the cave below from where he believed the mercenaries were operating. He had potholed while in military service and understood the rudiments of exploring rock tunnels, however he lacked a rope and therefore knew that he might encounter difficulties that would force him to climb back up and out. Seizing a pen torch from his slung bag, he switched it on, shoved it between his lips and then slid forward, suspending his bodyweight on his sturdy arms to spin his legs around and gently lower himself, feet first to search for toe-holds.

The heat from the vents increased but it wasn't unbearable as he sank down step by step, squeezing himself round several turns in the unforgiving rock, to come to rest on a small flat boulder. Straining, he could make out indistinct sounds, possibly voices, and he steeled himself, quietly lowering onto a strip of rocks that sloped gradually downwards, figuring that he could slither along its path toward the noises. But if it turned out to be a dead-end there was no way of turning around in the cramped space and he would be stuck without hope. He took the choice and manoeuvred forward to find the passage bending sharply around and then opening up so that he could come to squat on his knees, all the while the faint echo of a man's voice reverberated around him. He turned to sense the direction of the sound, crawling towards a fissure on its far side as hot air and the distinctive acridity of burnt logs now teased his nostrils. He pulled at his neckerchief to smother his nose and throat, preventing any cough that might alert those to his presence and then squeezed through the gap. Beyond was a cavern, its sheer walls caught the flickering orange-yellow light from the basic hearth, 30 feet or more below, constructed for warmth and cooking. At the centre of the floor space were large cardboard boxes of provisions, stacked four or five feet high. *What are these doing here?* He was taken by their number and suddenly cognizant of the operation's scale to capture Ivan Yegorovich. *He would never have revealed his secrets though.* But that hadn't explained how or why he had been left to rot in a shallow grave. Renewed anger had him now scouting the arena. Despite the earlier noises there was no sign of life, so he took the opportunity to perch his legs over the edge and with one breath, pushed himself off. Plummeting, he crashed through the top box of the stack as the others broke his fall and the sharp impact had him winded, spread-eagled on his back for some seconds. His actions were not noiseless, and shortly a sleeveless man carrying a slung automatic rifle stepped out into the place from an alcove that apparently led to another part of the complex. Boris quickly slid down hidden, to the ground and span around behind their bulk to hide, bristling with a heightened state as the mercenary examined the dented boxes poking them with the rifle's barrel and staring up at the naturally vaulted ceiling, his logic vexed. The Buryat was poised to strike as the figure neared but then footsteps brought in another fellow, shouting news that their fallen comrade had been found in the river and then exchanged muttered conversation. He was now in a difficult place and needed to act before the others returned. Picking up a small rock, he tossed it at the wooden door to the cave. The sound resonated loudly, causing an instant reaction from the mercenaries, crouching low to turn and point their weapons. Then he sprung from his lair, seizing the rifleman's trigger hand and firing off shots directly into the other, felling him. The thug, surprised, swung a reflex punch to the Buryat's chest, but it was instantly ridden as the local thrust his own hunting knife up and under the man's ribs. There was stillness, the figure staring in abject shock as he dropped to his knees.

'Did you torture the old man?' Boris shouted. A brief shaking head answered the question and then filled the air with a sharp exhalation as he expired. He hardly had time to process its impact as, attuned to the very real danger, he picked up the automatic weapon and pounced over the short distance to slam his body up flat against the coarse rock wall before poking his head slowly around the alcove, snatching a glance into the tunnel beyond. It was empty, and he wasted no time charging down it and then halting as it opened out onto a small zone. Three metal-framed bunk beds greeted him and along the wall's edges, rucksacks were slung around. The lack of any other mercenaries hackled his senses as he cautiously stepped around, aiming the rifle up close from his shoulder, spotting a bolted door. He was soon inside, waving the gun around, wary of the unexpected; what he found left him breathless. A young woman was bound feet and arms, in a chair, her head slumped with blonde hair dark dangling, clumped in her own dried blood. The Buryat, reached for a pulse as he simultaneously slipped his knife's edge under the cords to cut her free. She was alive, her heartbeat still strong; and gingerly, he lifted her chin to wipe the bloodied matted mass from her battered face. Slowly her mature features drew his horrified recognition. *It can't be!* But it was Lena Isotova.

Twenty Nine

Xinjiang

The roar of the jet's twin engines and the sudden surge of power tilting the fuselage up, gave Carty a perverse sense of freedom even though the raw impact of Lisa's disingenuous character and disturbing insouciance, sat like a knot in his stomach. He ran several scenarios in his head of how he would speak with Green and convince him that the only thing that mattered was Lena's release, not the blueprints to the machine. He was sure his friend would recognise this and agree but his real concern was the seriousness of Lisa's narcissistic madness and if she would keep her side of the deal, not to force him to return with her to set up the prototype while keeping Lena captive, indefinitely. He trembled with pained anguish that his woman was suffering somewhere, having been put through this bizarre nightmare again. *Overunity* may never be accessed in Xinjiang and that might result in both of their deaths, regardless of the Chinese authorities being put under pressure by Whitehall Jack's people to find and release them.

'I'm too tired to sit here,' Lisa uttered, flashing her pearly incisors as she unbuckled and pulled herself away from the table separating them, deliberately letting her hair tumble over her shoulder and shaking it out with a toss. Carty hadn't reacted, remaining lost to playing back images of his life with Lena against the rapidly vanishing city below.

'Are you tired, Scott?'

He quickly glanced up at the veiled comment, noticing the now unbuttoned blouse exposing the cup rims of an exclusive flowered bra

'I'm good thanks.'

She frowned, and in the sun's low light, the darker side to her character seemed agitated.

'So, you don't want to sleep?'

Blinking back at her, he shrugged. 'No.'

'What does a woman have to do to get Scott Carty?' she forcefully asked. 'Is your Lena that perfect that you don't want me?'

He was in trouble. The woman's ire was up, and Lena's life depended on keeping on the right side of her capricious decision-making. Thoughts ploughed as their gazes locked together and she lowered her face to his, engulfing him with her overpowering fragrance. He shot a look past her, noticing that the minders who had joined the plane with them were now strangely absent and then she forced her lips onto his, slipping her tongue between them. He reciprocated coldly in a mock act of compliance, grasping her toned upper arms to prevent her full-scale descent on to his lap.

'You see. It's not so bad after all, is it?' Her warm breath was tinged with garlic as she shook her head rubbing her nose against his.

'Not so bad,' he agreed, still strategically supporting her as she pushed for more.

'Lisa.' His voice was firm, and he smiled openly. 'Have you ever been in love?'

Her expectant eyes widened at the unexpected question.

'Possibly, why?'

Carty let out a sigh. 'That's not the right answer.'

She pulled back, stunned by his retort.

'Are you playing games with me?'

'No, all I'm saying is that if you genuinely had been, then you would have answered differently.'

'Excuse me, Scott Carty, the master of love,' she barked. 'You don't have any idea about how a woman's heart ticks.'

'I agree. It's impossible for me to know that but by the same token also, it's impossible for you to know how a man's ticks.'

'Hah,' she guffawed. 'You men only think with your dicks when it comes to pussy, regardless of the love you claim to hold. Your friend Nick was too easy while you're a little harder to crack but believe me, you're no different, Carty. I could make you mad with passion if I focused my efforts on you.'

Carty now feared her unhinged mind and what she might be capable of doing to prove her point. He quickly decided to placate her. 'I have no doubt about that, Lisa. You're stunningly attractive, and I admit it's hard not to have bad thoughts about you.'

'How bad? Do you want to show me?'

'Not on this plane. I'm not comfortable with the surroundings and I'm also exhausted. You forget what you've put me through in the last day, Lisa. Those drugs that were forcibly administered, have sapped my energy and I would never get aroused enough to please you.'

She grinned garishly. 'Let's see, shall we?' Swiftly moving her palm down over his groin, she rubbed him aggressively as her nose moved in to touch his again. He went with it, his mind thinking only of Lena and how her passion was so different, like a rose releasing its delicate scent in the morning sunlight, enthusing joy and love, the gifts of a true bonding of souls. He had never enjoyed a woman who forced herself and it showed.

'Hmm, I suppose you're right.' She pulled her hand back up to stroke his cheek. 'We can get to know each other better when we've landed in London. I'm sure after a good rest you'll be more responsive.'

'I'm sure I will be.'

She seemed satisfied and ran her palms over her temples, weaving her long fingers back and twirling the strands of hair up and back into a high ponytail which she fastened with several twists of a golden band. Then, raising her chin in a display of conquest, she swivelled on her heels and sashayed down the aisle to the private bedroom. She didn't glance back but simply closed the door behind her.

Thirty

Siberia

There wasn't time to squander on anger or small talk as the Buryat caught her glazed eyes and the pain they registered.

'Lena. It's me Boris. Can you stand?'

Her chin hung with the full weight of her skull as she tried to grunt something from her smashed mouth. He had to act fast, dripping water onto her lips, tempting her to lick.

'Can you feel if any part of your body is damaged..., broken bones?' he asked, smiling and keeping eye contact as he felt along her limbs and then gently prodded her torso. She yelped with the latter, forcing him to palm around the area with him sensitive hands to gauge if splintered ribs might be close to puncturing her organs. She was strong enough, though, to tentatively reach out, wrapping her thin arms around his neck and allowing his stocky build to pull her up out of the chair onto her shaking legs.

'Here, you must drink more water.' Cradling her head back on to his shoulder, he held the army issue flask to her lips once more, allowing a steady trickle to run as they parted while his other hand swept away the sticky mass of hair. Then he clearly recognised those glorious profiled features that he had patiently waited for with a heightened sense of longing when she was vacationing at her grandparents in Siberia. That his affections were not reciprocated in the manner a young man had wanted was almost past him, but a wave of emotion hurtled him back to those few, short summers of his youth, reminding him of the pain of first love and knowing that it could never be. She gazed up at him with those blue eyes, cracking a weak half-formed smile as if silently acknowledging his reminiscences, but the moment was lost on their predicament. She was in need of medical help and they had to exit the cave complex before the other mercenaries, having heard the shots, arrived. If not, they had little chance of surviving.

'Are you ready?'

She nodded, and he clipped the flask back onto his leather belt, feeling for his knife and then scoping the place for the automatic weapon. But his stare was drawn to something that could be far more useful and a counterintuitive notion sprang into his head.

'Lena, how many men were there? Can you remember?' he asked placing an ear to her lips. She faltered for some seconds and then uttered, 'Five.'

So that leaves two of them alive and they're both outside.

He sat her down again on the chair, softly gripping her chin to prevent it falling back to her chest. 'Lena, I want you to trust what I'm about to do,' he quietly said, simpering again as their gazes met.

She let out a huff of air and he began to loosely bind her wrists and ankles with what remained of the cord. He winked at her and then turned to trot out along the short tunnel to the main cave and the packing boxes. Minutes later he was hauling the cadaver of one of her captors back in by the arms and then up onto another chair facing her, positioning the slumped body to suggest that he might be sleeping with the automatic in his arms. Satisfied, he then moved over to the door where, propped against the wall, was the weapon that had caught his attention earlier: a SV-98 sniper rifle complete with folded tripod legs. He had used this extensively during military service, earning honours for specialising in remaining hidden camouflaged in the taiga for days on end in order to find his target and complete his orders. He slung its strap over his chest and turned back to face the woman.

'Don't worry, Lena. I will take us out of here. You can be sure of that!' His large moon face cracked into a serious smile and then he spun about. In the main cavern he grabbed at the other fallen mercenary's arms and dragged him out of sight behind the boxes as the bashing of a rifle butt against the cave's jammed door meant he was running out of time. It had been locked from the inside by the members as a matter of protocol, and he had wanted to leave it open before they retunred, to simulate the possibility of one of the men going rogue, but his plan had been scuppered. Now, his only hiding place was up and he began to scale the boxes as firearm shots from more than one weapon, splintered the huge wooden entrance. Then the men booted their way in, firing continuously. Lying flat on his back on the top of the provisions, four metres above them with the rifle by his side, Boris calmly breathed, slowly circulating his *Qi* and mentally waiting for the moment. The two newcomers soon spotted the legs of their dead comrade; the broken boxes drew their frantic looks up at the cave's roof, understanding that someone could have possibly entered from the ledge way above them, dropping down on to the packing but could not have left in the same manner. Clearly shaken, one of them gesticulated with practised military hand signals for the other to scout out the area while he went to check on his female captive, stealthily padding along the hewn tunnel towards Lena. Boris was suddenly nervous wondering if he had made a mistake in leaving her. What if they had already retrieved everything they had wanted, his hasty plan failed, and she was shot in cold blood. *But they would have already done that,* he reasoned, calming himself again. Curiosity, though, was claiming the brute left behind as he noticed the barrel of Boris' rifle protruding from the top edge, urging him to climb upon one of the fallen boxes as he called out to his mate and pointed his machine gun up, confused whether to shoot or not. The Buryat had inched himself on his belly out of sight and then slid back down the rear side, waiting. Then, as the killer wandered around, he leapt forward, grasping at the barrel with his left hand, the hidden blade in his right, and with a lightening scissor move, severed the man's carotid artery while pulling the gun from his trigger finger. The mercenary let out a gurgled cry that was instantly smothered as Boris clamped his palm over the figure's mouth spinning him around and pulling the gun across his windpipe, crushing it. He held the killer close in a sodden, bloodied hold for seconds until the cry of his fellow mercenary calling out for confirmation, triggered him to drop the body and scale back up the boxes to grab the sniper rifle. He instantly positioned its barrel tip between the joins of the packaging, hidden, and then exhaled, becoming one with the moment and the target as the other killer captor gingerly stuck his head around the tunnel's wall, screaming to his comrade to answer. Boris' finger had moved at the same instant, a bullet piercing the man's temple and splattering the rough cave backdrop with white brain matter and plasma. Instantly, he was down and skittering between the bodies, carefully looking through the pockets of their jackets to understand exactly who they were. But there was nothing except rouble notes and cigarette packets leaving him in no doubt that they were hired Special Forces from outside the region and they had been lax. Perhaps it was the length of time they had spent in the taiga, unused to its deceptively powerful ways and steeped in the immeasurable energy of plants and trees, which, along with the effect of alcohol, had blunted their discipline. As he moved to the entrance, he also knew that it was usual practice to leave a hidden sentinel standing guard, so he knelt, slipping his head out and scanning the scene to ensure that there were no others waiting to pick him and Lena off as they left. He then slid the rifle butt into the crook of his shoulder and cocked his head to look down the sight as he panned its barrel painstakingly slowly through almost 180 degrees, seeking any tiny sign of trampled or broken vegetation or disturbed animals. His hearing picked up a faint rustle and he swung the weapon around in the same direction adjusting the sight's focus until he could clearly see a head and shoulders tramping through the undergrowth near to a path approximately a quarter of a mile away. The figure stopped to look over his shoulder, his body language and facial expression wracked with urgent tension. *Interesting,* the local thought as he pulled back and looked ahead into the distance as the stranger turned again and paced off. The path he was on led up to a flat-topped hill where the helicopter had landed, and Boris registered that the man was its pilot; the team had left him on watch to contact back up if required. The figure might have witnessed Boris' handiwork and having no stomach for death, had made a getaway. *He would've already raised the alarm,* Boris reasoned, making a spit-second decision to re-sight the rifle and take aim. The man couldn't be allowed to escape and while it had been many years, the Buryat's skill hadn't been lost as he caught the man in the cross hairs, adjusted himself for the distance and the slight breeze and then squeezed the trigger, letting out a short inaudible breath as the silenced barrel recoiled. His quarry went down instantly.

Unswayed, the Buryat looked about again making doubly sure there were no others; he allowed a short moment of silence to reflect on the position before rushing on. Sweating with his fatigues encrusted in congealing blood, he pulled at the flask for a sip of water. He had never become used to the stench of death, despite the countless times he had hunted animals and carried their carcasses across his body. But always to him the lingering putrid odour of human plasma smelt far worse, and the cool water helped dismiss his nausea to focus instead on the daunting task ahead.

He soon had Lena up and walking aided by his arm slung under her shoulder and with hers around his neck. Struggling with pain she had seen the dead bodies and understood that there was no choice: more brutes would soon arrive to finish them, and despite her old friend's extraordinary abilities, he would not be able to save her.

The path up to the chopper was gruelling, compelling her to stop every ten or so steps to gather her energy but, finally, she was lifted into the ageing aircraft and laid across the seats, using the belts to secure her. Gripping her forearm, he winked to bolster her spirits and then turned to the cabin. He had flown MIL Mi-8s on a number of occasions, but it had been several years ago and he could only pray that those skills and his memory would serve them well.

Thirty One

The familiarity of Oleg Lubimov's face had Lena beaming at him early that evening as she was carried down from the helicopter on a stretcher by several of the team from *Sphinx*. Boris waved to her from the cockpit, mouthing something inaudible. He hadn't cut the engine and didn't intend to but planned to fly out as soon as possible to prevent dangerous attention being drawn to Lubimov's research centre, rendezvousing in a remote yet agreed location with his air-force comrades who would then take the chopper.

She watched the aircraft rise and bank out over the tree-line to head north as her porters delivered her into the small surgery. Lubimov himself examined her while a female assistant swabbed her face and hair to remove the encrusted blood then prepared a needle and thread to stitch one large gash to her cheek. Lena winced at the sight and another handed her sweetened kefir to drink.

'Please set up the laser therapy room for tonight,' Lubimov requested to his staff. 'Lena, you have a number of bruised ribs and swollen liver along with many contusions but thankfully nothing is broken.' His tired face showed despair at her beautiful features now swollen and bruised but relief that any further beating might have killed her.

'Are you going to give me the same treatment as last time?'

'Yes, the laser acupuncture, overnight when you're asleep. It should help you recover very quickly.'

She simpered as she gripped his hand, noting how much older he looked. He reciprocated shallowly, waiting for the young subordinates to leave.

'My God, you're lucky to be alive,' he exclaimed in a lowered tone, his demeanour clearly perplexed. 'I thought we had agreed that you could never come back here.'

'I didn't plan to. I was tricked.'

'By whom?'

'Vladislav. Do you remember him?'

Lubimov's face visibly darkened as he nodded.

'I received a note in London. It was handwritten in Russian and supposedly signed by you, stating that Ivan Yegorovich was desperately ill and that I needed to come as soon as possible without telling anyone.' Her voice faltered as she pulled the bed sheet to her face and sobbed. The old man threw his arms around her, consoling the woman he had known since she was a child.

'You don't need to say anymore,' he attempted to calm her knowing that at some stage he would have to tell her that her grandfather had been abducted.

'But I do,' she wailed, searching his eyes. 'Ivan Yegorovich is dead.'

Lubimov stared back, frowning. 'How do you know that?'

'Boris told me. He was being held captive and tortured,' she stuttered, her voice punctured by gasping spasms between the sobs, 'and then he had a fatal heart attack.'

The old man's head lowered and he shed a tear for his mentor as they held each other quietly for some minutes until Lena glanced up at him again, clearing her throat.

'Vladislav led me into a trap. He believed I had information about the machine he could trade.'

'And what did you tell him?'

'Nothing! He got nothing from me and when his paymasters came to take me, they shot him in cold blood. He was a fool thinking that he could have negotiated with them.'

'And were you about to divulge what you knew?'

'Never. I don't know enough about the machine and anyway they would have killed us both, regardless.

'It was a blessing that Boris found you.' Lubimov realised that his friend would have the answers to the difficult questions that he was not about to ask her. He took a swab and gently wiped her cheeks free of tears.

'And how is Scott?' he uttered.

'I don't know. I left him behind in London with a story that I was going to meet with some university friends in Dubai - that's where Vladislav said he would meet me but instead he sent his associate to bring me into Russia.' Her voice faltered again.

'You haven't been in contact with him since leaving England?'

'No, I lied to him and kept this secret for fear of exposure of my being in Russia. He must be worried sick and hating me, but I had to come, I had no choice.' She instinctively placed a hand on her belly, and the new life that was growing inside her. 'Is it possible to contact him from here?'

'That would be a mistake until you are well and ready to return. It's far too dangerous.'

'But there must be a way to get word to him that I am safe.'

'Let me consider how to do that without risking all of our lives. We don't know who may be listening or may have followed you. For now, though, you must rest.' He nodded reassuringly and moved over to open the door, peaking momentarily outside for insurance and then closed it. 'Lena, do you know about the books?'

'Containing the blueprints? Yes, we found them quite coincidentally embedded within the Dostoyevsky novels.'

'It's strange because only recently, Ivan Yegorovich asked me to get word to you about their location, if anything happened to him. He must have had a premonition about what was to come but anyway, he would have been happy to know that you and Scott had already found them,' he uttered, nervously pulling open the door again and noticing that the young research doctor was returning up the corridor, he hurriedly turned to back to her, his face now burdened. 'There's something I need to tell you about the machine and those blueprints before you leave, but not now.'

* * * *

The following morning, she woke late, her still body sore and aching as the memories of the rape and the beatings came flooding back. The mechanical booms holding the same lasers that had saved both hers and Scott Carty's life, as they hung in the balance a few years before, were perched overhead and all around her, their nozzles positioned to focus coloured laser light exactly over vital acupuncture points on her skin. They had been switched off some hours earlier but their healing effect had boosted her energy levels and feeling of recovery almost beyond her belief. Pulling herself up, she pressed the buzzer on the cabinet and shortly the clacking of heels could be heard as a nurse approached to administer water and several concoctions recommended by Lubimov.

Afterwards, she sat upright quietly for an hour or more gazing out into the meadow bordering the taiga, absorbing the fresh air that breezed in through the window and appreciating the homeland she had been missing. The distinctive noise of a truck's engine disrupted her peace, reminding her once again of the violent abduction in the cabin and she tensed, expecting trouble, now aware of the very real danger threatening her here. But then she heard Boris' voice, loud and melodious as he chatted with his few colleagues. Jubilant, she was keen to leave her bed to greet him, although knew she couldn't.

'How's the invalid?' the Buryat shouted from outside the door before entering carrying a posy of wild flowers in an old jam-jar topped up with water.

'Thank you. I'm feeling tired but recovering.' She took the flowers and attempted to smile through her broken face. 'Boris, I can't thank you enough for risking your life to save me.'

He sat alongside and took her hand to acknowledge her sentiment.

'Where have you been, though?' she asked.

His head dipped. 'The guys dropped me near to the spot in the forest, where I found Ivan Yegorovich's body. We've bought it back for burial. I'm sorry, Lena.' His voiced hung with sadness. 'But I'm not sorry I finished off those mercenaries. They were lost souls, paid to kill without any thought or mercy.

My worry now is that their paymasters will send more out looking for you.'

'Could they trace me here?'

'Possibly, but in any event, we need to move you tomorrow, even if you haven't fully recovered.'

'Where to?'

'Somewhere only I know you'll be safe. Whoever it is who wants information about the machine will not stop until they have you.'

'But I told Lubimov that I know hardly anything about it, not least its location.'

'I don't understand it either. Ivan Yegorovich's original machine was decommissioned in the early 1990s, and then reassembled almost a 100 kilometres from here. It doesn't make sense why, after all this time, they would have hunted him down?'

'Perhaps they want *overunity*?'

Ah, so Scott did tell her about the phenomenon, but does she know that a newer prototype is still operating below our feet?

'That's the conclusion I came up with too, but my instincts are still screaming that there's another, more convoluted aspect to all this,' he followed.

'Do you have any clues?'

'Only one. The imports of spent nuclear waste into the region have slowed to a trickle in recent months and the Chinese material has stopped entirely.'

'Do you think the original machine has malfunctioned..., stopped working, and that they wanted my grandfather's expertise to solve their problem? Is that possible?'

'I don't know. We will have to ask Lubimov.'

'But if it is the case, then Lubimov and Scott will be the next kidnap targets.'

'Oleg Matissevich was already debriefed about six months ago by the Russian Intelligence agencies, but they quickly released him when he reminded them that he was a doctor even though his father was Ivan Yegorovich's right-hand man.'

'So, they may visit him again?'

The Buryat grunted as a slight tap sounded through the door. Lubimov entered almost immediately, wiping his lenses on the old woollen jumper he wore.

'I hope that I'm not interrupting?'

'We were just discussing the possibility of you being a target for these criminals who want the machine.'

'And Scott too!'

'That's why Lena needs to leave first thing tomorrow,' the older man stated and then cleared his throat with a cough. 'But why don't you tell us about your good news, Lena?'

She flushed. *How does he know?*

Boris searched his friend's face and then Lena's, shrugging.

'I'm...,carrying Scott's baby,' she whispered, staring back at them.

Both men cracked huge grins and moved to kiss her.

'But how did you find out?'

'We made a full analysis of your blood when you went under the laser therapy last night. Does Scott know?'

'I only found out after I left London and thought to keep it a surprise until I returned.'

'He's going to be a very happy man I'm sure, and it's all the more reason to get you back to him as quickly as possible.'

The Buryat held her hand maintaining his grin. 'Is Lena in a fit state to leave so quickly?'

'Yes, as long as she is very careful and takes it easy. The laser treatment has helped already.'

'So how do you plan to get me to London?'

'Simple really,' Lubimov responded. 'Fly you back to Novossibirsk, like we did with Scott.'

'Won't that be dangerous?'

'Not if Boris ensures that you're safely on the flight.'

Her face lit up. Boris hugged her. 'Well, you need to excuse me. I'm going to make preparations to bury Ivan Yegorovich's body this afternoon.'

The words drew sadness back into her expression. Having narrowly escaped death she couldn't bring herself to be joyful.

But he would have been thankful that I survived with my unborn child. The thought gave her strength and a resolve for her return.

'And now it's time for a little more treatment,' Lubimov prompted as he swung the booms to focus on specific acupoints on her body and then chose the varying sympathetic shades of laser light that his ground-breaking research had defined, to help regenerate her health.

That afternoon Lena was able to pull herself off the bed and with the nurse's help, dress and then walk out along the rough concrete path to the open space where a small congregation was gathering.

'Ah good. Lena is here,' Oleg Matissevich announced. Several of the faces turned to smile and offer sympathies as they waited for Boris and his two friends to tramp back in from the taiga.

'Would everyone follow us please?' He waved his arm to show the direction back into the forest. Lubimov led the way and as soon as Lena reached the Buryat, he took over from the nurse, in supporting Lena's weight as she lent on him, walking behind the others through the foliage. Any low hanging branches had been cut away as had the litter of dead logs, to create a passage up to a set of granite sarsens. It wasn't a long journey, but Lena was struggling as they reached the clearing and the team gathered in a circle around the excavated hole, allowing her to take a position close to Lubimov who had begun to sing a rustic melody, telling a story of the adventurers of these parts. Then he invited those who knew Isotov, to recount memories and stories of his life. Lena's knees buckled with the impact of an overwhelming surge of emotion, an odd blend of love and anger at her tragic loss. This man, her grandfather, had, with his team, pioneered one of the greatest technologies unknown to humanity, and as a testament to him, it was operating clandestinely somewhere not far away, transmuting nuclear waste with its furtive potential to change the world, only secretly known to a handful of people. Boris had a strong arm under her shoulders and kept her close as she turned her injured face and buried her tears into his military jacket, sobbing almost inaudibly. He then spoke, and then it was Lubimov who gave the signal to the men to lower the hastily made wicker casket down into the depths as each member took some earth and quietly said a prayer before tossing it after the box. Lena was still resting her head on the Buryat as the party slowly broke away, some hugging and kissing her as they did. She thanked everyone and then tugged at Boris to escort her back, taking one last look over her shoulder at the men now refilling the hole.

'Will you leave a marker so that anyone who passes knows he's buried and so that I may revisit his grave at a future date?'

'I will make it myself from carved larch,' he answered. An extended silence tied their gaze, and the Buryat's smile grew to consume his large face, his brown eyes shining at her.

'So, what would you like, a boy or a girl?'

'I would be happy with either' she grinned back.

Thirty Two

'Sshhh,' the Buryat whispered, slipping into Lena's darkened cabin and disturbing her slumber. 'We have unwanted guests,' he whispered, in answer to her searching blue eyes. 'Get up and get dressed, now. Make sure you're as quiet as possible. Lubimov is waiting for us at the edge of the forest.'

She struggled in her physical condition, to comply but had soon pulled on a pair of jeans and trainers, throwing on a second-hand sweat top over her vest. All the while the local man had been angled to the window, scanning the hinterland beyond the Institute's makeshift timber gates.

'Good, now follow me and keep to the shadows,' he primed, stealthily pulling open the door and waiting for the moment before stepping out. Within a few paces they had disappeared into the overgrown passageway alongside the cabin, towards the forest, moving across the small arena of wild grass, hidden in the moonless environment. The Buryat had lived here most of his life and navigating in the near absence of visibility was second nature as he homed in on the spot where he had left Lubimov minutes earlier.

'Where are we going?' She was puffing, still not yet fully recovered and holding out her fingers to feel the older man's arm to greet him.

'Somewhere safe,' Lubimov's familiar voice comforted her.

'Are the visitors part of the same gang that held me hostage.'

'No, they're members of the local Governor's team. We're worried by his sudden announcement to visit at this late hour.'

'Do they think that I'm hiding here?'

'They've probably guessed,' Boris whispered. 'It's not difficult to trace where the helicopter landed, nearby.'

'But I can't see or hear any vehicles arriving.'

'That's because they're still on their way,' Lubimov responded.

'How do you know that?' she blurted. 'I thought you said that we *had* unwanted visitors.'

'A tip off. Oleg Matissevich has helped many people with their health over the years and has a lot of friends in high places. The visitors, however, are a two-man party, sent in advance to stake out if anyone is here who shouldn't be.'

She trembled, partly out of fear but also due to the early summer's cold nights in the taiga.

'Don't worry. Where we're going, no one will find us.' Lubimov hugged her.

She strained to make out the Buryat's eyes in the dark shroud of the taiga. 'I hope you're right. I'm not sure I can face another attack.'

Boris gently held her arm. 'That's not going to happen.' He stripped off his belt. 'Now, I want you to hold on to this end loosely while I hold the other and lead the way, slowly. Don't hang on to it with you weight but sink into your legs, stay centred, and allow yourself to just follow my steps. Oleg Matissevich will have his hand on your shoulder. If there is any problem, just tug on it and stop but on no account should you say anything. Your life may be at risk if these strangers are the people I think they are.'

'Assassins?'

'Ssshh.' He took her hand. 'Hold on to the belt and let's go.'

He smoothly turned, gave the belt a quick tug to ensure she had a grip on it and then stepped out precariously into the inkiness. She sensed the breeze, and a myriad nocturnal sounds muffled by the wild rhododendron, but she couldn't feel or hear the Buryat's feet push through the moss or the rising and sinking of his body with each step. The experience was uncanny as if he was somehow levitating very slightly above the ground. *That's impossible!* She dismissed the notion, putting it down to her weakened state, *but there's no other logical explanation,* she thought, wanting to turn to Lubimov but remembered the deep seriousness of her position and retained her hard focus on keeping the belt slightly taut so that she could follow. Mosquitoes had now filled the void with their incessant whining, growing in intensity, as they closed in on her exposed skin areas. Then she was bitten, not once but a few times in succession on the ankles and wrists, frantically wanting to hit out and squash them, but forced herself instead to bite her lip with frustrated agony, praying that they would ignore her bruised face.

By the time the Buryat had halted, she was subject to the rising itchy bumps of her immune system reacting to the bites. Boris pulled her close.

'These intruders are not far away and sound travels easily in the forest, so we can only whisper,' he said reaching out for Lubimov's arm. 'I will leave you with Oleg Matissevich. He will take care of you.'

'But where are you going?' she begged, desperate not to lose her guardian.

'To find them and understand what their intentions are.'

She couldn't see his eyes, but his words resonated chillingly.

'Come, my love,' Lubimov hushed under his breath. 'We're going inside here.'

Where? Almost everything was still invisible to her sight, but she could hear the faintest jangling of a chain as he pushed her arm up through the overhang of birch branches and leaves, forcing her to brush them to one side. Then she felt the coarse exterior of a wooden upright hidden underneath. He fingered around for some time, searching for the securing brackets through which a padlock was fastened and quickly released it, pulling the crude door open. Instantly the interior's mustiness burst out into the fragrant forest. She restrained a cough as she noticed the subdued flickering green light now reflected back in Lubimov's eyes.

'Inside please!'

She moved ahead of him into the dim, surprised by what she thought was just an old hidden cabin as behind her, Lubimov secured various bolts and then sighed as he switched on a torch. Taken at the sight of heavy dust-laden blankets covering the windows and a bank of meters covered in light linen sheets, Lena turned to Lubimov and clocked his craggy expression. He was clearly strained, and she felt an eerie sense that there was more about this place's existence to be revealed.

'What do we do now, wait?'

He seemed unsure of what to say as a moment passed before stuttering, 'No, we go down into the cellar.'

Her frown spoke volumes as he bent down on a knee, keeping her eye for some seconds before pulling at the rug and folding it back to one side to expose the hewn floor boards beneath. He raised a palm and then, with a loud slap, one of them moved smartly down on a spring system so that he could now put his arm into the void that had appeared.

'Are you ready for this?' his words echoed around her as he looked up again. A frisson gripped her. *Why is he asking that?* she thought, surmising that he may have some further secret documents and data outlining the operation of the machine, hidden in a room below the floor. But a creaking sound pulled her awareness to the floorboards as they moved as one, sliding under the adjoining planks in a smoothly engineered fashion, to leave a metre-square gap in the centre of the room.

'Here,' Lubimov offered her his hand as she peered at the narrow concrete steps descending away in the pit.

* * * *

Boris' position, sitting in the boughs of an ancient cedar pine gave him an unequivocal edge in the blackness. Lubimov had left instructions for his staff to shut off the few outside lamps at the Institute, allowing them to slip away unseen to the concealed cabin and the vast secret over which it sat sentinel. The Buryat quietened his senses and blended in with the deep intelligence surrounding him, assuaging his focus to indirectly survey the landscape below and feel any sign of human presence. The wait could take him well into the early hours. He hadn't heard any noises or seen truck headlights flickering up the recently built track and reasoned that the intruders were already in the vicinity, mistakenly thinking that they had an advantage in stealthily moving in to scope the place while the impending local Governor's late visit kept Lubimov's team busy. And if they found Lena, as their brief was to do, they would silently take her captive and slip away again.

His breathing had almost stopped, as he tuned into the nocturnal activities of the forest's fauna, observing them unnoticed. A bear below him, halted to nose the old tree, scratch at its bark and then leave its scent by rubbing his back and hind regions against the exposed layers for several minutes until satisfied, before trudging on. He felt a deep association with the animal, intuiting its instincts and inwardly grinning as he sent it a mental message before slipping back into a state of timelessness. Suddenly, there was a wild shout and then two shots from a pistol followed by the screams of mauled death as the bear found one of the strangers. Now it was the Buryat's turn as he watched for the desperate acts of the fallen man's comrade. His acute hearing tracked a rustling sound in the space where the taiga thinned out to the meadow and locking on to the co-ordinates, he slung his belt around the trunk and silently edged down to the ground, in readiness to hunt.

* * * *

The sharp crack from somewhere in the taiga, jolted Lena. Then it came again, the sound of gunshots.

'Quickly!' Lubimov insisted, grabbing at her arm. 'They may be here in minutes.'

Fright had her backing down the stairs with him holding on to her legs as a guide. Once she was in the small space, Lubimov swiftly moved back up and roughly pulled the rug over the gap before slipping back down a step to thrust the hinged boards back into place.

'There,' he uttered, taking a breath and flicking on the light. 'We should be safe down here.'

'What about Boris? He may have been shot at.'

'If I know Boris, he should be very safe. It would be hard for anyone to better him on his home territory.' As his words ended, she found herself sneezing. A whiff of pungency hung in the air, a faint smell she recognised but couldn't quite place as she glanced around at the jars of pickled cabbage and other vegetables lining the room's two parallel rendered walls. *How long do we need to stay holed up in here?* The question lingered with her growing feelings of disquiet and claustrophobia in the small space but then a strident click followed by a low trundling noise, which set the jars lightly rattling, drew her focus. *Am I imaging that?* She glanced at Lubimov who was now wearing the subtlest of grins. The far wall, devoid of shelves, appeared to be travelling very slowly, away from her. Then after a minute or two, the vibrations stopped and so did the apparent movement, but a more worrying, low frequency drone now resonated through the room and with it the increased pungency of the air. Lubimov meanwhile was sorting through a medium sized box.

'Come, let me show you something very few people have seen.' He passed her a rubber gas mask and winked to allay the concern etched into her expression. Despite the covert language she now had little doubt of what it was he was about to show her.

At the end of the cellar, he pressed his thin bony frame against the wall and edged himself sideways into a narrow gap that had opened up. He shot a look back to gently inveigle her into suspending her disbelief and follow him. She did, fighting against the damp coolness of the rock's face and the nauseous desire to vomit as they inched along the ten feet or so of narrow passageway until it opened out into a large cavernous hall, filled with a multitude of brilliant quartz crystals reflecting a pale blue glow that appeared to emanate from somewhere beyond the cave. Stunned, the intense fumes were causing her eyes to weep and the elderly Russian indicated that they should now place the masks over their faces. Once on, he adjusted her straps and then took her hand, so she could follow him over to a huge stone archway as the alien mechanical drone began to intensify and disturb her sense of calm.

'Be careful here, Lena,' Lubimov advised, his breathing barely audible as he turned his silhouetted face to her. 'Scott would want for me to show you your grandfather's legacy.' He quickly slipped on his mask and Lena gripped his hand tightly as she visibly shuddered.

They passed through into a separate natural chamber, smaller and longer than the first, negotiating a narrow man-made concrete plinth that stood proud of shallow pools fed from the dripping ceiling above. The Russian trod on unrelentingly into the luminescence which he seemed to know well, and she wondered how Scott had felt, tracing this same path. He had never told her of the exact details of the cavern nor what the machine looked like and now here, in its obvious presence, she struggled to regulate her breath with the consternation, feeling the copious beads of perspiration gather on her temples under the mask's rubber rim as its aged smell did little to comfort her against the increasing resonance now pulsating through her ribcage. Salty sweat ran down into her eyes, stinging them and, holding her palm to shield her view against the intense glow, she could see that the walkway ended before an opening in the rock face, less than a hundred feet away, and as they neared it, the Russian turned and clocked her nervousness. He smiled and formed his thumb and forefinger into an O sign before signalling for her to step up the roughly carved steps in the natural wall. She panicked, trepidation freezing her legs as she snatched a look at the man's kindly eyes and took his hand. He nodded his encouragement that he would not have brought her here if it meant endangering her or her unborn child. She lifted a foot on to the first step and leant on his frame to lever herself up, gripping the cold stone so that she could then manoeuvre herself though the aperture. Lubimov watched as her body, bathed in the intense light, froze momentarily and then disappeared into its brilliance.

Oh my God! The sight was all-consuming, mesmerizing her senses as the contraption before her appeared to hover in an otherworldly blue glow, defying gravity and suspending her belief. But she knew it was real and then slowly, fear rapt her with a bizarre loathing for this cold, metallic orb, regardless of the love for her grandfather and his genius in harnessing nature's ethereal powers through it.

Thirty Three

'So now you know Scott's little secret,' he said smiling, as he pulled off his mask, once more back in the safety of the cellar. Lena nodded in stunned silence, still nauseous from the odour of the mask's worn rubber as the wall began to rattle back into position.

'He told me he had seen the machine, but I could never have imagined that,' she uttered after a brief pause to regain her thoughts.

'And I'm also sure he must have told you how Ivan Yegorovich had given me the essential information needed to assemble this second prototype.'

'And it's exact positioning at this spot, accesses *overunity*?'

'Yes, that along with the extraordinary properties of Baikal's water. There are few places on the planet where it can be accessed and so, thank God, it is protected from those who would wish to abuse it potentially unlimited power.'

'Is it because of the purity of the water?'

'Yes, in part; it exhibits a strange fourth phase which is neither solid nor liquid but a kind of gel. We believe that this same water gel exists within the fascia and musculature of our bodies, sustaining life though the ability to transmit electrical charge to all of its cells. Sunlight appears to be the major factor in driving its kinetic energy within the human organism allowing blood vessels to move through capillaries that ordinarily, would be too small to allow their passage.'

'And all that has been shown through your research at the medical Institute here.'

He gazed at her face, still damaged yet radiant, admiring her mind and the fact that she would soon be having a baby with Carty. Clearly, their destinies were woven together and perhaps for the reason of bringing these important discoveries to the fore, in modern society.

'It has. In fact, we can demonstrate so many healing properties with this fourth phase of water that it might replace pharmaceuticals altogether one day, as the medicine for the 21st century.'

His words echoed around the small empty chamber as if emphasising his point.

'Does Boris know about the machine?'

'He knows of it but has never seen it..., he's chosen not to.'

'Why is that?'

The deep blue eyes of the older man were unwavering as he processed the question. 'I believe you will have to ask him that yourself.'

The answer mollified her curiosity and she calmly held on to his forearm. 'How long do we wait down here in this cellar?' She had grown pale with the noxious environment.

'Until Boris gives us the all-clear.'

There was no doubt in Lubimov's mind that the Buryat would prevail against any intruder, and true to his word, they didn't have to wait long before a sequence of pre-agreed knocks sounded on the outside of the cabin's walls, above them.

'Ready to go?' he announced, shifting agilely up the solid steps and manoeuvring the floorboards to one side on their mechanism. The immediate rush of the cooler yet musty air was a welcome relief and drawn to it, she followed.

He no sooner had the floor back in place and rugged than he was opening the bolts, pushing the entrance ajar on its worn hinges. The Buryat's large face was vaguely clear in Lubimov's torch light.

'V*ser harosho*?' [All okay?] he quizzed.

'*Otleechna,*' [Fine] came the man's familiar reply as he pressed himself through the narrow space into the room.

Lena was sat on a stool her forehead sunk into her palms, gently sobbing. Boris instantly squatted and placed his strong arms around her shoulders. Her tired eyes lifted, filled with tears shining in the mute darkness and she trembled violently, letting out a shriek. Boris held on to her, tightly. He and the older man understood that the unspoken ordeals she had been through would have cracked most individuals and now, within this sanctuary, she had broken down, releasing the horrors of the last few days.

'There's nothing to worry about,' Boris whispered, 'tomorrow we will have you in Novossibirsk and then shortly after, back in London with Scott. It's being arranged as we speak.'

She soon calmed and apologetically asked for forgiveness. None was needed.

'I almost can't believe what I saw down there.' She stared at Lubimov. His face lit up, consoling her. 'That's just what Scott said in this same room, not long ago.'

'And will it ever stop running?'

'Eventually it should, we just don't know when. But while it's running, it's producing almost limitless clean power, using the same principles of nature that drive this planet's systems.'

'You said earlier that it can only exhibit *overunity* at certain locations.'

'That's my hypothesis based on the Flower of Life.'

Boris who had been silently listening with his arm still around her shoulder, turned to face her.

'It's perhaps difficult to believe that the ancient cultures had created visual representations to encapsulate what they perceived coming from a deeper dimension and flowing throughout the natural world. Leonardo da Vinci was fascinated by the Flower of Life and its elegantly simple depiction of the sacred geometry that permeates and connects all living things.'

As the Buryat relayed this, Lubimov was unfolding a yellowing poster and in the faint light she noticed that its creased edges were so worn that holes had appeared in the image as he laid it out across the bank of meters.

'This is the Flower of Life,' he announced, his face glowed as he gazed upon its image superimposed over a map of the world.

'It is very beautiful,' she murmured, entranced.

'You can see the nodes at the centre of each flower?'

She gestured an affirmative.

'We can't be certain exactly how many nodes there are on the earth because we don't know of any other location where *overunity* is being accessed, if at all. Some are undoubtedly over the oceans, but we can place the central node over our co-ordinate here, at Baikal.' His gnarled jointed finger tapped at the location on the paper.

'Don't you have any idea how many...,a rough estimate perhaps?'

Lubimov swung his head to the Buryat, prompting his response.

'The ancients say that there are 13 node points on the planet with at least one on each continent,' Boris advised. 'The issue is that with the recent and sudden increase in the Schumann Resonance they may be shifting locations. Given our experience here at Baikal, Ivan Yegovorich and I came to the hypothesis that they must be centred over, or close to ancient bodies of water.'

'Because of the need to have water's fourth phase present?'

'Exactly!' Lubimov beamed, touching the back of her palm, excited to be sharing this cryptic information with an honest mind he knew he could trust. There hadn't been many.

'I want you to take this back to Scott. It's the key to everything.'

She sat upright, taken aback by the request. 'I'm happy to but what if like last time, I'm searched, and it's taken from me.'

She was referring to her escape into China, when she was detained and the plans for Lubimov's revolutionary solar heat pumps were temporarily taken from her and copied by officials.

'It's unlikely anyone is going to understand the significance of an old drawing like this. But you will, now that you are also aware of the fourth phase of water.'

'Do you mean Scott isn't aware of it?'

'We did discuss the relevance of Baikal's unique water exhibiting unusual properties as well as the exact node point's location on the planet being essential for *overunity* and he was aware that there must be other node points but unaware of this map and its possible use in locating them.'

'But it is just a hypothesis, isn't it?'

'Nature and science always have a slight mismatch, like the ghost in the machine that always causes a glitch but thankfully, it's never too much of one to prevent man's evolution. So, what I'm trying to tell you is that this map will be essential in the future.'

All this while Boris had slipped back outside to ensure that there were no other intruders lurking around. Then a fan of light shot up above the trees and he understood that the formal visitors had arrived.

'Time for you to meet the Governor,' he stated calmly, poking his head back inside.

Lubimov patted her wrist and stood, wiping the creases from his shiny aged trousers and straightening his jacket. Lena raised a finger.

'Don't make yourself look too presentable. You're supposed to have been woken up by this unannounced arrival.'

They laughed, and he messed up his snowy hair with a sweep of his hand before undoing several buttons on his shirt.

'Stay here in the cabin with Boris until the morning, just to be sure.' The instruction sounded ominous, but she knew that if there was one person with whom she could be safe, it was the Buryat.

Thirty Four

The dirty crimson cloud-base looming low on the distant horizon signalled to Carty that London was approaching, offering the promise of home and relative safety. *If we could just reach it without any last-minute change of plan.* It seemed to be Lisa's wicked speciality, raising expectation and then dashing it spitefully, at the penultimate moment of elation, only to then bask in the ineluctable and utter sense of desperation she had engendered. *But did I manifest her?* Carty now certain that the recurring dreams and visions of the serpent dragon were a warning of her nature and perhaps also the dark part in himself that was so attracted to her in the first place. Hafeza and the elderly Ludmilla Anatolivna had advised him in so many words that he had been neglecting the work he had been thrown into, to bring his unconscious powers to the fore and assist humanity. Green, Lubimov and Boris had started him on this unchosen quest but, having lapsed, the manifestations had jolted him unwittingly back into action, reminding him of what it was that fed his soul. *And where were Hafeza and her grandmother now?* he ruminated. Had they too been subject to Lisa's dysfunctional behaviour, suffering without any hope? But then he recalled the young woman's incredible skills, which would make her capture difficult, and that of the older woman who had likely, already transcended into *tudkum* somewhere in the Flaming Mountains, supporting life in this world as a Bodhisattva.

He deliberated on how he would relay all this to Green; the ordeal with Lisa along with the necessity to give up the books to save Lena. *Where was she now? In Dubai still, or possibly being held in London, ready for the handover?* He was shaken from his thoughts by the sudden movement of the Mongolians, further up the cabin as they stood and stretched out their huge frames from the eight-hour journey, before replacing their oversized jackets. There was a beep on one of their mobiles, a text instructing them to open the cream leather padded door to the two cabin bedrooms. Lisa strode out without care like some queen, in a powder-blue linen suit, the jacket of which was fine tailored into her tight waist while its slacks hung a perfect length over suede woven wedges.

My God, how many changes of clothes does she have?

'Did you sleep?' she called out with nonchalant irrelevance. Carty breathed deeply, audibly sighing as he let the air out.

'Look, there is your fabulous city and soon, all this will be over for you.'

'And Lena, too?'

'Of course, Scott. That's the agreement.' She backed it with a controlled grin, but he knew her word was dirt and she could just as quickly change her plans, depending on a mood swing or the wrong comment or smile. It seemed that she had already switched her plan from the previous day when she threatened to force him to return with her to Xinjiang to build her dream, kept as some lackey or sex slave to pleasure her mind and body, all dangling on the threat to Lena's freedom.

'We'll both be winners.'

I'll have to play this cruel bitch carefully, he resolved, smiling casually and avoiding direct eye contact, preferring to gaze out at the lit sky *Soon.*

Her fingers snapped loudly. One of the men kicked into action, pulling something from his jacket and placing it in her ritually held out palm.

'And here is your passport.'

He took it silently nodding his appreciation as he flicked through it to double-check the photograph page and if it was actually his. She visibly puffed up her slight breasts in muted annoyance before taking the seat across the aisle and belting herself in.

The landing was routine into the same small airport from where they had taken off, just outside London, catering for the private jets of the elite. They were met at the foot of the stairs by the open door of a limousine that drove them the few hundred metres to the customs hall where the night shift wore friendly faces, familiar with her regular comings and goings.

'Where are we heading to now?' Carty buzzed, joining her across the line, onto English territory having had the passport routinely scanned and passed back to him.

'You don't need to know that. Just follow this gentleman to the car. I will join you later today.'

A burly suede-headed figure hovered nearby, clearly known to her as she voiced what seemed to be instructions.

The vehicle, another limousine, sped up the M3, a motorway Carty didn't know well but recognised place names on the large blue placards along the side of the road. Dawn was not for some hours yet and he felt the fatigue of being held captive, more relaxed as he was now home, although not out of danger, yet.

A shrill call tone disturbed him as he began to nod off.

'Please sir, Miss Lisa. She wants to talk,' the driver garbled in his pidgin English, before passing the phone over his shoulder. Carty took it, frowning.

'Hello, Lisa.'

'Scott, you're about to be handed an envelope.'

The driver then consequently passed it to him, a large, bulky manila type.

'Yes, I have it.'

'Good. In it there's a phone and instructions on what to do. I will call you soon to find out if you've completed the task.' She hung up without his counter and he hastily tore it open, pouring its contents on to his lap. There was a generic cell phone along with a small sealed envelope bearing his handwritten name. He pulled up a flapped edge and slid a finger along its length. The single page inside read with typed words:

CALL GORDON GREEN NOW. TELL HIM THAT YOU'LL MEET HIM AT 10:00 AM AT A LOCATION IN CENTRAL LONDON TO BE ADVISED AND HE IS TO BRNG THE DOCUMENTS.

TELL HIM THAT LENA ISOTOVA IS BEING HELD CAPTIVE AND THAT SHE WILL BE RELEASED UNHARMED SOMETIME AFTER THE DELIVERY.

IF HE ATTEMPTS TO INVOLVE THE SECURITY SERVICES OR FRUSTRATE THE SITUAITON IN ANY WAY THEN SHE WILL NOT BE COMING HOME AND YOUR LIFE WILL ALSO BE FORFEITED.

DO NOT CONTACT ANYONE ELSE, EITHER BEFORE OR AFTER THIS DEAL HAS BEEN SUCCESSFULLY COMPLETED.

IF BOTH YOU AND HE COMPLY WITH THESE INSTRUCTIONS ALL WILL GO SMOOTHLY AND NO ONE WILL BE HURT.

AFTER YOU FINISH THE CALL TEAR UP THIS LETTER, OPEN THE BACK OF THE PHONE TAKE OUT THE BATTERY AND SIM CARD AND THEN HAND ALL BACK TO YOUR DRIVER.

How did Lisa know it was Green who holds the books? He was stunned at her audacity and cunning. *And what if I refuse to call him?* He toyed with the notion like a tantrum-driven teenager for some seconds, before a chilling sense of foreboding followed and he decided to follow the instructions.

'Gordon, is that you?'

'Who's that? Scott?' His friend croaked. The call was unexpected and had woken him.

'Yes, it's me. I'm sorry but I don't have time to explain in detail everything that has happened, I just need you to do something urgently for me..., okay?'

'Dear boy, what do you mean you don't have time? We thought you...,'

'Sorry to interrupt Gordon,' he shouted with an urgency that the man immediately understood. 'The books, I need you to deliver them to me in the morning, 10 am sharp.'

'Where?'

'I haven't been told yet but it's a location somewhere in central London. I'll advise you immediately the minute I know.'

'What are you talking about, Scott. Where are you and who wants these books?'

'Look Gordon, Lena's life is at risk. If I don't hand over those books, she and I will be assassinated.'

'You do know what you're asking don't you, Scott?'

'That's irrelevant.' His voice heightened. 'They know that you have them. Just do as I ask. Her life depends on you doing this one simple thing..., please, it's not a joke. I'll text you the co-ordinates once I have them.'

'Alright, Scott, I understand. I'll meet you wherever you want at 10 am.'

'And, Gordon, come alone and do not contact anyone regarding this..., you know who I mean without saying any names. These people holding Lena are deadly serious.'

'Are you with Lisa Taylor?'

'Gordon, I'm hanging up now. I will see you in a matter of hours as agreed, okay?

'Okay, but...,'

But Carty had already cut the line, and begun to dismantle the cell phone.

Gordon Green shook himself as he hauled his body out of bed, trying not to disturb his wife any further. Certain things in his life he could not share openly, even if she knew about Carty and Lena and the troubles they had shared. He quickly robed and moved downstairs anxiously ruminating over the call and what he needed to do. What if he was being watched or monitored at this moment? Padding into his wooden-panelled study, he flicked on a desk lamp and turned the key to the lock of a pedestal cabinet, pulling a drawer open. Its felt-lined interior contained nothing other than a nondescript cell phone that had been given to him by Whitehall Jack for an occurrence such as this. It carried a SIM that was not registered to anyone and therefore could not be listened or tracked. He fumbled to turn it on and waiting for the brand to light up, so that he could activate the SMS function and type a sentence.

Subject has returned under duress. Will meet him at 10 am in London at a location to be advised. Serious - lives at risk!

The air was still as he pushed the chair back and stared into the shadows where he and Carty had spent many an hour discussing unusual topics but never the books – that was reserved for the privacy of the steam room at the Iron Monger Row Baths. A tiny bleep responded, and he called the number shown.

'What is the situation?' Jack's eloquent voice quizzed, economically.

'Subject called from an anonymous number telling me that his woman is being held hostage.' Green whispered, careful not to mention any names. 'His handler wants me to deliver some of his books.'

'Books! What kind?'

'This is not the time to explain, suffice to say that what they contain means that I don't keep them at the house but at a safety deposit box. The problem is that it's not open – it's Sunday.'

'We can solve that very easily with a phone call, if you give my people the exact location and contacts.'

'I don't think we should do that.'

'So how do you want to play it?'

'I have to follow the instructions by turning up on time and hope that they will buy the story.'

'10 am you say...,where?'

'At a location to be advised.'

'Once you have it let me know immediately, and we'll put full covert surveillance in place. But when were you going to tell me about these books?'

'Never. I was leaving that for the subject to explain to you when he is ready. I haven't seen inside them but am aware of what they contain.'

'I can only guess what that is. Let's meet later in the day once you've met the subject. Take the phone and if there's even a whiff of danger, press the hash key three times.'

'I know.'

'Good. Just take care of yourself.'

The phone clicked off abruptly leaving Green alone with his thoughts in the pale light.

Where's Lisa Taylor in all this? he wondered as the prospect began to surface of what that morning would bring and how his friend Scott Carty would react when he turned up empty-handed.

Thirty Five

Siberia

Lubimov's mood was heavy as they sat in the canteen eating a breakfast of *kasha* and coffee.

'What did the Governor's people want?' Lena gently probed in her sweet yet direct way.

'To shut us down. The funds have been lacking for years, and we have survived purely through donations from wealthy business people who have benefited from my treatments over the years. It seems that his people have found this out and he's jealous.'

'But it doesn't make any sense to close the Institute if it's also providing an essential medical service locally.'

'That's what I also argued but it's fallen on deaf ears, and I fear that other forces want to remove me and my team and then reopen the cavern from its original entrance that was blasted shut over 25 years ago.'

'Why?' She asked, shaking her head at the comment and frowning.

'Probably to reinstall Ivan Yegorovich's original machine that operated in the cavern at that time. I have a suspicion that they must have learnt something from him during his torture and have realised that its positioning is crucial to its continual running for their transmutation business.' He faltered, removing the rimmed spectacles to pinch at his nose bridge. 'I just pray that he didn't yield and tell them about the *overunity* effect.'

'I doubt that he did, but what will happen to the machine that's there now?'

'That's the problem. Only you, Boris, Scott and I, know that it exists. It will have to be decommissioned and removed, secretly, but that will take many months and require a team to do so.'

Boris joined them at that moment, through the old metal-framed French windows that opened out onto the small gardens between the Institute's blocks.

'The guys will be landing in an hour or so, and we have a fine weather window for flying,' he announced.

'Good, we have time to talk a little more. Lena doesn't have many possessions to pack,' he said attempting a laugh but wavered with sight of her sad demeanour.

'What will happen to you all?' she asked

'I have no idea but I can guarantee that the machine you saw will never fall into anybody's hands, nor will I give any information to those seeking its secrets.'

'That is exactly what happened to Ivan Yegorovich and he had to run away into exile with my people,' Boris interjected, 'until somehow they found him.'

They chatted about their memories of her grandfather until the coffee had become cold and after a while, seeing Boris hovering at the door, she was prompted to go into the canteen's kitchen to collect a rucksack, packed with *pirogi* pies that were still warm to the touch. Then she heard the distinctive and not too distant clattering of rotors and froze to the spot, realising the imminence of events, her stomach now sent into sudden spasms as it dawned on her she might never see them or this place ever again.

Outside, there was time only for the briefest kisses of cheeks and a hug with the old scientist as Boris placed a palm over her head to gently drop her into a hunkered posture under the down-draft of the hovering copter. Stepping on its foot rail, the local held out his arms to carefully help her up. Then the craft incrementally rose, allowing her screamed farewells to the older man from the entry hatch. He solemnly stood there, a lone figure in his threading grey jacket, his hand held high.

Boris buckled her into one of the rear seats, his russet eyes conveying an absolute lack of fear in their mission.

'Sleep. It's going to be a while before we land to refuel,' he said, struggling against the drone. He winked and slid the side entry shut before slumping down alongside her. She wanted to surrender to his suggestion but first had to peek down at the array of buildings rapidly diminishing in size beneath them.

'Boris.' She pulled herself close to him so that she could speak directly into his ear. 'Why have you never seen the machine?'

'I don't need to..., or want to.'

'But aren't you just a little bit intrigued by it?'

'I was but I feel that it's not my story.'

Her blue eyes flexed wide with surprise. 'Not your story?'

'No, I work with nature and my dream is to relieve the collective damage humanity is causing to itself and this planet. It's the way of the shaman; even in these modern times there is a desperate need for our work. Some choose to sit in deep silence to influence the world, but my inner nature is to be actively engaged in changing things.'

'And the machine can't actively change things for the better?' she strained over the background noise.

'I'm not hopeful. Look at the way humanity treats nature, like children greedily seeking new toys, regardless of the sacrifice of this irreplaceable resource. We are just not evolved enough as a race to let it loose on the world and besides, there are many conventional technologies that can shift us from the wasteful way we consume energy and exacerbate climate change, but that's only one aspect of the problem. Oceans are under threat from pollution and plastics that are dumped into them and which have now entered the food chain. Here in Russia we also see the looming threat from information technology becoming sentient. Scott may know that the father of the computer, Alan Turing, stated that a computer would deserve to be called intelligent if it could deceive a human into believing that it was human – that is a major threat to life itself.' He glanced askance at her, pulling himself up using the cabin's handgrip, his soft mongoloid features seeming to harden as he patted her leg. 'But don't let this weigh on you. There are many of us working on the energetic level to avert a crisis and we trust that the spirit of humanity will be with us. Get some rest.'

He bounded forward and glided down onto the co-pilot's chair, pulling on the headgear as his friend gave him the thumbs up. The unchanging scenery below drew Lena's attention, a green carpet undulating to the horizon, punctured occasionally by granite bluffs poking their jagged edges free to nest eagles and crows. Its pleasant monotony finally put her into slumber, which was only temporarily broken by the refuelling stop, and then they were on their way again.

A slight nudge brought her round.

'We're coming into land.'

'Novossibrisk?'

'Yes, nearby, at an old military landing strip. My friends are waiting for us.'

Her fleeting smile lit up her otherwise pallid appearance as she stretched out her arms and legs and rapidly took in the approaching concentration of settlements around the city in the distance. She hadn't been there since her early teenage years when she would visit her grandparents at Academgoradok, the former Soviet centre of excellence in the sciences nearby, and then spend the short summer with them in the taiga, at their privileged *dacha*. Memories of happy innocent times swamped her; travelling on the train alone with packed food and being swept into her protective grandmother's arms as she arrived in the city. But in them she recognised that Ivan Yegorovich was, by that time, well into his research and soon to be exiled for his extraordinary claims, to *Sphinx*. Then her summers took on a different hue, travelling the extra 1,500 kilometres to Irkutsk to be collected by undercover security men and taken up the lake on a private boat. The location was remote and less pleasant, but she had grown to love Baikal's vast uniqueness and the small, close knit team around her grandfather, including the Lubimovs, senior and junior, and Boris, then a young ranger who was quietly enamoured by her clear-faced beauty.

'Hold on!' the Buryat shouted. The chopper was blown by a sharp cross wind as it hovered 60 feet above the ground and she gasped, fearful that after all this way they might be in danger of losing their lives in a crash landing. The pilot stabilised the craft and took them down swiftly, onto the disused strip, alongside the skeletons of Cold War military jets.

'Wow!' she sighed loudly. The Buryat, was already out of his seat and scoping the arena in front of them, pointing at the UAZ rapidly approaching them. Based on the same chassis as the famed Soviet GAZ jeep of WWII, it had become the loved utility vehicle of choice, capable of driving off road practically anywhere, even in low rivers. Boris' aspirated grin spoke of his relief as he turned to her.

'Yulia is on the way.'

Thirty Six

London

Gordon Green couldn't remember the last time he had visited the Landmark Hotel but was familiar with it being one of London's grandest Victorian train terminal hotels and that it had been remodelled and reopened in the 1980s. He had texted Jack just 20 minutes before his arrival, immediately after Carty's notification of the meet's location and pacing through its marbled entrance in his polished brogues, he fingered the phone in his pocket, hoping that it wouldn't be needed. Natural light was pouring down from the atrium roof over the courtyard onto a plethora of plants and flora, so arranged to make for discreet areas in which to meet clients or a lover. He wondered if it was Carty's choice or his oppressors' as he glanced at the waiters and odd clientele milling about, wondering exactly who was in the pay of Jack's people and who were the foreigners watching their meet.

As he neared the reception he clocked Carty sitting in the easy chairs. *This isn't going to be easy,* he muttered inwardly. Carty stood, hesitantly smiling through his stubble-heavy mien, his blue eyes dull and lacking the sparkle that portrayed his normally youthful soul. He thrust out a hand; Green reciprocated as they nervously locked stares and then both met shoulders in an attempt to re-bond, each placing an arm around the other.

'Thanks for coming.'

'Don't mention it. How are you?'

'I could be better,' Carty replied, noticing that the older man's hands were empty. 'Did you bring the books?'

Green placed both hands on his friend's shoulders. 'I wanted to, but the safety deposit box is locked over the weekend.'

'Shit! What am I going to do?' he blurted, his fatigued mind spinning with a myriad of scenarios. 'They'll kill Lena.'

'I'm sure they won't, Scott. They want those books so badly that they can wait another day.'

'But I can't believe...,'

The older man's squeezing of his upper biceps and slightest wink had stopped Carty mid-sentence. He understood that Jack had been engaged and that this episode had now stepped into a whole new territory where the stakes were all or nothing. In their last meeting at the Baths, the Whitehall man had implied his suspicion that there was more behind this technology, more than Carty had told him. He simply couldn't allow that to be handed over to a foreign agency regardless of the cost. A mounting anger bit into Carty as his cheeks grew florid masking the dull, exhausted pallor of emotional stress. He wanted to scream bitterly at Green for betrayal of his trust but then grasped that he might have done the very same thing, if in his shoes.

'I suggest that you call the people who have put you in this predicament and tell explain why it was impossible for me to bring the books. I'll collect them first thing tomorrow morning and deliver them to you at a location of their choice.'

'But I can't call them. I don't have a phone or a contact number.'

'Scott,' he uttered, holding his friend's gaze. 'Once I leave here without having handed anything over you're going to be contacted. Are you staying at the hotel?'

'Yes.'

'Then all you need to do is sit and wait. Have courage, and we will see this thing through so that Lena is safely returned. You have my word and another's.' He winked again. 'Do you have any funds?'

'Nothing.' He picked nervously at his nails. 'But Lisa's people have paid for a room.'

'I thought she was behind this. Relax and sleep as much as you can. You look like you need to but whatever you do don't leave the hotel,' he said, with a limp smile.

Carty slowly slipped back down into the seat, watching his friend, Green, awkwardly pace back out into the summer sun and the morning traffic chaos on Marylebone Road.

'Excuse me sir, Mr Carty?'

He glanced up blearily at a smoothly-suited Mediterranean-looking man carrying a hotel name tag on his lapel, who was offering him a cell phone. 'I was asked to hand this to you.'

'By whom?'

'It was apparently left by the person who pre-booked your room yesterday.'

'Did they pay with a credit card?' he sleuthed, accepting the phone.

'I wasn't on duty but I can check it, if you wish me to.'

'Yes, if you wouldn't mind.' He assumed it was the driver but wanted to know, just in case Lisa had slipped up.

The man didn't return, and he guessed it was a ploy, leaving him to stay in his room and sleep. He toyed with the cell phone switching it on and off and replacing the SIM card, but despite his attempts the device was not allowing him to make any calls.

Lying on the bed he tried to calm his racing mind but couldn't and decided to find solace in the mini-bar, downing several of the small spirits before stretching out again. The effect of the liquor quickly numbed his senses, causing the weariness to overcome him.

He shook his legs violently and woke up, confused that the Buryat was silently looming there in the room.

'What is it, Boris?'

The figure remained silent, his eyes boring into Carty's as all around, the familiar voice of Ludmilla Anatolivna sounded once again, reminding him that he was not alone. The Englishman then understood that his suspicions were being confirmed; his old friend and the local woman were of the same tradition and with that recognition, Boris' smiling features rapidly started to fade away into nothingness and the wall's bland backdrop sprung into life, displaying a graphic scene that gripped Carty once more. The earth was still held by the serpent, writhing madly within its own coils, but they were rapidly unravelling from around the planet's delicate circumference, repelled it would appear by an invisible force. Then he felt his mouth gape at the sight. In the midst of its thrashing, wild fury the beast seemed to be devouring its own tail. In that instant, a flash of realisation told Carty that soon it would consume itself completely.

He was woken by a Turkish rap song, the phone's ring tone.

'Hello.'

'Scott. I hear that your Mr Green has let you down badly.' Lisa's delectably galling tone was pitched to exact anguish.

'He hasn't exactly.'

'What do you mean? Of course he has, and that has put your lovely Lena's life in jeopardy.'

'Lisa, look!' Carty blurted. 'Green couldn't get access to a safe deposit box where the documents are stored because it's Sunday. It's not his fault.'

'That's a wonderful excuse, Scott, and totally unbelievable, but we will give him one last chance; then we will act. You need to understand that if we press the Russians harder, I'm sure we will have the technology anyway. It's just a matter of time. But I would prefer to have it now. However, if you and Green fail me, I'm not sentimental...,do you understand me, Scott?'

I understand you only too well.

'Do you understand me?!' she pressed, infuriated by his silence.

'Of course, Lisa,' he replied gently, the vision of the dragon consuming itself, still with him. 'I don't want this to end badly and I believe that somehow, you will succeed in your plans to change the world for the better, with or without me.' Humouring her was his only tool.

'Good boy,' she purred. 'Someone will be in contact with you in the morning to advise where to meet and remember any tiny deviance from the instructions and the deal is off. You know what that means.'

The line went dead.

I only hope that Green and Jack know what they're doing. The worry hovered as he tried to shake the dream's images but deep down he knew they were relevant, that the serpent's intent on all-consuming power would end up consuming itself. It gave him succour that possibly, forces beyond his comprehension were hinting at the outcome, if he could just hold on.

A sharp knock startled him. He was in two minds whether to answer it but then understood he must. It was the same man who had approached him hours earlier, obviously in the dual employ of the hotel and Lisa.

'The phone please, sir, if you will.' He stepped slightly forward into the room and held out a tray with a tea cloth folded neatly upon it, forcing Carty back to the night stand to retrieve it and place it as requested. The figure routinely folded the cloth over it and, thanking him strolled effortlessly out and down the corridor.

Thirty Seven

'I'm not happy about this at all, Gordon. You've been keeping this information from me all this time,' Jack uttered, coolly.

Green balked. 'It wasn't my place to divulge it to you. That responsibility lies with Scott Carty.'

'But even when I declared that our government boffins had begun to suspect that low energy nuclear reactions were being produced by that machine, both of you decided to remain silent about these books and the blueprints they contain.' He frowned as he fingered the bridge of his heavy framed glasses.

'As I said, Jack, that was Scott's choice and I gave him my word. Anyway, I have no knowledge of what is in those books.'

'You've never opened them out of curiosity?'

'Never!'

'Well, we would like to before you hand them over, Gordon.'

'We can't. They're locked away in a security deposit vault.' His ruddy face was defiant.

'And as I said, that's easily solved. Now, I'm afraid that I'm calling rank on you. This is strategic information of significant importance to the State. You must understand that.'

'I do.'

'So, let's have it, Gordon. The location and the security pass. We need to take a look at them tonight.'

'I was afraid you'd say that.' A vein pulsed beneath his silver temple as he slipped a hand inside the old golfing jacket and then cast the key card across Jack's desk.

'And where exactly is the location?' the man quizzed, his black shining hair already lowered as he punched in a number on the landline phone. Within seconds he was firmly placing instructions for a team to immediately pick up Green's pass, go to the address and then await orders. He then advised his Number 2 to find the managing director of the security company warning that, regardless of it being a Sunday, it was a government matter of the utmost urgency, and refusal would be met with penalties. 'Find out where he or she lives and send a car there. Got it? Good!'

He looked back up maintaining his severe countenance as he characteristically wiped a hand over his locks and down to his nape. 'Now, Gordon, we have to think through your actions tomorrow and try to second guess what these lunatics are up to.'

'I'm waiting for Scott to give me instructions on where to meet.'

'Yes, but regardless of where they agree to meet, they will change the plans last minute, otherwise they risk a prearranged stake-out and exposure. We're having The Landmark Hotel monitored now.'

'How are your people doing that?'

'Sorry, can't tell you that, but it appears that Scott has been receiving instructions on a phone that's been provided to him by a member of the hotel staff. My people can't act and pull that person in as it will blow the game, but they will try to monitor the phone to get a trace on who is calling and giving Carty these instructions.'

Green's large face seemed to harden. 'Is Lisa Taylor behind this?'

'Of course, she has been from day one with her uncle. That ruse to change directions mid-flight into Urumqi was the start of a plan to ensnare Carty and blackmail him.' His eyes rolled. 'He really should have learnt his lessons by now!'

'It wasn't obvious to him that he was being tricked.'

'It never is. Remember D'albo's shenanigans?'

He grinned soberly. 'How could anyone forget?'

'By the way, there is something I need to tell you about D'albo, rumours that we recently heard, but it can wait for another day.'

Green's eyes grew in size at the blithe statement, wanting answers but Jack raised his thin hand. 'Not now, Gordon, there's too much to focus on. Now, where was I?' he questioned, as the same hand then pulled at his glasses as his other flourished a hanky from a breast pocket.

'Talking about Scott being led into a trap by Lisa Taylor,' Green rejoined.

'Yes, and hence the ruse to have Lena fly into Dubai and then into Russia. We don't know how well Lisa is linked to Koshechenko's mob but it's obvious that they are working together to get their hands on the technology's blueprints.'

'But Kosechenko already has the technology and it's transmuting waste,' he stated frowning as he gently shook his grey, shorn head.

'And that's the issue we don't yet understand. All our leads have dried up, but what we do know is that the Chinese have unofficially banned the export of any spent waste. From the scant information available, we know that uncle Ong, was heavily involved in that business, and we are guessing there's been a power struggle to take control of it.'

'And Ong's being able to solve Sole Carbon's problems in Xinjiang?'

'That was the bait to trap Scott. What worries me now, though, is have Kosechenko and Ong found out about *overunity*?'

'Even if they did, what would they plan to do with it?'

'You tell me. I thought it had the ability to generate a new form of emission-free power that wasn't reliant on the existing framework,' he said sardonically. 'It's a power game of immeasurable dimensions and may turn the world on its head.'

'That is what I told Carty. I felt it was a few hundred years premature, and if unleashed, would be pyrrhic, fracturing the existing economic paradigm and sending it into a downward spin that might take a generation to recover from, regardless of its utopian ideals. I reminded him that there are other interim and benign energy technologies just waiting to be deployed that could achieve the same sustainable future for everyone. They just require a fraction of the level of focus and finance that the nuclear industry has benefited from in the post-war years.'

'I tend to agree with you, but the urgency now is that there are others who don't care for our form of democracy, who would relish the thought of removing the hegemony of fossil fuel economies overnight. That's why it's so important that we see what's in those books.'

Green's stare affirmed his friend's summing up, but his expression conveyed something else.

'You know, Jack, the Russians who developed the machine were worried about a much greater threat to civilisation, in general.'

'Really? And what was that?'

'You mean what is it..., the threat from a volatile sun..., a super solar flare such as the one that enveloped the planet in the 1850s, the so-called Carrington Event. Its impact with the atmosphere lit up the skies for many months and the ground induced electric currents it caused, created havoc with the simple telegraph systems and ships' compasses of the day. If a similar sized flare impacted the earth nowadays then those same currents would blow most of the global grid infrastructure resulting in months without power. Chaos and a loss of life on an unprecedented scale would result until grids could be rebuilt, which might take many months. Imagine if basic heating and light, fresh water, sewage-pumping, refrigeration, the internet, to name just some – all the things we are totally dependent on day to day, and which define our modern world...,imagine them stopping in an instant. These men Carty met in Siberia believe that when it does occur again, and it will, then *overunity* might have a chance to be implemented in a new energy paradigm.'

'Sounds like science fiction to me.'

'But it's not, the threat is very real. You should check it with your analysts, I'm sure they know all about it.'

'Alright, I will, but that doesn't solve our immediate problem.'

'Getting Lena back?'

Jack finished off cleaning the glasses and replaced them, his now magnified eyes glaring impassively back. 'Not really, Gordon. Unfortunately, our aim is not to let those books get into the hands of Lisa and her people. We must stop them at all costs.'

'You mean even if Lena's life is at risk.'

‘I do.’

‘Jack, you can’t be serious. You were responsible for getting her back safely to the UK and from the grip of Kosechenko.’

‘That’s why I’m taking no chances and pulling out all the stops. We’ll have full back up at all times and if necessary, we’ll take Lisa and force her to tell us where Lena is.’

‘And if you can’t achieve that or if in the event she’s captured or killed, she’s given instructions for Lena to be finished off?’

‘That’s a chance we have to take, Gordon. The stakes are too high. God forbid it, but there may be a chance that Lena has already been eliminated.’

Green drilled his friend with a stare of abject contempt. He had always known where the man’s loyalties lay and hadn’t ever questioned them but hoped that an appeal to his emotions might change the strategy. It hadn’t and now Green understood that there was only one avenue open to him. He would sit in quiet contemplation and ask the unconscious for help.

Thirty Eight

Carty had received another phone with an early morning knock at his hotel door. He had been going stir crazy, spending the night sitting in the room or anxiously wandering around the hotel's impressive glazed atrium courtyard, unable to eat or sleep through the pressure of nerves and the nagging pains of his injuries.

The room's landline trilled.

'Morning, Scott.' It was Green. 'I have the package and will wait for you downstairs by reception.'

As he replaced the receiver, a retching sensation had him dashing into the bathroom, vomiting bile, his eyes streaming with the reaction of his body to what he was experiencing and about to go through. He cleaned his face with a damp flannel and gazed at his reflection in the mirror struggling to identify the image, believing that the specks of grey in his chestnut hair and washed-out complexion were a bizarre construct that merely masked the man he thought he knew. His bloodshot eyes, though, gave the game away; the two light-blue star gates to his soul were now looking back at him with a calmer countenance that he recognised. *Silence is the key to action.* He took courage and sucked in air, expanding his chest and taking his mind to his practice, the silent standing that Boris had taught him in the taiga. In it, he instinctively knew that he had to live in the moment and act with the flow of events, not try to predict the outcome and fret about things that may never occur.

'Hi, Gordon,' he calmly stated as he approached his friend, his eyes glancing to the man's satchel and guessing that he had brought the items. Green reached out his hand, but before he could speak, the small cell Carty had been given rang on cue.

'Do you have the books yet?'

As if she doesn't know that!

'Yes, they're just being handed to me,' he answered.

'Check that you haven't been given some duds, please.'

Carty looked sheepishly at his friend. 'Sorry, Gordon, I'm being asked to check the contents.' He pointed. 'Do you mind?'

'Of course not,' Green snorted and handed the weighty bag to him.

Carty sat and held it between his shins as he flipped open the straps and felt inside. There they were, the two tomes that he and Lena had first perused after their escape from Russia, three years before. He glanced up to see Green casually scoping out the surrounds.

I'm sure Jack's people are here watching this.

'They're all in place as I expected,' Carty replied to a waiting Lisa.

'I want you to hand this phone back to the passing waiter, but before you do please tell your friend, Mr Green, that if any of his friends attempt to detain the man or take the phone, then the deal is off, but I will have the books. Do I make myself clear?'

'Crystal clear.'

'Now, move to the back lobby. A cab will pick you up outside. Just follow the instructions and everything will work out just as we agreed. Scott, don't forget that we have something special: we both share the same ideals and hopes for this planet. Let me, at least, achieve those aspirations.' The words echoed around his head as she hung up and the same attendant moved in with his tray to collect the cell. He then signalled for Carty to follow him outside with a flourish of an arm.

'I guess this is it,' he stated.

'Don't worry, Scott. This isn't over yet,' Green retorted, pulling the slightest of winks.

Carty followed the man's rapid pace through the courtyard, to the hotel's back entrance where a cab was waiting as advised. The attendant reached for the door to open it for him and as he poked his head inside first, to check it, he found the gruff face of a London taxi driver, staring back at him over a shoulder. 'You getting in, then?' he barked.

Carty did so, and the cab took off, the door slamming shut with its momentum, forcing him to crane back to catch Gordon Green's image through the back window, approaching the attendant on the taxi rank. The man, though, had hurriedly dismantled the phone and was dropping its contents down through a drain's grate.

'Any idea where we're going?' Carty quizzed.

'No idea yet, mate. I'm waiting for a call on this phone I've been given.'

Here we go again!

'They paying you well?'

'Handsomely.'

'What if I told you that they're criminals sought by the police?'

'Sorry, mate, I've been told to ignore anything you might say and just drive you to the destination they tell me to.'

Carty stifled a sarcastic splutter and looked behind again, noticing a dark blue Audi racing up to slow behind them.

I wonder?

As the lights went amber-red, the cab flicked on its left indicator and pulled round on to the Marylebone Road, just managing to slip through the next set of traffic lights as they changed to amber, to swing left again onto Great Central Street, alongside the hotel. Carty was still glancing back watching the Audi as it missed the timing of the lights and pulled to a halt, as they switched to red. The cabbie slowed the taxi and swung another left so that they were back where they started, in the drive-through outside the hotel. Neither Green nor the assistant were there, and the cab simply sped along, past the others waiting in rank, to turn left down Harewood Avenue and back down to the Marylebone Road, once again. It was clearly a ruse to throw off any tail, but as the traffic lights turned green, they pulled right across the road into the filter lane to turn right, down Upper Montague Street. Carty was still scoping the cars behind, noting that the blue Audi was nowhere to be seen. *Just a coincidence?* he thought as the driver's new phone rang, shrilly.

'Hello..., yes, love, got it!'

'So, any clues as to where we going?' Carty probed anxiously.

'Sorry, mate, you couldn't pay me what they're paying, so I suggest you sit back and shut it!'

The vernacular took him by surprise and he understood that this wasn't a regular cabbie but a criminal posing as one. He took the cue and sank into the threading leather.

The route was circuitous, weaving back on itself several times, but Carty guessed that despite this, there would be a helicopter somewhere overhead, keeping track of their moves and location. *But if I know that, then so does Lisa..., so what's her end game? How is she going to collect the books and then escape the country?* Then a worrying concern brought his focus back to Lena and how she was coping with the abduction. He had no idea where she was or how she was being treated but he had experienced her mental strength first-hand and that fortified him. The thought of her ordeal at the hands of a jealous narcissist such as Lisa, who had her sights on removing any lover of Carty's, was a terrifying notion and one he decided to park along with the possibility that Lena might be already dead. He had to focus on the now, on charming Lisa and he had little idea yet how he was going to do that.

The cab was now in The Strand, having briefly negotiated the many cyclists on Trafalgar Square taking their lives in their hands, as they navigated its circus. The phone rang again and answering it, the cabbie passed it back to Carty.

'You're almost there. When the cab stops, do exactly what my waiting colleague tells you and do it as rapidly as possible.' Lisa barked and then hung up as the cab shot down through several traffic lights and then instantly pulled a right onto Savoy Court., the only road in London where cars drive on the right-hand side of the road, a tradition borne in the days of horse and carriage, dropping off passengers. Carty knew the place well, having been to countless business functions at the world class hotel as well as taking Lena, and in the past, Diane, to its theatre.

'This is where you and I leave each other, mate. No need to pay,' the cabbie announced, chortling as he slowed in front of the uniformed attendant. The door was pulled rapidly open, though by another bearded man who had appeared from nowhere and grabbed Carty's arm to pull him out.

'This way,' the stranger whispered, leaving Carty little chance to catch the eye of the doorman as he was rushed through the revolving entrance and then down the staircase to the lower levels, where the fellow barged through a set of double doors leading into a back corridor, used by the semi-invisible staff providing its renowned service. *He can't be a member of staff but must be in Lisa's pay, just like the other guy at The Landmark,* Carty conjectured, wondering how they got away with it. *Money talks, as always.*

They paced past a number of the employees and then through another set of doors to find themselves at the rear entrance, on the lower level to the Embankment. The rear gate to a waiting Mercedes Benz V350 was already open and its driver standing alongside, carrying a blanket under which he the hidden nozzle of a pistol was pointing directly at Carty.

'Get in and lay down,' the man growled in an accented deep voice as Carty was marched a few steps forward and bundled straight into the back of the vehicle. The blanket was then thrown across him. 'Remain still and hidden until I say otherwise.'

Why haven't they simply taken the books from me? He was confused, *maybe Lisa wants to enjoy the thrill of taking them personally,* he reasoned clutching the satchel tightly, safe in his assumption that she wouldn't have trusted such valuable assets in the hands of mere hired hands.

Then, the foreign chatter of a family pulling themselves up into the vehicle with an assortment of luggage concerned him. *Do they know I'm here?* The notion prompted him as the driver loaded one of their suitcases next to his head. Then the doors slammed, and it started up. To all intents and purposes, it appeared to be a hired taxi, collecting tourists from the hotel to take them to the airport. *Is that possibly where we're going? To the airport, to meet Lisa's corporate jet so that she can fly out immediately?* But he knew that Jack would have already known that, and all airports would be on high alert. *I hope to God they don't try to stop her.* A sudden wave of sheer hopelessness washed over him. If they did try, Lena's life would be forfeit; he could only trust that Jack and Gordon Green already understood this. The kid passengers' laughter threw him, reminding him of his own son James and how he had missed him too, in these last few days. Then he wondered how these poor children would feel knowing there was a hostage hidden in the back of the vehicle but as he tuned in and listened more distinctly, he caught odd words that he thought he recognised and slowly it dawned on him that this family was speaking the distinctive Uyghur that he had heard from the market in Turpan. A worrying perception came to him. *They might even be members of Lisa's family – she could trust them.*

He remained motionless as the vehicle stopped and started repeatedly for what seemed like half an hour, before the engine picked up a fast, constant speed. *We must be on a motorway,* he gleaned. But it didn't last for long, and very shortly, they had slowed again before coming to a halt and the passengers disembarked. After a short pause, the blanket was stripped away and he was hauled out by two unshaven thugs. He blinked several times, remaining silent but locking into his mind's eye where he now was, the ground level car park of a building. Walking towards them was what appeared to be a security guard, hurriedly beckoning them as Carty wistfully thought he heard the faint sound of a helicopter, somewhere overhead. His captors were ruffians who smelt rank and allowed him no luxury, manhandling him straight along the stained concrete wall of the parking lot and through a set of plastic strip curtains to an empty loading bay, following their guide. It wasn't an industrial location but some small commercial centre, by the sound of trucks and the forklift machinery he glimpsed as he swung a look behind him, causing his face to be slapped hard to remind him these men meant business. Then the guide swiftly ushered him through a narrow and unrendered passageway that could barely take two of them abreast. Beyond its strip-lit confines, about 100 paces ahead, he gleaned that they were entering the working heart of this small complex. The guard had already reached the tight space, a central point with several other much wider passageways branching out from it, where he was waiting with his hand holding open the stainless steel doors of a service lift. Its interior was battered and scarred from the continuous movement of goods and components. Carty scanned the men's bizarre visages reflected back in the dull steel encasement wall as it jerked from floor to floor. The overwhelming rancidity of unwashed body odour exacerbated in the close confines, blended with industrial volatiles, created a cocktail that forced a similar retching sensation to the one he had experienced that morning. *When is this going to end?* Sheer exhaustion had now begun to sap his legs and his jangled mind. With an abrupt clunk the lift stopped and stepping out, he recognised the paraphernalia of a huge plant room, filled with looped air-conditioning ducting and hydraulic machinery, all part of the running of a large concern below them. Then a veil of Chypre pricked his nose and he spun about, holding on to the satchel.

'Well, Scott. It's lovely to see you again.'

For a moment her vision was lovely until his tired mind recalled the angst of the last few days. She flourished her hand for his escorts to back off, allowing her two Mongolians to fill the space.

'I hope it's all been worth it, Lisa.' His sarcasm seemed wasted on her as she glided up to him and shook her hair out so that it flailed his face. Her gaze wandered up and down his loosened physique for a moment before her expression became stern.

'Have you brought them?'

'Yes, here,' he said presenting the worn satchel.

She clicked her fingers and one of the Mongolians took the carrier from Carty's shoulder while the other dropped a small black industrial briefcase on the floor and twirled its combinations into place, momentarily checking before flipping its lid open. Its dark foam interior was precisely hollowed out to house a strange pistol shaped apparatus.

Meanwhile the other of Lisa's manservants had taken the unusual weight of the books in his trunk-like forearms and she was already examining one of them, flipping pages and nodding her head.

'Hmmm, very interesting,' she uttered as he watched on, suspended. 'They look authentic enough, although, I can't read Cyrillic that well. You're a very dark horse, Mr Carty, hiding these away from the world and trying to fool us with that buff English persona of yours.'

'I haven't tried that hard!'

'We'll see,' she remarked waving her hands for her other man to sweep the first tome carefully with the contraption. A loud bleep registered over its speaker as he centred it on the book's spine. Her green eyes narrowed. 'What's this? Are your friends planning to catch me?' she hissed as the tiny tracking device was pulled from the binding and passed to her. She held the mechanism up, in her polished nails in front of the Englishman's face. *Shit, Jack's people must have planted that.*

'Any more, I wonder?'

'Lisa, really, I had no idea that that was placed in there. I haven't seen these books for some years. They've been locked away and only handed to me this morning, in this satchel, which has been strapped shut all the time.'

'Don't worry, Scott. I'm not blaming you but I'm just wondering who would have done such a thing..., Mr Green perhaps? I very much doubt it.'

A wave of panic gripped his expression. 'Lisa, please don't let this spoil the deal.'

'Ah,' a cruel grin now reappeared, 'that depends on my leaving without being hassled by Mr Green's friends.'

'No one is going to hassle you. He's well aware of what is at stake and has promised me that nothing will hinder your passage.'

'Oh..., but what's this?' she cackled, as the machine's whine rose to a crescendo, passing over the other book's spine. 'Is there another?!' Within seconds she had a further tracker between her fingers and was giving Carty a look of smug disdain as she gently shook her head. She gave a sideways nod to the two men and one gripped his arms, tersely manhandling him into a fixed position so that the other could sweep him with the device. He slowly passed it over his collar and down one side of his body, up his legs into his crotch and then down the other side leg, following up the outside and across his jacket. Then came the distinctive loud beep and the brute slowed its passage further, honing in on his jacket's outside pocket and then thrusting his hand in to pull out a similar looking tracker to the other two. He held it up.

'Ha ha!' Her freckled nose scrunched with mock laughter. 'I wonder who put that in there?'

Carty shrugged, holding his hands up, his eyes registering exasperation as the examination continued.

'So now that we've cleaned you we can get on with our business,' she said, the corners of her mouth dropping, as she silently held out her palm to one of her henchmen. Her eyes seemed troubled, and he felt in her, a wave of sadness, a plea for help to be released from the dark spells that flooded her soul and fuelled her mad persona. A silenced pistol was placed into her delicate hand and she gripped it, turning to position the barrel against Carty's cheek and stroking its hard gunmetal up and down and then across his mouth, puckering his lips. The action froze him to the spot, petrified as a ridge of heat, building from his belly, shot out into his palms covering them in a patina of sweat. He was now fully aware that this woman was possessed and there was no reasoning with her.

'Such a shame..., you and I, we could have been a perfect match..., we are a perfect match, but you let that Russian bitch spoil it all.' Her eyes had glazed over as he clocked them. 'She could have gone free you know.' She smiled vacantly. 'All you had to do was genuinely show that you wanted me, and I would have given you everything.'

'Everything?' Carty uttered in muted defiance as his mind recalled the emotion of facing death once again and he prepared to face her down. The minder sensed it and forced out an arm to hold him back. 'Lisa, you can do what you want with me but when you're alone at night and that serpent demon visits you, sucking at your soul, think of the little girl that has been lost to it. Remember what it's like to be powerless and at the mercy of a force you cannot contain. The more you run from it, the more it will consume you and then the greater the loss of that little girl will be, which will, inevitably force her to end it all. And then where will your dream of creating Green Eye be?'

Her face froze and she pulled the gun away. 'Thank you for those beautiful lines, Mr Carty. Now, please kneel down.'

He did, slowly bending to place his weight on one knee then the other. She ran her hand behind his skull and played with his locks, pulling at them and forcing his face into her crotch as she threw her head back skyward, letting out an inaudible wail. Tear-stained, she collected herself and placed a palm on his crown as an axis point around which she paced in her stilettoes, until she stood behind him. Then she leant and whispered.

'Why are you so wholesome, so good?'

He shrugged.

'For being these things, I will release your Lena.'

Then she pushed the silencer barrel into his skull. 'Goodbye, Scott Carty.'

His eyes squeezed in readiness. Her trigger finger hovered and with one sweet move, she pulled the gun away and then violently swung it back down again, with the full momentum of her small frame, to deliver a blow to his nape its handle. Carty's head slumped and then he crashed forward, out cold.

* * * *

Lisa wasted no time in having her men lock Carty's unconscious body into a utility room stacked with large tubs of cleaning fluids. *He might die from the off-gassing if he's not found soon,* the thought pricked her guilt. *But finally, I have them*! she gloated, stroking the tomes covers and then hugging their weight in her slender arms, her mind meandering along her pre-prepared strategy for global change, starting in Xinjiang. The two hulks stood primed for instructions as they watched her theatre. Then she shook her head and bent to place the books in a small wheelie suitcase, zipping it back up and locking the tabs into the combination lock. One passed her a large clear bag, full of effects. She stripped off, pulled on a pair of worn baggy jeans, old trainers and a blonde wig, taking a few moments to change her lip gloss colour and then donned a pair of regular sunglasses.

'Here, take this,' she instructed, in dialect, handing Green's leather satchel to one of them as she dropped a tracking device inside. He took it, placing it on the floor and inserting two large dictionaries inside, giving it the same effective weight as the books. 'And this.' She passed him the bag now filled with her clothes. 'Go, as fast as you can!' she barked and instantly his bulky mass was making for the elevator. She turned to the other, handing him the two remaining trackers.

'Here, put these in your pocket and do as instructed.'

That Mr Green is very cunning, but he's fallen foul of me. The tracking devices had not been unexpected; she'd simply had to adjust her strategy for this outcome when Carty hadn't shown up with the books the morning before. Now she had to move quickly, tracing her pre-planned route down some fire stairs, giggling quietly to herself at a vision of the confused mess anyone tracking them was about to encounter in the midst of one of London's busiest out-of-town shopping centres. At the bottom of the last flight, she pushed open a fire door that had been previously deactivated for a small fee and joined the main staircase and a stream of ladies heading for the cloakroom. But she continued straight on to the main exit and the taxi rank, waving at a moderately old jeep that was hovering, timed perfectly to her texted instructions. She pulled open the rear tailgate and stowed her own bag before jumping into the passenger's side and pecking the swarthy-looking driver on the cheek. It was all theatre again, for the centre's camera surveillance system when, no doubt, they would be monitored, at some later point, to understand how she had vanished.

Thirty Nine

Novossibirsk, Siberia

Yulia shook out her shaggy, peroxide-blonde hair, unembarrassed by its darkening roots, as the two women shook hands, eyeing each other reservedly, both aware of the other's connection with Scott Carty.

'You're not leaving now, are you?' Lena asked Boris as she caught his diffident smile, the chopper's rotors droning nearby; they hadn't stopped.

'Yulia will take you on to the UK contacts in the city.'

Shorter than Lena and much stockier, the local woman commanded the space and the situation. 'Come, Lena,' she uttered, her frothy nature now shining through as she began to understand the woman's distressed state from the purple bruising around her face. 'We have a short journey to make and another day before a new passport will be ready. There is also someone who wants to meet you.'

'Who?' Lena resisted, nervously shooting a double-take at Boris.

'It's fine,' he said holding her shoulder. 'Yulia is like a sister. She'll take as good care of you as she did when she helped Scott.'

'We've already contacted a senior member of the British Embassy in Moscow to advise him of your predicament. He flew in last night and is waiting for you,' Yulia advised.

'But he could be anybody pretending to be an official,' Lena uttered, well aware of the games the authorities could play to ensnare her.

'That's unlikely.' The woman flexed her mousey brows. 'My contacts know exactly who he is and his excuse for being here is to meet with the Mayor of the City to discuss inward investment from British companies. It's something he's been working on for the last year, in a few regions of Siberia and he is very well connected. As soon as you've met with him, he will set the wheels in motion to get you out of the county.'

'So, you're going to be safe from here on but please do not try to contact Scott or anyone else for that matter!' Boris added. 'It may jeopardise your escape home.'

Lena shrugged. 'How can I? I don't have a phone!'

'I'm just making the point.' His hand squeezed her shoulder to reinforce it.

The local woman then reached out to the Buryat, grasping him around the neck and then fondling his copper cheeks passionately as she pecked his lips. He reddened, his flat features rounding into a smile, pulling her hips close to his before nodding sideways, signalling that she should leave. Lena understood that these two had shared a close relationship that wasn't quite over, and it meant that she would not betray Boris or her.

'So, shall we go then?' Yulia held out a hand to Lena.

Boris gently hugged his charge. 'Take care and do everything Yulia tells you to.'

Then he spun around and began trotting back in a low run, springing back into the hatch to sit with his legs overhanging the craft as it slowly rose. They waved frantically and he reciprocated by blowing kisses back at them.

It was now early afternoon and the air was sticky as Yulia stripped off her fleece to reveal her toned arms and the outline of a flat stomach.

'Not very far to go from here,' she articulated, casually opening the vehicle's passenger door and ushering Lena up into the seat.

'How are you feeling, physically?' she asked putting the vehicle into gear and slowly moving off, back across the strip.

'I've felt better.' Lena attempted a smile, winding down the window for fresh air. Yulia's musty odour was overwhelming. 'Thank you for helping me.' She removed the tired combat jacket to reveal her lean frame beneath the light blouse.

'It's a pleasure,' she bounced back. 'I would do anything for Boris and Scott.'

'Yes, I heard all about how you smuggled him into Kazakhstan. It must have been terribly fraught.' She turned to catch the local looking her up and down and she self-consciously looked away, concerned that her naturally stunning figure would cause an unconscious jealousy. She had forgotten about her looks in all the mayhem.

'I can see you've been beaten up pretty badly. Do you know who did it?'

'I was betrayed by someone..., a man.'

'Men, eh? Can't ever trust them..., with the exception of Boris and Scott, of course.'

'Why would you say that?' Lena fired back through a quirky grin as she played with her braided hair, conscious of the swelling across her cheek and eye socket.

'They don't see every woman who smiles at them as a conquest.'

Lena quietly held the grin. 'Are you and Boris in a relationship?'

She laughed loudly and then winked. 'We see each other from time to time. He's a natural man of the forest and can't be trapped in an apartment, like an animal in a cage. That would kill him.'

'So, you're happy with that?'

'I guess I am. It allows me to also be free.'

'You don't want children?'

'With him? I'm not sure that he does but yeah, sure, I would love a child although, he wouldn't be around much to help. Different to Scott, eh?'

Lena snorted a laugh, relaxed and now drawn to the woman's natural warmth as Yulia switched up gears in rapid succession to open up the truck's engine.

'Do you smoke?' Yulia pointed at an unopened packet on the dash.

Lena's hand ran down to her belly. She had in the past and was now tempted but aware of the life that was blooming inside her, she resisted. 'No..., thanks. Scott doesn't like it.'

'Ah ha!' she exclaimed, holding on to the primitive steering wheel, gripping and turning it firmly like a sailor working the capstan of a ship. The air pouring in carried a whiff of industry about it and Lena let her eyes wander out onto the familiar scene; tired telegraph poles supporting an intertwined array of cables, shooting out to each of the haphazardly situated *dachas*, in the thinning forest. Ahead the city beckoned, and brick and concrete houses were becoming the norm as they sped past small trucks that appeared to be on their last legs, belching out black *mazut* fumes. Their choking smell was nauseous, and she had always hated this undeveloped part of her Russia, the stupidity and ignorance of the State and the population in general, to abuse the sheer natural beauty they were privileged to live with. *But I guess it's the same all over the world.*

True to Yulia's words, the journey was short. They had pulled up outside a small modern hotel on a street running near to the River Ob's wide passage through the city.

Checking-in had all been prearranged without the need for an internal passport but in the lift, Lena appeared anxious.

'The clerk at the desk may report me for not showing my documents.'

'No, she won't. Those old Soviet requirements are being relaxed. You shouldn't concern yourself with them, and anyway she thinks you've run away from you wife-beating husband and are hiding here for a while.' She grinned.

'That's a good cover story.'

'Yes, this hotel is normally used for wealthy businessmen to meet their high-class hookers. So she may suspect that I'm using this story as a cover. But it's the ideal place to be discreet, no questions asked.'

Lena gaped at the candid response, pausing for a second to consider her next question. 'Tell me, Yulia, who's paying for all this?'

'That's something else you shouldn't worry about!' she retorted, manoeuvring the key with its bulbous lacquered wooden into place in the lock and pushing the door open to reveal a very modern interior, in severe contrast to building's shoddy common areas.

'Why don't you have a shower and I will pop out for some food. Would *plov* be okay?'

Lena perched down on the bed, nodding an affirmative. She was famished and relished the thought of the Central Asian rice dish sold at most kiosk stands throughout Siberia.

'I will give two sharp knocks when I arrive back,' Yulia said firmly, fixing her with a hard stare. 'Don't respond at all but wait for 30 seconds and then I will give another two knocks followed by the word *Plov*. If I say anything else don't utter a word and for God's sake don't open this door. Here, you'll need this.' She pulled a Nugent revolver from her rucksack and offered it. Lena's eyes grew as she gingerly held out her palm to receive the familiar cold metal shape with its silencer barrel.

'Don't worry about what might be happening to me, if anyone comes through that door, shoot them.'

Her head dropped as she surveyed the weapon recalling how she had fired rifles and pistols in her basic intelligence training and how, being blindfolded in her dismantling and reassembling of a Kalashnikov, she had failed to do so inside the set time. There were many attempts made before she succeeded. It had been the most difficult part of the course, loathing the thought of having to use a weapon to kill or maim another person. Now, she was being told that, if need be, if Yulia was compromised, then she had to use it to prevent being taken again. The notion had her quaking with a dread that she had all too easily forgotten. The men who had held her, even Vladislav, had been hired to extract information in any way possible. Ivan Yegorovich had died at their hands, and if it hadn't been for Boris, she might well have too.

'What are the chances of that happening?'

Yulia shrugged as she held the handle to the door. 'This is Russia. We can never be too sure who has been paid to betray the trust of others.'

Lena did as Yulia suggested, putting the scenarios to the back of her mind and luxuriating in a long steamy shower, rinsing out the sweat of the journey from her hair and pores. She then switched on the air-conditioning and sat up against the headrest in two towels; one wrapped around her curves, the other around her golden locks. Yulia had been gone for a considerable length of time, too long just to collect food, and nerves began to eat at her. *What if this is another set up? Perhaps Yulia has a price too?* She wouldn't believe that Boris had been duped by this woman who had a strong moral compass and obviously was too much in love with the Buryat to ever contemplate such a thing, regardless of whatever offer was made. Then she realised the thought didn't make any rational sense. *Yulia wouldn't have given me the gun to defend myself if she was planning to have me abducted.*

She settled waiting for the knock.

It came some minutes later and as instructed, she said nothing but heard the key going in the lock and fleetingly thought it might be another guest mistakenly trying their key in the wrong door or perhaps the chamber maid. *But a chamber maid would ask aloud if it's convenient before entering.* She understood as the door handle turned and she leapt across the bed, grabbing the revolver and lying down, flat on her back on the floor, hidden and waiting for the inevitable. If she had to shoot she would, she resolved, trying to take control of her pounding heart and gasped breaths as she mentally took herself back to the firing range and the instructions of her trainer to breathe calmly and squeeze the trigger, not pull at it. She now waited, hung by the heightened suspense of nothing. The door had opened but there had been no movement, no familiar call from Yulia. Nothing.

And then the slow thud of footsteps, more than one person's, sounded and she could hear gasping and the figures then inched past the bed. Yulia's eyes were wide with pain and horror as a huge man, towering over her had an arm around her torso with such strength that she was almost lifted off the ground. His other hand held a silenced revolver to her temple and her mouth was gagged with a small towel soaked in the blood from her broken nose. He grinned callously; many of his front teeth were gold-capped or missing.

'Throw the gun away and get up,' he growled at Lena.

She hesitated, remembering Yulia's words. *Shoot them.* A clammy sweat covered her trembling hands as she held on and aimed. *Squeeze the trigger, don't pull at it.* The trainer's words played back. Yulia's eyes bore into hers willing her to take a shot, any shot as the thug drilled the silencer further into her temple, causing her to wince and then scrunch up her eyes.

'I said throw it away or I will kill your friend.'

Something else overcame Lena and she lowered the barrel.

A strange muted thud then sounded out and momentarily she thought he had shot Yulia but it came again and then something splashed across her face. The brute's brains were sprayed against the wall and mod cons. Yulia forcefully pulled away from the felled man as he crashed down onto a chair, shattering it. The door then slammed shut and she turned her face, still gripped with fear, before relaxing her frame and throwing her hand out to Lena.

'What happened?' Lena blurted.

Yulia pulled the towel from her mouth, her voice muffed by the mucus and plasma running down into her throat. 'We had some help from the British.' She attempted a grin as she pulled Lena up.

By the door stood a non-descript suited man of average height and weight, probably in his early forties by the looks of his greying hair and freckled pallid face. She looked questioningly at him unscrewing the weapon's suppressor from its barrel, but his expression remained stony.

'Lena Isotova?' he asked, calmly.

'Yes,' she answered in a hushed tone.

'I'm Hedditch. Scott Carty is safely in London and I aiming to get you back there as quickly as possible.

Hedditch..., Hedditch. Lena mentally churned the name. It rang a bell. 'Do I know you?' she quizzed, wondering exactly who this man was who, with his slight frame and wispy locks, had been bold enough to shoot a man dead in broad daylight and shrug it off as if it was another day in the office.

'I don't think we've ever met.'

'But I remember, Scott told me about you.'

'Well, he shouldn't have. He was sworn to secrecy.'

She raised her still trembling palms and shrugged.

'We can discuss that another time. Right now, I have to make a secure call.'

He took off the rucksack he was carrying over a casual linen shirt and rummaged, retrieving a small device.

'It's a satellite telephone,' he answered their stares as he punched at the buttons. 'Amazing how small they can make them nowadays. These things used to require a suitcase of electronic paraphernalia.'

But Lena wasn't interested; instead she moved to the bathroom to soak a hand towel in cold water. 'Here, let me help you.' She gently removed the one that Yulia was holding and placed the cold fabric over the bridge of her nose. 'You're going to need to have this looked at.'

'I know,' said Yulia, 'once you're safely out of the country.' She winced with the pain.

'I'm sorry this has happened.'

'It not your fault, and thank God for Hedditch, we're both alive.

'Not for long if we don't get a move on,' Hedditch interjected as he waited for the line to pick up. 'Hello. Yes, Mountain Lion here. Need to speak with the Crow,' he responded to the receiver trying not to look too sheepish as the women stared at him.

'Yes, all fine here thanks. The bird has been retrieved and is back in the cage.' He hung up.

'What kind of bird am I?' Lena asked, coyly.

He ignored her. 'Now, Yulia, help me dump this body in the wardrobe.' His matter of fact approach chided, but the local woman complied, shaking off her pain, taking hold of the cadaver's legs while he took the arms and between them they sat the body sideways and quickly closed the doors before it slumped out.

'What happens when they find him in there?'

'That will be sometime later tomorrow, and by then you should be safely on the way home.'

It had all become too much for Lena and her knees buckled causing her to stumble back onto the bed. Yulia, caught her arm and then sat alongside, hugging her.

'Right, let's get Lena into a change of clothes and then we can go through the plan.'

Lena was handed a bag, which she emptied out on the bed to find her own blouse, skirt, tights and high heel shoes. 'Have you been through my wardrobe in London?'

'Naturally. They're all a perfect fit. Please don't take too long,' he added smugly and despite his heroics, Lena hadn't warmed to him. She gathered them up and made for the bathroom, remerging some minutes later, glamorous even with a puffy, bruised face.

'We will have to put some make up on you to cover that bruising. You've been through the wars. Do you want to tell me what happened?'

Lena burst into a nervous laugh to which Yulia joined. 'Not particularly!'

He stared blankly back, passing her a familiar looking hand bag, which she instantly recognised as hers too.

'In that you'll find an English passport. We've changed your family name to Hardy. The story is simple, if you're pushed, and there's no reason why you should be, you're married to a Mr Hardy. If they ask for your original maiden name I suggest that you make one up now and stick to it, and state that you grew up in Moscow.'

She sighed, flicking through the document, noticing the recent photograph of herself on the details page. 'I don't understand,' she stammered, 'how could you have organised all this so quickly?'

'Ah well, it's amazing what one can do when you have the right resources. As soon as our people heard from Yulia, I flew straight in from London. Before that, I had one of my team, a lady, go into your house and pull your things together,' he scratched at his hair and half-cocked a smile, as if to show the importance of his position. 'I had to sight you before I could make the confirmation back to my superiors. It was critical, you see. Scott's life depended on knowing if it you were alive – we thought that you had probably been abducted and then killed. Next time let us know, before you give us the slip and leave Dubai.'

'But this passport photograph. It's very recent. Have you been watching me, us?

'Yes, you are always under surveillance and so that's how I know you are the real Yelena Isotova, but that photo was lifted from Scott's laptop. It's the most solemn one we could find as you appear to be smiling in all the rest.'

'Is Scott in danger?'

'Less so – now that we know you're safe with us. But I can't tell you any more than that. It's not plain sailing for either of you until you're out of Russia.'

'And how do you plan for me to leave.'

'By plane, the same one that brought me here in the early hours, but this time we'll fly back via Kazakhstan. It's the nearest foreign territory and it will give me an alibi when talking to the mayor's team in a few hours' time. I will excuse myself and advise that I must travel to Astana for a few days.'

'But aren't you part of the Embassy staff?'

'I suggest you don't ask me any more questions about what I do. There's a dead man in the wardrobe and it's likely that if he was able to trace yours and Yulia's arrival here, then there will be others who have done the same. With blood splattered across the walls and furniture, we have a limited window before the alarm is raised, so we need to move down to the basement carpark where my driver is waiting.'

They gathered their scant belongings and Lena felt the cold dead weight of the pistol in her moist palm.

'Thanks for this.' She hurriedly handed it to Yulia as if it was a contaminated.

The woman squinted very slightly. 'I knew you would have used it.' She leant over to grip Lena's shoulder. 'You were just bluffing that bastard by dropping the barrel, weren't you?'

There was a slight pause as Lena dropped her eyes. 'That's right,' she responded.

Outside in the corridor, Hedditch, shut the door firmly and then, after double locking it, forced the heel of his palm across the key's protruding end, sharply snapping it off to leave the end flush inside the lock.

'There, that should buy us some time,' he said knowing that things worked differently in Russia and room service in this hotel knew only too well not to disturb guests who wanted privacy, believing they had locked the door from the inside. It would be a day or so before anyone took serious notice and forced an entry.

'Does the hotel have cameras on the different floors?' Lena asked as they made their way through the fire doors.

'No, and for obvious reasons,' Yulia whispered. 'If they did, they would lose their particular clientele.'

'There are cameras in the basement carpark, but we found that these have been switched off permanently for the same reason.'

The car waiting for them was an aged black Mercedes saloon, typically ubiquitous on the streets of the city so wouldn't raise any attention.

'Where shall we drop you, Yulia?' Hedditch asked, craning his head back over the edge of the passenger seat.

'At the entrance to Berezovaya Rosha Park, near Zolataya Niva metro station. There are fewer people there and I can catch a local bus service out of town.'

Hedditch nodded to his driver, an Uzbek to whom Yulia then spoke to, briefly, in Russian. He smoothly swung the car around and across onto the opposite carriageway, heading out of town.

Soon the two women were hugging as if they had been long lost friends. Tearful, Lena pulled back. 'Thank you for risking everything to help me.'

'Everything?' Her bleary eyes were moist. 'Tell Scott to take very good care of you. You're a special woman!' Her hand gently patted Lena's stomach as she winked knowingly.

Nodding madly back, Lena let out a small sigh of despair. 'I will, and please ensure that Boris takes care of Lubimov.'

Yulia then stepped out, slammed the door and turned towards the main gate of the park, to lose herself among its many visitors as the car raced off to Hedditch's appointment at the Mayor's office.

Forty

London suburbs

Gordon Green sat in the front seat of the packed Range Rover as it raced into a shopping mall's main carpark and pulled up to a waiting security officer.

'Give me a status,' Jack shouted before the window had fully retracted.

'Our guards are on all doors and monitoring anyone who fits the descriptions given.'

'Good, but make sure none of your people approach the suspects.'

Jack didn't normally handle an operation live in the field but with these high stakes he needed to be on the front line and Green hadn't forgotten his friend's words the previous evening. Jack was going to take Lisa down or try to, regardless.

A call came in on his walkie talkie. 'What's that? I see. Any sign of the satchel? Ah ha.' His expression hardened. 'Okay, take them in for questioning.'

He turned to Green. 'We've been played very nicely. Two women have been apprehended. One roughly fitted Lisa's description and had two of our trackers in her pocket. The other was carrying your bag, which had another tracker sitting loose at the bottom. The books were replaced with dictionaries.' He sighed.

'And there's no sign of Lisa anywhere?

'The team is looking at the camera records now.'

At that moment the speaker kicked into life again. 'You found Carty...,where? Okay we're coming in, stay where you are.' He turned to his two colleagues and shouted, 'Go!'

Green was waiting by the ambulance as Carty lying inside, was tended. Next to him, one of the officers briefed Jack.

'Looks like our ruse of placing a tracker in chewing gum under the arch of Carty's shoe worked. It wasn't picked up like the others were,' Jack announced to his friend.

'How on earth did your people manage to do that?'

'We have our ways. Anyway, it allowed us to find him quickly. He's carrying a wound to the head and has a serious concussion.'

'So, we've lost the books?' Green continued the broken conversation of earlier.

'Yes, it would appear so. But the good news is we have Lena.'

'What?' Green gaped widely back at the man who was coolly flattening his hair, restraining the temptation to hug him. 'I can't believe it! When did you find this out?'

Early this morning we received a call from one of my subordinates in Novosibirsk.' He raised a finger to his mouth, nodding sideways. 'Let's not say anything to Scott now. He's been through a lot in the last few days and it's better he rests. She's still not safe until she's back in London.'

'Is that why you decided to move today on those women?'

Jack cocked his head. 'As I told you, we were going to act anyway. We couldn't afford to let those books disappear, at least without knowing what they contained.'

'What are trying to tell me? Have you...,' he stalled, clocking his friend's grinning eyes enlarged through the heavy lenses.

'Yes, Gordon, I had them scanned yesterday at the same time as our techies we were putting the tracker in their spines. It's amazing how small these handheld scanners are nowadays.'

'And I suppose the information is with your specialists already?'

'Yes, those same scientists who believed that Carty's device exhibits some form of cold fusion. That's all I can ever tell you.'

'So we'll never know if they decide to construct such a machine.'

'That's correct.'

'But if it could transmute spent nuclear waste as the Russians were using it for, then surely it should be pursued by UK interests for that same purpose?'

'That is out of my hands. I'm just the civil servant who collects the information and protects our security at the highest level. The important thing is that we now know what the Russians and Lisa have.'

'But you can't let Lisa get away with this information.'

'If she's as smart as she appears to be and with the resources of her uncle, then she's probably far away by now. Saying that, there's a security brief to watch out for her at all borders.'

'And Lena, can your people fly in and pick her up?'

'They can but won't do so until absolutely sure it's safe. It requires some delicate timing and if we draw the attention of the authorities they will pull her in. Remember she is Russian despite having travelled on her English passport.

The doors of the ambulance were being shut in readiness to take Carty with his armed protection officer to hospital.

'Just a minute,' Green called to the attendant. He winked at Jack. 'I want a word with him before you leave.'

'Alright, but remember, hold back on the news of Lena for now.'

But Green had already climbed inside to find his friend wired up with a saline drip.

'Hi, Scott,' he uttered holding the man's hand.

'The books?' Carty whispered, his eyes still semi-closed.

'Don't worry we've dealt with them.'

'They're safe?'

Green simpered. 'Yes, they're safe.'

Forty One

Novossibirsk, Siberia

'My driver, Farrukh, will take you for a brief tour around the City and order some food for you. There shouldn't be a problem, if you need anything. Just don't get out of the car for any reason, got that?'

'How long will you be?'

'A few hours and then we'll head to the airport.'

'What if I need the bathroom?'

'Now?'

'Yes.'

'Okay, change of plan, come with me and I will introduce you as my assistant to the Mayor's people, you can use the loo, and then I will walk you back to the car.' He nodded again at the man. 'Please park and wait for my call.'

'Just act cool and casual and don't speak in Russian. If any official we meet takes an interest in the bruising on your face you can tell them politely that you do kick boxing and recently lost a competition.'

'Really! Do I look like a kick boxer to you?'

'Not at all, but if you don't like that excuse you'd better come up with a better one and fast.' He sniped as they stepped through the giant oak-panelled double doors of the local State building.

A young man presented himself and Lena was shown by a female staff member to the Ladies bathroom. As she reappeared she was briefly introduced as Mrs Hardy to the Mayor and some influential businessmen from the Novosibirsk Oblast and made brief but pleasant small talk before Hedditch walked her back out to the car.

'They liked you,' He uttered. But then he understood that she oozed a certain charm and her unspoken idiosyncrasies could have only come from being a native woman in the presence of powerful Russians.

She dozed on the back seat, her appetite lacking with the weight of the recent events pressing her emotions. She had faced a plethora of death and violence in just a few days, the like of which she had not understood, even though she had been amongst it with Kosechenko's people before. Her escape was now behind her shut lids, visualising Carty's smiling blue eyes shining back at her.

Hedditch slamming a side door shook her awake.

'All good?' he asked, generally.

She remained silent, absorbed by the imagery reeling through her waking mind.

Soon, Farrukh had pulled up the car and indicated to the airport staff to notify the officials of a VIP exit. Hedditch meanwhile passed her a small carry-on bag from the trunk which she immediately recognised as her own.

'You really don't leave anything to chance, do you?'

'We try to think of everything. It's full of your things. Now, as we go through the VIP channel don't be pulled into any discussion of why you're here. Just let me do the talking.' His small eyes flicked sideways at her as he spoke, they betrayed a cold English ruthlessness that she had experienced before with visitors to her country. It was, in truth the conditioning that had led her to be so harshly blunt with Carty on first meeting him, then regretting it an hour later as his quirky smile lingered in her mind.

'I understand.'

An official shook hands with Hedditch and asked for their passports as he introduced her as his personal assistant. The man simply indicated for them to pass their bags, phones and paraphernalia through the X-Ray scanner in the usual way before being ushered into a small exit lounge. Lena sat down, her body and mind sapped, as she then spotted the official's stern gaze from a glazed office, making her self-conscious. She brushed her loose blonde mane across her face to partially hide the marks and her anxiety.

'I'm sorry, Mrs Hardy, there appears to be an issue. We can't let you leave the country until we resolve it.' The man's quiet accented English then beckoned to her from its open door.

'What's that?!' Hedditch boomed, 'what's the problem?' He stood and turned on his well-practised and stealthily belligerent tone.

'We have no record of Mrs Hardy arriving on our computer.'

'That's can't be right. Please check again.'

'You can travel, sir, but she cannot until we clarify her entry date on the computer.'

'But that utterly ridiculous. She arrived with me last night through this very VIP lounge,' he bluffed hoping that they wouldn't pull the video footage. 'We have to leave sharp, our jet has a short window of time in which it can take off.'

The man suddenly became dark and officious. 'I'm sorry, sir, but we cannot allow it.'

'I see. Then you'd better call your superior down here and I don't want just anyone, I want to the head of the airport.' Hedditch matched the younger man's demeanour. 'And hurry up, please.'

Lena looked hopelessly at him as he rummaged in his bag pulling out an envelope and his phone. *Who does he think he is, talking to a Russian official like that? He's a relic of the British Empire.*

'Here, hold that.' He placed an envelope in her hand and flipped open the Nokia, walking away over to the corner of the small room, talking firmly to whoever was listening.

The official reappeared to wait patiently while Hedditch finished up his call.

'Well?'

'The airport chief is on his way, sir,' the young man stated, his speech now very nervous, as he shiftily flicked his gaze between the two visitors.

'Good, then it should all be resolved, shortly.'

A group of holstered black clothed paramilitaries burst through the door a few minutes later. Lena squirmed in her seat, fearing that they had been rumbled and it was now over.

Was it a Russian thing to unconsciously succumb to the forces of the State and not show the bravado that Hedditch and her love, Scott Carty, displayed in buckets. The thought gave her a burst of confidence as she shot her eyes up and caught Hedditch's willing her to be brave and act with him. Fingering the unsealed flap to the envelope, she suddenly flipped it open to find the neatly folded paper embossed with the hotel's insignia and bill receipt stapled to its top left hand corner. She scanned the first two lines of service details.

King Size Double Bed – two persons.
1 x night – US$ 500.00

Grinning, she resisted an urge to shake her head as she glanced again at Hedditch. He winked back and then turned to the approaching five men entourage, headed by a fat suited one with a sagging double chin and dark blue lines etched below his sunken lids. Surrounded by his obvious security, he lacked any real authority but was going through the motions. The younger official introduced the man as *acting* airport chief, and translated as Hedditch explained the situation, casually pointing to the seated woman twice. The official shook his head, defiantly as Hedditch held out his hand to her. She took it and stood up on her heels, causing the plump man to scope her up and down as his mouth hung slightly open.

'You see,' Hedditch said taking the paper from her while placing an arm loosely around her hips, 'My assistant and I shared a room last night, but we wanted to be discreet.' He waved it at the younger man pointing out the mention of the double bed. The man flushed and looked awkward as he conveyed the words in Russian, to his superior and at that moment the Englishman's Nokia rang again. He answered it, paused and then handed it theatrically to the burly official.

Lena sank into the pose, playing acting at being a mistress and catching the younger man's florid looks, sensing that he was toying with the possibility that the bruising had been caused by Hedditch beating her. She looked away, embarrassed, noting his boss' subservient responses and contorted expression when he handed the phone back to the Englishman. Eyeing them both he then ordered the young man to apologise for the mistake he had made. Clearly demolished, the youthful official profusely stated that he regretted his actions. Hedditch registered his acceptance with a dignified nod to the older man.

'Good, so perhaps you'll hand us back our passports and we'll be on our way.'

Bloody Englishman, they're so smug and self-righteous and I'm pregnant with one of them! Lena thought, restraining an outward giggle.

'Who was that phone call from?' she asked as they were safely in the air bound for Kazakhstan.

'One of the men you met this morning is a very influential businessman here in Siberia.'

'Oil or coal?'

'Neither, he's into the emerging tech industry and a supplier of mobile networks – made a small fortune in a few years. He's interested in developing business ties with the UK.'

'So what did he say to that official?'

'I think he called rank on the man, threatening to strip him of his job.'

'Why?'

'He was taken by you and was rather impressed with the fact that you were my mistress. Sorry, Lena but it was a necessity.'

She grinned. 'And the hotel booking?'

'A ruse which we needed as back-up. It's obvious, though, that I can never return to Russia. It's just a matter of time before they bust my story and find out that you were in the country,' he cracked a wry smile at her, 'apparently, it was worth it. The folks in London are very keen to have you back.'

Forty Two

The jet's layover in Astana, Kazakhstan's capital had lasted two hours. Hedditch's ploy was clever, allowing his Russian counterparts to believe that he had urgent meetings there and would return. Now, though, half a day later, they had already cleared the English coastline on a cloudless May afternoon and the descent into Stansted airport was imminent. A sensation of weight lifted from her shoulders. Even though she had left behind her friends, she couldn't bring herself to wonder what might become of them, now that Kosechenko and other forces understood that *Sphinx* might hold a darker secret concerning the machine.

Hedditch passed the plane's internal phone to her.

'Hi, Lena.' It was Jack. 'How are you feeling?' he asked, his tone remaining measured

'Good, I think.'

'Hedditch suggests a doctor at the airport. What do you say?'

'No, that won't be necessary, not until I'm home. I need to see my own doctor.'

'Well, if you say so.'

'How's Scott? Is he there, can I speak with him?'

'He's here, resting and nothing to worry about. We'll take you to see him as soon as you land.'

****

Stansted Airport, London

The journey through the security channels of the airport was well oiled. Just minutes after touching down and taxiing, Jack and Gordon Green were waiting inside a mediocre greeting room, carpeted with blue and industrial purple patterning.

'Lena!' Green shouted with an unrestrained joy, gently pulling her into a hug. She reciprocated smiling and as he stepped away, Jack moved in to place a hand on her shoulder, his large lenses revealing the relief in his eyes that she was now safe.

'And Scott?' she begged.

'He's in hospital having a few tests done but they're all routine, nothing serious,' Green answered.

'I must see him?'

'And you're going to but just a quick check up first,' Jack answered. A lady, clearly a doctor with a stethoscope was present as Lena knew she would be. Jack was too thorough not to have seen to that. 'I'll be back shortly,' he instructed, stepping outside to catch a waiting Hedditch and the man's rapid debrief of the situation. Green's large frame, though, remained firmly fixed as he held her palm in his fingers. She gazed back, pulling a quirky smile, her blue eyes welling-up with the release of emotional tension and in turn, his ruddy demeanour cracked with the realisation of what she must have endured.

The doctor, moved between them shining a torch in Lena's eyes, consecutively monitoring each for concussion and satisfied, wrapped a blood pressure sleeve around her upper arm while listening to her heartbeat.

'Hmmm, slightly elevated. Pop this thermometer in your mouth please,' she prompted, poking the thin phial towards her. After some seconds she examined it and frowned. 'Your temperature is a bit high,' she remarked knowingly, and Lena shrugged, lowering her eyes.

'I'm pregnant.'

'I thought so. How far gone?'

'A month, perhaps six weeks.'

'It's usually a little early to have a scan but after your traumatic experience, I suggest you have one straight away.'

Green's face registered surprise at her sudden announcement. 'Scott's going to be ecstatic!' he sang. 'We'll ask

Jack to have his people organise that scan immediately. You can see Scott later.’

Forty Three

Some days later

'So, finally, I'm more than pleased to have you two safely back together, in one room and without all the frightful stress of the last week,' Jack said, smiling and fingering the bridge of his glasses. 'And such good news about your pregnancy, Lena.'

She dropped her eyes, embarrassed by all the attention as Carty squeezed her hand gently.

'Tea, anyone?' Jack asked, already placing a fine china cup from its stack onto a saucer and then lifting the milk jug to pour, before stopping and raising his glistening head to see who was taking.

'Yes please,' replied Green. Carty and Lena smiled their acknowledgement in response to the Whitehall man's etiquette, a well-practised ritual to have everyone feeling comfortable before he delivered his intentions.

'I'm intrigued, Jack. Why did your people move on Lisa when they did?' Scott Carty was keen to get into the details.

'We had the call from Hedditch that he had sighted Lena.' He pointed unconsciously at her as he relayed the story.

'But you were already tracking Lisa and me via the bugs in the books. Were you going to move in anyway?'

Jack stopped stirring his tea and seemed to freeze for a second, considering his response. 'With hindsight it's easy to see it negatively,' he uttered, bluntly.

Carty fidgeted but Lena gripped her man's hand, indicating that he should restrain from further questioning. Green read the body language between them.

'Scott, the important thing is that Lena, you and your unborn baby are now safe. It's useless to pick over the bones of what might have been.'

Carty's shrug and a wry smile softened the atmosphere.

'But what I would like to tell you about is Lisa's back story,' Jack said. 'In the debrief, Scott, you told us about her family's research institute and the advanced technology they are developing, including a new generation of Thorium nuclear power plants funded by the Chinese government.'

'Thorium, really?' Green interjected.

'I'm sure that Scott will brief you on all that another time,' Jack fired back.

Carty winked at his older friend, taking it as his cue to fill in some of the gaps. 'Despite Thorium, Lisa is really an environmental fundamentalist, hatching an incredible scheme to *green* the Taklamakan desert by irrigating it and growing hemp. It seems that China is still the world biggest producer of that crop. She's really incredibly persuasive and driven.'

'And manipulative,' Green added.

'How can they green a desert?' Lena piped up. 'By definition it hardly has any water, that's why it's a desert!'

Carty tilted to face her. 'Apparently there have been recent discoveries of huge..., and I mean huge, aquifers hundreds of metres below its terrain, the result of many thousands of years of run-off from the mountain range on the its southern edge.'

'Good, I'm glad you confirmed that Scott,' Jack uttered.

'Why?'

'It's what our intelligence has been telling us. While Lisa has some very noble, utopian plans, it would appear that she has been the main victim of a huge deceit.'

The younger man's face drew a blank. 'I don't follow.'

'No, I don't suppose you would, but anyway she's been duped by her uncle, Ong and the group that surround him, although, it is true that he had been side-lined by those in power, preventing him controlling the shipments of spent nuclear waste. We're guessing that once he discovered the Russians were transmuting it, he got greedy and wanted to form a joint venture company with Kosechenko to ensure he had a large chunk of the revenues. He was entrenched and had his own power base, bribing relevant Party members, probably cutting them into the business too.'

Jack is good. That's almost exactly what Hazeza and I believed had happened. Carty ruminated, although somewhat still confused. 'But how is that duping Lisa? Surely she was well aware of all that.'

'Here's the rub. We've obtained information from another source that Ong was planning to create a breakaway state, bringing Xinjiang Province under his autonomous control with the pretense to support Uyghur ethnics like himself.'

'That's incredibly hard to believe; the Chinese government would never allow that.'

'Well, we've passed on what we know to our counterparts there.'

'And what do you know?' Green's curiosity had got the better of him.

The Whitehall man slipped back into his seat, drumming his long pointed fingertips together in an open prayer in front of his mouth, gazing at the man.

'You said Ong *was* planning to create a breakaway state. Has he been stopped?' Green persisted.

'We understand he has but it was a very dark business he was engaged in and frankly, Scott, you're lucky to have got out of there. For some time, you were suspected of being part of Ong's team and his plan.'

'And just exactly what was this dark business,' Carty asked. He had met Ong and had been told of his history by Hafeza but he still couldn't believe Jack's comment about Lisa being duped by Ong.

'He was to move his local militia in a sudden coup, taking control of the Lop Nor nuclear test facility while at the same time notifying the authorities in Beijing, that a number of dirty bombs had been delivered to major cities in China, threatening to detonate them during the Olympic games later this year.'

Green frowned. 'Dirty bombs?'

Jack cocked his head nonchalantly back at his friend. 'Yes, they're devices typically containing very small amounts of low-level radioactive material, detonated in or over cities or places of strategic importance, rendering them uninhabitable for many years.'

'That's horrendous,' Green blurted.

'Ong's using to his advantage the methods of the growing extremism that's infiltrating that region from neighbouring Afghanistan. With control of a Thorium reactor and its raw material supply in Xinjiang, along with access to these newly discovered saline aquifers allowing him to pump the local oil reserves, his grand scheme was to create an energy independent fiefdom, his own, free of governance from Beijing, or at least that was his plan.'

'The Chinese intelligence services stopped him?'

'We understand that they moved on him in the last 48 hours. Scott, we had no idea where you were, and the plan was for them to also find and free you. Instead, and as I should have guessed, you found your own way home!'

'And you suspect that Lisa wasn't aware of this masterplan?'

'It's unlikely. She was being fed information and a huge promise to lure you in for your information. As you said she had a utopian vision for the region, not one of political separation.'

'But she has those blueprints and she's probably back in the region by now, with Ong.'

'If she is, then she'll be arrested.'

'I doubt that,' Carty said shaking his head at the man, his face a picture of fear. 'And the machine will soon be in the hands of fundamentalists in Central Asia. Lisa was naive enough to believe that she could have provided free energy to the region and then the world. Despite her English upbringing, her mind-set was all about overthrowing the western veneer on life, even though she had hugely benefited from its privileges.' Carty refrained from divulging all of her perverse games in front of Lena but he knew that shortly he would need to fully brief Jack.

The man depended on having this information in order that he could trade with his counterparts in other security agencies around the world.

'I guess Ong thought that having the machine operational in Xinjiang would give him a huge revenue stream to transmute nuclear waste from all over the world.'

'But they will never have *overunity,*' Lena added in a hushed tone. Green swung around to catch her knowing glance at Carty.

'What do you mean, Lena?' Jack articulated, pulling himself forward on the edge of his seat. 'I gather that you know about the peculiar phenomena the machine displays as it was you that discovered the diagrams in the books.'

'Yes, but I hadn't even bothered to look at them until Scott and I moved in together.'

'And what you just said about Lisa and her people not having *overunity* ..., what was that all about?' He squinted, his nous now keen as Carty and Green drilled her with looks, willing her not to say too much. But she understood the cat was out of the bag and that Jack now deserved to know the truth.

'In Russia I was told that the machine will only generate *overunity* at precise points on the earth's surface where the energetic aspects of nature are strong enough to support it. Except for the exception of Baikal, the other locations are, as yet, unknown and it's unlikely given the huge challenge, that they will be discovered any time soon.'

'Really?!' He pushed his specs up onto his forehead. 'And did you know about this too, Scott?'

Carty dropped his gaze and coughed. 'Erm..., well come to think of it, I do remember hearing something along those lines but couldn't really understand the pidgin English and so it slipped my mind.' His appearance was challenged with the lie and he resisted the urge to blush, glancing instead at Green who was raising his hands with a light shrug, attempting to look astonished at the announcement.

‘That’s a hell of a point to let slip, don’t you think?’ Jack’s measured retort was pitched so eloquently that it could have cut Carty and he wouldn’t have felt a thing. ‘Be honest, you’ve been holding back on all this since day one, haven’t you?’

‘Jack,’ Carty took a breath. ‘You must understand that the life of Lena’s grandfather and anyone else associated with that machine, was at risk. I was made to promise to those that saved my life..., and Lena’s, not to give its secret away.’

‘And I suppose now that the secret has revealed itself in another manner, you haven’t broken any trust. I do understand and respect both of you and would have most likely acted similarly.’ He flipped the specs back down and glanced at his friend, chameleon-like.

‘Gordon, what do you make of all this?’

‘It sounds like good news,’ he answered. They all frowned in varying degrees at him but secure in his own mind, he countered. ‘Look, if the machine has to be situated at specific locations, as Lena has just told us, then there’s a fair chance they will never find them. It would be like looking for a needle in a haystack.’

‘Any idea of the coordinates of those other locations, Lena?’ Jack smoothly asked, simpering at her.

‘No.’ She shrugged, keeping her gaze neutral and on her partner. Even though Hedditch and his team had looked through her scant possessions, they had overlooked The Flower of Life poster as some mere decorative picture to frame on her wall and not as the code for unlocking the possible sites. *Not even Scott knows that, yet,* she ruminated, unaware that he had seen that very same picture twice, in the last week.

‘We just have to keep an eye on spent nuclear waste shipments to see where they are ending up,’ Jack said, thinking out loud and now slipping back in his seat again.

‘Well, with Ong being held and Lisa on the run, it’s unlikely any shipments at all will be moving out of Xinjiang,’ Carty conjectured. ‘Do you think that Lisa will trade the books with those in power in China, in order to secure her pardon?’

'Who knows? I doubt it very much, though.'

A melodic ring tone emanating from Jack's mobile, punctuated the conversation. Recognising the number, he flipped it open. 'Yes?' he nodded and then dropped his head, placing one palm on his cheek, his expression one of cast seriousness.

'Ah ha, I see. Are there any leads?'

The caller continued for some seconds.

'What about the books…, no? Okay, I'm going to wind up a meeting and then I will be there as soon as I can,' he said closing the call and holding the phone a short distance from his ear for some seconds, contemplating the news as he gazed unfocused through the window. It was a bright afternoon and the tempting warmth of the early summer sun now bathed him.

'What is it?' Gordon quizzed softly. Jack spun about, running both hands back across the tightly greased hair as he caught Carty's searching gaze.

'Lisa Taylor's body has just been found in the Thames…, her throat has been slit.'

'Oh no.' Lena pulled her hand up to cover her mouth. Despite never knowing the woman, the thought of such a barbaric act filled her with horror. Carty reacted, placing and arm around her so that she could bury her face in his shoulder. 'Any ideas who might have done that?' he asked bluntly.

'Too early to say, but my hunch is the Triads. They often take care of Chinese business overseas.'

'And the books are lost, I suppose?'

'It would appear to be the case,' he answered, 'so it's unlikely that Central Asian fundamentalists will be seeing them anytime soon.'

I guess Lisa was playing too close to the edge, Carty surmised, as the image of the vision's young girl sitting with her legs dangling above the writhing serpent in the blackness of the pond, filtered back. *She had it all but at the same time had nothing.* Lisa's narcissistic, cruel behaviour wasn't lost on him; he just wasn't ready to analyse the madness of the experience she had subjected him to with her warped controlling affections. He ran a palm over the blonde mess of Lena's bowed head and glanced at Gordon Green who was solemnly shaking his head at the news.

'Alright, well let's wind this up for today. I will put an extra guard on the safe-house and Scott, please, I must insist that neither you nor Lena try to leave without receiving permission from your minder that it's safe to do so,' Jack chided.

Lena lifted her shining eyes. 'How long will we have to stay there for?'

'Until all this has blown over…, a month perhaps.' He turned to the older man. 'Gordon, we'll talk soon.'

Forty Four

One week later

The safe house had been a wise precaution if not an unwanted one, Carty surmised, as he and Lena stepped back into the emptiness of their home. *I wonder how many bugs Jack's had put in this place.* The false security needed to be kept at the forefront of his mind when they were to share particular aspects of their recent adventures, which neither Jack nor Green needed to know. He filled a kettle and took her in his arms, cupping her jaw with his palms to closely examine the yellow bruising.

'Scott, there is someone, I need to tell you about..., a man.'

'Who is he?'

'Someone I was in relationship with before you.' The treachery of Vladislav preyed heavily as she began to share the story and its weight and many minutes later, Scott Carty tried to make sense of his welling tears and unfamiliar anger. He should never have left her at Heathrow that day; he should have remembered the danger of their previous lives, listened to his instincts and not been complacent. But with the emotions came the voice of Hafeza Bazareva, quietly reminding him of the story of Fate and Destiny again and, in sipping his tea he understood that these recent trials that he and Lena had endured were for reasons he was only just beginning to understand. A part of their lives had been left unfinished at Baikal and he had an inkling of what it was. What if a similar machine was tapping into *overunity* somewhere else on the planet? Then perhaps those books had to have been taken and exposed to others, in order that the technology couldn't be held in the shadows any longer. Perhaps, as Hafeza had told him, the dramatic increase in the Schumann Resonance in recent years was a reflection of humanity's consciousness rising to a new vibration in preparation to meet the challenges, one being the deployment of free energy without greed and control. Green had dismissed this as nonsense; that the collective shadow was still long and had not yet been satiated. But the older man's view, wise as it was, did not ring true with Carty. Ludmilla Anatolivna and an unseen army of Bodhisattvas sat in silent contemplation, calling on the Kuan Yin, the Anima Mundi – the feminine soul of nature - to tend the unheard cries of humanity and guide those willing to listen.

He snapped out of his long thought, to see a faded poster, laid out over the kitchen table

'Scott, this is The Flower of Life,' she calmly advised. 'It represents the soul of the earth.'

'I know,' he stuttered. It was as if she had just read his thoughts and stunned by the synchronicity, his blue eyes searched hers, not quite able to process how or why this familiar image was now again in front of him. He then proceeded to tell her when he had been shown it as he pondered the drawing, noticing that under the worn fold creases and smudged finger marks that marred the image, the delicate intersecting circles had been superimposed over the earth in a very odd, yet specific orientation. She leant over and whispered directly into his ear and then pulled back, leaving him grinning at her.

Her invitation to join him in the shower meant learning of the secrets she had gleaned in Russia about that picture, which couldn't be openly shared with anyone listening. The ensuite bathroom was steaming up as he gingerly tried the pounding water and adjusted it to a bearable temperature. Lena strolled in naked, humming to a Stan Getz number that sounded loudly from the bedroom. He loved that she remembered the little details that gave him a sense of who he was and a memory of where he came from. His father had been an avid jazz saxophonist, casually playing around the house ad hoc, to his favourite musician, Getz. Coyly, she approached and draped herself on him, her lips millimetres from his, running her fine fingers through his hair and then down over his face to his shirt.

Passion sucked them into an insatiable kiss and she tore at the garment, ripping it and tossing it to the floor, her seductive look inveigling him to take her. He pulled at his trousers and soon he was naked and grinding against her cool milky flesh.

'Shower?' she muttered with a teasing giggle as her hair stuck to her glistening face. Then her demeanour slipped from the playful as she tugged his arm and stepped one foot into the torrent, pulling him with her. Her long braids hung in soaked strands and she grabbed at his shoulders sinking her un-manicured nails into his bare pale skin while burying her tongue in his ear. Then she whispered. 'The Flower of Life has a hidden pattern within it, which is the key to locating the co-ordinates of the other nodes.'

He tilted his face and kissed her deeply, the information's importance somehow reinforced by the water's refreshing pummelling of his skin. She pushed him back after some seconds and took his hands in her palms. 'You understood what I just said, didn't you?'

'Of course, I will study it a little later,' he answered, moving to nuzzle her gazelle-like neck and grabbed at her thighs to lift her. She wrapped her legs around his and squeezed, she could wait no longer for him.

They remained under the hot water without a care for time or the world, laughing and giggling. She leant in and pecked his cheek, leaving her mouth close to his ear again.

'Lubimov and Boris wanted me to give you their strongest best wishes.'

'You saw them?' he whispered.

'Yes, and Yulia.'

'Ha!' His guffaw confused her. 'How are they all?'

'Okay but could be better.' Her lips downturned as she gazed at him, telepathically suggesting there was more.

'What?' he probed.

She rubbed her nose against his jaw. 'I saw the machine,' she barely uttered against the shower's pounding, the words momentarily suspended within an invisible bubble before their impact registered through his wide-eyed expression.

'Lubimov told me that there's a deliberate flaw in the blueprints in those books. They're incomplete.'

'I can't believe it. Why?' he murmured, wanting to cry but continuing with the covert game they were playing.

'It's a form of insurance. Anyone trying to construct it would be unsuccessful at the least and at worst, the machine would implode, catastrophically.'

'But what if that had happened to us?'

'He told me that he would have sent word in good time before we had a chance to construct it.'

Carty paused to stare at her. 'And you recognise what this means? Those who have the books will fail.'

'Exactly! And that includes Jack's people.'

'You believe Jack had time to copy those books?'

'If I could have copied them, then he most certainly must have,' she uttered.

'You copied them?!'

'Yes, scanned them actually. I knew that they would be at risk at some stage, so I did it before you gave them to Gordon.'

'How did you know that I was going to give them to him?'

'Come on, Scott. You should give me a little more credit.'

'I'm sorry. I shouldn't have kept that a secret from you. I never wanted to.'

'It's fine. I understand why you trusted him with them, and I would have done the same, in your place. The problem is...,' she hesitated with the gravity of the thought, 'someone is going to get hurt trying to build and run that thing.'

'That's not our problem,' he fired back. 'And, Lena, you need to hide that picture.'

'I will, in plain sight. I'm going to have it framed and put on the wall in the kitchen.'

'Sshh,' he hushed her tone. 'How on earth did Hedditch not take it from you?'

'He examined it when they debriefed me but seemed more interested at the Russian handwriting written on the back.'

'What did it say?'

'Just my grandfather's words, gifting it to my grandmother for one of her birthdays in the 1970s.' She giggled and scrunched up her nose to rub it against his. 'I'm tired, let's sleep,' she murmured.

Under the smooth cool of Egyptian cotton sheets, she lay on his hairless, muscled chest noticing that he had lost weight. They snoozed on and off for most of the afternoon, he allowing her comments to filter through his unconscious mind. The lengthening days had turned to dusk when he woke, hungry, and with her resting on her elbows, observing him with an enthusiast's passion for a rare curio. She placed her fingers on his cheekbone, luring him into a kiss and then slid on top of his warm body and nibbled his lips. Then a thought crashed into his mind. *That's it! The Tree of Life, the picture in Green's book – it must the key to locating the exact coordinates if it's superimposed over The Flower of Life.*

He would have to contact his friend and gently suggest he borrow the book, praying that the folded pieced of paper with the picture, was still within its pages.

Forty Five

A day later: The Ironmonger Row Baths

'I can't believe that you found yourself stuck in a foreign country without your passport, again.' Gordon Green said, quietly gasping in the heat as he rubbed his palms over his chest and shoulders.

'I know,' Carty acknowledged, slumping forward, the intensity of the hot room almost too much for him.

'Cold dip?'

'Yeah,' he grunted. But standing up too fast had his head turning giddy and immediately he bent over, leaning down with his outstretched palms onto the wooden-slatted plinth.

'Steady.' Green grabbed him.

'I'm fine, Gordon.'

The plunge pool's icy water instantly revived him and he made a point of standing under the ludicrously oversized faucet that fed it. Green had already dipped in and out within seconds and was stretching his toned frame on one of the wicker loungers, wrapped in a robe.

'So, do you want to let me in on what happened with Lisa?' he probed.

'Didn't Jack tell you? He debriefed me for long enough.'

'Scott, you know what I asking about?'

'Are you suggesting that I had mad and abandoned sex with her?'

'Possibly, she was an attractive woman and obviously very predatory.'

'Well, she really didn't light my candle,' he countered. 'The woman was crazy, slipping me a drug in the drinks and then coyly claiming the next morning, that we had spent the night together and that I was acting like a complete bastard in not acknowledging it.' His raised voice while echoing around the empty chamber hadn't convinced his friend of her wicked and total betrayal of his trust.

'Through it all, it was clear she was drunk on the power she believed her family's vast wealth wielded and which perversely distorted her ability to feel any empathy.'

'That's very common psychopathic behaviour. In fact, it is claimed the majority of CEOs controlling international corporations display similar traits. Let's not forget Arthur D'albo!'

Carty rolled his eyes at the remark. 'Despite all that, it's a huge loss. Ong's research facilities were incredible, developing a number of advanced materials from graphene and hemp to produce supercapacitors and plastics, among other things.'

'Ah yes, you did mention hemp and Lisa's desire to green the dessert with it. Have you discussed any of this with Nick?'

'No, I haven't had the chance, and strangely he isn't returning my calls. He must be on one of his overseas jaunts again.'

'You're probably right,' Green said, springing up lithely. 'I'm ready for a steam, if you are?'

The confines of the familiar small room and its dense moist atmosphere comforted Carty. It was where they had first shared his dreams in relative privacy and had cemented their uncommon bond. As a blanket of scalding vapour enveloped them, Carty gasped. 'Do you recall the dream I relayed to you before I left?' he quizzed.

'About the demonic serpent-dragon?' Green resounded as he flicked his towel down and sat, pulling his legs up into a lotus posture, his outline now somewhat muffled by the swirling mist given the impression he was hovering in its opaqueness. 'We both came to the conclusion that it was a warning, didn't we?'

'We did and how true that was. It became a recurring vision throughout my ordeal in Xinjiang.'

'Really?'

'Gordon,' he blurted, eyes shining with the palpable anxiety of another secret. 'Hafeza, the executive running Ong's facility saw the dragon around me and took me to visit an old woman, a member of her family, who,' he said, pausing to breathe audibly, 'was a mystic holding an unusual Tibetan Buddhist lineage called *tudkum,* a tradition of sitting in deep meditation for many, many years.'

'I've heard of it,' Green uttered, gently, wiping his forehead.

'Apparently she was about to enter it but appeared to be waiting for me to arrive, as if she had to give me a message first.'

'And did she?'

Carty slowly lifted his wilting head, recalling the image of the woman's radiant face against the hazy backdrop, as she came to his aid while he was under the effects of Lisa's truth drug. But that, he reasoned, was a story he would tell Green on another occasion, as he caught the man's expectant eyes. 'Yes. She sensed that I was the keeper of an immense secret which could change the course of humanity and told me that a Bodhisattva – the Kuan Yin – was protecting the earth from the serpent - prompting me to walk a path between my own concepts of good and evil in order to manifest it.'

'Manifest your secret..., the machine?'

'Either that or the opportunity to bring it to the world's attention.'

'I see,' Green wiped his face with his towel, 'and what's this about protecting the earth from the serpent.'

'In a vision, I saw that it was encircling the planet with its coils, literally squeezing all life away and that's when the Kuan Yin emerged as a tiny figure, a lone force against the beast.'

'Except that she is not alone.'

'No, and in a more recent dream, it appears that she had prevented it from doing so. Instead, the dragon had begun to devour its own tail. I had a feeling that it would soon consume itself and then all would be well.'

'My God, Scott, you've witnessed something rather magical!' he blurted out, excitedly. 'The tail-eating snake – the *Ouroboros* – is a powerful alchemical symbol, signifying that a process has become conscious or complete. The fact that you saw it encircling the world, though, is profound, don't you think?'

'Are you implying that the planet has become more conscious?'

'It already is conscious, No, I mean mankind may have become more conscious so that the beast no longer has power, and that the old outdated ways are losing ground. Perhaps your journey in the last few years has helped tipped the scales.'

'The makeweight that tips the scales and shifts the planet into a whole new reality?' he bounced back.

'Indeed.' Green smiled broadly at the comment, recognising it as one of Jung's.

'And something to tell my children,' Carty followed, grinning back at this friend.

Quiet and exhausted by the steam, they strolled back to the pool and jumped straight in. It took some minutes before they had sufficiently cooled and were back up the steps again, heading for the hot rooms.

'So, Jack suggested that you might tell me more about the thorium nuclear plant that Ong was building,' Green probed. 'I've made a brief research on the internet and am stunned at the simplicity of this technology. It should be more commonly deployed instead of uranium reactors.'

'Try telling that to those running that industry. Thorium produces far less nuclear waste and while I'm no fan of nuclear, and nor are you, the facts are sobering. It's considered to be one of the most abundant, cleanest and safest energy sources readily available, and it's estimated that one ton of it can produce the equivalent amount of energy as 200 tons of uranium or more than three million tons of coal. Staggering, isn't it?'

Green nodded an affirmative. 'It does seem to present a feasible low-carbon bridge to a sustainable energy future.'

‘If that isn’t enough, it’s been postulated by the scientific community that its natural radioactive decay keeps the earth’s iron core molten.’

‘And without that, human life would not exist,’ the older man sighed, ‘but the question begs itself, why thorium has not already replaced uranium as a nuclear fuel. Call me a sceptic, but perhaps it’s because it’s so plentiful, and as a fuel, produces hardly any plutonium, it’s of no use to weapons manufacturers. The dark side of humanity always holds an incredible power over those who wish to control others,’ he added, pulling back the clear plastic curtain to enter the sweltering dry rooms. ‘We’ve discussed it so many times, but it’s clear that fossil fuels are not losing any ground to alternatives. In fact, with shale fracking they appear to be gaining momentum again despite the rapid uptake of technologies like electric vehicles.’

‘Electric vehicles need to be charged, and that’s where the change can be made.’

‘I see. Thorium does seem like a viable solution to the poor legacy associated with nuclear electricity generation, but the hydrogen economy is still a simpler and more sustainable bet in the long term.’

‘And Nick was hoping to develop that with Lisa’s people.’

‘You mean with Brown’s Gas?’

‘Yes. She had convinced him of her uncle’s programme to convert diesel marine engines to using Brown’s Gas instead. Nick reckoned that efficiencies are massively improved and carbon emissions almost eradicated.’

‘That’s an important play.’

‘Ong’s influence was such that apparently, he was able to convince the Chinese navy to convert a number of its ships to use Brown’s Gas. I actually saw one of the operational marine engines being tested at the research facility.’

‘But were you sure it was actually running on Brown’s Gas?’

Carty rolled his eyes. ‘No, I took Hafeza’s word for it. She, like her aunt, had very unusual powers and helped me escape the attack on Lisa.’ Again, he resisted the urge to tell Green of her supernatural skills. 'I knew instinctively that I could trust her,' he said, convincingly. 'There's also something else, though, Gordon. The Chinese claim that Brown's Gas can transmute nuclear waste to safer isotopes and that in some cases it displays *overunity.*'

'Did you also hear that from this woman Hafeza?'

'No, from Nick, on the day he introduced me to Lisa, but I fear that he may have succumbed to her romantic designs and in a mad moment slipped up, telling her about the machine and its ability to also transmute nuclear waste.'

'He's a fool and should have seen that woman for what she was.'

'That's easy for you to say. She was so charismatic and so compelling with the lies that she told.'

Green exhaled a huge sigh. 'Well, that information about Brown's Gas is hugely important. Nick needs to make Jack aware of it as soon as possible.'

'I've already told Jack.'

'During his debrief?'

'Yes.'

'Then you ought to know as we're speaking of Jack, that he had the books scanned before I handed them to you that morning. There was nothing I could do to stop him,' he blurted before lowering his head.

Carty shrugged, inwardly simpering. *Lena had already guessed that.*

'I can't blame him, Gordon, and I would rather they were with Jack than with anyone else.' His words seem to hang in the sweltering air with Lena's message that they were of no use anyway, vital elements of the blueprints had been deliberately omitted as an insurance policy by the machine's inventor.

'While we're on the subject of books, do you think I could borrow *The Secret of the Golden Flower?*'

Green glanced up at him. 'But you have it,' he said with a quizzical smile. 'You took it on that day that I gave it to you.'

'I did?' Carty frowned, believing that the heat had confused the older man's memory, but it hadn't.

Epilogue

London, Late August 2008

The summer had been quiet, alone with Lena, forbidden to travel or contact friends. All Scott Carty had been able to do was work on the overhanging legal issues associated with the embezzlement of his Xinjiang projects. It seemed that the unwanted notoriety hung around him like a bad smell, prompting investors in Sole Carbon to seek redemption – the repayment of their investments – regardless of the assurances he and his legal team had given that the funds were safe and would be returned with interest, within a few months. He knew in his heart that he couldn't persuade anyone to stay invested for the agreed term. Such bad publicity would also hasten the end of the fund, forced to sell the projects at just cents in the dollar to Chinese industrial groups now circling like vultures. *No smoke without fire* had been the rumour passing among the ranks of suited City bankers when they heard Carty's name. They considered him a reckless fool and a flake, unable to gauge risks and becoming embroiled in deals reeking of corruption and deceit. Hindsight for them was a wonderful thing, but none had been stranded in such a position as his, forced to endure life-threatening and terrifying scenarios, and putting complete trust in his instincts to save himself regardless of the consequences. Carty had and was now contemplating all this philosophically, thankful for his bizarre luck which had saved him from death on more than one occasion, and which had ultimately, brought joy in the form of his soulmate Lena Isotova.

But why has all this madness happened to me? The notion challenged as he panned through the TV's channels, fixing on the spectacle of the Beijing Olympics' closing ceremony and wondering what might have been if Ong had carried out his threats to detonate dirty nuclear bombs. The man was now probably incarcerated in the worst jail the Chinese authorities could find and, no doubt, doing hard labour so that he wouldn't live for too many years. This and the episodes in Xinjiang stubbornly hung in Carty's mind, particularly Lisa's psychopathic drives, at the expense of all else. For her the end would be justified by any means, however cruel, and he wanted to hate her for the genuine physical and psychological pain she had caused to both Lena and himself. But he couldn't bring himself to do so. Not all of her soul had been corrupted by her mad lifestyle, some part genuinely wanted to action environmental change through transforming the Taklamakan desert into a huge green eye at the centre of the world. It was a noble, even if misguided ambition and one that she had also abused – the carrot used to entice Carty to give up his technology. And he might have succumbed if he hadn't had the guidance of his dreams, faith in Lena's love and help from two mysterious women. *And what of Hafeza and her aunt, Ludmilla Anatolivna?* he wondered. Were they now suffering at the hands of the authorities for helping an alien, *or were they simply in self-exile, solitary silence in the mountainous caves of Central Asia, sitting in tudkum?* Clearly, with Ong's funding now frozen, the research centre would likely fall into the hands of the State or asset strippers, eager to steal the extraordinary technologies already developed there. *Perhaps graphene, hemp plastics and Brown's Gas will still emerge as game changers?* But without Ong's presence, Lisa's hedonistic leadership and Hafeza's focus, the environment would surely lose out to the commercial exploitation of Xinjiang's vast mineral wealth above all else.

He rose and went out into the garden, greeted by an unseasonal chill as the evening's skies began to close in and the sun's dying rays were masked by purple thunder clouds. The scene stirred a further anguish. A storm was brewing in the US retail mortgage markets and had been since the previous summer. Word was out that contagion had already begun to whip up a wild fire through the banking world and despite all efforts, could not be put out. His beloved carbon credits and their derivatives were about to become casualties too, as worthless as toilet paper in a world reeling from the foreboding collapse of global blue-chip financial institutions.

Will this be just the beginning of a global realignment, a process that may take a generation to complete? Ever since he had met those Russians at Baikal, his world sense had changed and despite wanting to shrug off any notion of it over the last few years, events or Fate had metaphorically dragged him back by the hair, screaming, to admit the same conviction.

But then a smile quietly crept over his tired face with the joyous expectation of his baby arriving early in the New Year. Lena was now showing and he understood that his life's focus had to change to ensure that this unborn child had the best start and that his son James would still feel wanted with a sibling. It would soon be their world and Carty's role would be to hand over to them and their peers, when the moment was ripe, the arcane knowledge he had acquired. That thought sent a chill through him. All he had was the guidance of his inner self to help steer their generation to care for the world. He took succour at the memory of his vision of the Kuan Yin, sitting at the heart of the planet whose presence prevented all life being squeezed away by the serpent's encircled tail. With it, a numinous understanding came that left a fleeting sensation of pure calm.

An overwhelming fragrance of roses roused Carty from his brief slumber on the couch, and he pulled himself up to sit. He didn't grow roses and his searching stare, out through the French Windows into the twilight, left him bewildered–it wasn't his garden but aspects of it he seemed to recognise and then suddenly, he became cognisant that he was awake in his own dream. With that he caught a slight movement against the bushes at the far edge of the long lawn and turned to squint into the shadows. Among them, he could just make out an outline and recognised instantly that it was the hooded revenant Basilides, waiting for him again. Then he found himself being magically transported across the grass to meet the figure, who quickly swung away to float off through the dense overgrowth.

Carty pursued him, sure that he was about to be shown something of great relevance, ignoring the pressing worry of having his skin gashed open in pushing through the rosebushes. But uncannily, they parted to allow his unhindered passage as all birdsong evaporated to leave just the faint yet distinct tumbling of water from a fountain playing somewhere in the background. He watched as his otherworldly guide stopped just short of an ancient crumbling wall, pointing at its large gnarled oak gate and Carty now understood that he was being brought to the walled garden he had visited in the earlier dream. The choice to pass through was his alone, but if he did he knew he was to face the watery serpent once again. That and the prospect of discovering if the young girl had been devoured had him steeling himself against a tightening apprehension. Then he turned the gate's bulbous bronze latch.

The inner garden was much like before, although now a mass of blooms and heady rich fragrances that momentarily distracted him until, in the rising moon's shafts, he glimpsed the dense ivy shrouding the pool's vast stone perimeter. A cool breeze played against his back and he momentarily shuddered but stepped on, drawn towards the sound. Basilides was nowhere to be seen but he felt the being's presence close by and took heart, placing a foot on to the lower step that ran around the pool's base while taking purchase of its top ledge to pull himself up, trembling at the expectation of what he imagined encountering on the other side. Peering over its edge he scanned the arena, noting the huge baroque stone carp as its centrepiece, cascading waters spewing from its mouth as if it was somehow alive. Sitting on a wide plinth was the young woman, her legs casually paddling in the water, but her appearance couldn't have been more different to his last visit: in a short summer frock with her auburn hair neatly tied back in a ponytail. Almost instantly she spied his moving head reflected in the water's surface and began to hum a melody that filled the space. The childlike innocence she had exhibited before, in the presence of the imminent danger of the dragon lurking in the pool below her, was now absent. In its place instead she carried an aura of nonchalant radiance which set his being at peace as she busied herself reaching forward into the depths with both hands. It appeared she was enticing whatever it was floating just beneath the waters and for a moment, Carty feared that it was the beast but something then quietly broke the surface, reflecting a flicker of scant light from its form as it did, signalling that it was probably a fish. But whatever the creature was, it was soon scooped gently up into the maiden's palms and she formally presented it up towards her silent onlooker. Carty was taken aback by the sight – a frog, the size of a small football with its limbs splaying from her hands as she struggled with its slippery mass. Soon, it started to vibrate its throat so that it drowned out her humming, and then with a large belch, it spewed up a shining orb onto her lap.

'You did your part in turning the dragon from its path of destruction.' Ludmilla Anatolivna's words telepathically arrived out of nowhere. 'And the beast has been transformed to deliver up the pearl that it holds.'

The dream left him with a sense of bewildered satisfaction that the old mage had not only been a guiding hand in helping him to survive his ordeals, but was now implying that the dragon had been defeated, transformed. *But into a frog! I wonder what Gordon will make of that.* The thought hovered momentarily and then set in motion the recollection of the Chinese legend Lisa had recounted – "*that each dragon carries a pearl beneath its chin, a secret prize for only the most worthy.*" It seemed ironic that she had worn with great pride, a South Sea Pearl necklace, no doubt purchased at an exorbitant price and yet, the dragon's pearl she spoke of was not something that could be obtained with money. It had him pondering again the whole mess she had fallen into and how she might have transformed herself for the better. But that was all moot, now. *Am I being offered the pearl?* He then pondered, prompting him to switch off the television and arrange to meet his mentor. He missed Green's company and wanted to discuss the symbolic aspects of this dream.

'Gordon, I trust all is well with you? Do you have time to meet this week?'

'Hah!' Green uttered. 'I was just about to call you. Jack wants to see us tomorrow. He's sending a car to pick us up in the morning. We'll be with you at around 9, if that's okay?'

* * * *

The next morning

'Hello Jack,' Carty greeted the man as they were ushered into the small office.

'Morning gentlemen, take a seat.'

They did and Carty glanced around, noting that nothing there had changed much since the last few times that he had visited. He understood that in this backwater of Whitehall, the old ways of calm, measured intellect still prevailed in defiance of an intelligence world in the throes of tectonic change. The internet and the dominance of cyber espionage were now seeking huge resources to monitor a beast, which while having remained constant in its appearance since the Cold War, was now changing masks every month or so - a demanding challenge to those responsible for security.

'I'm guessing something important has cropped up for you to call us in so urgently?' he asked meeting Jack's eyes searching him through the lenses.

'Hmmm,' the man replied, pulling some papers together from the desk and joining them to sit on the Barcelona chairs 'Right, I'm not going to waste time asking how yours and Lena's day-to-day lives are, Scott. My people update me if anything out of the ordinary is happening and that's why you're here, now.'

'Something bad?' Carty blurted, and then hesitated, waiting for Jack to reply.

'I'm afraid so. The fraud case at Albion has been reopened,' he said, pausing to read from the page of notes on his crossed legs. 'Albion has never really recovered from the damage

D'albo inflicted and in light of a looming financial crisis, banks are calling in their loans. I have it on good authority that Albion is facing collapse.'

Green's tousled brows flicked up in mock surprise. 'And why, exactly, does that concern Scott? He was cleared of any fraud.'

Jack's annoyance was tempered by a sharp knock followed by the door opening. Tea was about to be served and he allowed his assistant to perch the tray down and then leave.

'It appears that senior members of Albion had hidden a slush fund in a Panamanian account, syphoning-off millions of US dollars per year from fictitious option trades.

Carty's expression became stony. 'Smells of D'albo's shenanigans, all over again.'

'They never stopped, even after his supposed death.'

'*Supposed...*, what are you implying?'

'I'll get into that in a minute. What I'm being told is that some of the scams D'albo set up were hidden from the Fraud Office investigators who were focused on unravelling the trail of bogus Russian trades at Albion in which he had framed Scott as the fall guy. Two of Albion's former employees have just been arrested in the US and the information we have is that the Panamanian accounts are managed by one person only, as the authorised signatory for the funds disbursement to other accounts, mainly to BVI shell companies.'

'D'albo?'

'No, Scott, you. Your signature is all over the accounts. Someone is posing as you, obviously.'

'What!' Carty rasped, his throat tight and his face now a picture of abject horror as he stared across to Green.

'And it goes back a long way, well before the CentralniySib fiasco that almost ruined your career.'

'And D'albo?' Green interjected, 'you mentioned his supposed death.'

Jack turned to the man, nodding slowly. 'You will recall that Arthur D'albo died mysteriously from a fall off a horse while in the USA and that he was then rapidly cremated. We understood at the time that his ashes were scattered over a lake by the mother of his illegitimate daughter and there was no reason to doubt her.'

'Are you now proposing that he faked his death?'

'Pretty much. We believe he was controlling these funds and paid off a number of people to hide the other option scams at Albion as well as hiring an actor pretending to be you, Scott.'

'But that's madness. The financial world knew my face, after all the notoriety of the Albion fraud case and TV interviews.'

'Not in Panama and not if the account manager was in the pay of D'albo. Anyway it's a moot point now even though the funds were stolen from Russian and Chinese counterparts who had little idea of the investments' complexities and were probably trying to hide illicitly earned funds anyway. Albion is on the point of ruin. Its lines of credit are being foreclosed based on this revelation.'

'There's going to be a lot of angry people after D'albo's blood, if he is still alive.'

'It's clear he is, still. We just don't know where yet, and a number of different intelligence services are working together to close the trail. We should have him soon enough. But what this means Scott is that you'll probably have to appear in court at some future point, as a witness when these Albion employees are tried.'

'Really..., I can't believe my luck.'

The sarcasm didn't register in Jack's demeanour.

'Again? Is that really necessary?' Green added.

'That's not up to me, you know that, Gordon!' Jack uttered, pausing to pour from the covered tea pot, his look beckoning from the others to confirm that they also wanted their cups filled. They both nodded silently, allowing the ceremony to provide a needed breather to digest the shocking news.

Jack remained emotionless as he slipped back into his seat with the bone china in his palm.

'I will keep you briefed on any outcome once I think it is right to do so. Of course, not a mention of this to anyone, please. The newspapers will be all over the Albion collapse and very soon will be asking you for your comment, Scott.'

Carty lowered his eyes, in acknowledgment but not quite able to accept that D'albo and the Albion fraud had erupted into his life, yet again. He looked back up, catching Green's wink.

'And there's also another small point,' Jack added.

'What?'

'We're holding a man who was found unconscious on your garden patio several nights ago. Thankfully, you and Lena were staying at the safe house. I think that you should remain there for the immediate future.'

'Who found this man and who is he?' Carty probed.

'He's an assassin and we've yet to find out in whose hire he was in. The surveillance team picked him up on the camera monitors but before they could act, they saw another figure appear from nowhere to incapacitate him.'

Green chortled. 'What do you mean, from nowhere?' he blurted, doubt obvious in his voice. 'Was this other person intercepted?'

'No, whoever it was, they vanished almost immediately.'

Carty glared at the man. 'Even from the cameras?'

'Yes, I can show you.' He reached for a laptop sitting on his desk and opened it up, waiting for some seconds for the programme to run. 'Now watch this bit carefully,' he instructed as he turned it around to face them. Carty recognised his Highgate garden despite the odd green glare of the infrared night image. Clearly an intruder was trying to force open the patio doors. But then, as Jack has said, a ghostly shadow seemed to materialise from the edge of the shot.

'Pause it, please,' Carty cried. He wanted to take a closer look. The images were blurred but he could see the assassin being chopped across the neck by the mysterious figure. 'Okay, thanks, play it further.'

Jack hit the play button and the video carried on for another couple of seconds.

‘Hold it! Can you re-run that last bit?’ Carty prompted as he looked over to Green, in astonishment.

‘That defies belief,’ his friend uttered, slowly shaking his head at the screen. Then they watched it again and again. The blurred last few seconds of the stranger's outline didn’t exit the screen but just appeared to vanish or become invisible.

‘Was there a problem with the camera recording this footage?’ Green asked.

‘That’s what our team thought but there wasn’t anything faulty otherwise it wouldn’t have recorded at all and no one has tampered with it since. Why would they?’ He stared at Carty. ‘Any ideas?’

‘None, none at all,’ Scott Carty replied, hearing the words leave his mouth as if he was observing himself from somewhere else in the room. None of it made sense and for a second he almost suspected that the revenant of his dreams, Basilides, had materialised in this world to assist him, but then he understood that was impossible. His logic, though, slowly presented a clearer notion to him. Only one person he knew could possibly exhibit such skills. *The Buryat..., but if he is here then there must be danger coming,* the thought dawned on him, eliciting a very queer sensation of angst with the almost certain expectation that another challenge, one much bigger than any he had faced and survived so far, was looming large in his life.

Afterward

In 1927, the Dashi-Dorzho Itigilov, the 12th Pandito Hambo Lama, then 75 years of age and the last patriarch of Tibetan Buddhism in Russia, gathered his monks. Announcing that he was about to die and that they should visit his body 30 years in the future, he sat in a full lotus asana, began to meditate and chanting a prayer for the dead, died. Sometime in 1956 or 57 - the exact date is not known - he was exhumed. To the shock of the monks, it appeared that he was not yet dead but had achieved *sunyata* - the state of a living saint. They quickly reburied him in a box packed with salt, in an unmarked grave for fear of retribution by the Soviet regime. He was finally exhumed in September 2002 at almost 150 years of age and his apparent non-death state: flexible hands and joints, nail growth and soft leathery skin, stunned the scientists of the day. He is venerated at the Ivolginsk monastery–the Russian Lhasa, not far from Lake Baikal, in Buryatia, Siberia, and continues to remain an inexplicable enigma to this day.

Jules Verne, in his 1884 novel, *The Mysterious Island,* predicted that the inevitable evolution of water as an alternative fuel to coal would emerge and be made real, 200 to 300 years into the future. Was he eerily foreseeing Brown's Gas and the very real threat of fossil fuels exacerbating Climate Change? *'Yes, my friends, I believe that water will one day be employed as fuel, that hydrogen and oxygen which constitute it, used singly or together, will furnish an inexhaustible source of heat and light, of an intensity of which coal is not capable.*

Glossary

Readers may wish to look into some of the more unusual topics cited below, which are developed in *Green Eye*.

The Hydrogen Economy

The hydrogen economy was first proposed and coined by Professor of Chemistry John Bockris in 1970, as a system of delivering hydrogen gas as a replacement to fossil fuels, for energy supply with little or no CO2 footprint. Opponents of this system have argued that Hydrogen does not occur naturally as a fuel in its own right but is a transfer medium of energy, too costly to supply and too difficult to transport. Proponents argue that with investments a fraction of the subsidies given to the nuclear and fossil fuel industries, methods for economically and safely producing/storing Hydrogen can be developed using renewables and water electrolysis. Recent developments in fuel cells and catalyst technology in the US, Japan and China as well as the use of cheaper and more efficient materials and renewables such as solar, are bringing the Hydrogen Economy closer to deployment. A further promising prospect in achieving this is the cheap production of Ammonia which can be easily shipped and stored and then 'cracked' to produce Hydrogen in situ. This can then be introduced into the existing natural gas infrastructure pipe system, creating a 'synthetic-gas' mixture, which when burnt will substantially reduce CO2 and other greenhouse gases. The existence and effectiveness of Brown's Gas is still to be formally verified, but perhaps in some remote lab, it's already operating.

The Schumann Resonance

The, German physicist W.O. Schumann first hypothesized, in 1952, that measurable electromagnetic waves existed between the surface of the earth and the ionosphere 30 miles above it.

He subsequently proved the existence of a standing wave resonance at a main frequency of approx. 8 Hz (7.83 Hz) which has since, been loosely dubbed the electrical heartbeat of the planet, the tuning fork for life - a background frequency influencing the biological circuitry of the mammalian brain. The ancient yoga Rishis expressed this frequency in their chanting of OHM, the incarnation of pure sound. Interestingly, 7.83 Hz is at the upper range of theta and low range alpha brain wave states, associated with hypnotism, suggestibility, meditation, cerebral blood-flow rates and increased human growth hormone levels. In recent years the Schumann Resonance's frequency has intermittently spiked to between 13 Hz and as much as 32 Hz, the latter being in the top range of Beta brainwave states associated with overwhelming stress and anxiety. Some are suggesting that the Earth (and Heaven) is organising a trial of cleansing in preparation for a new frequency above 40z which would resonate with Gamma brainwaves responsible for super-consciousness. This is what appears to have been foretold by the indigenous traditions as a fifth song of consciousness, one that has not yet been heard.

The Fourth Phase of Water

Gerald Pollack, Professor of Bio-engineering at University of Washington has in recent years, developed a revolutionary theory based on the work of Sir William Hardy who, in the early 1900s argued that water exhibited a separate phase from its usual three states, a so called ordered" or "structured" 4th state of water. This 4th state explains many of the anomalies that water possesses and is very possibly a fundamental structure underlying all life. See his intriguing brief presentation on TEDx talks, or: https://www.structuredwaterunit.com

Overunity

Overunity is term coined to describe the function of a machine that somehow has the ability to produce more energy than that put into it. According to the laws of physics, this contravenes the

First Law of Thermodynamics and is theoretically impossible. However, what most people forget is that these laws apply to closed systems. The Earth, however, is not a closed system. As conjectured in *Blue Eye*, is Overunity simply utilising energy that is returned to its source on a much longer time frame? Many inventors claim that they have produced such machines that access the quantum flux, the aether which holds the stuff of matter and the universe together. Other terms that have been used to describe similar disputed phenomena are Zero Point Energy, Cold Fusion and LENRs (Low Energy Nuclear Reactions).

Neijia

Neijia is a Chinese word which roughly translated means the internal arts, the underlying body framework of healing and martial arts that develop and harness the breath, mind and Qi as opposed to just pure physical calisthenics. Yoga and other similar arts could be considered neijia.

Thorium

The Thorium fuel cycle nuclear reactor was developed at approximately the same time at the Uranium fuel cycle but despite several pilot reactors being successful built and run, it was overlooked for Uranium for reasons that are unclear. Many believe that Thorium is key to developing a new generation of cleaner, safer nuclear power stations. According a group of scientists at the Georgia Institute of Technology, considering its overall potential, Thorium-based power can mean a 1000 plus years solution or more significantly a quality low-carbon bridge to truly sustainable energy sources, solving a huge portion of mankind's negative environmental impact. The Thorium fuel cycle offers several potential advantages over the Uranium fuel cycle, including much greater abundance of raw material Thoria, superior physical and nuclear fuel properties, greatly reduced nuclear waste production and the important fact that it is almost impossible to build a nuclear weapon from a Thorium reactor's by-products. However, like the Uranium nuclear industry, the development of Thorium power has significant start-up costs. The UK's Parliament did establish an All Parliamentary Party Group ('APPG') to discuss and understand the merits and feasibility of establishing Thorium as a fuel source for powering the UK. http://www.appg-thorium.org.uk/

Hemp & Graphene

The history of hemp and its supposed suppression is explained in fair detail by Lisa, in *Green Eye*. Hemp may yet provide the solutions for sustainable plastics and fuels. Graphene's potential will truly revolutionise the modern world.

The Carrington Event

The Sun's solar storm of 1859 spewed out massive coronal mass ejections (solar flares) which directly engulfed the earth. The same events will one day, happen again, and as described in *Blue Eye*, could incapacitate the electrical grid and other technological systems of the modern world. The implications of this would be quite extraordinary.

Acknowledgements

My heartfelt thanks to my family who have been a source of inspiration and love, and who have generously allowed me the time to complete this work, and to the late Rodney Love, genius artist to whom this book is dedicated.

My special thanks to Olivier and Barbara for their editing brilliance, Wayne Dorrington for the incredibly inspired book cover and to Neil Fox, Dr Anthony Soyer, Jim Uglow, David Guyatt, Karen Scott, Richard, Diana, Angela, Sarah, Tony, Tibor, Merritt, Simon, Guy, Liz, Stefan, Sean, and Holly Brink for their dear friendship, love, teaching and spiritual support.

My appreciation to Justine Solomon's *Byte the Book* - the friendliest forum in town and finally, eternal gratitude to Carl Gustav Jung, pioneer of the unconscious, the late Graham Gordon-Horwood, kindred spirit, dream-worker and friend who first fired my inspiration, and The Yang Family who have preserved and handed down their extraordinary *neijia* for future generations.

About Green Eye and the Author

Green Eye continues where *Blue Eye* left off, weaving a modern day thriller concerning the global energy paradigm, sustainability, international business, love, and the journey of transformation for its hero, Scott Carty, and raises some possibilities that defy this consensus scientific age. If you wish to know more about *Green Eye* and its prequel *Blue Eye*, please visit: http://www.blueyethebook.com and follow on Twitter @blueeyethebook

Tracy Elner grew up in London intrigued with natural philosophy and inspired by conjuring, the Taoist martial arts and some great friendships. In an international career spanning almost 30 years, in which he spent time as a material scientist, a commodities trader and a pioneer in the fledgling emissions markets, he has visited some lesser-known parts of the world, including the former Soviet Union and China, as they stumbled into the free-market. More recently, he consults to the environment sector, using his real-world nous of business commerce and culture to help meaningful projects balance their expectations. He is also an ambassador of the Going Blue Foundation – the first global campaign to fight water pollution at source. In his personal life, he finds himself most comfortable with conscious, creative people with whom he can enjoy the mutual sharing of knowledge. He has been practising and teaching the *neijia* healing arts for most of his adult life and appeared on the TV programme *01 for London* in the 1990's, showing how they can be used to re-balance and energise daily life. He has also spent a similar number of years striving with dream-work for personal wholeness and wellbeing.

concentrate on

FRENCH Writing FOR GCSE

PETER DAVIES

SERIES EDITORS:
STEVEN CROSSLAND
AND CAROLINE WOODS

Hodder & Stoughton

A MEMBER OF THE HODDER HEADLINE GROUP

Orders: please contact Bookpoint Ltd, 78 Milton Park, Abingdon, Oxon OX14 4TD. Telephone: (44) 01235 827720, Fax: (44) 01235 400454. Lines are open from 9.00–6.00, Monday to Saturday, with a 24 hour message answering service. Email address: orders@bookpoint.co.uk

British Library Cataloguing in Publication Data
A catalogue record for this title is available from The British Library

ISBN 0 340 75841 4

First published 2000

Impression number	10	9	8	7	6	5	4	3	2	1
Year	2005	2004	2003	2002	2001	2000				

Typeset by Wearset, Boldon, Tyne and Wear.
Printed in Great Britain for Hodder & Stoughton Educational, a division of Hodder Headline Plc, 338 Euston Road, London NW1 3BH by J.W. Arrowsmiths Ltd, Bristol.

CONTENTS

Introduction to the Concentrate on French series

The *Concentrate on French* series is designed to provide reinforcement and practice materials in each of the four Modern Language skills – Listening, Speaking, Reading and Writing. The books can be used at any appropriate time in Key Stage 4 and can complement any commercial course or scheme of work.

Within each of the 10 units, exercises are carefully graded to target particular levels of attainment at GCSE as follows:

Section One – GCSE grades G, F and E.
Section Two – GCSE grades D and C
Section Three – GCSE grades B, A and A*.

The exercises are designed to reflect the test types used by GCSE and Scottish Standard Grade examination boards. They can be used by teachers with a whole class or by individual students working at their own speed. To this end, a record sheet is included at the end of the book on which the student can record progress through the exercises.

Mark schemes, hints and model answers are provided at the end of the book.

Notes to the student

As you cover individual topics during your GCSE Modern Languages course or your revision programme, use the exercises in this book to gain further practice. Look at the contents page and select the topic area you wish to practise or revise.

Each unit is divided into three sections according to the level of difficulty: exercises in Section One target GCSE grades G, F and E, Section Two exercises target grades D and C and those in Section Three target grades B, A and A*.

The exercises are designed to resemble those that you might come across in the GCSE examination. Specific instructions on the skill area practised in this book can be found overleaf. When you have attempted the exercises in one section, consult the answer section at the end of the book and find out how well you have done. If you were successful in all the exercises in a particular section, try those more difficult exercises in the following one.

We hope you find this and the other books in the series useful. Good luck!

Introduction to this book

As explained on the previous page, this book contains ten units, each divided into three sections of exercises graded in difficulty.

Section One
The exercises in this section begin with simple lists and progress to short messages. When you answer the latter you should aim to write in complete sentences. Marks in this section are normally awarded for communicating the message. You should try to be as accurate as possible, checking spellings carefully and not missing out any of the tasks.

If there are ten items requested, there will be 1 mark for each; if there are five tasks, then each will probably be worth 2 marks.

Section Two
At this level you are expected to write approximately 90 words. The questions are a mixture of letters, reports and accounts, usually with four, five or six different tasks to complete. Keep your answers relevant; do not waste your time writing at great length as you will not gain more marks by doing so. It is far better to concentrate on the quality of an answer of the required length.

If you are writing a letter, remember to use an appropriate beginning and ending as there are usually some marks allocated for this part of the answer. You should also remember to use *vous* in a formal letter.

You should aim to write some complex sentences; there are many examples in the model answers at the back of this book, in which the relevant key words are in *italics*. The Appendix also has a short list of some of the possible ways of developing your style.

The other important element is your success in using a range of tenses. In the model answers, verbs in the past, future and conditional tenses have also been put in *italics*. Marks are generally given for communicating the message and for the accuracy of the language used, in roughly equal proportions.

Section Three
There are a range of tasks in this section, all of which invite you to give your own opinion and comment. This is a significant element of work at this level; if you do not address these points,

you are likely to have a lower mark. In the model answers opinions and attitudes are in *underlined italics*.

As in Section Two, a range of language and structures are essential; you should strive to bring as much variety and sophistication to your work. There is advice in the model answers on how to avoid repeating yourself.

The recommended length is approximately 130 words. You will not gain more marks by writing more than is required. At this level there are normally more marks for language than for content, possibly as high as a 75%:25% ratio.

Answers

For each question there is a model answer which provides a guide to what is expected. Where a question asks for specific detail, the answer identifies possible answers. In some cases there is a choice of interpretation. The model here may well be quite different in detail from yours; however, it will give you some invaluable help on relevant vocabulary, sentence structure and tense usage. Some of the model answers are long; this is simply to provide you with as much helpful information as possible.

Using a dictionary

The dictionary is obviously helpful in writing exercises. You should use it firstly to check the spellings and gender of words that you know. If you need to use an unfamiliar word, be careful when looking it up in the dictionary. Many students lose marks because they choose the wrong word from those listed. Remember that the dictionary has a key, often in abbreviations, to identify the use of a word (e.g. *n*: noun; *v*: verb). Students frequently mistake words which have more than one use – for example 'work' can be both a verb (*travailler*) and a noun (*le travail*). It is important that you know what you want, and that you can choose the correct word from the list provided.

UNIT 1 MYSELF AND OTHERS

Section One

Exercice 1

Le correspondent/ la correspondante

Tu cherches un(e) correspondant(e) français(e).

Remplis la fiche en français.

Demande de correspondant/correspondante

Date d'inscription: le 14 mai 2000

Nom de famille: ______________________

Prénom: ______________________

Date de naissance: ______________________

Famille: ______________________

Caractère: i ______________________

ii ______________________

Langues parlées: i ______________________

ii ______________________

Sport favori: ______________________

Autres loisirs: i ______________________

ii ______________________

Animaux: ______________________

Matières préférées: i ______________________

ii ______________________

PAGE 53

Section One

Exercice 2
Ma famille

Réponds en français aux questions de ton ami(e) belge.

1 Combien de personnes y a-t-il dans ta famille?

2 As-tu des frères pi des sœurs?

3 Ton père/ta mère, comment sont-ils?

4 Tes parents, que font-ils dans la vie?

5 Quels animaux as-tu?

Exercice 3
Mon animal favori

Tu as des animaux?

Envoie-nous une photo!

Fais une petite description en français de ton animal favori pour accompagner la photo. Il faut mentionner:

A son nom;

B son âge;

C sa couleur;

D son caractère;

E son repas favori.

UNIT 1 MYSELF AND OTHERS

Section Two

Exercice 1
Une lettre

Vous avez reçu une lettre de votre nouveau correspondant français/nouvelle correspondante française. Voici les questions dans sa lettre.

- Parle-moi de toi.
- C'est quand ton anniversaire?
- Où es-tu né(e)?
- Comment es-tu physiquement? Tu es grand(e)?
- Tu as les cheveux comment? À qui ressembles-tu?
- Et ton caractère?
- Quels sont tes loisirs? Qu'est-ce que tu as fait récemment?

Écris-lui en français et réponds à toutes ses questions.

Écris une lettre en français à ton ami(e) en France.

- Commence et termine la lettre avec les formules nécessaires.
- Dis merci pour la carte/le cadeau.
- Dis quels autres cadeaux tu as reçus.
- Explique où et quand tu as fêté ton anniversaire.
- Dis ce que tu as mangé.
- Dis ce que tu as aimé le plus.

Section Two

Exercice 3
Vos animaux

Vous avez des animaux à la maison?

Écrivez un article en français au sujet de votre animal domestique. Il faut mentionner.

A une description de votre animal;

B comment vous vous occupez de votre animal;

C ce qu'il faut faire tous les jours;

D pourquoi l'animal est si important pour vous et la famille.

PAGE 56

Section Three

Exercice 1
Au revoir!

Ta meilleure amie/ton meilleur ami est parti(e) vivre aux États-Unis Écris une lettre en français à ton ami/ton amie suisse.

- Commence et termine la lettre avec les formules nécessaires.
- Décris ta meilleure/ton meilleur ami(e).
- Dis ce que vous avez fait ensemble et pourquoi vous vous entendiez si bien.
- Décris comment tu te sens depuis son départ.

PAGE 57

Section Three

Exercice 2
Une dispute

Vous vous êtes disputé(e) avec un(e) ami(e) d'école. Écrivez en français à votre copain/votre copine suisse et expliquez-lui pourquoi vous vous êtes fâché(e)s. Dites-lui ce qui s'est passé et comment vous avez résolu la situation.

Exercice 3
Ma vie dans 20 ans

Participez à notre débat!

Comment vous imaginez-vous la vie dans 20 ans?

Serez-vous marié(e)?

Serez-vous célibataire?

Pour quelles raisons?

Écrivez vos opinions et vos projets en français.

UNIT 2 AT HOME

Section One

Exercice 1
My home

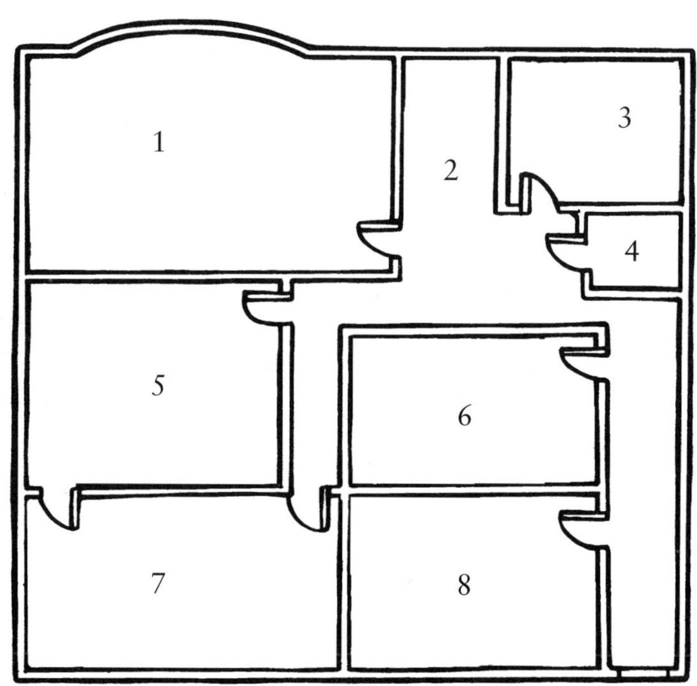

Label five different rooms in French. For each room, write the name of a piece of furniture/equipment in it.

Example: **1** le bureau – un ordinateur

PAGE 60

Exercice 2
Ma ville/ mon village

Écris 5 phrases en français sur ton village ou ta ville.

Exemple: Mon village est à la campagne.

PAGE 60

Section One

Exercice 3
Aider à la maison

Comment-aides-tu à la maison?

Remplis l'agenda de la semaine en français.

Exemple: Lundi – je débarrasse la table.

lundi...
....
mardi...
....
mercredi...
....
jeudi...
....
vendredi...
....
samedi...
....
dimanche...

PAGE 60

UNIT 2 AT HOME

Section Two

Exercice 1
Votre région

La classe prépare une brochure sur votre région pour les étudiants qui arrivent avec l'échange.

Écrivez un article en français. Il faut mentionner:

A où se trouve votre région en Grande-Bretagne;

B des détails sur les activités qu'ils pourront faire;

C des informations sur les monuments qu'ils pourront visiter;

D vos recommandations et les raisons de votre choix.

PAGE 61

Exercice 2
Ta routine

Quelle est ta routine les jours scolaires? Et le week-end? Réponds en français aux questions de ton ami(e) de Monaco. Dis-lui:

A à quelle heure tu te couches/tu te lèves;

B ce que tu manges d'habitude;

C comment tu vas au collège et combien de temps tu y restes;

D ce que tu fais le soir;

E ce que tu as fait le week-end dernier.

PAGE 62

Section Two

Exercice 3
Les jeunes

Les jeunes, êtes-vous paresseux ou aidez-vous à la maison?

★ Que faites-vous exactement?

★ Combien de fois par semaine? Quels jours?

★ Avant ou après l'école?

★ Est-ce que vous recevez de l'argent?

★ Et pendant les dernières vacances, qu'est-ce que vous avez fait?

Écrivez une lettre en français à la revue et répondez aux questions.

Section Three

Exercice 1
La décoration

Les jeunes, que préfèrent-ils comme décoration?

Donne-nous tes idées!

PAGE 64

Tu as décoré ta chambre. Écris un article en français pour la revue des jeunes. Explique pourquoi tu as changé de décoration, ce que tu as fait et qui t'a aidé. N'oublie pas de donner ton avis du résultat. Tes copains/copines, qu'en pensent-ils?

Exercice 2
Faire la cuisine

Tout le monde doit savoir faire la cuisine.

Écrivez un article en français. Il faut mentionner:

A comment vous avez appris à faire la cuisine;

B ce que vous avez comme expérience;

C ce que vous aimeriez pouvoir préparer;

D ce que vous pensez de l'idée.

PAGE 65

Exercice 3
Où j'habite

La ville?

La banlieue?

La campagne?

Écrivez un article en français pour donner vos opinions. Expliquez où vous habitez en ce moment, où vous aimeriez habiter plus tard et pourquoi.

UNIT 3 RELAXING

Section One

Exercice 1
Les distractions dans ta région

Fais une liste des distractions dans ta région.

Nomme 10 activités en français.

PAGE 67

Exemple: un bowling

Exercice 2
Mon week-end

Remplis ton agenda du week-end en français.

PAGE 67

Exemple: vendredi soir – aller chez ma copine

Exercise 3
A trip to France

Send a postcard in French to your friend.

1 Invite her/him to meet you.

2 Suggest a place.

3 Tell her/him the date and time.

4 Say what you would like to do in the afternoon.

5 Ask what she/he wants to do in the evening.

PAGE 67

Section Two

Exercice 1
Sondage: la télévision

TÉLÉVISION

INFORMATIONS	☐
DOCUMENTAIRES	☐
FILMS	☑
BANDES DESSINÉES	☑
ÉMISSIONS DE SPORT	☐

Tu écris en français à ton ami(e) français(e) pour lui parler des émissions que tu regardes. Commence et termine ta lettre avec les formules nécessaires. Dis-lui:

A combien d'heures par jour tu regardes la télé;

B les émissions que tu préfères et pourquoi;

C les émissions que tu n'aimes pas et pourquoi;

D ce que tu penses des actualités;

E ce que tu as regardé hier soir.

PAGE 68

Section Two

Exercice 2
Argent de poche

Les 14–18 ans, combien d'argent de poche ont-ils? Comment le dépensent-ils?

Écrivez un article en français sur votre argent de poche. Il faut mentionner les aspects suivants:

A combien vous recevez, quand et de qui;

B comment vous dépensez votre argent d'habitude (disques? vêtements? sorties?);

C quelque chose que vous avez acheté récemment;

D si vous faites des économies et pourquoi (vacances? voiture? université?).

PAGE 68

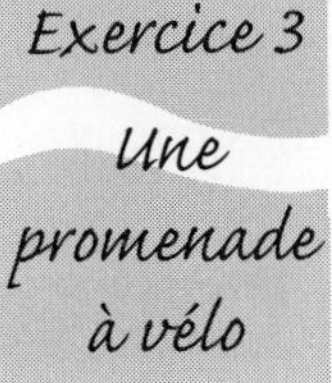
Exercice 3
Une promenade à vélo

Vous avez fait une longue promenade à vélo pendant les vacances. Écrivez une lettre en français à votre ami(e) en France. Commencez et terminez votre lettre avec les formules nécessaires.

Donnez les détails suivants:

A où vous êtes allé(e)s et quand;

B quel temps il faisait;

C ce que vous avez fait le matin;

D où vous avez déjeuné/ce que vous avez mangé;

E comment vous avez passé l'après-midi;

F à quelle heure vous êtes rentré(e)s;

G comment vous vous sentiez.

PAGE 69

UNIT 3 RELAXING

Section Three

Exercice 1
Le week-end dernier

Vous avez passé un week-end magnifique avec vos copains et copines. Vous écrivez un article en français. Expliquez ce que vous avez fait, comment vous vous êtes amusés et pourquoi c'était un plaisir.

Exercice 2
Tes loisirs

Ton correspondant/ta correspondante t'a posé des questions sur tes loisirs.

Dans ton temps libre, que préfères-tu?

Sortir ou rester à la maison?

Écris-lui en français pour lui raconter comment tu aimes passer les soirées et les week-ends. N'oublie pas de lui dire pourquoi.

Exercice 3
Mon ami(e)

Récemment vous avez fait la connaissance d'un nouvel ami/d'une nouvelle amie. Vous écrivez une lettre en français à votre correspondant(e) en Belgique. Il faut mentionner les aspects suivants:

A où et quand vous avez rencontré cette personne;

B ce que vous avez fait ensemble;

C pourquoi vous vous êtes bien entendus;

D vos projets pour le/la revoir.

UNIT 4 HOLIDAYS

Section One

Exercice 1
À l'Hôtel Bellevue

Tu commandes le petit déjeuner pour ta famille. Choisis 4 boissons et 4 plats. Remplis la fiche en français.

Hôtel Bellevue

Commande de petit-déjeuner

Les clients sont priés de remplir la fiche avant 21h. Merci.

Date: le mardi 4 août

Chambre no: ....

À boire .... À manger ....

....

....

....

....

PAGE 73

UNIT 4 HOLIDAYS

Section One

Exercise 2
My holiday photos

Write a caption in French for five of the photos.

Example: je danse à la discothèque

Exercice 3
Au camping

Vous êtes au camping. Vous envoyez une carte postale à votre ami(e). Il faut mentionner les détails suivants:

- la situation du camping
- ce qu'il y a au camping
- le temps
- les activités
- les repas

Section Two

Exercice 1
En vacances

Vous partez en vacances en France. Vous écrivez une lettre de réservation en français. Commencez et terminez la lettre avec les formules nécessaires.

Hôtel-Restaurant
Les Sables Blancs

Ouvert mars – décembre
Avenue de la Plage
Bénodet

Voici les détails:

A nombre de personnes 

B nombre de chambres/lits 

C équipements 

D dates 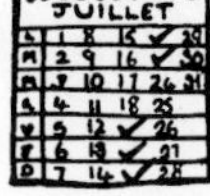

E paiement 

F transport 

PAGE 74

Exercice 2
Des vacances en France

Tu vas aller chez ton ami(e) en France. Écris-lui une lettre en français. Commence et termine ta lettre avec les formules nécessaires. Dis-lui:

A la date de ton voyage;

B ton moyen de transport (avion? bateau?) et l'heure de l'arrivée;

C ce que tu as acheté pour les vacances;

D ce que tu aimerais faire;

E et posez une question à ton ami(e).

Section Two

Exercice 3
Les échanges scolaires

Les échanges scolaires! Parle-nous de tes expériences!

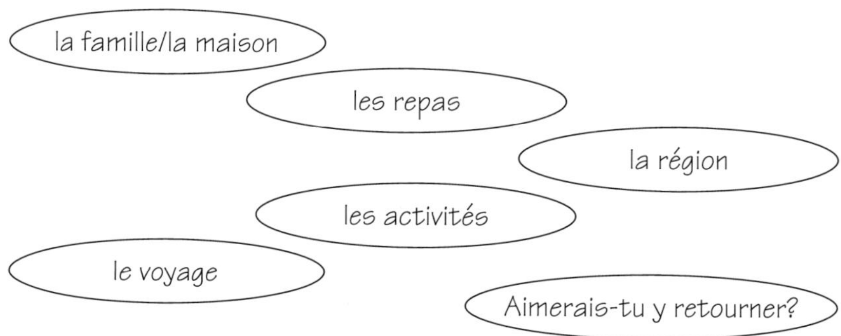

Écris un reportage en français sur ta visite.

PAGE 76

Section Three

Exercice 1
Une auberge de jeunesse

Vous avez passé quelques jours avec des amis dans une auberge de jeunesse en France. Vous avez été déçus. Écrivez une lettre en français au père aubergiste pour vous plaindre. Il faut mentionner les aspects suivants:

- **A** qui vous êtes et les dates de votre visite;
- **B** le mauvais état des équipements (les douches, la cuisine, les toilettes, autres?);
- **C** les différences entre cette auberge et les autres que vous avez visitées.

N'oubliez pas de lui expliquer combien vous êtes déçus et pourquoi.

PAGE 77

Exercice 2
Vive les vacances!

Vive les vacances!

À la mer ou à la campagne?

Avec qui?

À l'hôtel ou au camping?

Vos meilleurs souvenirs?

Écrivez un article en français; donnez les détails de vos expériences (destination? logement? activités? temps?) et notez vos préférences et votre opinion.

PAGE 78

Exercice 3
Un gîte

Vous avez passé des vacances dans un gîte en France. Vous vous êtes beaucoup amusés et vous étiez très contents du gîte et de la région. Envoyez une lettre en français à la propriétaire pour la remercier. Racontez vos expériences et dites-lui ce que vous avez apprécié le plus, pourquoi vous aimeriez y retourner et si vous allez le recommander à d'autres personnes.

PAGE 79

Section One

Exercice 1
Aux objets trouvés

Tu as perdu ton sac à dos.

Fais une liste en français du contenu. Donne dix articles, vêtements ou affaires de camping.

Exemple: lampe de poche

PAGE 80

Section One

Exercise 2
Lost property

On holiday in Dinard you lose your wallet and its contents.

The police ask you to complete this form in French.

Commissariat de Police
Bureau des objets trouvés

Ville de: Dinard

Nom de famille: .... **Prénom:** ....

Objet perdu: ....

Date de la perte: ....

Lieu de la perte: ....

Description de l'objet (deux détails): ....

....

Contenu: ....

Valeur: ....

Signé: ....

Date: ....

PAGE 80

Section One

Exercice 3
La carte postale

Ton ami(e) envoie cette carte.

Rencontre-moi à
la plage samedi
à 11h 30
à bientôt
Cathy

Tu es malade. Écris une carte-postale en français pour expliquer les détails ci-dessous.

Exemple: 

le mercredi 2 septembre

Section Two

Exercice 1
La montre

Vous avez passé un week-end à l'hôtel mais, malheureusement, vous avez perdu votre montre. Écrivez une lettre en français à l'hôtel.

- Commencez et terminez avec les formules nécessaires.
- Expliquez ce que vous avez perdu.
- Donnez les dates de la visite et le numéro de votre chambre.
- Faites une description de la montre (donnez deux détails).
- Précisez pourquoi la montre est importante.
- Dites comment on peut vous contacter.

PAGE 81

Section Two

Tu as fait une promenade à vélo. Malheureusement tu as eu un accident. Écris une lettre en français à ton ami(e) au Canada. Il faut mentionner les aspects suivants:

A où et quand tu as eu l'accident;

B comment cela s'est passé;

C tes blessures;

D comment tu es rentré(e) chez toi;

E les précautions que tu vas prendre à l'avenir.

Exercice 3
Des vacances désastreuses

Un jour pendant les vacances en France il a fait mauvais. Quand tu es rentré au camping tu as trouvé ta tente renversée. Écris un compte rendu en français pour ton correspondant.

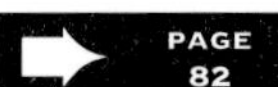

Section Three

Exercice 1 Malade!

Tu as été malade et tu vas retourner au collège après une absence de quelques jours. Écris une lettre en français à ton ami(e) belge. Il faut mentionner les détails suivants:

A tes symptômes et depuis combien de temps tu souffres;

B comment tu as passé le temps;

C comment tu te sens maintenant;

D quand tu vas retourner en classe;

E pourquoi tu t'es inquiété(e).

PAGE 84

Exercice 2 La fuite

Vous êtes en vacances en France dans un gîte. Un soir, en rentrant, vous trouvez la maison inondée, il y a eu une fuite. Vous écrivez un rapport en français pour la compagnie d'assurance. Décrivez ce qui s'est passé et expliquez quelles pièces et quels meubles ont été touchés. N'oubliez pas de mentionner combien vos vacances ont été gâchées.

PAGE 85

Section Three

Exercice 3 Un accident (2)

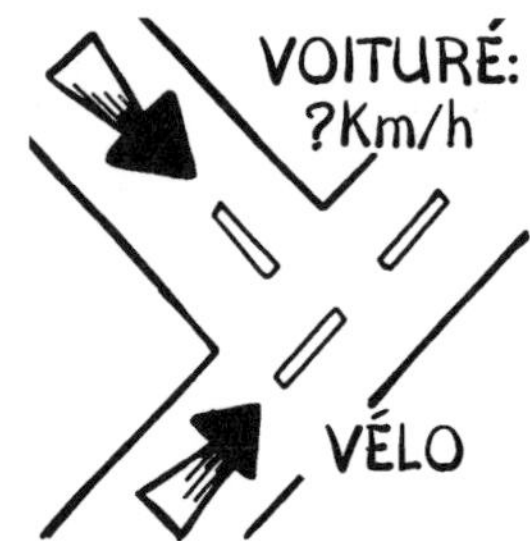

Vous avez vu un accident de route dans le village de Theix en France. Voici le plan des policiers du lieu de l'accident. Écrivez un compte-rendu en français de l'accident. Il faut mentionner les détails suivants:

A une description de la voiture et de la personne qui conduisait;

B une description de la personne à bicyclette et ce que cette personne a fait;

C ce que vous avez fait après l'accident;

D votre opinion sur ce qui s'est passé.

PAGE 86

UNIT 6 SHOPPING

Section One

Exercice 1 Des cadeaux

Tu achètes des cadeaux. Fais une liste en français de cinq cadeaux/souvenirs de vacances. Dis pour qui est le cadeau.

	cadeaux	pour qui?
Exemple:	une affiche	pour ma copine Annie
1	______________	______________
2	______________	______________
3	______________	______________
4	______________	______________
5	______________	______________

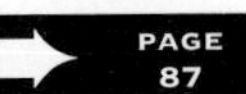
PAGE 87

UNIT 6 SHOPPING

Section One

Exercice 2
Des courses

Vous faites des courses en France. Écrivez une liste en français de cinq articles et cinq magasins.

Exemple: des bonbons à la confiserie

You are going shopping. Leave a message in French for your penfriend. Tell her/him:

A where you are going;

B what you are going to buy;

C what you are going to get for dinner;

D ask him/her to meet you;

E at what time.

Example: say how you are travelling – *je prends le bus*

UNIT 6 SHOPPING

Section Two

Exercice 1
Les magasins chez toi

Ton ami(e) à la Martinique t'a posé des questions sur les courses. Écris-lui une lettre en français et réponds à toutes ses questions.

A Il y a des magasins près de chez toi?

B Qu'est-ce qu'on peut y acheter?

C À quelle heure ouvrent et ferment les magasins en Grande-Bretagne?

D Les vêtements sont chers?

E Qu'est-ce que tu as acheté récemment?

PAGE 88

Exercice 2
Des cadeaux de Noël

Tu es allé(e) en ville pour acheter des cadeaux de Noël. Tu écris une lettre en français à ton ami(e) au Canada. Commence et termine ta lettre avec les formules nécessaires. Dis-lui:

A où et quand tu as fait tes courses;

B ce que tu as acheté et pour qui;

C combien d'argent tu as dépensé;

D comment c'était dans les magasins;

E ce que tu espères recevoir à Noël.

PAGE 89

Section Two

Exercice 3
Une plainte

Vous avez acheté un vêtement dans un magasin en France. Malheureusement, vous n'êtes pas content(e). Écrivez une lettre en français au directeur du magasin pour vous plaindre. Commencez et terminez votre lettre avec les formules nécessaires. Expliquez-lui:

A ce que vous avez acheté (donnez deux détails);

B combien vous avez payé;

C quand vous l'avez acheté;

D pourquoi vous n'êtes pas content(e);

E et posez lui une question au sujet de ce vêtement.

PAGE 90

Section Three

Exercice 1
Faire le shopping

Les jeunes, vous aimez faire le shopping?

Vous aimez les grandes surfaces ou vous préférez les petits magasins?

Écrivez un article en français pour donner vos opinions. Dites où et quand vous avez fait les courses la dernière fois. Expliquez ce que vous pensez; c'est une perte de temps ou un plaisir?

PAGE 91

Exercice 2

Les vêtements de marque

Les vêtements de marque

Vous aimez la mode?
Vous portez les vêtements de grande marque?
C'est une perte d'argent?
Écrivez un article en français pour donner vos opinions. Expliquez ce que vous aimez porter et pourquoi. Dites ce que vous aimeriez faire si vous aviez plus d'argent.

PAGE 92

Exercice 3

Les magasins chez toi (2)

Faire du shopping dans votre région, c'est facile? C'est agréable? Écrivez un reportage en français sur les possibilités. Expliquez ce qu'il y a comme magasins près de chez vous et s'il faut faire une grande distance pour acheter certaines choses. Dites ce qu'on pourrait faire pour améliorer le choix de magasins.

PAGE 93

UNIT 7 FOOD AND DRINK

Section One

Exercice 1

Tu aimes manger ...?

Tu vas chez ton ami(e). Envoie une liste en français des choses que tu aimes manger et que tu n'aimes pas manger.

Il faut mentionner 10 choses.

	j'aime	**je n'aime pas**
Exemple:	la salade	les oignons

PAGE 94

UNIT 7 FOOD AND DRINK

Section One

Exercise 2
A picnic list

1 kilo

Prepare in French a shopping list of five items for a picnic. Include the quantity/container for each.

Example: des canettes de coca

Exercice 3
Gardez la forme!

1

2

3

4

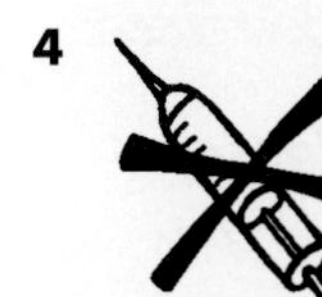

5

6

7

8

Donnez cinq conseils en français pour avoir la forme.

Exemples: Ne prenez pas de drogues! (4) Dormez bien! (8)

Section Two

Exercice 1
Le barbecue

Vous avez fait un barbecue chez un ami. Écrivez une lettre en français à votre ami(e) suisse. Expliquez:

A où vous étiez et qui était là;

B pourquoi;

C quel temps il faisait;

D ce que vous avez mangé;

E ce que vous avez fait après;

F votre opinion des repas barbecue.

PAGE 95

Exercice 2
Faire un repas

Tu as préparé un repas.

Écris un article en français pour décrire tes expériences dans la cuisine. Explique:

A quand et où;

B pourquoi (anniversaire? Noël? quelqu'un de malade?);

C ce que tu as préparé (viande? poisson? dessert?);

D qui t'a aidé;

E si c'était un succès.

PAGE 95

Section Two

Exercice 3

Un repas de vacances

Écrivez un compte-rendu en français. Il faut mentionner:

A où vous avez mangé (fast food? crêperie? restaurant traditionnel?) et avec qui;

B à quelle occasion;

C ce que vous avez pris (entrée? plat principal? dessert? boisson?);

D si c'était un grand plaisir/un désastre? pourquoi?

PAGE 96

Section Three

Exercice 1

Pour garder la forme

Les jeunes, vous gardez la forme?

Vous avez changé de routine?

Votre régime?

Vos activités sportives?

Écrivez un article en français pour en expliquer les avantages et pour donner vos conseils. Expliquez ce que vous avez déjà fait, ce que vous mangez d'habitude et ce que vous avez l'intention de faire à l'avenir pour garder la forme.

PAGE 97

Section Three

Exercice 2
Fumer

Ton ami/ amie fume!

Écris un article en français pour donner ton opinion. Il faut mentionner les aspects suivants:

A qui c'est et son état de santé;

B depuis quand et combien de cigarettes elle/il fume;

C pourquoi elle/il fume;

D ce que tu as fait pour la/le décourager;

E ton opinion sur la cigarette.

PAGE 97

Exercice 3
Végétarien?

Tu manges de la viande?

Tu es végétarien ou végétarienne?

Écris un article en français pour la revue. Donne des détails sur ce que tu manges, si tu suis un régime et donne ton opinion sur la viande/le régime végétarien.

PAGE 98

UNIT 8 STUDYING

Section One

Exercice 1
Ton collège

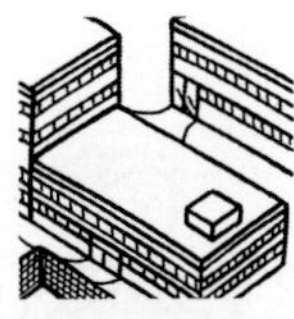   

Tu donnes des détails sur ton collège. Choisis cinq images et écris une phrase en français pour chacun.

Exemple: il y a 650 étudiants

Exercise 2
Homework

Your penfriend has asked about your homework. Write a short note in French and tell her/him:

A how much homework you have;

B where you do your homework;

C which nights you do not do homework;

D which homework you like;

E which homework you do not like.

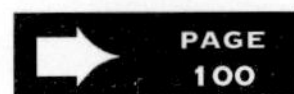

Section One

Exercice 3
À l'école

Réponds aux questions en français.

A Que portes-tu comme vêtements?

B À quelle heure quittes-tu la maison?

C Comment vas-tu à l'école?

D Où manges-tu à midi?

E Quelle est ta matière favorite?

Exemple: À quelle heure commencent les classes? – Les classes commencent à neuf heures.

PAGE 100

UNIT 8 STUDYING

Section Two

Exercice 1
Une visite scolaire

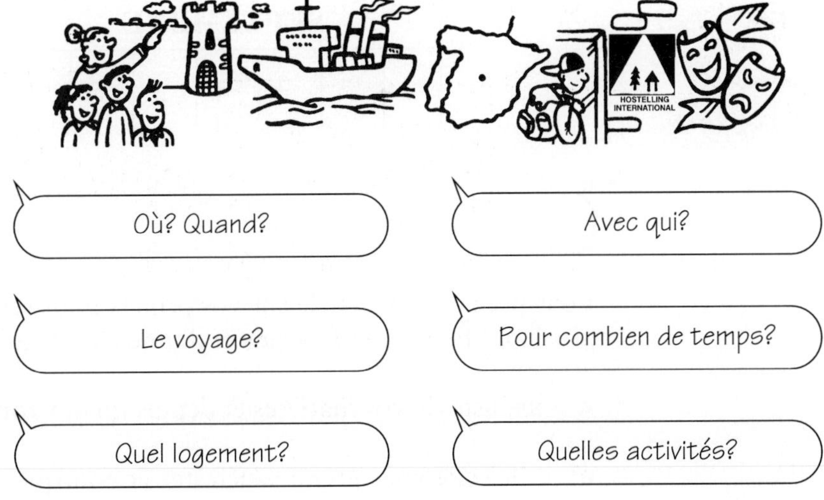

Écrivez un reportage en français sur une visite que vous avez faite avec l'école.

Exercice 2
Les examens

Les examens approchent.

Tu envoies une lettre en français à ton ami(e) français(e) pour lui parler de ta routine. Il faut mentionner:

A quand les examens vont commencer;

B combien d'heures tu travailles par jour/semaine;

C les préparations que tu as déjà faites;

D ce que tu vas faire comme révision;

E ce que tu fais pour te reposer/t'amuser.

Section Two

Exercice 3
L'année prochaine

SEPTEMBRE						
1	2	3	4	5	6	7

les études?

l'emploi?

Vous préparez un article sur vos projets pour septembre prochain. Écrivez en français et donnez les détails suivants:

A une liste de vos matières et depuis quand vous les étudiez;

B celles que vous préférez/détestez et pourquoi;

C ce que vous allez faire l'année prochaine;

D où vous allez étudier/travailler et pourquoi;

E votre ambition.

PAGE 103

Section Three

Exercice 1
Mon activité

Tu as participé dans une activité sportive (un match?) ou dans une activité culturelle (un concert? une pièce?). Tu en écris un rapport en français. Donne des détails sur l'activité que tu as faite. Donne tes impressions, explique si c'était un succès et pourquoi. Aimerais-tu le refaire?

PAGE 104

Exercice 2
L'uniforme scolaire

L'uniforme scolaire, vous êtes pour ou contre?

Écrivez un article en français pour donner votre opinion. Expliquez les règlements dans votre collège. Décrivez ce que vous portez normalement et dites ce que vous préféreriez porter et pourquoi.

PAGE 105

Exercice 3
Les règlements au collège

Les règlements au collège – sont-ils nécessaires?

Tu envoies une lettre en français à ton collège jumelé en France. Décris les règlements dans ton collège, dis ce qu'en pensent les étudiants en général et donne tes propres opinions. Sont-ils nécessaires?

PAGE 106

Section One

Exercice 1 Demande d'emploi

Tu cherches un emploi pour les grandes vacances. Remplis ce formulaire en français.

Date de la demande: le 12 mai 2000

Nom de famille: ______

Prénom: ______

Nationalité: ______

Date de naissance: ______

Caractère: i ______

ii ______

Expérience: ______

Langucs parlées: i ______

ii ______

Sport favori: ______

Autres matières étudiées: ______

Mois libre(s): ______

PAGE 107

Section One

Exercice 2
Les emplois des jeunes

Sondage sur les emplois des jeunes

Dis-nous ce que tu fais!

A Où?

B Quels jours?

C De quelle heure à quelle heure?

D Quel salaire?

E Comment dépenses-tu ton argent?

Écris cinq phrases en français sur ton job.

PAGE 108

Exercise 3
Life in 10 years' time

1 
2 
3 
4 
5 

6 
7 
8 

What are your plans? Make a list of five details in French.

	Je voudrais	Je ne voudrais pas
Examples:	gagner beaucoup d'agent	être étudiant

PAGE 108

Section Two

Exercice 1 Votre stage en entreprise

Écrivez un article en français sur votre stage. Il faut mentionner les aspects suivants:

A où vous avez travaillé;

B quand et pour combien de temps;

C ce que vous avez fait exactement;

D comment était le patron/la patronne;

E si vous allez faire le même travail plus tard.

PAGE 109

Exercice 2
La colonie de vacances

Colonie de vacances 'la vieille ferme'

à Ainay-le-Vieil

cherche

personnel de cuisine, animateurs, surveillants

pour juillet et août

jeunes personnes, âge minimum 16 ans

Répondez en français à l'offre de travail. Commencez et terminez avec les formules nécessaires. Dites:

A quel job vous désirez;

B quelle expérience vous avez;

C quand et pour combien de temps vous voudriez travailler;

D pourquoi vous voulez travailler en France;

E et posez une question au patron.

PAGE 110

Section Two

Exercice 3

L'avenir

Étudiants, qu'est-ce que vous allez faire après l'école?

Écrivez un article en français et répondez à toutes les questions.

A Vous quitterez l'école à quel âge?

B Vous allez continuer vos études?

C Vous désirez gagner beaucoup d'argent?

D Quelle sorte de travail voulez-vous?

E Pourquoi?

PAGE 110

Section Three

Exercice 1

Vos projets

Aller à l'université ou chercher un emploi?

Quels sont vos projets? Écrivez un article en français pour donner vos opinions et les raisons pour votre choix.

PAGE 111

Section Three

Exercice 2
Une difficulté au travail

Tu as eu une grosse difficulté au travail.

Dans une lettre à un/une ami(e), décris la situation en français. Il faut mentionner:

A où tu travaillais;

B ce qui s'est passé et quand;

C ce que tu as fait (téléphoner? à qui?) et qui t'a aidé;

D comment tu te sentais à l'époque;

E comment tu as résolu la situation.

PAGE 112

Exercice 3
Votre carrière

Quelle carrière choisierez-vous? Qu'est-ce qui est important pour vous?

L'argent?

Aider les gens?

Travailler en équipe?

Avoir votre propre compagnie?

Choisirez-vous une carrière seulement si c'est bien payé?

Écrivez un article en français et expliquez vos intentions pour l'avenir. N'oubliez pas de donner les raisons de votre choix?

PAGE 113

Section One

Exercice 1
Le recyclage

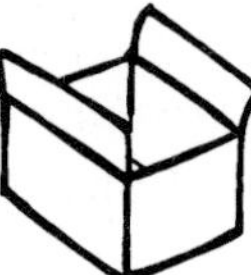

Faites une liste de dix choses en français qu'on peut recycler.

Exemple: **1** le carton

PAGE 114

Exercise 2
Animals in danger!

Animal: le panda

Continent/pays d'origine: la Chine

Couleur: noir et blanc

Taille: très grand

Nourriture préférée: le bambou

In French, draw up a similar profile for three other endangered animals.

PAGE 114

Section One

Exercice 3
L'eau

L'eau est essentielle à la vie!

Faites une liste en français de dix activités où il s'agit d'utiliser de l'eau.

Exemple: **1** boire de l'eau

PAGE 114

Section Two

Exercice 1
En vacances

Vous avez visité un pays en vacances. Écrivez un reportage en français. Expliquez où vous êtes allé(e). Il faut mentionner:

A le temps qu'il fait normalement;

B ce qu'il y a à faire dans la ville;

C ce qu'il y a à voir pour les touristes;

D la cuisine typique de la région;

E ce que vous avez particuliérement aimé.

PAGE 115

Exercice 2
La fête de Noël

Tu écris une lettre à ton ami(e). Dis-lui en français comment tu fêtes Noël dans ta famille: les traditions, les repas, les cadeaux. Explique-lui comment c'est différent de la fête en France.

PAGE 116

Section Two

Exercice 3
Un article sur votre région

Parlez-nous de votre région/de votre quartier.

Écrivez un article en français sur votre région/votre quartier. Il faut mentionner les aspects suivants:

A situation (centre-ville? banlieue? rurale?);

B inconvénients (peu de magasins? graffiti? crimes?);

C avantages (distractions? transports? centres commerciaux? espaces verts?);

D pollution (usines? circulation? beaucoup de bruit?).

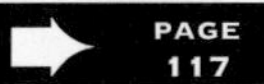
PAGE 117

Section Three

Exercice 1
Un grand supermarché

On va construire un grand supermarché près de chez vous. Vous envoyez une lettre en français à votre ami(e) à Bordeaux pour lui en parler. Il faut mentionner les aspects suivants:

A ce qu'on va faire et où;

B les raisons pour cette construction;

C les opinions des habitants, pour ou contre?

D ce que vous en pensez, c'est un avantage ou un inconvénient?

PAGE 118

Section Three

Exercice 2
Is recycling important?

Do you recycle ...
bottles ...?
newspapers ...?
boxes ...?

Write an article in French giving your opinions on recycling. Explain the recycling policy of your school or what you do at home. State why you think recycling is important.

PAGE 119

Exercice 3
Les transports en commun

Les déplacements en voiture ou en train/en autobus – qu'en pensez-vous? Devrait-on laisser les voitures à la maison? Écrivez un article en français pour donner votre opinion. Expliquez comment vous voyagez normalement et dites ce que vous pensez des transports en commun.

PAGE 120

UNIT 1 ANSWERS

Section One

Exercice 1
Le correspondant/la correspondante

Each detail given in French will be awarded 1 mark.

Nom de famille: your surname

Prénom: your first name

Date de naissance: your date of birth

Famille: mère, père, frère, sœur, grand-mère, grand-père [as appropriate]

Caractère: gentil/le, aimable, sympa, sportif/ve, branché/e, paresseux/se, travailleur/se, bavard/e

Langues parlées: anglais, français, allemand, espagnol, italien

Sport favori: natation/basket/équitation/cyclisme/patinage/planche à voile [many sports are the same as in English]

Autres loisirs: cinéma/télévision/musique/danse/animaux/lecture/art dramatique

Animaux: chien/chat/lapin/souris/cheval/hamster

Matières préférées: anglais/français/allemand/histoire/géographie/dessin/musique/art dramatique/informatique/mathématiques/chimie/ biologie/physique/EPS (the equivalent of PE)/EMT (the equivalent of D&T)

Exercice 2
Ma famille

You will gain more marks if you write in full sentences.
Answers should follow this pattern:

1 Il y a trois/quatre/cinq personnes dans ma famille.
2 J'ai une sœur/un frère/une belle-sœur/un beau-frère/deux sœurs/deux frères *or* Non, je n'ai pas de frères ou sœurs.
3 Mon père est sympa. Ma mère est travailleuse.
4 Mon père travaille dans un magasin/mon père est électricien; ma mère est au chômage/ma mère est médecin.
5 J'ai un chat/un chien/un poisson rouge/un hamster.

NB if you have no brothers or sisters, or no pets, you should say so; you will gain full marks for a statement such as: Je n'ai pas d'animaux.

UNIT 1 ANSWERS

Section One

Exercice 3
Mon animal favori

Whatever animal you choose to write about, your sentences must follow these patterns. If you have a female animal, your sentences will begin *elle*. You may find these feminine words helpful: *ma chienne*, *ma chatte*, *ma lapine*. Remember that the word for mouse is feminine, so it is always *ma souris*.

A Il s'appelle Benjie.
B Il a cinq ans.
C Il est blanc et noir.
D Il est gourmand/mignon.
E Il aime la viande et les biscuits.

Section Two

Exercice 1
Une lettre

In this answer you will see alternative spellings, the first for a boy, the second for a girl.

Salut!/Bonjour! Cher . . ./Chère . . .

Mon anniversaire est le 18 juin.

***Je suis né/née* dans une ville dans le sud-ouest de l'Angleterre *qui* s'appelle Stroud.**

Je suis assez grand/grande; je mesure 1m65.

J'ai les cheveux marron. Je ressemble à mon père *qui* a aussi les cheveux courts et frisés.

Je suis calme et aimable; je suis un peu timide aussi.

***Comme* loisirs, j'aime sortir avec mes amis le week-end, faire du vélo, écouter de la musique; je fais collection de cartes postales.**

La semaine dernière, *je suis allé/allée* au cinéma vendredi soir et puis samedi *j'ai joué* au tennis.

Amicalement . . .

Section Two

Exercice 2
Mon anniversaire

In this answer you will see the alternative spellings for the verb *aller*, the first for a boy, the second for a girl. Note the simple ways of expressing your opinion in the final paragraph.

> **Salut!/Bonjour! Cher . . ./Chère . . .**
>
> **Merci beaucoup pour la jolie carte et ton cadeau d'anniversaire. Le poster est superbe et *je l'ai mis* dans ma chambre.**
>
> ***J'ai reçu* de l'argent de mon grand-père.**
>
> ***Ma mère m'a donné* un stylo et *mon père m'a offert* un disque.**
>
> **Pour fêter mon anniversaire, *ma famille et moi sommes allés/allées* à la pizzeria où *j'ai bien mangé*. J'adore les pizzas.**
>
> **Puis, vendredi soir, *je suis allé/allée* à la discothèque avec mes copains.**
>
> ***J'ai aimé* la soirée à la discothèque le plus *parce qu'il y avait* une bonne ambiance et *j'ai* beaucoup *dansé*. *C'était chouette*.**
>
> **Amitiés . . .**

je l'ai mis – I put it (i.e. the poster)
ma mère m'a donné – my mother gave me
mon père m'a offert – my father gave me (NB: The French often use *offrir* rather than *donner* when it comes to giving presents.)

Section Two

It would be easy to answer this question in very simple fashion and in far fewer words. Remember that you should aim to write the required number of words, otherwise you may not score very highly. You should use every opportunity to show more complex sentences: notice how you might achieve that here.

Nous avons un chien à la maison. Il s'appelle Growler. Nous l'avons *depuis deux ans et demi*. Growler, *qui* a trois ans, est un petit chien noir et blanc. Il est adorable et très marrant. Tous les jours, *avant d'aller* à l'école, je promène le chien. Ce matin *je suis allé/allée* au grand parc près de chez nous. Growler aime jouer avec sa balle. Le soir, *quand* je rentre à la maison, nous allons faire une longue promenade dans le bois.

Maman lui donne à manger à midi; il aime la viande et les pâtes! *Il faut le brosser* tous les jours; il aime être propre.

Growler est important *parce qu'*il protège la maison; il aboie toujours *quand* il y a des gens *qui* viennent à la porte. En plus, il nous fait rire. Moi, *j'aurai* toujours un chien chez moi.

il nous fait rire – he makes us laugh
Maman lui donne à manger – Mum feeds him
il faut le brosser – it is necessary to brush him

Section Three

Exercice 1
Au revoir!

This letter is written by a girl; a boy would use the masculine form of adjectives and verbs. Make sure that you express your feelings about the situation. Note the variety of ways of conveying the idea of 'we': *mon ami(e) et moi/nous/on* . . . The imperfect tense is important in this answer as you need to refer to what regularly happened in the past.

Chère Cécile,
La semaine dernière *ma meilleure amie, Laura, a déménagé* pour aller vivre aux États-Unis. Son père travaille à Boston *depuis quelques années* et *la famille a* enfin *décidé* de s'installer là-bas parce qu'*ils n'aimaient pas* être séparés pendant longtemps.

Laura est gentille et très dynamique. *Comme* moi, elle a les cheveux longs et marron en queue de cheval. <u>*Je pense que*</u> nous nous entendons bien *parce que* nous sommes toutes les deux filles uniques. Nous sommes amies *depuis douze ans*.

Tous les matins, *nous allions* au collège ensemble. *Comme nous n'étions pas* dans la même classe, *nous nous rencontrions* à la cantine et puis *nous allions* jouer au hockey ou travailler dans la bibliothèque. Le week-end, *on allait* en ville, *on faisait* du cheval, *on jouait* au tennis. *On s'amusait* beaucoup, *on avait* le même sens de l'humour et on *riait* souvent. *Nous nous entendions* si bien *parce que Laura et moi aimions* les mêmes choses, la musique rock, les films d'horreur. L'été *nous allions* en vacances ensemble avec mes parents ou avec les siens; par exemple, l'année dernière *je suis allée* en Écosse avec la famille de Laura.

En ce moment <u>*je me sens un peu triste, Laura me manque beaucoup*</u>. J'ai d'autres copines mais <u>*nous passions tant de temps ensemble que c'est dur*</u>. Heureusement *la famille m'a invitée* à leur rendre visite pendant les grandes vacances.
Amitiés . . .

nous nous rencontrions – we used to meet
nous nous entendions bien – we used to get on well
la famille m'a invitée à leur rendre visite – the family has invited me to visit them

Section Three

Exercice 2
Une dispute

This letter is written by a boy. A girl writing a similar letter would need to make the necessary agreements. Feelings/emotions are very important in this response.

> **Salut Marc!**
> **L'autre jour *je me suis disputé* avec un ami d'école. *J'étais vraiment énervé* et *il était fâché*, lui aussi.**
> **Mon ami est capitaine de l'équipe de rugby et *il m'avait dit* que *je serais* dans l'équipe pour la finale du tournoi des collèges dans notre région. *Je me suis entraîné* régulièrement et *je me sentais* en pleine forme. Deux jours avant le match, *j'ai dû* aller chez le médecin pour me faire vacciner contre le tétanos – nous habitons une ferme et *j'y* travaille souvent; c'est pour cette raison que je suis en si bonne santé. Malheureusement, *cet ami a entendu* parler de ma visite chez le médecin et *a supposé* que *j'étais* souffrant. *Il a donc décidé* de me remplacer dans l'équipe. Tu peux imaginer *comme j'étais furieux* *quand je n'ai pas trouvé* mon nom dans l'équipe affichée au collège. *Je suis allé* chercher mon ami pour lui demander *ce qui s'était passé*. *Je n'arrivais pas à me contrôler* et *on a failli* se battre. *Après nous être disputés* pendant quelques minutes, *nous avons commencé à rire* *car c'était* un simple malentendu. Et finalement, *j'ai pu* jouer *puisque* la personne *qui devait* me remplacer, *partait* pour le week-end avec ses parents.**
> **Amitiés . . .**

comme j'étais furieux – how mad I was
on a failli se battre – we almost came to blows
un malentendu – a misunderstanding

UNIT 1 ANSWERS

Section Three

Exercice 3
Ma vie dans 20 ans

You will need to use the future and conditional tenses. Note the various ways of expressing your hopes/plans for the future (see also the Appendix), these structures express your feelings/ attitudes. Remember the patterns of the verb to use with *si*.

si + present tense + future
si je gagne beaucoup d'argent, j'achèterai une maison en France – if I earn a great deal of money, I shall buy a house in France

si + imperfect tense + conditional
si je gagnais beaucoup d'argent, j'achèterais une maison en France – if I were to earn a great deal of money, I would buy a house in France

Ma vie dans 20 ans
Dans vingt ans *j'aurai* 36 ans. À 36 ans on est toujours jeune, on est plein d'enthousiasme et d'espoir. *J'espère que* *je pourrai* continuer à profiter pleinement de la vie.

J'ai l'intention de partir à l'université pour faire des études de comptabilité. Après, *j'aimerais* trouver un emploi dans une grande compagnie; *je rêve de* gagner beaucoup d'argent et de voyager partout dans le monde. *Si je réussissais*, *ça me plaîrait d'avoir une jolie maison*, ainsi qu'une belle voiture.

Est-ce que *je serai* marié? Qui sait? *Si* je rencontre quelqu'un avec qui *je pourrai* partager la vie, *ce sera* possible. *Aurai-je* des enfants? En principe, oui, *surtout que* je suis enfant unique; mais cela dépend. Est-ce que ma femme *voudra* des enfants? Avoir des enfants c'est une chose très sérieuse et cela demande du temps et de l'énergie; on perd aussi un peu son indépendance.

surtout que – especially as
avoir des enfants – having children (French uses an infinitive in this situation, e.g.: *apprendre une langue est très important* – learning a language is very important; *s'entendre avec ses parents est essentiel* – getting on with your parents is vital).

UNIT 2 ANSWERS

Section One

Exercise 1
My home

Make sure that you use different words in an exercise like this; you are not likely to gain marks twice for identical information.

Possible rooms	*Possible furniture*
la cuisine	le four/la cuisinière
le salon	la table/le fauteuil/la chaise/la télévision
la salle à manger	la table/la chaise/le buffet
la salle de bains	la douche/le lavabo/la baignoire
ma chambre	le lit/la table/l'armoire/la lampe/l'étagère
la chambre de mes parents	le lit/la table/l'armoire/la lampe/l'étagère
la buanderie	la machine à laver
la véranda	la chaise/la table

Exercice 2
Ma ville/ mon village

There are various ways of writing your sentences. Your first answer could be about where you live: *J'habite un petit village/J'habite une petite ville/J'habite une grande ville.* To describe what there is in the village/town, use this familiar pattern:

Il y a une patinoire.
Il y a une piscine.
Il y a un terrain de sports/un stade.
Il y a des magasins.
Il y a une disco.
Il y a une bibliothèque.

You may want to say that there is *not* a particular facility:
Il n'y a pas de piscine.
Il n'y a pas de terrain de sport.

Exercice 3
Aider à la maison

These are the answers which correspond to the pictures: you should have any five of them.
Je fais du jardinage.
Je passe l'aspirateur.
Je mets la table.
Je range ma chambre.
Je fais les courses/le shopping.
Je fais la vaisselle.
Je lave les fenêtres.
Je fais les lits.
Je lave la voiture.

UNIT 2 ANSWERS

Section Two

Exercice 1
Votre région

Notice the simple ways of expressing an opinion.

J'habite une région industrielle dans le nord-ouest de l'Angleterre. *La ville la plus importante* est Liverpool. C'est un grand port et la ville est un centre commercial très important. Et, bien sûr, nous avons deux grandes équipes de football.

Comme distractions, il y a des cinémas, des centres sportifs, des théâtres, une patinoire, des piscines et beaucoup de magasins; vraiment, il y a beaucoup de choses à faire.

Dans la région, il y a de vieilles maisons en noir et blanc, comme Speke Hall et un grand musée des beaux-arts *qui* s'appelle The Tate *où* on peut voir des peintures modernes.

*Je pense qu'*il faut aller à Southport, une ville au bord de la mer qui a une très grande plage. On peut aussi visiter la ville de Chester *où* on peut faire le tour de la ville sur les anciens murs romains. *C'est magnifique.*

There are two useful patterns here, which are slightly different from the English and which you can use in a variety of contexts:
on peut voir – you can see
on peut visiter – you can visit
il faut aller à . . . – you should go to . . .

UNIT 2 ANSWERS

Section Two

Exercice 2
Ta routine

This answer is rather longer than is necessary; you should have some of the suggested detail. Take note of the various time phrases (see also Appendix).

> Salut!
> Tu m'as posé des questions sur ma routine, voici mes réponses. Normalement je me lève à six heures et demie en semaine, mais le week-end plus tard, surtout le dimanche. Les jours d'école, je me couche à environ dix heures, mais le samedi je me couche à minuit.
>
> Pour le petit déjeuner, je prends toujours des céréales, du pain grillé et de la confiture et je bois du café. À midi, je mange des sandwichs au fromage ou au jambon et une pomme ou une banane. Le soir, nous mangeons un repas chaud vers six heures.
>
> D'habitude je quitte la maison à huit heures moins le quart; je prends le bus pour aller au collège. La journée scolaire commence à neuf heures moins cinq et finit à trois heures et demie.
>
> Le soir, je fais mes devoirs et je regarde la télévision ou je lis un magazine. Je ne sors pas beaucoup en semaine.
>
> Le week-end dernier, *j'ai travaillé* au supermarché toute la journée et samedi soir *je suis allé/allée* au cinéma avec mes copains. Dimanche, *j'ai joué* au tennis dans le parc près de chez moi.
>
> Que fais-tu le week-end?
> Amitiés . . .

Section Two

Exercice 3
Les jeunes

This letter is written by a boy; a girl would use *paresseuse* (on the first line). Note the time phrases (see Appendix).

Monsieur/Madame
Moi, je ne suis pas paresseux du tout. Tous les jours j'aide à la maison. Le matin je fais mon lit *avant de quitter* la maison. Le lundi et le jeudi soir, après le dîner, je fais la vaisselle; les autres jours mes sœurs la font. Le week-end, en été, je travaille dans le jardin, je tonds la pelouse.

Mon père me donne dix livres par mois *comme* argent de poche; ma mère me donne de l'argent de temps en temps *si* je l'aide à faire les courses ou à passer l'aspirateur.

Pendant les vacances du mi-trimestre, *j'ai fait* du babysitting *parce que mes parents travaillaient.* Mes sœurs sont plus jeunes que moi.

Veuillez agréer, Monsieur, l'expression de mes sentiments distingués, . . .

Note the word order in these statements:
mes sœurs la font – my sisters do it (the washing up)
mon père/ma mère me donne – my mother/my father gives me
si je l'aide – if I help her

UNIT 2 ANSWERS

Section Three

Exercice 1 La décoration

This is a long answer and you would not be expected to write at this length in the examination. However, you can learn much from the variety of structures and verb forms. The writer is a girl.

Je viens de faire du bricolage; *j'ai changé* toute la décoration de ma chambre.

Nous habitons une maison assez moderne et j'ai une petite chambre au premier étage *qui donne sur* le jardin. *J'aime bien* ma chambre mais *le décor était* assez enfantin. *Mon père avait peint* la chambre il y a cinq ans et depuis *j'avais* les mêmes murs roses, des rideaux à fleurs et un tapis gris. En plus, *j'avais* un petit lit et *comme j'ai* beaucoup *grandi*, *je* le *trouvais* trop petit.

Mes parents étaient d'accord et *ils avaient dit* qu'*ils* m'*achèteraient* un grand lit. *J'étais ravie*, mais *il fallait* garder le tapis gris *parce que cela aurait coûté* trop cher, heureusement il est gris clair.

Comme la chambre est plein sud, il y a beaucoup de soleil et *je voulais* un store au lieu des rideaux. *J'ai choisi* un beau tissu jaune, ma couleur favorite, et ma mère *qui* est très douée en coûture m'*a fait* le store.

Mon père était très occupé, donc *il n'avait pas* le temps de repeindre les murs; *il* m'*a dit* que *je devais* apprendre à le faire et *c'est ce que j'ai fait*, avec l'aide de mon ami, bien sûr.

Après avoir rangé tous les meubles au milieu de la pièce, *nous* les *avons recouverts* d'un vieux drap. Ensuite *nous avons lavé* les murs; *mon père a dit* qu'il faut toujours bien préparer les murs. *Nous avons mis* deux jours à faire la peinture; *j'étais contente* du résultat, mais *j'avais mal* au bras!

Après avoir fini la peinture, *on a nettoyé* le tapis et *on a remis* tous les meubles. *La chambre était* transformée.

J'ai un gros bouquet de fleurs sèches sur ma commode en pin, une belle glace en face de la fenêtre et, bien entendu, mon nouveau lit.

ma mère m'a fait le store – my mother made me the blind
il m'a dit que – he told me that
c'est ce que j'ai fait – that is what I did

UNIT 2 ANSWERS

Section Three

Exercice 2
Faire la cuisine

This is written by a boy.

Moi, *j'étais* nul en cuisine. Quelquefois *je préparais* du pain grillé pour le petit déjeuner et chaque fois *il était* brûlé!

Puis, l'année dernière *mes parents sont partis* pour le week-end et *je suis resté* à la maison avec ma sœur aînée. *Elle travaillait* mais *elle ne savait pas* faire la cuisine non plus. Alors *c'était* moi *qui devais* préparer à manger. Nous habitons près du centre-ville, heureusement! *On a* bien *profité* des restaurants chinois et indiens, et des pizzerias! Ou *j'ai* tout *brûlé* ou *ce n'était pas* assez cuit, *c'était* un véritable désastre. Le dimanche, *je suis allé* déjeuner chez ma grand-mère et *je* lui *ai expliqué ce qui s'était passé*. Elle est très bonne cuisinière et *elle* m'a *dit* qu'*elle* m'*expliquerait* comment faire. Et voilà, maintenant je sais ce qu'il faut faire; l'important c'est de bien s'organiser, de calculer le temps *qu*'il faut.

De temps en temps je prépare un repas le week-end et tous les mercredis je fais le dîner, quelquefois du poisson avec une sauce piquante ou un ragoût. Je dois bien réussir *parce que* tout le monde semble très content du résultat. En plus, *si* je fais la cuisine, je n'ai pas à faire la vaisselle!

La cuisine *que* j'apprécie le plus c'est la cuisine thaïlandaise *parce que* c'est très fin, j'adore le goût des épices.

Cela me *ferait* plaisir d'apprendre à faire quelques plats simples.

ou . . . ou . . . – either . . . or . . .
ce qui s'était passé – what had happened (compare *qu'est-ce qui s'est passé?* – what has happened?)

Note the word order:
on a bien profité de – we took great advantage of
j'ai tout brûlé – I burned everything

Note the use of the object pronoun:
je lui ai expliqué – I explained to her
elle m'a dit – she told me
elle m'expliquerait – she would explain to me
cela me ferait plaisir – that would please me

Section Three

Exercice 3 Où j'habite

This has been written by a boy. Note the ways in which he expresses his opinions/feelings. There are a number of complex sentences which you should be able to use; there are also some useful adjectives and time phrases (see Appendix).

J'habite dans une assez grande ville; la plupart de mes amis habitent dans les banlieues de la ville. Ils se plaignent toujours que c'est ennuyeux, que c'est trop calme, qu'il n'y a rien à faire. En plus, ils dépendent beaucoup de leurs parents pour le transport *quand* ils veulent sortir, surtout le week-end, *car* il n'y a pas de bus après sept heures le soir.

Quant à moi, j'ai de la chance *parce que* je suis en plein centre; tout est à proximité et je peux aller partout à pied. La ville n'est pas très animée, mais du moins je peux profiter des distractions *sans avoir à* demander à mes parents de me déposer quelque part ou de venir me chercher. Samedi dernier, par exemple, *je suis allé* à la discothèque et *je suis rentré* à minuit sans problème. Cela est appréciable *quand* on a 16 ans.

La campagne ne m'intéresse pas beaucoup; c'est bien pour une sortie à vélo de temps en temps, mais *je ne pourrais pas* y vivre, *ce serait* trop calme pour moi et *je perdrais* beaucoup de mon indépendance.

Plus tard, j'espère avoir une maison ou un appartement dans une grande ville. *Je n'aime pas du tout* l'ambiance des banlieues où tout semble endormi. *Je préfère* l'animation de la ville; d'ailleurs on perd moins de temps et d'argent *car* tout est sur place, et en plus cela a l'avantage d'être plus écologique.

ils se plaignent toujours – they are always complaining
sans avoir à – without having to
je ne pourrais pas y vivre – I could not live there
venir me chercher – to come and fetch me
me déposer quelque part – to give me a lift somewhere

UNIT 3 ANSWERS

Section One

Exercice 1 Les distractions dans ta région

You should include 10 different places. You may have others, check them carefully in the dictionary.

un théâtre
une piscine
une discothèque
un musée
une patinoire
un stade
un cinéma
un château
des magasins
une promenade en bateau
un gymnase
une piste de ski artificielle

Exercice 2 Mon week-end

As you are asked to write about activities, aim to produce more than a one word answer so that you convey clearly what you do. Possible answers suggested by the pictures:

écouter de la musique
jouer au tennis de table/au ping-pong
aller aux magasins/faire des courses/du shopping
aller au cinéma
regarder la télévision

You might have some of your own, e.g.:

faire du babysitting
rester à la maison
aller/manger au restaurant
aller au club de jeunes
aller au match de football
danser/aller à la discothèque

Exercise 3 A trip to France

You must use sentences if you are to communicate the information clearly.
Your answers should follow these patterns:

1 Tu veux venir me voir? (Do you want to come to see me?)/On peut se rencontrer? (Can we meet?)

2 Rendez-vous dans le jardin public/devant la Poste/à la piscine (you may choose any place provided that you follow the pattern of these answers).

3 . . . samedi (any day) à deux heures (any time) – this information can be added to the previous sentence.

4 Je voudrais faire du vélo/aller au parc d'attractions (any suitable activity would gain marks, look at Exercise 2 for some other correctly written activities).

5 Qu'est-ce que tu veux/voudrais faire le soir?

UNIT 3 ANSWERS

Section Two

Exercice 1
Sondage: la télévision

It would be possible to answer this question in very few words. Notice here how relevant detail has been added and how opinions have been expressed and some more complex language used. Note also the time phrases (see Appendix).

> **Bonjour cher ami/chère amie**
> ***J'aime beaucoup* regarder la télévision. J'ai un poste dans ma chambre. D'habitude, je regarde la télévision deux ou trois heures par jour.**
> **Je regarde surtout les émissions de sport, d'habitude le mercredi et le dimanche. Mon émission préférée c'est *Friends*, c'est une comédie américaine. *Je l'aime bien parce que* c'est très amusant et les personnages sont amusants. *Je n'aime pas* les actualités *parce que* c'est toujours barbant. Je ne les regarde pas.**
> **Hier soir, *il n'y avait pas* d'émission de sport, alors *j'ai regardé* un film policier. *C'était* passionnant.**
> **Amitiés . . .**

je l'aime – I like it
je ne les regarde pas – I do not watch them (news bulletins)

Exercice 2
Argent de poche

There are four separate tasks and within each there are a varying number of details to give; you should include all of these points, otherwise you may lose marks. What follows is a guide as to what you might include; if you have your own ideas and you can express them, then do so. Note the variety of time phrases (see Appendix).

Mon argent de poche
D'habitude je reçois cinq livres par semaine. Pour cela je dois faire la vaisselle tous les matins. *Je pense que* ce n'est pas assez *parce que* ma mère me donne l'argent le vendredi soir et souvent le lundi je n'en ai plus! Heureusement, je gagne deux livres par heure *quand* je fais du babysitting.

Normalement, je vais en ville le samedi et j'achète un magazine ou peut-être un CD, *si* j'ai assez d'argent. Samedi dernier *j'ai acheté* un petit cadeau d'anniversaire pour mon père, *c'était* une boîte de ses chocolats favoris.

Je voudrais acheter une moto plus tard, alors pour Noël ou pour mon anniversaire je demande de l'argent. Comme cela je fais des économies.

je dois faire la vaisselle – I have to do the washing up (You could practise this pattern by making a list of things that you have to do at home/in school/at work.)
ma mère me donne – my mother gives me
je n'en ai plus – I have none left
comme cela – in that way

Exercice 3
Une promenade à vélo

This letter has been written by a boy; a girl would need to remember to make the agreements, e.g. *je suis partie*. Note the different patterns of the verb in the perfect tense.

Cher/Chère . . .
Pendant les vacances de Pâques *je suis parti* faire une promenade à vélo à la campagne avec des amis. *Nous sommes allés* dans les collines *qui* se trouvent à Malvern; elles sont à quinze kilomètres de chez moi.
***Comme il faisait* beau et chaud, *nous avons quitté* la maison à neuf heures du matin. En route, *nous nous sommes arrêtés* dans un village à côté de la rivière *où nous avons regardé* les bateaux *qui allaient et venaient*. Ensuite *nous avons bu* un coca *avant de* partir.**
***Nous sommes arrivés* en bas des collines à midi. *Nous avons décidé* de grimper au sommet tout de suite; en haut, *il y avait* une très belle vue de la campagne. Là, *nous avons pris* notre pique-nique et puis *nous nous sommes reposés* un peu au soleil.**
L'après-midi *on a fait* une promenade sur les collines *avant de* revenir à la maison. *Il était* cinq heures *quand je suis rentré* chez moi et *j'étais* fatigué mais content de ma journée à la campagne.
Amitiés . . .

qui se trouvent – which are situated
avant de partir – before leaving
avant de revenir – before coming back

Section Three

Exercice 1
Le week-end dernier

A question such as this allows you to write about any weekend which has a particular significance for you. This is rather long, too long to produce in an examination; however it shows you a number of structures and details which you should be able to produce accurately. This account was written by a girl.

Un week-end magnifique
Cassie, ma meilleure copine, *avait décidé* d'aller à un concert de musique pop pour fêter ses seize ans, le vendredi 25 novembre. *Elle* m'*avait invitée* à la joindre, *ainsi que* deux autres de ses amies.

Nous sommes allés à la grande salle d'exposition près de Birmingham voir un groupe *qui* s'appelle Boyzone, c'est un groupe de jeunes irlandais *qui a eu* beaucoup de succès en Angleterre.

Le concert *devait* commencer à huit heures. C'est le père de Cassie *qui* nous *a emmenées* en voiture. Déjà dans le parking *on sentait* l'ambiance; *il y avait* une énorme foule de jeunes *qui chantaient* et *qui riaient*.

Je dois avouer que *je n'aimais pas* tellement ce groupe, mais *je ne voulais pas* râter l'occasion. *Quand j'ai aperçu* tous ces gens *qui s'amusaient*, *j'étais ravie* d'être venue.

À l'intérieur de l'immense salle, *il y avait* un bruit fou; *tout le monde sautait* et *dansait*. *Dès que le groupe est arrivé* sur scène, *les gens se sont mis* à hurler. *Lorsqu'ils ont commencé* à chanter, *la foule* aussi *a chanté*. A la fin de chaque chanson *on s'extasiait*. Vraiment, *je n'avais jamais rien vu* de pareil.

Le père de Cassie est revenu nous chercher et *il était* minuit passé *quand nous sommes arrivées* chez Cassie, *car on allait* passer la nuit chez elle. *Nous étions* épuisées!

Le lendemain *on a continué* la fête; *les parents de Cassie* nous *ont emmenées* à un restaurant italien au centre de Birmingham. *Comme j'adore* la cuisine italienne, *cela a fait* un week-end sensationnel.

Note the use of the pronoun:
les parents de Cassie nous ont emmenées – Cassie's parents took us (What other examples of this pattern are there?)

Note also the addition of the 's' – this is the agreement required when the pronoun precedes the verb. (Which other verb in the text has a different agreement? Can you work out why?)

il était minuit passé – it was gone midnight

Section Three

Exercice 2 Tes loisirs

This may appear to be a very simple response; however, although the range of tenses used is quite limited, the text displays some good structures.

Salut!
Tu veux des détails de mes passe-temps. Alors les voici!

Tu sais que je suis très enthousiaste et j'aime bien profiter de la vie. Alors ma passion c'est le cyclisme; tous les soirs, après le collège, je saute sur ma bicyclette pour faire une grande tournée d'une vingtaine de kilomètres.

Bien sûr, l'hiver il fait nuit trop tôt pour faire cela, alors en novembre, décembre et janvier, je peux sortir à bicyclette seulement le week-end. Pour maintenir la forme l'hiver donc, je vais à la salle de gym *où* je m'entraîne pendant une heure, deux fois par semaine. Je prends cela très au sérieux et mon ambition c'est de devenir cycliste professionnel. *J'ai* déjà *fait* des courses et *j'ai eu* quelques succès.

***Quand* je ne fais pas de vélo, *j'aime* jouer aux jeux électroniques. Je sais que pour certaines personnes *c'est une perte de temps*, mais cela me détend. *La télévision ne m'intéresse pas*, il n'y a jamais d'émissions intéressantes, *sauf* les émissions de cyclisme, mais il y en a très peu. Le week-end, de temps en temps, je sors avec mes copains au cinéma ou en boîte; mais je fais attention de ne pas trop boire, la forme m'importe trop.**
À bientôt . . .

les voici – here they (the details) are
mon ambition c'est de devenir . . . – my ambition is to become . . .
cela me détend – that relaxes me
la forme m'importe trop – keeping fit is too important for me

Section Three

Exercice 3 Mon ami(e)

A very long answer – it is quite difficult at times to restrict yourself; a plan is essential if you are going to confine yourself to the requested number of words. However, there is some good material for you to imitate here. The letter was written by a girl.

Cher ami . . ./Chère amie . . .
Au mois de novembre de l'année dernière *une jeune fille est arrivée* dans notre classe. *Sa famille avait quitté le Canada où ils vivaient depuis dix ans*. Elle s'appelle Marie, ses parents sont Écossais.

Bien sûr *elle n'avait pas* d'amies dans le collège et *le professeur* m'*a demandé* de l'aider à s'installer. *Nous avons* vite *trouvé* qu'*on avait* beaucoup en commun. Marie adore la musique et joue de la clarinette *depuis quatre ans*; moi aussi je suis musicienne, je joue de la flûte. Marie est douée, donc *le professeur de musique lui a demandé* de faire partie de l'orchestre.

Marie est venue chez moi et par la suite *elle* m'*a invitée* chez elle. *Nous nous sommes* bien *entendues parce que nous avons* non seulement les mêmes intérêts, la musique, la lecture, la danse classique, mais aussi on a un peu le même caractère. Imagine donc *comme j'étais déçue quand elle* m'a *annoncé* qu'*elle allait* encore déménager *parce que son père avait trouvé* un poste à Edimbourg.

Heureusement on peut s'écrire et se parler au téléphone et cet été *je passerai* quelques jours chez elle. *Comme* je ne connais pas cette ville *ce sera* génial.
Amitiés . . .

je joue de la clarinette – I play the clarinet (Notice how this pattern is slightly different from that used for sporting activity – *je joue au tennis*.)
elle m'a invitée – she invited me
elle m'a annoncé – she announced to me (Although the *me* refers to the same person, the girl writing the letter, there is no agreement here as the pronoun is indirect; similarly, *elle m'a écrit* – she wrote to me/*elle m'a parlé* – she spoke to me/*elle m'a expliqué* – she explained to me.)

UNIT 4 ANSWERS

Section One

Exercice 1
À l'Hôtel Bellevue

Make sure that you complete each part of the form.

A Chambre no. 24 [any number will do, you are not likely to gain marks as there is no word given in French].

B Possible answers suggested by the pictures:
À boire: café, thé, lait, jus d'orange/de pomme, chocolat
À manger: croissant(s), pain, confiture, yaourt, céréales, pommes

Exercise 2
My holiday photos

These are the answers which correspond to the numbered pictures. Remember to write a sentence if you can; the example will show you what is expected.

je mange au restaurant
je joue sur la plage/au bord de la mer
je visite un château
je fais du vélo/de la bicyclette
je vais au parc d'attractions
je me bronze
je fais des courses au marché

Exercice 3
Au camping

You should aim to write in sentences; you will communicate the message more effectively. These are the details suggested by the pictures:

A je suis sous une tente/j'ai une tente;
B je suis avec mes trois amis/amies/copains/copines;
C il fait très chaud/il y a du soleil/il fait beau;
D je joue sur la plage;
E je mange à la terrasse du restaurant.

UNIT 4 ANSWERS

Section Two

Exercice 1
En vacances

It is often quite easy to write a short formal letter in answer to a question of this sort. Make sure that you do not omit any details as you will lose marks if you do. Note how you can use 'nous' and 'on' to express 'we'.

Monsieur/Madame
Nous avons l'intention de **venir en France pour les vacances cet été. *Je voudrais* faire une réservation pour cinq nuits à partir du 19 juillet.**

Nous serons **quatre, deux adultes et deux enfants. Il nous faut deux chambres, une chambre avec un grand lit et une chambre avec deux petits lits pour les enfants. *Si possible, nous aimerions* des chambres avec douche et balcon.**

Nous arriverons **en voiture. Est-ce qu'il y a un parking?**

On voudrait **payer par carte de crédit. Vous les acceptez?**

Veuillez agréer, Monsieur/Madame, l'expression de mes sentiments distingués . . .

nous serons quatre – there will be four of us
il nous faut – we need

Section Two

Exercice 2

Des vacances en France

The tasks are straightforward and they could easily be answered in fewer words; remember that it is in your best interests to write a sufficient amount. Get used to adding relevant detail, for example by adding a variety of adjectives as this girl has done. There is a good range of tense; she has shown that she can use simple verb forms confidently.

> **Chère amie,**
> **Je t'écris pour confirmer les détails de mon voyage.**
> ***J'ai pris* mon billet d'avion pour le 2 août et *j'arriverai* à l'aéroport de Bordeaux à 14h 30. *J'ai réservé* ma place pour le voyage du retour pour le 14 août, *le départ sera* à neuf heures et demie. *Ce sera* mon premier voyage en avion, alors *je l'attends avec impatience*.**
> ***J'ai acheté* un nouvel appareil photo pour les vacances; on peut faire des photos panoramiques, alors *j'en suis vraiment contente*. J'ai aussi un beau maillot de bain *parce que tu as dit* qu'*on ira* souvent à la plage. *J'adore* faire de la natation et j'espère que *nous allons nager* dans la mer.**
> ***Tu seras* à l'aéroport à mon arrivée?**
> **À très bientôt . . .**

j'ai réservé ma place – I have booked my seat (You could also say: *J'ai réservé ma place.*)
je l'attends avec impatience – I am really looking forward to it
j'en suis vraiment contente – I am really pleased about it

Section Two

Exercice 3

Les échanges scolaires

This boy has clearly enjoyed himself; he has found much to write about. Your account will probably be shorter.

Note how he uses the imperfect tense to describe the place and the family, especially the difference in ending *-ait* (singular)/*-aient* (plural).

Mon échange scolaire

En 1999 *je suis allé* chez mon correspondant Alain, *qui* habite dans une petite ville en Bretagne.

J'ai eu de la chance *parce que la famille était* très gentille; *il y avait* trois enfants, Philippe, le frère aîné d'Alain et sa sœur cadette, Sophie. *Je m'entendais* bien avec toute la famille.

Ils avaient une jolie petite maison près du centre-ville et *il* m'*ont donné* une chambre pour moi tout seul.

Le seul problème *c'était* les repas. Je suis végétarien et dans la famille *toute le monde aimait* la viande, *ils en mangeaient* deux fois par jour. *Le fromage était délicieux et très varié*; quant aux desserts, *ils étaient super*.

C'est une ville historique avec beaucoup de petites maisons anciennes située à quelques kilomètres de la mer. Donc *il y avait* plein de choses à faire – le cyclisme, la natation, la planche à voile.

J'ai voyagé par le tunnel jusqu'à Paris *où j'ai pris* un train de la même gare, donc *c'était* assez facile.

Si possible j'y retournerais l'année prochaine *parce que* la famille est tellement accueillante et *je me suis bien amusé*.

je m'entendais bien avec – I got on well with
deux fois par jour – twice a day (Practise some more phrases following this pattern.)
à quelques kilomètres de la mer – a few kilometres from the sea
la même gare – the same railway station
la famille est tellement accueillante – the family is so welcoming

UNIT 4 ANSWERS

Section Three

Exercice 1
Une auberge de jeunesse

When writing a letter of complaint remember that you should be polite. Explain simply and clearly what problems you encountered.

The verb *se plaindre* (to complain) and the expression *porter plainte* (to lodge a complaint) will be useful.

> **Monsieur,**
> **Pendant ma visite en France *j'ai passé* trois nuits à votre auberge de jeunesse avec trois de mes amis. Je m'appelle William Hughes et *je suis resté* à l'auberge de jeunesse *du 12 juillet au 14 juillet.***
>
> ***Malheureusement, nous avons été fort déçus.* Au cours de notre séjour en France *nous avons logé* dans plusieurs auberges, *on a* toujours *été* content de l'accueil et de l'état de l'auberge, *on n'a jamais eu* l'occasion de nous plaindre. Cependant *nous avons trouvé* les conditions chez vous inacceptables; *deux des douches étaient* cassées et *deux autres ne donnaient que* de l'eau froide. Pire encore, *les toilettes étaient* sales, *comme si on ne* les *avait pas nettoyées depuis longtemps*. Dans la cuisine, *une des cuisinières ne marchait pas* correctement, alors *nous avons brûlé* notre dîner. *On n'aurait jamais trouvé* de telles choses en Grande-Bretagne.**
>
> ***Après avoir quitté* votre auberge, *nous sommes allés* à Blois *où nous avons logé* dans une auberge *qui offrait* des équipements tout à fait corrects, *c'était* très propre et bien agréable. *On a pu* finir nos vacances sur une bonne impression des auberges françaises.**
>
> **Veuillez agréer l'expression de mes sentiments distingués . . .**

Note the word order in these phrases.
nous avons été fort déçus – we were extremely disappointed
on a toujours été content – we have always been pleased
pire encore – worse still
deux autres (douches) ne donnaient que de l'eau froide – two other (showers) only gave cold water
on n'aurait jamais trouvé de telles choses – we would never have found such things/such a state of affairs
des équipements – facilities

UNIT 4 ANSWERS

Section Three

Exercice 2
Vive les vacances!

Note how the writer, a boy, conveys his feelings. He uses a variety of language and he gives examples of past experiences.

À mon âge <u>*je préfère*</u> les vacances avec mes copains. *Je me suis* beaucoup *amusé* en vacances avec ma famille *quand j'étais* plus jeune. Cependant actuellement, mes parents aiment des séjours plus tranquilles, dans une petite station calme et paisible. Pour moi, il me faut un centre animé *où* on peut faire du sport et *où* il y a des discothèques et des boîtes de nuit.

L'année dernière, *je suis parti* avec quatre de mes amis à Newquay, dans le sud-ouest d'Angleterre. *Nous sommes allés* à un terrain de camping à côté de la mer. <u>*C'était vraiment génial*</u> *car le camping était* plein de jeunes. *Tout le monde était* passionné des sports nautiques; *j'ai essayé* le surf pour la première fois, <u>*je l'ai trouvé vraiment grisant*</u>. *Il y avait* une ambiance magnifique sur le camping.

<u>*Je préfère*</u> ce genre de vacances *parce qu'*on a plus d'indepéndance; pour le moment le confort de l'hôtel ne m'intéresse pas. *On a eu* de la chance *parce qu'il a fait* beau et chaud pendant notre séjour; *s'il avait plu cela aurait été* sans doute très différent.

grisant – exhilarating
tout le monde était passionné de – everyone was passionate about
(Remember that *tout le monde* is singular.)

Section Three

Exercice 3
Un gîte

If you are able to write from experience it makes it much easier. You have only to transpose the details of a visit in whatever country to France. This is an enthusiastic response which will give you some good descriptive vocabulary.

Chère Madame,
À notre retour en Angleterre *mon père* m'*a demandé* de vous écrire pour vous remercier de notre séjour dans votre gîte à Mauzé.

<u>*Nous avons été tous ravis*</u> de nos vacances. *Le gîte était* vraiment confortable et bien aménagé. <u>*Tout le monde a apprécié*</u> le décor simple et rustique. En plus, *le jardin était* très bien fleuri et agréable; *il y avait* tout ce qu'*il fallait* pour des vacances reposantes.

***Ma mère*, *qui* aime faire de la peinture, *a* beaucoup *aimé* la vue de la campagne et du village; *elle* en *a fait* une belle peinture *qui* est un souvenir charmant de notre visite.**

Grâce aux VTTs *que mon frère a trouvés* dans le garage, *on a pu* explorer le village et les environs. *Mon frère pensait* qu'*il allait* s'ennuyer, mais en fait *il s'est fait* de nouveaux amis et il parle déjà d'aller les revoir.

Quant à l'année prochaine, *on aimerait* retourner dans la région; *ce serait* un plaisir de revenir passer des vacances chez vous.

***Nous n'hésiterons pas* à recommander votre gîte à nos amis francophiles.**

Veuillez agréer, Madame, l'expression de mes sentiments distingués . . .

bien aménagé – well equipped
que mon frère a trouvés – which my brother found (The additional *s* refers back to *que*, which in turn represents *VTTs*; this is known as the object pronoun agreement.)
il s'est fait de nouveaux amis – he made some new friends
il parle déjà d'aller les revoir – he is already talking of going to see them again
francophile – this adjective is used to describe people who love France and all things French

UNIT 5 ANSWERS

Section One

Exercice 1
Aux objets trouvés

Any 10 of the following words would earn 1 mark each: you may have thought of others, check them carefully in the dictionary.

carte
brosse à dents
serviette
stylo
assiette
couteau
fourchette
cuillère
lunettes de soleil
argent
appareil photo
passeport
maillot de bain
livre
cartes postales

Exercise 2
Lost property

You have some choice here; each appropriate detail would each gain 1 mark.

Commissariat de Police

Bureau des objets trouvés

Ville de Dinard

Nom de famille: Hughes **Prénom:** Amy

Objet perdu: porte-feuille

Date de la perte: le mardi 3 août

Lieu de la perte: plage

Description de l'objet (deux détails): petit; noir; cuir

Contenu: billets; cartes de crédit; argent

Valeur: 20 livres sterling

Signé: Amy Hughes

Date: le 4 août 2000

UNIT 5 ANSWERS

Section One

Exercice 3
La carte postale

You must write a sentence for each of the answers. However, if you give some relevant information in note form, you will probably gain some marks.

Exemple: le mercredi 2 septembre

je suis malade/j'ai mal à la tête
j'ai de la fièvre/j'ai très chaud
je suis/je reste au lit
je ne mange pas/je n'ai pas faim
rendez-vous à la plage jeudi prochain/20 septembre

Section Two

Exercice 1
La montre

In a formal letter, you should remember to use the *vous* form and to use the formal etiquette. This straightforward response, by a girl, gives all the required detail; it is just short of the 90 words. Note the way in which she describes the watch.

> **Brackley**
> **le 8 avril 2000**
>
> **Monsieur/Madame,**
> **Malheureusement *j'ai perdu* ma montre à l'hôtel Richemont. *Je suis descendue* à votre hôtel *du 3 au 6 avril. J'ai eu* la chambre numéro 14 au premier étage.**
> **C'est une montre suisse en or avec un bracelet en cuir noir. La montre est très importante *parce que c'était* un cadeau de ma grand-mère. *Elle* m'*a donné* la montre à Noël.**
> **Vous pouvez me contacter chez moi, le soir. Mon numéro de téléphone est le 9936540.**
> **Je vous remercie d'avance.**
> **Veuillez agréer Monsieur/Madame, l'expression de mes sentiments distingués.**

du 3 au 6 avril – from the 3rd to the 6th of April (This pattern is important.)
je suis descendue à votre hôtel – I stayed at your hotel (This is the correct verb; avoid *rester* in this situation.)
elle m'a donné la montre – she gave me the watch (Note the word order.)

UNIT 5 ANSWERS

Section Two

Exercice 2 Un accident

In an informal letter, you may use *tu* or *vous*. This letter from a boy shows you a wide range of detail. There is a short paragraph on each of the points in the question.

Bolton
le mardi 25 mai 2000

Salut!
***Il y a une semaine, j'ai eu* un accident de vélo.**

***Je suis parti* de chez moi pour faire une promenade à la campagne. Malheureusement *je descendais* une pente trop rapidement et *comme les freins n'ont pas marché, j'ai perdu* contrôle du vélo. *Je me suis fait* mal au bras et à la tête.**

***J'ai dû* marcher *jusqu'à la maison. J'étais* très fatigué *quand je suis arrivé* chez moi.**

Plus tard, *je suis allé* chez le médecin. Heureusement, *ce n'était pas* grave.

La prochaine fois *je ferai* attention et *je porterai* un casque.
Au revoir!

comme les freins n'ont pas marché – as the brakes did not work
j'ai dû marcher jusqu'à la maison – I had to walk all the way home (*jusqu'à*: see Appendix.)

To practise 'I had to . . .', you could make a list of things you have to do at home, at work, at school.

Exercice 3 Des vacances désastreuses

The question gives you a clear picture of the kind of detail required. Note how the use of time phrases (see Appendix) helps to structure a logical account. In this account there are alternative spellings for certain key words: the second version is for a girl.

Je suis arrivé/arrivée au camping avec mon copain vendredi dernier. Pendant le week-end *il faisait* beau et chaud et *nous nous sommes* bien *amusés* sur la plage.

Lundi matin *j'ai loué* un vélo et *j'ai fait* une promenade le long de la côte. À midi, *il a commencé* à pleuvoir. *Je suis* donc *retourné/retournée* au camping pour chercher mon copain *qui voulait* rester à la piscine.

UNIT 5 ANSWERS

Section Two

Tout d'un coup, *il y a eu* du tonnerre et *je suis entré/entrée* dans un café *où j'ai bu* un chocolat chaud.

Quand je suis arrivé/arrivée au camping une heure plus tard *je n'ai pas pu* trouver la tente. Enfin *j'ai vu* mon copain *qui ramassait* nos affaires près de la piscine.

Nous ne pouvions pas passer la nuit au camping et *nous sommes allés* en ville chercher un hôtel. Le lendemain *nous sommes rentrés* à la maison. *C'était une grosse déception.*

nos affaires – our belongings
nous ne pouvions pas passer la nuit – we could not spend the night (Think of some statements you could make beginning *j'ai pu*; each time you will need to follow it with the infinite form of the verb.)
une grosse déception – a big disappointment

UNIT 5 ANSWERS

Section Three

Exercice 1
Malade!

The topic of health is an important one. You could make a list of useful phrases used here and add to it as you come across others.

> **Cher ami,**
> **Je suis au lit *depuis cinq jours* et je m'ennuie terriblement. *J'ai eu* une forte grippe, et les premiers jours *j'avais* très mal à la tête et de la fièvre. *Je n'avais pas* faim et *j'avais* toujours soif. *Je n'avais* même *pas* la force de me lever. <u>*C'était vraiment ennuyeux.*</u>**
>
> ***Papa, qui était* en vacances, *a été* sympa et *il* m'*a tenu* compagnie au lieu d'aller jouer au golf. *On a joué* aux cartes! Normalement, je n'y joue jamais.**
>
> **Bien sûr, *j'ai regardé* un peu la télévision, mais les émissions dans la journée sont nulles, il n'y a rien d'intéressant. En plus, je suis vite fatigué *si* j'essaie de lire un livre. Il fait tellement beau que *j'aimerais* sortir faire une promenade en plein air. *Quelques amis sont venus* me voir *il y a deux jours*. <u>*C'était agréable*</u> d'avoir des nouvelles. Pendant la semaine, *ils ne peuvent pas* passer *parce qu'*ils ont trop de travail. *J'ai parlé* au téléphone à ma meilleure copine, *qui* m'*a dit* qu'*on a commencé* à préparer les examens. Je m'inquiète un peu *parce que j'ai manqué* beaucoup de cours.**
>
> **Aujourd'hui je commence à me sentir un peu mieux. *J'ai pris* un petit repas à midi et encore ce soir.**
>
> **J'espère retourner en classe au début de la semaine prochaine; *après avoir manqué* tant de cours *j'aurai* du mal.**
>
> **Tu vas bien, j'espère!**

la grippe – flu
j'ai eu une forte grippe – I have had a bad bout of 'flu
je n'avais pas faim – I was not hungry (*avoir soif*, *avoir froid*, *avoir chaud*, *avoir de la fièvre*: do you know all of these? What others do you know? They are all very useful.)
au lieu d'aller jouer au golf – instead of playing golf (an easy pattern to use: *au lieu de* + infinitive.)
je n'y joue jamais – I never play it (i.e. cards)
des nouvelles – news
je m'inquiète un peu – I am slightly worried

je commence à me sentir un peu mieux – I am beginning to feel a little better
après avoir manqué – after missing
j'aurai du mal – I will find it difficult

Exercice 2
La fuite

Here is a detailed and quite long account of a rather unpleasant experience. Note the variety of structures used.

En rentrant à la maison à vingt heures le mardi 4 août, *nous avons trouvé* de l'eau partout dans le gîte. *Le salon et la cuisine étaient* inondés et dans la salle de bains, au premier étage, il y avait de l'eau *qui coulait* du plafond. *On ne savait pas* que faire.

Après avoir fermé le gaz et l'électricité, *nous avons téléphoné* à la propriétaire *qui* habite à quelques kilomètres du village. *Elle est arrivée* quelques minutes plus tard *accompagnée de* son mari. Tout de suite *elle a coupé* l'eau et puis *elle a fait* le tour de la maison. Bien sûr, *elle était* très ennuyée.

Nous avons aidé à sortir les tapis dans le jardin et ensuite *nous avons essayé* de rassembler les meubles dans un coin du salon. *Nous avons ouvert* toutes les fenêtres et *la propriétaire a décidé* d'allumer le chauffage central pour faire sécher la maison.

Comme il n'y avait ni eau, *ni* électricité, *nous ne pouvions pas* rester dans le gîte. Alors, *nous avons dû* partir à l'Hôtel Richemont *où nous avons passé* trois jours.

Note the patterns in the following two statements:
elle a coupé l'eau – she turned off the water
après avoir fermé le gaz – after turning off the gas
Note the patterns in the next three statements (see Appendix.)
nous avons aidé à sortir les tapis – we helped to take out the carpets
nous avons essayé de rassembler les meubles – we tried to get the furniture together
la propriétaire a décidé d'allumer le chauffage – the owner decided to switch on the heating
il n'y avait ni . . . ni . . . – there was neither . . . nor . . .

Section Three

Exercice 3 Un accident (2)

You are asked for quite precise information and in a question of this sort you should provide what is requested. You should not make up your own version of an accident; do not revamp an account you have already written, as an examiner will spot this and will likely mark you down.

Note how the use of time phrases helps to give a logical account of what happened. You could make a list of vocabulary associated with road traffic used in this account (written by a boy) and add to it as you meet any new ones.

Le vendredi 15 avril, *après avoir fait* des courses au supermarché, *je suis descendu* le long de la rue de la Poste. *Il était* environ onze heures et quart. *Il y avait* beaucoup de circulation, comme toujours le vendredi, *parce que c'était* le jour du marché. *Je venais de passer* devant la boulangerie *quand deux jeunes filles* à vélo m'*ont dépassé. Elles ne roulaient pas* très vite.

Je me suis arrêté pour traverser la rue. Tout d'un coup, *j'ai entendu* un klaxon et un bruit de freins. *Une grosse voiture bleue*, une voiture allemande peut-être, *est arrivée* à grande vitesse. A ce moment-là, *j'ai eu* très peur *car le conducteur n'avait pas remarqué* les deux cyclistes *qui attendaient* aux feux. Heureusement *la voiture n'a pas touché* les filles, mais *l'une d'entre elles a dû* avoir très peur car et *elle est tombée* sur la chaussée. *La voiture a ralenti* un instant *avant de repartir* très rapidement. *J'ai pu* voir le conducteur *qui avait* l'air assez jeune. *Il avait* les cheveux courts, blonds et *il avait* des lunettes; *il portait* une chemise noire. *J'ai noté* le numéro d'immatriculation de la voiture, *c'était* 43567 NG 23. À mon avis, *elle roulait* beaucoup trop vite.

J'ai couru immédiatement vers la fille *qui pleurait. Elle était* en état de choc mais *elle ne semblait pas* être gravement blessée. *Je suis resté* avec elle *jusqu'à l'arrivée de l'ambulance.*

il y avait beaucoup de circulation – there was a lot of traffic
je venais de passer . . . – I had just gone past . . .
la chaussée – the roadway
la voiture a ralenti – the car slowed down
elle roulait trop vite – it (the car) was travelling too fast (Use *rouler*, never *voyager*, when referring to a vehicle.)
jusqu'à l'arrivée de l'ambulance – until the arrival of the ambulance/until the ambulance arrived

UNIT 6 ANSWERS

Section One

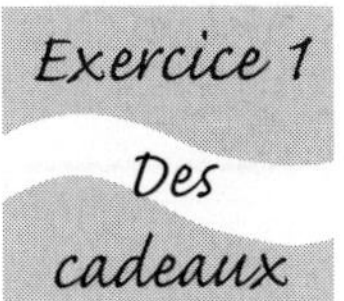

Remember that you will receive marks for writing in French. In the example, writing only *pour Annie* would not necessarily gain a mark, so make sure that you use a word which makes it clear who the person is; remember not to repeat a word.

The pictures suggest the following items, you may have quite different answers for the people:

une carte-postale — pour ma sœur
des chocolats — pour ma mère
un livre — pour mon père
du parfum — pour ma grand-mère
un crayon — pour mon oncle
une écharpe — pour ma tante
un bol — pour mon père
une affiche — pour mon ami

Exercice 2 Des courses

The answers given are based on the pictures provided. You may have a variety of items from any of the shops.

des timbres à la Poste
une carte postale à la maison de la presse
un poulet à la boucherie
des croissants à la boulangerie
des pommes au marché
de l'aspirine à la pharmacie
du dentifrice à la pharmacie
un journal à la maison de la presse
du bœuf à la boucherie
du pain à la boulangerie
des gâteaux à la boulangerie
des tomates au marché
des bananes au marché
du sparadrap à la pharmacie

Exercise 3 Shopping

Aim to write in complete sentences, in this way you will make your plans clearer.

A *Any shop relevant to what you want to buy would be correct.* Je vais en ville/au marché/aux magasins/au supermarché.

B *Any appropriate item correctly spelt would gain marks.* Je vais acheter une carte postale.

C *Any recognizable item of food would gain marks.* Je vais prendre du jambon.

D *Here are two useful ways of arranging a meeting:* On se retrouve – we'll meet. Rendez-vous – meeting place. Rencontre-moi/Rendez-vous devant le cinéma/à la Poste/au café . . .

E You may give the time in French using numbers, provided that you follow the French pattern *à 4h15*; remember that the French never use a.m. or p.m.

UNIT 6 ANSWERS

Section Two

Exercice 1

Les magasins chez toi

You need simply to respond to the questions posed. The writer has added a few extra details in paragraphs 2 and 3.

Cher ami/Chère amie,
Tu **m'*as posé* des questions sur les magasins en Grande Bretagne.**

Nous habitons à trois kilomètres du centre commercial. Près de chez moi, il n'y a pas beaucoup de magasins. Il y a seulement un salon de coiffure et un petit magasin *où* on peut acheter des journaux, des bonbons, du tabac et du lait.

En ville les magasins ouvrent d'habitude à neuf heures et ferment à cinq heures et demie le soir. Il y a de petits magasins *qui* ouvrent plus tôt et *qui* ferment à dix ou onze heures du soir.

Quant aux vêtements, cela dépend. Il y a des magasins *où* on peut acheter des habits peu chers; mais *si* on veut des vêtements de marque, comme Lacoste, ils coûtent très chers.

Quand je suis allée **en ville samedi dernier, *j'ai acheté* une revue et des bonbons. *J'ai* aussi *acheté* un cadeau d'anniversaire pour mon père.**
Amitiés . . .

There are two words for clothes: you can avoid repeating yourself and improve your style.
des habits – clothes
des vêtements – clothes

Here is a useful structure which you can adapt for any number of situations:
où on peut acheter . . . – where you can buy . . . (où on peut jouer au golf/où on peut faire des promenades/où on peut visiter un musée).

UNIT 6 ANSWERS

Section Two

Exercice 2

Des cadeaux de Noël

You are asked for particular information about Christmas shopping; make sure that you restrict yourself to those details.

Note how this writer adds variety by using other verbs than *acheter*: to avoid repetition, you can also use *choisir*, *prendre* and *trouver*.

> **Salut!**
> ***Je suis allé* à Birmingham pour faire des courses. *Je voulais* des cadeaux de Noël pour ma famille. Pour ma grand-mère *j'ai pris* une boîte de chocolats et pour mon grand-père *j'ai acheté* des chaussettes. Ma mère adore le parfum, alors *je* lui *ai acheté* du parfum italien. Mon père lit beaucoup, donc *j'ai choisi* un roman policier. *J'ai trouvé* une affiche pour ma petite sœur. En tout *j'ai dépensé* quarante livres sterling.**
> ***Les magasins étaient* décorés et *c'était* très joli, mais *il y avait* beaucoup de monde. Pour Noël, *je voudrais* un VTT ou un ordinateur; je ne peux pas me décider.**
> **Amicalement . . .**

une affiche – a poster (You may also use *un poster*.)
j'ai dépensé quarante livres – I spent forty pounds (Remember that *passer* is used for time: e.g. *j'ai passé une semaine* – I spent a week.)
il y avait beaucoup de monde – there were a lot of people
It would be helpful to remember these variations:
il y avait tant de monde – there were so many people
il y avait trop de monde – there were too many people
il y avait peu de monde – there were few people

Section Two

Exercice 3
Une plainte

A formal letter can be difficult because of the need to write sufficient detail; it is important to keep to the point. Whenever you wish to make a complaint, you should make certain that you are polite. Remember to use *vous*.

> **Monsieur,**
> **Il y a deux semaines *j'ai acheté* un pull vert en laine, taille moyenne.**
> ***Je** l'**ai payé** 250 francs.*
> **Malheureusement *quand je suis rentré* à la maison, *j'ai sorti* le pull du sac et *j'ai trouvé* qu'*il y avait* un petit trou dans le dos. Je ne sais pas *comment c'est arrivé*, mais *le trou devait* être déjà dans le pull au magasin.**
> ***Comme* je ne peux pas le porter dans cet état, je vous demande de le remplacer.**
> **Pouvez-vous me téléphoner au plus vite au numéro indiqué?**
> **Veuillez agréer, Monsieur, l'expression de mes sentiments distingués . . .**

j'ai sorti le pull du sac – I took the pullover out of the bag (Compare: *Maman a sorti la voiture du garage* – Mum got the car out of the garage; *Papa est sorti en voiture* – Dad has gone out in the car.)
le trou devait être déjà dans le pull – the hole must already have been in the jumper
Note the word order in this statement:
je vous demande de le remplacer – I ask you to replace it

UNIT 6 ANSWERS

Section Three

Exercice 1 Faire le shopping

You have the opportunity here to give your opinions and feelings about shopping. If you are able to write from experience you are likely to be more convincing.

You may not agree with the writer of this account but the structures/vocabulary used are useful and adaptable.

Les jeunes, vous aimez le shopping?

Je vais rarement dans les supermarchés *parce que* <u>*je déteste*</u> l'ambiance là-dedans. Cependant la semaine dernière, *comme ma mère avait* la grippe, *j'ai dû* aller faire les courses. Pour commencer, *je ne trouvais rien*; *il fallait* faire tout le tour du magasin pour chercher les provisions sur la liste *que ma mère* m'*avait donnée. Comme je devais* m'arrêter devant chaque rayon, *j'ai perdu* énormément de temps.

C'était une expérience à ne pas répéter. <u>*Je trouvais les gens désagréables*</u>; *les allées étaient* bloquées par les chariots des gens *qui discutaient* quel produit *ils allaient* prendre. Et puis, bien sûr, *il y avait ceux qui parlaient* au téléphone; <u>*je trouve cela inacceptable*</u>. Le téléphone portable devient un véritable fléau.

Pour moi *ce n'était* sûrement pas un plaisir; *ma mère s'est fâchée parce que je suis rentré* plus tard que prévu. Par conséquent *on a dîné* très tard ce jour-là, donc *tout le monde était* de mauvaise humeur.

Quant aux grandes surfaces, <u>*je ne les aime pas*</u> *parce qu'*on perd du temps à chercher ce qu'on veut et il y a tous ces gens *qui* semblent errer sans but. Il y a peut-être plein de choix; pour certaines personnes c'est peut-être pratique; moi je les évite. Le shopping c'est une nécessité, pas une distraction.

un rayon – a shelf/a department (in a store)
une allée – aisle
un fléau – a scourge
plus tard que prévu – later than expected
on perd du temps à chercher . . . – you waste time looking for . . .
sans but – aimlessly
plein de choix – plenty of choice (*plein de* is a useful alternative to *beaucoup de.*)

Section Three

Exercice 2 Les vêtements de marque

Everyone has opinions about clothes. Here is your chance to give yours: even if you do not share the views of the writer, there are some useful structures and adjectives here which you can use.

La mode

En ce moment, mes amis sont tous obsédés de vêtements de marque; ils sont habillés des pieds à la tête en vêtements extrêmement chers. Ce n'est pas simplement les vêtements, il faut aussi les eaux de toilette, les chaussures et les baskets. J'avoue que ces habits sont assez élégants, que les couleurs sont belles, mais tout cela coûte une fortune. *<u>Je préfère</u>* garder mon argent pour acheter une voiture. Je cherche des habits moins chers.

Le week-end dernier par exemple, *je suis allé* faire des courses avec mes amis: moi, *j'ai acheté* un pull, un jean et quelques t-shirts pour cinquante livres; pour ce même prix, *mon meilleur ami n'avait qu'*un sweat.

À la longue, je pense que c'est moi *qui* gagne. *Comme* je ne paie pas cher ce que j'achète, je peux me permettre d'acheter de nouveaux vêtements plus souvent. Mes amis, par contre, *ayant payé* beaucoup, continuent à porter des affaires *qui* sont un peu démodées.

<u>À mon avis</u>, on exploite les jeunes; ils n'ont pas les moyens de changer continuellement de vêtements et de toutes façons, ce n'est vraiment pas nécessaire. *Même si j'avais* beaucoup d'argent, *je ferais* toujours attention; les vêtements, cela s'use! La possibilité de m'acheter une voiture est plus importante.

des pieds à la tête – from head to toe (Literally: from the feet to the head.)
les vêtements de marque – designer labels
à la longue – in the long run
je peux me permettre . . . – I can afford to . . .
cela s'use – it wears out

Section Three

Exercice 3 Les magasins chez toi (2)

You are asked for your opinions on the facilities in your area. This writer gives a highly personal view; note how he makes comparisons. The variety of structure is excellent, although it is a longer piece than is required.

Le shopping dans ma région

Comme nous habitons une région agricole, les courses c'est toujours un problème. Le village le plus près a simplement un petit magasin *qui* vend de tout. Donc *non seulement* le choix est très limité *mais aussi* on doit payer plus cher que dans les magasins en ville.

La ville la plus proche est à 18 kilomètres; *il faut* une bonne demi-heure pour aller au supermarché, *qui* se trouve, malheureusement, de l'autre côté de la ville.

Pour nous la situation est assez difficile; mon père travaille de six heures du matin *jusqu'à la nuit tombante* à la ferme, *tandis que* ma mère est réceptionniste au cabinet du médecin dans le village. Ils ont tous les deux des journées très chargées.

Heureusement les supermarchés et les autres grandes surfaces ouvrent le dimanche. Donc nous allons souvent faire les courses le dimanche, *comme nous avons fait* la semaine dernière et *comme on a été* obligé de faire pour préparer la fête de Noël.

Pourtant, le dimanche *c'était* le seul jour de la semaine *où mes parents pouvaient* se reposer ou faire quelque chose *qui* leur *faisait* plaisir, rencontrer les amis, visiter un château ou simplement s'endormir devant la télévision!

Je crois qu'il faut encourager les commerçants à ouvrir plus de magasins à la campagne *au lieu de* construire toujours des supermarchés gigantesques *qui* se trouvent tous les uns à côté des autres.

jusqu'à la nuit tombante – until nightfall
le cabinet – the surgery (You could check in the dictionary to find what other meanings there are for *le cabinet.*)
les grandes surfaces – large stores (usually used for out-of-town shops)
c'était le seul jour de la semaine où . . . – it was the only day of the week when . . .
au lieu de construire – instead of building

UNIT 7 ANSWERS

Section One

Exercice 1
Tu aimes manger … ?

Here is a list of food items suggested by the pictures, singular or plural words would be acceptable. If you have used any others you can check the spelling in your dictionary:

yaourt	**fromage**	**tomate(s)**	**bifteck/steak/viande**	
poisson	**oignon(s)**	**carotte(s)**	**petits pois**	**poulet**
œuf(s)	**lait**	**café**	**thé**	**laitue**

You should have ten, but where you have put the words will depend on your personal likes/dislikes.

Exercise 2
A picnic list

Notice the words for containers and amounts in italic; these will give you some help in forming your own answers. The pictures suggest these answers.

une boîte de sardines
un paquet de chips
une bouteille de lait
un morceau de fromage
un kilo de pommes
une tranche/des tranches de jambon

Exercice 3
Gardez la forme!

The numbers match the pictures.
In the negative advice notice how to express 'do not':
1 ne fumez pas de cigarettes
2 ne buvez pas d'alcool/ne prenez pas d'alcool
3 ne mange pas trop de bonbons/chocolat.
Here are the positive pieces of advice:
5 faites du sport/du jogging/de l'exercice
6 mangez de la salade/des légumes/des fruits
7 buvez de l'eau.

UNIT 7 ANSWERS

Section Two

Exercice 1
Le barbecue

Each of the points is answered simply and logically. Note how you can use the question to help frame your answer.

> **Salut!**
> **Vendredi soir *nous avons fait* un barbecue dans le jardin chez mon ami Tom *qui* habite Wellingborough. *Il y avait* une douzaine de copains et de copines de ma classe.**
> ***Nous avons décidé* de faire un barbecue *parce que c'était* la fin du trimestre et *les vacances commençaient.***
> **Heureusement *il faisait* beau et chaud. *Nous avons préparé* des saucisses *parce que tout le monde* les *aimait*. Après, *nous avons écouté* de la musique et *nous avons dansé.***
> **Moi, *j'aime* les repas barbecue, surtout en été, mais je ne mange jamais les biftecks.**
> **Amitiés**

une douzaine de – a dozen/about twelve (Remember that you can add *-aine* to a number to suggest an approximate amount, e.g. *une vingtaine*, *une centaine*; you will need to remove the final *e* of some numbers, e.g. *une quinzaine*, *une trentaine*, *une cinquantaine*.)
tout le monde les aimait – everyone liked them (i.e. sausages.)

Exercice 2
Faire un repas

Note how this writer decides to use his own experience to answer the question: the suggestions in brackets are there to stimulate ideas, you can use ides of your own if you wish.

The opinions/attitudes expressed follow a simple pattern, *c'était ennuyeux*; *c'était délicieux*; *j'étais content*; *c'était assez facile*: you should be able to use these and to develop more of your own.

J'ai préparé un repas
Le mois dernier *ma mère a commencé* un nouvel emploi dans un grand magasin en ville. Le jeudi soir le magasin ferme à huit heures, donc elle arrive à la maison trop tard pour préparer le dîner.

Alors c'est moi *qui* fais la cuisine le jeudi. Quelquefois ma sœur m'aide, mais d'habitude je prépare le repas et elle fait la vaisselle.

Au début *je n'aimais pas* cuisiner, donc *je faisais* des salades; mais *c'était ennuyeux* de manger toujours la même chose. Donc jeudi dernier, *j'ai décidé* d'essayer quelque chose de différent. *J'ai fait* un plat avec des pâtes, des champignons, du bacon et du fromage. *Toute le monde a trouvé* que *c'était* délicieux. *J'étais content parce que c'était* assez facile à préparer.

c'est moi qui fais la cuisine – it is me who does the cooking
ma sœur m'aide – my sister helps me (Note the word order.)
manger toujours la même chose – always to eat the same thing

Exercice 3
Un repas de vacances

This person has written about a meal while abroad. Where you were does not matter, but if you can write from experience, you are likely to give a more interesting account. Note how the person has highlighted what was special about the occasion.

Je passais les vacances en Italie avec mes parents, mon frère et mes grands-parents. À la fin de notre séjour, *nous avons décidé* d'aller au restaurant une dernière fois. *Nous avons choisi* un petit restaurant à côté de la mer *où nous avons réservé* une table à la terrasse. C'est ma mère *qui a choisi* ce restaurant *parce que la spécialité était* les fruits de mer et tout le monde dans la famille aime le poisson.

Nous avons pris un menu à 90 francs. Pour commencer, moi *j'ai eu* des crevettes, après *j'ai choisi* un plat de pâtes avec du poisson, des champignons et une sauce à la crème et puis une salade verte. *C'était vraiment délicieux.*

Mon grand-père a voulu faire une surprise, alors *il a commandé* du champagne avec le dessert! *Comme* dessert, *j'ai pris* une glace à la framboise. *Tout le monde était enchanté, nous avons* bien *fêté* la fin des vacances.

un menu à 90 francs – a set meal at 90 francs (A useful pattern to remember, the price is normally added after the item *une glace à 6 francs.*)
une sauce à la crème – a cream sauce (Remember this pattern, *une sauce à la tomate, une sauce au fromage, une sauce au poivre.*)
nous avons fêté – we celebrated

UNIT 7 ANSWERS

Section Three

Exercice 1
Pour garder la forme

There is plenty of guidance in the visual clues and in the questions about what is expected.

Comment garder la forme!
Depuis quelques années je fais toujours attention à *ce que* je mange. J'évite les matières grasses et je ne mange pas trop de sucreries; avant, *j'adorais* les bonbons et surtout le chocolat, mais maintenant, *si* j'ai faim entre les repas je prends un fruit.

Quant aux activités sportives, c'est une autre histoire; *je n'aimais pas le sport* au collège, *je n'étais pas* du tout sportif, mais *mon père* qui *avait décidé* de faire du jogging deux ou trois fois par semaine et *il disait* que *cela* lui *faisait* du bien. Donc, un jour *je* l'*ai accompagné* et maintenant on sort régulièrement. De retour à la maison, je prends une douche et *je sens vraiment que cela me détend.*

Bien sûr *il ne faut pas* se laisser tenter par les cigarettes et l'alcool; *je n'ai jamais fumé* et *je ne vais* certainement *pas commencer*. Quant à l'alcool, *il faut* consommer avec modération; on dit que le vin rouge peut avoir un effet bénéfique.

Les drogues? N'en parlons pas!

de retour à la maison – back home (This is a useful phrase to start a sentence.)
cela lui faisait du bien – this did him good
je l'ai accompagné – I accompanied him/ I went with him (cf. *il nous a accompagnés* – he came with us; how would you write 'she came with me', using this pattern?)
bénéfique – beneficial

Exercice 2
Fumer

This is an issue of great concern and there is plenty of advice in the question about what is required; make certain that you give your opinions.

Note how the writer, a girl, expresses attitudes, feelings and opinions. You could make a list of the phrases and sentences which she uses to do this.

Mon amie fume
Quand j'étais à la discothèque vendredi dernier avec quelques amis pour fêter mon anniversaire, *ma meilleure amie* m'*a offert* une cigarette! *J'ai été un peu choquée parce que je ne savais pas* qu'*elle fumait*.

Bien entendu *j'ai refusé*. À ce moment-là, *Sara a commencé* à rire; *elle s'est moquée* de moi, *en disant* que *j'étais* prude.

J'ai découvert que *Sara fumait depuis plus d'un an* et qu'*elle fumait* au moins cinq cigarettes par jour. Certainement *ses parents n'étaient pas au courant. Elle* m'*a dit* qu'*elle avait commencé* à fumer *quand elle était sortie* pour la première fois avec son petit ami. *Elle fumait parce que son ami fumait* et *elle voulait* faire comme les autres. En plus, *elle trouvait que cela la détendait lorsqu'elle était stressée.*

J'ai essayé de la décourager *en lui expliquant* que *c'était* nuisible, qu'*elle risquait* de tomber malade. *Elle a* simplement *dit* qu'*elle ne fumait pas* assez pour mettre sa vie en danger.

Moi, *je ne suis pas d'accord; à mon avis,* une cigarette par jour c'est une cigarette de trop. *Je pense que c'est une habitude dégoûtante; je hais* l'odeur des cigarettes. *On devrait* bannir les cigarettes de tous les endroits publics.

elle s'est moquée de moi – she made fun of me
prude – prudish
cela la détendait – that relaxed her
nuisible – harmful
une habitude – a habit (Remember that the French word *habit* means an item of clothing.)

Exercice 3
Végétarien?

An issue of contemporary concern about which you should have some ideas and opinions. This girl makes some interesting points using quite familiar language.

Pour ou contre la viande
Dans notre famille c'est toujours un grand débat. Mes parents mangent de la viande mais ma sœur et moi sommes végétariennes. Moi, je mange du poisson, mais ma sœur refuse d'en manger.

Je n'ai pas mangé de viande *depuis cinq ans*. Quelquefois la variété et même le goût de la viande me manquent, mais *je n'*en *mangerai plus*.

J'ai décidé de devenir végétarienne *quand j'ai entendu parler* de la maladie de la vache folle. *Cela m'a fait peur*. À cette époque, *quand je sortais* avec mes amis, *je prenais* souvent des hamburgers. Ensuite, *j'ai découvert comment on élevait* les cochons et les poulets; *cela me révoltait, je trouvais que c'était vraiment cruel*. Je sais que certains fermiers essaient de faire de l'élevage biologique, mais *je me suis habituée* à ce régime. J'espère que *les restaurants s'adapteront* à nos goûts.

ma sœur refuse d'en manger – my sister refuses to eat it (fish)
la variété et même le goût de la viande me manquent – I miss the variety and even the taste of meat
je n'en mangerai plus – I will never eat it again
j'ai entendu parler de . . . – I heard about . . . (When it is simply a noise, then you should use *entendre*, however, when it is a question of information then *entendre parler* is more correct.)
la maladie de la vache folle – 'mad cow disease'
cela m'a fait peur – this frightened me (Compare *faire peur* 'to frighten' and *avoir peur* 'to be afraid'.)
je me suis habituée à . . . – I have got used to . . .

UNIT 8 ANSWERS

Section One

Exercice 1 — Ton collège

Here are some sentences suggested by the pictures:

c'est une grande école	**c'est une école moderne**
c'est une petite école	**il y a un terrain de sports**
il y a une bibliothèque	**il y a une salle d'informatique**
il y a une piscine	**on porte l'uniforme scolaire**
c'est une école mixte	**c'est une école pour garçons et filles**

Exercise 2 — Homework

Your sentences should follow these patterns. The information you will give may vary.

- **A** J'ai une heure/deux heures de devoirs.
- **B** Je fais mes devoirs dans ma chambre/dans la cuisine/dans la salle à manger.
- **C** Je ne fais pas de devoirs vendredi/samedi/dimanche soir. [NB: *nuit* is not correct here.]
- **D** J'aime les devoirs de mathématiques/de dessin/d'anglais/d'histoire.
- **E** Je n'aime pas les devoirs de biologie/d'espagnol/de géographie/de musique.

Exercice 3 — À l'école

Your sentences should follow these patterns. The information you give may vary e.g. different colours of uniform/different times.

- **A** Je porte un uniforme, une chemise blanche, un pull rouge et un pantalon noir/une jupe noire.
- **B** Je quitte la maison à huit heures/huit heures et quart/huit heures et demie.
- **C** Je vais à l'école à pied/à (en) vélo/à bicyclette/en bus/en voiture/en train.
- **D** À midi, je mange à la cantine/à la maison/chez moi/chez mon ami(e)/en ville.
- **E** Ma matière favorite est l'anglais/l'informatique.

Section Two

Exercice 1 Une visite scolaire

You are asked to describe a school trip; the pictures are there to provide a few ideas, but the questions are more important so do not miss out any information. However, if it was a day trip, make certain that you make that clear, as this will explain why you have not responded to *quel logement?*.

Cher . . ./Chère . . .
L'année dernière, au mois de juin, *je suis allé* dans la région des montagnes dans le nord du Pays de Galles.
***J'y suis allé* avec mes amis de classe et les professeurs de géographie. *Nous avons voyagé* en car. *C'était* un voyage assez long. *Nous sommes restés* cinq jours. *Nous avons logé* dans une auberge de jeunesse.**
Pendant la journée, *nous avons fait* des randonnées dans les collines et *nous avons fait* du canoë sur un lac.
Le soir, *nous avons fait* une promenade dans la ville de Bangor.
Amitiés . . .

j'y suis allé – I went there (Note the word order: *y* meaning 'there' goes in front of the verb.)
nous avons logé – we stayed (It is far better to use *loger* rather than *rester*.)
nous avons fait des randonnées – we went rambling/hiking (Note how frequently you need *faire* to refer to outdoor/sporting activities. However, if you are writing about a game, you would use *jouer*, e.g. *jouer au tennis*, *jouer au basket*, *jouer au volley*.)

UNIT 8 ANSWERS

Section Two

Exercice 2
Les examens

It is important in this question to make sure that you distinguish between what you have already done and what you are going to do.

Note the ways of referring to the future: *je vais passer* – I am going to take; *nous aurons* – we will have. Pick out other examples and practise by writing the other version, e.g. *je vais passer* – *je passerai*.

Salut!
Alors cette année, au mois de juin, *je vais passer* des examens importants. *Il y aura* douze examens en tout *parce que* pour certaines matières *comme* les maths, l'anglais et les sciences *nous* en *aurons* deux.

En fait *nous avons* déjà *commencé*; *j'ai passé* mon examen oral en espagnol la semaine dernière et hier *j'ai passé* l'examen oral en français. *Comme* j'aime les langues, *j'ai fait* beaucoup de préparations et *cela s'est* bien *passé*.

Normalement j'essaie de faire une heure de révisions tous les jours et un peu plus le week-end, le samedi ou le dimanche. *Je préfère* garder un jour de libre pour faire du sport ou sortir avec les copains.

***Je vais continuer* à faire cela et puis, au mois de mai, *nous aurons* une semaine pour travailler à la maison avant le commencement des examens.**

D'habitude, *j'aime* travailler pendant une heure et puis faire autre chose, *autrement* c'est trop fatigant, par exemple hier soir *j'ai promené* le chien et ce soir *je vais regarder* une émission de musique à la télévision.
Amicalement . . .

cela s'est bien passé – it passed off well
un jour de libre – a free day/a day off
autrement – otherwise

Section Two

Exercice 3 L'année prochaine

Note how this writer expresses opinions and attitudes. You may not have quite the same range; however, you should have used some of these patterns.

Mes études

Cette année j'étudie l'anglais, les maths, la biologie, la géographie, le français, l'allemand, le dessin et l'informatique. Je les étudie *depuis plus de quatre ans*, *sauf* l'allemand et l'informatique *que j'ai commencés* l'année dernière.

La matière *que je préfère le plus* c'est l'allemand *parce que* le professeur est dynamique et très marrant; j'apprends très vite et je suis doué en langues modernes. *J'aime* aussi le dessin, cela me détend et *j'aime bien* cette façon de m'exprimer.

Je déteste la biologie; je dois suivre au moins une matière scientifique mais *je les trouve vraiment barbantes.*

L'année prochaine, j'ai l'intention de continuer mes études; j'espère faire l'allemand, le français et le commerce. *Je vais quitter* le collège *parce que* c'est simplement un collège pour les étudiants de 11 à 16 ans. *J'irai* au grand lycée en ville.

Mon ambition c'est de travailler pour une grande compagnie aérienne *parce que j'adore* voyager et recontrer les gens.

je les étudie depuis plus de quatre ans – I have been studying them for more than four years
sauf – except
que j'ai commencés l'année dernière – which I started last year (The added *s* refers back to *que* which in turn refers to *allemand et l'informatique*; this is known as preceding object pronoun agreement.)
cela me détend – that relaxes me
un lycée – this is the word which best translates Sixth Form College

Section Three

Exercice 1
Mon activité

You have a great deal of choice in this question. This person has chosen to write about her amateur dramatics; if you have chosen to focus on a sporting activity then you will have little in common. You will benefit from studying the answer, however, as there are many useful patterns.

Mon activité préférée au collège c'est l'art dramatique. *J'ai toujours aimé* être sur scène, *même quand j'étais* à l'école primaire; *si on ne* me *donnait pas* un rôle à jouer, *j'étais très déçue.*

Je fais partie du club au collège et on se rencontre tous les lundis soirs de sept heures à neuf heures pour répéter; normalement on présente une pièce toutes les six ou sept semaines. Le prof *qui* nous dirige est vraiment dynamique et tout le monde veut réussir.

Le trimestre dernier *nous avons présenté* une comédie par Oscar Wilde *qui* s'appelle 'The Importance of Being Earnest'. C'est une pièce très connue en Angleterre et elle attire toujours un grand public. *Comme* je suis assez forte de carrure, *on* m'*a demandé* de jouer le rôle de la matronne *qui* a environ soixante-dix ans. *J'étais ravie parce que* c'est un rôle important et en plus, le personnage dit des vers extrêmement drôles.

J'adore apprendre un rôle et répéter, après une répétition je me sens toujours bien. On s'amuse beaucoup, mais *si* on veut avoir du succès en si peu de temps, *il faut* travailler dur.

Tout s'est passé merveilleusement bien; *quand on est arrivé* au jour de la première représentation, *on se sentait* prêt à faire de notre mieux.

Normalement on fait trois représentations, jeudi soir, vendredi soir et samedi soir. *La salle était* complète chaque soir et l'*assistance a* bien *apprécié* notre travail. *C'était* une réussite et *tout le monde a reçu* les félicitations du directeur. *Après avoir fait* la dernière représentation samedi soir, *nous avons fait* une boum sur la scène, *comme* à chaque fois.

J'attends avec impatience la prochaine pièce, *ce sera* une pièce de Shakespeare.

je suis assez forte de carrure – I am quite well built
une pièce – a play (What other meanings does this word have?)
une représentation – a performance
faire de son mieux – to do one's best
la salle était complète – the hall/auditorium was full
l'assistance – the audience

Section Three

Exercice 2
L'uniforme scolaire

This is a familiar topic which arouses some passion; do not try to write as much as this person, but give your opinions, do not merely describe your uniform. Remember that there are a number of verbs you can use for 'to think', this person uses *penser*, *croire*, *estimer*. Note also that you can express 'have to' by using *il faut*, *on doit*, *on est obligé de*.

Mon collège est typique des collèges en Angleterre, il y a un uniforme *qu*'on doit porter; il y a une chemise blanche, une cravate bleue et verte, une veste bleu marine, et un pantalon ou une jupe pour les filles. On est obligé de porter des chaussures noires, pas de bottes, et jamais de chaussures marron. Ici, c'est vraiment strict, les filles n'ont pas le droit de porter de pantalon, même en hiver, *quand* il fait froid. Du moins, on n'a pas à porter de casquette ou de chapeau *comme* du temps de mes parents.

Le directeur et les professeurs croient que c'est plus facile *si* on est tous habillés de la même façon, que cela crée une bonne impression. Ils estiment aussi, sans doute, que c'est mieux pour *ceux qui* n'ont pas beaucoup d'argent.

Les étudiants s'en *sont plaints* plusieurs fois et *certains parents ont écrit* au directeur, mais il n'y a rien à faire, c'est le refus total.

À mon avis, je trouve que c'est ridicule de vouloir contrôler les éléves de cette façon. L'uniforme n'est pas confortable, on a chaud l'été et les filles ont certainement froid l'hiver. *J'ai vu* que dans quelques collèges il y a un uniforme, mais cela ne fait jamais élégant *parce que* chacun l'adapte *comme* il ou elle veut. Les filles, par exemple, ont des jupes courtes ou des jupes longues; les garçons portent une chemise blanche *qui* est souvent une chemise de grande marque.

Les professeurs devraient comprendre que cela fait démodé et que *les étudiants pourraient* travailler tout aussi bien *s'ils s'habillaient* autrement.

du moins – at least
on n'a pas à . . . – we do not have to . . .
comme du temps de mes parents – as in my parents' time

Exercice 3

Les règlements au collège

Keep to the point and ensure you give your opinions. Some of the points made in the introduction to question 2 are useful here.

Chers amis,
Dans toutes les écoles il y a des règlements; *étant donné qu'*il y a quelques centaines de jeunes *qui* travaillent ensemble dans le même bâtiment, *il faut* les contrôler d'une façon ou d'une autre.

À mon collège les règlements sont simples et pour la plupart, les étudiants les acceptent, *parce qu'*ils trouvent que c'est nécessaire. Cependant, il y en a un qu'ils détestent, celui de l'uniforme; *personne n'*aime porter l'uniforme.

Quant aux autres règlements, c'est du bon sens; *il s'agit* ou de la sécurité ou de la politesse. *Il ne faut pas* fumer, *si* on fume, on est renvoyé; *si* on emploie de la violence contre un autre, on est renvoyé définitivement, et *je trouve que cela est juste*. En plus, on n'a pas le droit de manger du chewing gum; *il ne faut pas* courir dans les couloirs; *il faut* se lever *quand* un professeur entre dans la salle de classe.

***Depuis quelques années* nous signons un contrat au mois de septembre; *en signant* ce contrat, chaque étudiant accepte de se comporter d'une façon convenable: on doit toujours faire de son mieux, compléter ses devoirs, se montrer respectueux envers les professeurs et les autres étudiants.**

De toute façon, les règlements sont essentiels partout, sur les routes, au lieu de travail, dans les transports, pourquoi pas au collège?

À bientôt . . .

étant donné que – given that
d'une façon ou d'une autre – in one way or another
renvoyer – to suspend
renvoyer définitivement – to expel

UNIT 9 ANSWERS

Section One

Exercice 1
Demande d'emploi

Make sure that you complete all parts of the exercise; you are unlikely to gain marks for information in English.

Nom de famille: [surname]
Prénom: [first name]
Nationalité: britannique/anglais(e)/écossais(e)/gallois(e)/irlandais(e)/indien(ne)/pakistannais(e)
Date de naissance: [date of birth using this pattern: le 9 février 1984]
Lieu de naissance: [place of birth]
Caractère: you should have two; if your answers are not in the list, you should check in the dictionary (girls should use the second spelling): gentil/gentille; bavard/bavarde; aimable; timide; sportif/sportive; gourmand/gourmande; sympa; généreux/généreuse; sincère
Expérience: there are various ways of gaining marks here:

- i you could mention a job – vendeur/vendeuse; caissier/caissière; garçon/serveur/serveuse;
- ii or you could mention a place – dans un supermarché/dans un hôtel/dans un restaurant/dans une station service/dans une bibliothèque
- iii or you might use a phrase such as – faire du babysitting/livrer les journaux

Langues parlées: anglais/français/allemand/espagnol/italien/russe/japonais/ourdou [any two]
Autres matières étudiées: dessin/musique/informatique/histoire/géographie/biologie/chimie/physique [any two]
Mois libre(s): juin/juillet/août/septembre

UNIT 9 ANSWERS

Section One

Exercice 2
Les emplois des jeunes

You should aim to write in complete sentences. If you cannot write a complete sentence, you should at least try to give some information; however, you may gain fewer marks. The pictures suggest the following sentences.

A Je fais du babysitting. Je travaille dans un supermarché en ville. Je fais du jardinage. Je travaille dans un restaurant.

If you have a different job and you can express it, then use it.

B Je travaille le vendredi soir/le samedi.
C Je travaille de six heures à dix heures/Je commence à huit heures et demie et je finis à cinq heures.
D Je gagne trois livres par heure/vingt livres par semaine.
E Avec mon argent, j'achète des disques et des vêtements.

NB: you could put the first two details in the same sentence and still gain full marks, e.g. Je travaille dans un supermarché le vendredi soir.

Exercise 3
Life in 10 years' time

If you have followed the ideas in the pictures and followed the pattern of the examples, then you may have these answers. You will gain marks for each answer, as the column only shows your personal preference.

1 être étudiant(e)
2 me marier/être marié(e)
3 avoir des enfants
4 avoir une belle/grosse voiture
5 partir en vacances/faire des voyages (en avion)
6 travailler dans un bureau
7 être maçon/travailler sur un chantier/travailler à l'extérieur
8 gagner beaucoup d'argent

Section Two

Exercice 1
Votre stage en entreprise

This person has given a straightforward account of his experiences in a supermarket. You may well have described experiences in a quite different environment; however, the structures are likely to be similar. Make certain that you do not confuse the verb *travailler* and the noun *le travail*.

Mon stage en entreprise

Vers la fin du trimestre l'été dernier *j'ai passé* une semaine à travailler dans un grand supermarché. *J'ai commencé* le lundi matin à huit heures et demie et *j'ai fini* le vendredi soir à cinq heures.

Chaque jour *j'ai fait* quelque chose de différent, par exemple le lundi *j'ai aidé* à remplir les rayons; le mardi *j'ai aidé* la personne *qui* s'occupe des produits frais, les fruits et les légumes. Le mercredi, *j'ai livré* les produits à domicile, puis le jeudi, *j'ai travaillé* au rayon charcuterie. *J'ai passé* la dernière journée avec le directeur. *Quand il a fait* son tour d'inspection, *je me sentais* important!

J'ai trouvé les employés très sympa surtout le directeur *qui* m'*a* tout *expliqué*.

C'est un travail assez fatigant mais intéressant. Plus tard, *je voudrais* travailler dans une banque ou dans un bureau, *je n'ai pas* encore *décidé*.

le rayon – the shelf/the department (This word has two meanings when referring to a store/supermarket.)
j'ai fait quelque chose de différent – I did something different
j'ai livré – I delivered

Section Two

Exercice 2 La colonie de vacances

As this is a formal letter, be polite and remember to use *vous*. Try to avoid repeating the same structure; this person has used *je voudrais* a number of times. Remember that you can also use *j'aimerais*.

Monsieur,
***Je voudrais* poser ma candidature pour le poste de plongeur.**
Je fais la vaisselle régulièrement à la maison et j'ai de l'expérience dans les restaurants. Pendant les vacances de Noël, *j'ai travaillé* dans la cuisine d'un hôtel dans la ville *où* j'habite. L'année dernière, *j'ai travaillé* le vendredi et le samedi dans un petit restaurant italien au centre-ville *où j'ai fait* la vaisselle et *j'ai* aussi *servi* à table.
Cette année *je voudrais* travailler pour quatre semaines au mois de juillet.
***Je voudrais* travailler en France *car j'aimerais* perfectionner mon français.**
Veuillez agréer, Monsieur, l'expression de mes sentiments distingués . . .

poser sa candidature pour le poste de – to apply for the post of
un plongeur – dish washer (person)

Exercice 3 L'avenir

You will need to be careful about the verb forms here; you must use the future tense. Notice below some of the alternative ways of referring to the future.

L'avenir
Moi, j'ai l'intention de continuer mes études l'année prochaine. Je compte étudier les maths, la physique et la chimie *parce que* *j'adore* les sciences. Donc, je *quitterai* l'école *quand j'aurai* 18 ans.

Alors, après le collège, *si* je réussis aux examens, j'espère aller à l'université.

J'ai toujours voulu devenir ingénieur des travaux publics *parce que je suis fasciné* par ce genre de travail. *J'ai l'intention de* voyager partout dans le monde et *je pourrais* travailler dans les pays pauvres, les aider à construire des maisons, des routes et des ponts.

Quant à l'argent, *j'aimerais* gagner un bon salaire pour pouvoir bien profiter de la vie.

je compte . . . – I expect to . . .
j'espère . . . – I hope to . . .
j'ai l'intention de . . . – I intend to . . .

UNIT 9 ANSWERS

Section Three

Exercice 1
Vos projets

The question raises an issue which many will face; here is your opportunity to organize your current thoughts. Even though you may not agree with this response, you will find some helpful expressions giving opinions.

La plupart de mes amis ont décidé de partir à l'université; ils parlent déjà de *ce qu'ils vont faire*, mais j'ai l'impression qu'ils ne prennent pas les études au sérieux. *Ce qui* les intéresse c'est plutôt de faire de nouveaux amis, de boire, d'aller en boîte, de s'amuser.

J'ai décidé, il y a longtemps, que *ce n'était pas* pour moi. Il n'y a plus de bourses; je ne veux pas demander de l'argent à mes parents et je n'ai aucune intention de faire des emprunts. *Je trouve que* c'est trop risqué: étudier pendant trois ans et se retrouver avec des dettes, *sans* travail peut-être, *cela ne m'intéresse pas*. En septembre, après les examens, *si* j'ai de bonnes notes, *je vais continuer* mes études; *je ferai* maths et informatique. Après cela, *je voudrais* travailler pendant une année pour une organisation charitable. Ensuite, *je chercherai* un poste *comme* stagiaire en comptabilité. J'ai l'impression que *j'aurai* un meilleur début dans la vie active.

je n'ai aucune intention de – I have no intention of . . . (The negative *ne . . . aucun/aucune* is more forceful than *ne . . . pas*.)
faire des emprunts – to take out loans
risqué – risky
une organisation charitable – a charity organization
un/une stagiaire – a trainee
la vie active – working life

UNIT 9 ANSWERS

Section Three

Exercice 2

Une difficulté au travail

Whether or not you are able to write from personal experience, make sure that you plan your answer carefully so that you produce a logical account. The writer has produced a rather long answer; this is often a danger with an open-ended question. You are unlikely to have chosen a situation such as this one. However, you should note how the writer expresses his feelings and emotions.

Salut!
***Comme* tu le sais déjà, je travaille le vendredi soir et le samedi dans un grand supermarché en ville. Je le fais *depuis presqu'un an* maintenant. *Je n'ai jamais eu* de problèmes et *j'ai* toujours *trouvé* les autres employés bien agréables.**

Normalement le vendredi soir j'aide à remplir les rayons. Alors, vendredi dernier, vers huit heures et demie, *je mettais* des boîtes de céréales sur le rayon *lorsque j'ai remarqué* un jeune homme *qui cachait* des affaires dans ses poches. *Il était* assez grand et *il portait* un sac à dos. Évidemment *il ne* m'*avait pas vu*. *Je ne savais pas* que faire *parce que j'étais* le seul employé dans cette partie du magasin. *Je pensais* que *si j'allais* chercher quelqu'un, *il quitterait* le supermarché pendant mon absence. *Je n'osais pas* lui parler, *j'avais trop peur*.

***Après avoir fini* de vider la boîte, *je suis allé* en chercher une autre. Par hasard *j'ai rencontré* le chef de service et *je* lui *ai expliqué ce que j'avais vu*. *Il est parti en courant* pour chercher le garde chargé de la sécurité. Bref, *on a arrêté* le voleur *au moment où il arrivait* à la caisse. Dans son sac, *il y avait* plusieurs produits qu'*il avait pris sans avoir* l'intention de les payer. Et moi? *On* m'*a donné* une récompense de vingt livres.**
Amitiés . . .

cacher – to hide
je n'osais pas lui parler – I did not dare to speak to him
il est parti en courant – he ran off (You could practise similar patterns using *traverser*, *monter*, *entrer*, *descendre*, e.g. *sortir*: *je suis sorti en courant* – I ran out.)
une récompense – a reward

UNIT 9 ANSWERS

Section Three

Exercice 3
Votre carrière

If you can focus upon your current career plans, you are likely to be able to write more convincingly. As with the previous question, however, there is a need to keep control of your answer. Plan carefully so that you do not produce an over-long, rambling answer.

Ma carrière

J'ai décidé il y a longtemps que *je voulais* une carrière *qui* m'*offrait* un bon salaire. Je comprends que certaines personnes sont prêtes à consacrer leur vie pour aider les autres, mais moi, je suis assez égoïste et *je voudrais* profiter pleinement de la vie.

J'irai à l'université pour faire une licence en droit international. *Après avoir fini* mes études, *je chercherai* un poste dans une grande entreprise ou dans une banque. Mon ambition c'est d'être millionaire avant l'âge de 30 ans, *ce qui* n'est pas rare de nos jours. Par la suite, j'ai l'intention de trouver un poste *comme* directeur général.

Si je réussis, *je pourrai* prendre la retraite à 50 ans et puis poursuivre mes intérêts: *j'adore* voyager et *j'aimerais* acheter un gros bateau pour faire des croisières ou dans la Méditerranée ou dans la mer des Caraïbes.

consacrer sa vie à – to devote one's life to
je voudrais profiter pleinement de – I would like to take full advantage of
une licence en droit – a law degree
une grande entreprise – a large company

UNIT 10 ANSWERS

Section One

Exercice 1 Le recyclage

You would gain a mark for either a singular or plural noun. These are the obvious answers:

journal/journaux; revue(s)/magazine(s); livre(s); papier; canette(s)/boîte(s) de conserve; bouteille(s); carton; pneu(s); bois; vêtement(s); voiture(s).

Exercise 2 Animals in danger!

If you follow carefully the pattern of the profile in the example, you should find it fairly easy to provide two sets of details. You would gain 1 mark for each item. There are many possible answers, here are three:

Animal:	lion	éléphant	ours
Continent/pays d'origine:	Afrique	Inde	Arctique
Couleur:	marron	gris	blanc
Taille:	grand	énorme	très grand
Nourriture préférée:	viande	feuilles	poissons

Exercice 3 L'eau

These are the answers suggested by the pictures: you would gain marks for each idea which you communicate completely. The numbers match the pictures.

1 boire de l'eau
2 prendre une douche
3 se brosser les dents
4 se laver
5 se baigner/prendre un bain
6 préparer un repas/faire la cuisine
7 faire du thé
8 arroser le jardin
9 laver la voiture
10 faire la vaisselle
11 laver les fenêtres
12 faire la lessive

Section Two

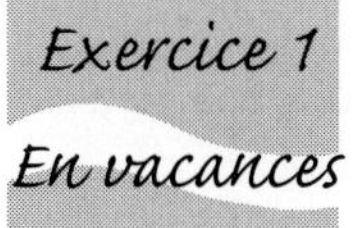

You have the choice of any country; whichever you choose, you will need the patterns used here. This is a simple response and includes all the details required. Note how the writer uses the imperfect tense to describe the place.

Une visite en Grèce
J'ai visité la Grèce pendant les grandes vacances l'année dernière. *Je suis allé* avec ma famille et *nous avons logé* dans un petit hôtel.

Normalement, il fait très beau en été; il y a beaucoup de soleil et il fait très chaud. *Nous sommes restés* une semaine dans une petite ville *où il y avait* quelques magasins, des restaurants, un petit aquarium et un musée. *Il n'y avait pas* de cinéma ou de théâtre. Pour les touristes, *il y avait* des promenades et des vues magnifiques sur la mer.

La cuisine typique de la région est bonne; on mange beaucoup de poissons. Moi, *j'aime* le poisson, mais mon père ne l'aime pas, alors *il était déçu*.

J'ai particuliérement aimé la mer. *J'aime* nager et faire des sports nautiques.

nous avons logé – we stayed at a hotel (*nous sommes descendus dans un hôtel* is also correct.)
nous sommes restés une semaine – we stayed for a week (You should avoid using this verb with *hôtel/camping*, etc.)

UNIT 10 ANSWERS

Section Two

Exercice 2
La fête de Noël

However you spend Christmas, you will find here the patterns you need to give the information requested. You could make a list of relevant Christmas vocabulary to learn.

> **Cher . . ./Chère . . .**
> **D'habitude nous fêtons Noël en famille, chez nous. Mes grands-parents viennent passer quelques jours, donc la maison est pleine.**
>
> **Pour nous, c'est le jour de Noël *qui* est le plus important. Nous nous levons de bonne heure pour ouvrir les petits cadeaux dans les chaussettes, puis on prend le petit-déjeuner vers huit heures. Ensuite, mes grands-parents vont à l'église. *Pendant* ce temps, nous préparons le repas traditionnel, la dinde, les légumes et puis le pudding *qui* est la spécialité anglaise.**
>
> ***Après avoir mangé*, nous ouvrons nos cadeaux et puis c'est l'heure du goûter. Nous mangeons des petites pâtisseries aux raisins secs. L'année dernière, c'est moi *qui* les *ai préparé*es.**
>
> **Le soir, on aime jouer aux cartes, au scrabble ou au monopoly; dans la famille on aime les jeux de société! Quant à la télévision, on ne la regarde pas, il n'y a jamais rien d'intéressant. Le lendemain, nous faisons une longue promenade au bord de la mer!**
>
> **Amitiés . . .**

(As the French do not have mince pies it is necessary to describe then; one way might be: *les petites pâtisseries aux raisins secs* – literally 'little pastries with raisins'. Remember that to the French *le raisin* is 'grapes' and le raisin sec is 'raisin'.)

c'est moi qui les ai préparées – It was me who prepared them (There are two things to note here: first, *qui* refers to *moi* and therefore the verb is in the form for *je*; second, the *es* added to *préparé* agrees with *les*, the preceding direct object, which refers to *les pâtisseries*, which are feminine plural.)

il n'y a jamais rien d'intéressant – there is never anything interesting

UNIT 10 ANSWERS

Section Two

Exercice 3
Un article sur votre région

You have the opportunity here to use familiar language to describe the area in which you live. The question gives you plenty of help. Use what you know. Note how the writer, a boy, incorporates opinions.

Ma région

J'habite une région industrielle dans le nord-ouest; on n'est pas loin de la mer mais *la région n'est pas tellement jolie*. Notre maison se trouve dans la banlieue; c'est à deux kilomètres du centre-ville et c'est assez calme dans le quartier. La banlieue est propre, mais le centre-ville est vieux et un peu sale. Malheureusement, beaucoup de magasins sont fermés et le choix est limité.

Ce qui est bien c'est qu'il y a des distractions pour les jeunes. Je vais à la piscine tous les mardis; aussi *le cinéma est assez bien*, j'y vais souvent et *je suis allé* au bowling *il y a une semaine*. Il y a aussi une patinoire, mais, je n'y vais pas *parce que je n'aime pas* le patinage. On peut regarder des matchs de rugby à treize au stade et bien sûr on peut toujours aller à la discothèque.

Il y a beaucoup de pollution *parce que* nous avons des usines dans la ville; quelquefois en été, l'odeur est insupportable.

le quartier – the district
la banlieue – the suburbs
ce qui est bien c'est que . . . – what is good is . . . (How would you write the following?: what is interesting is . . .; what is bad is . . .; what is curious is . . .)

UNIT 10 ANSWERS

Section Three

Exercice 1
Un grand supermarché

The question gives you a clear set of tasks, relating to a quite common problem. Ensure that you give your opinions. The writer has given a straightforward answer: note how he draws the reader's attention to the place in the second paragraph: *c'est là que nous avons joué au football.*

Cher . . ./Chére . . . ,
***On vient d'*annoncer qu'*on va construire* un énorme supermarché à côté de chez nous. C'est un quartier résidentiel assez tranquille à trois kilomètres du centre-ville. À part un petit magasin *qui* vend des journaux, des bonbons etc., il n'y a pas de magasins ici. Tout le monde va faire les courses en ville ou au centre commercial *qui* se trouve de l'autre côté de la ville.**

En ce moment, il y a des champs *où* on peut promener le chien et *où* les enfants peuvent jouer. *C'est là que nous avons joué* au foot *quand tu es venu* à la maison. En face des champs il y a une petite école primaire. C'est sur ces champs qu'on veut construire le supermarché.

La compagnie dit que *la ville a besoin d'*un nouveau supermarché dans ce quartier *parce qu'*il y a plus de gens *qui* habitent le quartier maintenant et que les magasins manquent.

***Comme* tu peux imaginer, tout le monde est contre ce supermarché. *Ce serait* dangereux pour les petits enfants; *on ne pourrait plus* profiter des champs et puis *il y aurait plus* de circulation et de bruit.**

Amitiés . . .

on vient d'annoncer . . . – it has just been announced that . . .
la ville a besoin de . . . – the town needs/is in need of . . .
les magasins manquent – there is a shortage of shops
c'est là que . . ./c'est sur ces champs que . . . – it is there that . . ./it is on those fields that . . .

UNIT 10 ANSWERS

Section Three

Exercise 2

Is recycling important?

Here is an opportunity for you to give your opinions on a major issue. Note the variety of ways in which the writer draws in opinions and attidues.

Recycler, c'est important?

Pour certaines personnes recycler c'est une perte de temps, c'est une activité *que* font les Verts. Moi, *je ne suis pas d'accord*; au contraire *c'est essentiel qu'on recycle* *tout ce qui* est recyclable, par exemple le papier, le verre, le carton, le caoutchouc. *Si possible on devrait* aussi utiliser les matières végétales pour faire du compost pour le jardin.

Si on jette tout, *il faut* trouver des champs ou peut-être une vieille carrière dans la région pour déposer les déchêts. Cela crée un endroit *qui* sent mauvais, surtout *quand* il fait chaud. En plus, c'est dangereux, *parce que* ces déchêts font un gaz très toxique.

Dans certaines villes, *on a trouvé* un moyen d'utiliser les déchêts pour faire de l'électricité; c'est bien, mais pour le moment c'est assez rare.

Chez nous, c'est moi *qui* m'occupe de transporter les bouteilles et les journaux au centre de recyclage; dans notre ville il y a des dépôts dans tous les grands parkings, alors c'est assez facile.

Au collège, nous avons des poubelles *où* on peut mettre les canettes; *il faut* encourager les jeunes enfants à tout recycler.

C'est important pour l'environnement de ne pas continuer à abattre des arbres.

une carrière – a quarry
les déchêts – rubbish
un gaz toxique – a toxic gas
un dépôt – a recycling point
abattre des arbres – to cut down trees

Section Three

Exercice 3
Les transports en commun

This question invites your thoughts on another area of current concern. Note how the writer states quite simply his personal circumstances and explains why certain solutions are impractical or impossible.

Les déplacements en voiture ou en train/en autobus
Comme j'habite à deux kilomètres du collège je prends le bus tous les jours pour y aller. L'inconvenient c'est qu'*il faut* quitter la maison de bonne heure; en plus, le bus est toujours bondé et quelquefois c'est sale. De temps en temps, il y a des embouteillages et on arrive en retard. *Je préférerais* aller à vélo, mais il n'y a pas de piste cyclable alors c'est très dangereux le matin. Je ne peux pas y aller en voiture *parce que* mon père part de la maison tôt le matin et ma mère amène ma petite sœur à son école *qui* se trouve dans un autre quartier de la ville. *Aller* au collège à pied, *il n'en est pas question*, je suis trop paresseux!

Quand nous sortons en famille nous prenons toujours la voiture, par exemple la semaine dernière *nous avons rendu* visite à mes grands-parents *qui* habitent dans le sud de l'Angleterre. On peut y aller par le train mais cela coûte cher et en plus, *cela prend* mettre plus de temps, *car* on doit aller à la gare, attendre le train *qui pourrait* avoir du retard, puis prendre un taxi ou un bus pour finir le trajet. La voiture est beaucoup plus rapide et pratique.

Bien sûr, pour protéger l'environnement *on devrait* moins utiliser les voitures, on gaspille l'essence, on pollue l'atmosphère, on bloque les rues, et il y a un manque de parkings. Pourtant les transports en commun ne sont pas la solution pour beaucoup de personnes *qui* doivent aller au collège ou à leur lieu de travail.

aller au collège à pied – walking to school (Note how the infinitive is used as the subject of another verb: *apprendre à conduire est important* – learning to drive is important; *protéger l'environnement est essentiel* – protecting the environment is essential; *utiliser les transports en commun n'est pas toujours possible* – using public transport is not always easy.)

qui pourrait avoir du retard – which might be late
NB: être en retard – to be late (For an appointment.)
le trajet – the journey (This is a useful alternative to *le voyage*.)
on gaspille l'essence – we waste petrol

Appendix

Time phrases

These will provide a framework for your accounts/letters. This list contains phrases used in the answers, it is not exhaustive, you will know others and you should keep your own list and add to it.

d'abord – firstly, first of all
d'habitude – usually
il y a – ago (il y a 10 minutes – 10 minutes ago)
depuis – since (depuis l'année dernière – since last year)
ensuite – then/next
puis – then
plus tard – later
bientôt – soon
tous les jours/matins/soirs – every day/morning/evening
chaque jour/matin/soir – each day/morning/evening
le matin – in the morning
l'après-midi – in the afternoon
le soir – in the evening
la nuit – at night
la semaine dernière – last week
le mois dernier – last month
l'année dernière – last year

Specific times and dates are also highly useful; you should be familiar with patterns such as these:

à sept heures et demie
le vendredi 18 juin

Expressions of quantity

These are often misused; they are always followed by **de** or **d'**, never by **du**, **de la**, **des**.

beaucoup de – many/a lot of
trop de – too many
plus de – more
tant de – so many

NB: *beaucoup de monde* – many people; *tant de monde* – so many people.

Adverbs of place

partout – everywhere
situé à deux cents mètres – two hundred metres away
à cinq minutes à pied – five minutes away on foot
à l'étranger – abroad
chez moi – at my house

Negative forms

ne . . . plus – no longer
ne . . . personne – nobody
ne . . . que – only
ne . . . aucun/aucune . . . – not one single . . .
ne . . . jamais – never
ne . . . rien – nothing
ne . . . nulle part – nowhere
ne . . . ni . . . ni . . . – neither . . . nor

Conjunctions

These are essential if you are to produce more complex structures; there are many examples in the answers.

qui – who/which
quand – when
pendant que – while
puisque – since
si – if
car – for
que – whom/which
lorsque – when
tandis que – whereas
comme – as
parce que – because
pourquoi – why

Verbal expessions

These are useful for stating your plans and hopes for the future: they are often followed by the infinitive.

j'espère – I hope to
je compte – I plan to
j'ai l'intention de – I intend to
je rêve de – I dream of

These are important for expressing your opinions:

je pense que – I think that
je considère que – I consider
je crois que – I believe that
je trouve que – I find that
j'ai l'impression que – I have the feeling that
j'estime que – I consider that

These verbs, sometimes referred to as modal verbs, are followed by an infinitive; there are many uses of them in the answers:

aller: je vais – I am going to
vouloir: je veux – I want to
savoir: je sais – I know how to
décider de: j'ai décidé de – I decided to
commencer à: j'ai commencé à – I started to
pouvoir: je peux – I am able/in a position to
devoir: je dois – I must/have to
falloir: il faut – it is necessary to
essayer de: j'ai essayé de – I tried to
réussir à: j'ai réussi à – I succeeded in

NB: *venir de*: (in present tense) *je viens de finir* – I have just finished
(in imperfect tense) *je venais de sortir* – I had just gone out

The perfect infinitive

This is an excellent way of establishing the sequence of events:
après avoir visité – after visiting
après être arrivé/arrivée – after arriving (you may need the plural agreement with 's')

The present participle

This is also a useful pattern for stating when events occurred (it has the meaning of 'by', 'on' 'while'):

en rentrant – on reaching home
en travaillant – while working